FOREWORD

It is extraordinary that the early Christian martyr, St. George of Lydda, who was called "Megalomartyros" or "Great Martyr", the "Trophy Bearer" and the "Victorious One" in the East should in the West today have his very existence in doubt. This was partly caused by an ignorant press reaction to the reform of the Roman Calendar in 1969, which removed his name from the Universal Calendar and reduced his feast to a local observance. This still saw his feast celebrated in Venice, Genoa, Portugal, Catalonia, Georgia, Lithuania, Greece, Sicily, Aragon, Barcelona, Valencia, Malta and England. He also remains the patron saint of soldiers, knights, archers, armourers and husbandmen, and is invoked against plague, leprosy and the pox.

There is more evidence for his authenticity than for some of the Apostles, whose existence has never been doubted. However, as is the case with the Apostles, there are also legends, such as his visit to England across the Irish Sea (hence it was named St. George's Channel). In the same genre, St. Andrew had a visit to Scotland. The science of historiography is a comparatively modern discipline, hence the ancients had no problem with a little judicious exaggeration and tendentious accounts of their great heroes in order to impress. Even the early Christians did as much in combating a pagan world.

The dragon story, however, is an allegory: George is the Church's champion who, in defending the maiden, defends the Church's teaching; and in slaying the dragon, overcomes, by his martyrdom, the pagan persecutors. Like the Gospel parables, such a story is simply a vehicle to convey a religious truth. *Saint George, Knight of Lydda* goes behind the parable of the dragon story to reconstruct a believable account of the "Great Martyr" George. For such inventiveness and masterly composition, Anthony Cooney is to be congratulated. He draws on the bare bones of what we know of St. George's life and makes a convincing account. His detailed historical setting provides a convincing background for the times in which the martyr lived, and his narrative sustains an interest throughout. He places George, as a Christian Roman tribune, on a posting to Britain; against tradition he has him travelling from the coast of Gaul and not from the West, nevertheless it is a feasible journey and makes historical sense.

The dénouement is set within layers of historical context which lend a veracity to the simple historical record of George's death. One thing that made him stand out at this period was that the largely Christian Nicomedia had remained silent in the face of the Emperor Diocletian's edict of Christian persecution – for it was George, the most prominent local citizen, who made a stand. His most memorable tearing down of the edict and his subsequent martyrdom put heart back into the Christian community.

1

Eusebius, Bishop of Constantinople, wishing to make the record known, wrote not long after the event that George at this time was the first of those who distinguished themselves as Christians. Moreover, St. Ambrose, Bishop of Milan, writing about the same time, stated that when others concealed their faith George alone adventured "to confess the name of God". Thus *Saint George, Knight of Lydda* fulfils all expectations of a well-informed, readable and plausible account of the "Great Martyr".

Mark Elvins OFM Cap

PREFACE

The Third Century A.D. is so deficient in sound historical witness and documentation, that it should not surprise anyone that, for the martyrdom of St. George, there is only one primary source, Eusebius, and one good secondary source, Ambrose of Milan. However, the brief passage in Eusebius, and the even briefer passage in Ambrose, tell us much more than we might at first suppose.

Eusebius writes that "A certain man of no mean origin, but highly esteemed for his temporal dignities, as soon as the decree was published . . . tore it to shreds as a most profane and wicked act." This, he tells us, took place when the "two Caesars were in the city". This establishes the date of the martyrdom as being after Diocletian's reorganization of the Empire. This man, Eusebius continues, was the "first that was distinguished there in this manner", that he freed his slaves and distributed his wealth and "after enduring what was likely to follow, preserved his mind, calm and serene, until the moment when his spirit fled". It is not now seriously contested that the "certain man" was George of Lydda. The passage from St. Ambrose indicates why George's martyrdom generated, within a few decades, widespread and intense veneration:

"George, the most faithful soldier of Jesus Christ, when religion was by others concealed, alone ventured to confess the Name of God, whose heavenly grace infused such constancy into him that he not only warned the tyrants, but was contemptuous of their tortures." Inference from subsequent developments, chiefly the Donatist schism, suggests that until George made his stand, apostasy was widespread, threatening the Church with catastrophe.

The other secondary sources for the martyrdom of St. George are the three documents discovered in Ethiopia, circa 1880, by Sir E. A. Wallis Budge, the leading Ethiopian scholar of his day.

The first is attributed to "Pasicrates", already known in the Greek "Acta" as the servant of St. George, rescued by him from pirates and depicted in Greek icons as a boy mounted behind the saint on horseback. The second is attributed to Theodosius of Jerusalem and the third to Theodotus of Ancyra. They are represented as the texts of "Encomiums", preached at Lydda and Nicomedia.

The texts Wallis Budge found are copies, as indeed are all our ancient texts, probably several times removed from the originals, and bear clear signs of interpolation and textual corruption by copyists. The account of the tortures St. George endured and the miracles he worked becomes, in Fr. Thurstan's words, "preposterous". However the texts are not historically worthless. Much has been made by sceptics of the fact that the Ethiopian texts and the various "Acta" assert things which the historian knows are simply not true. According to the Latin texts, George is tried before "Datian, Emperor of Persia". There was, the sceptics point out, no such person.

But "Datian" or "Dacianus" simply means "The Dacian", and Galerius was in fact a Dacian. Furthermore, he conquered more of the Persian Empire than any other Roman Emperor and so, after a century of confusion, he may well have been described by some Latin scribe, as "Emperor of Persia".

Diocletian's wife is named as the Empress Alexandra, and is converted after witnessing George's heroic constancy. As a result she also was martyred. History knows of no such "Empress Alexandra", and Diocletian's wife was named Prisca. However, Diocletian was awarded a Triumph after his victory at Alexandria, and in accordance with custom, the Senate would have added that name to his long list of titles. The name, "Alexandra" would be added to those of the Empress. Although a Christian, Prisca was, as Empress, pressured into sacrificing. Sometime later she repented. Galerius' successor, Maximin Daia, exiled her and her daughter, Valeria. After Daia's suicide, both were put to death by Licinius during a renewed persecution, so the story is not so much false as distorted by compression.

A similar situation arises over George's trial before the "Council of Seventy". There is no record of any such Imperial Council. However, the preamble to the first anti-Christian Edict states that the Emperor has sought the judgement of learned men throughout the Empire on the doctrines and practices of the Christians, and as a result of their judgement he is determined upon the suppression of the sect. It was the judgement of this "Council" which brought George to his martyrdom.

Another assertion of the sceptics is that there is no record of a Theodosius as Bishop of Jerusalem, nor of a Theodotus as Bishop of Ancyra. It would certainly be remarkable if complete records of bishops of any city other than Rome were still extant, but apart from that, both may have been presbyters elevated to the dignity of Presbyter Episcopi by the grandiloquent Pasicrates, for the names are common enough.

"Pasicrates" is clearly the source of the many "Acta", Latin, Greek, Coptic and Arabic, that circulated in the Fifth Century. They indicate that George endured torture, extreme even for the time, before finally being beheaded. From comparison of the texts with the "Acta", Wallis Budge constructed an outline of George's life and ancestry.

A tertiary source, if they can be considered as such, are the various "Acta", which purported to be histories of St. George, but which were altered and exaggerated with every version, especially, we may suspect, by copyists to enliven the tedium of their task. Because of our instinctive projection of the present into our interpretation of the past, we have difficulty in appreciating that these "Acta" were not written as "history", as we understand it, but as parable and entertainment.

They were, if not historical novels, then the historical romances of the day. Pope Gelasius, in A.D. 494, deemed it necessary to condemn those "Acta" relating, among others, to Saints Cyriacus Julitta and George as "fabulous" and "ridiculous"; the "work of heretics and schismatics", giving rise to "unseemly mirth" when preached from the pulpit. St. George, he declared, must be counted as one of those "whose names are justly reverenced among men, but whose deeds are known only to God". While the various "Acta", however exaggerated, do have features in common, which when sifted contribute to an overall picture, they are also the cause of our regarding

George as a figure isolated from the day-to-day life of the Later Empire, rather than, as Eusebius presents him, a provincial gentleman of wealth and standing, who accepted the ultimate obligation of giving up his life in defence of his friends.

Fr. Mark Elvins OFM Cap., in his excellent booklet *St. George – Who Was He?* writes: "The closest to any factual account of the life of St. George must be based on the features of his *cultus*, which can be corroborated by more than one authority." It is to the cultus that we must turn to get some idea of the sheer fame of St. George. He is venerated as the "Great Martyr", the "Trophy Bearer", "The Victor", as "Captain of the Noble Army of Martyrs", as "Husbandman of God", and as "Mighty Man of the Galileans". He is regarded as patron of agriculture, of soldiers, particularly of cavalry, protector of youth and chastity, protector of those in peril of storm and tempest, as curer of lunacy and as champion of the oppressed. These attributes and their universality must have a foundation in fact. Dr. Samantha Riches, at the conclusion of her book *St. George, Hero, Saint and Martyr*, says that, as the book progressed, St. George as a real person, knowable and admirable, emerged from the shadows of legend. That is the common experience of all who embark upon the study of his life.

Finally there are the legends of St. George, particularly the English legends. They have no historical foundation, but cannot be ignored by the novelist. The legends of George's service in Britain with the VI Victrix at York and the II Augusta at Caerleon are simply that, legends. The best that can be said of them is that they are not improbable and may even rest upon an oral tradition, for as a tribune in the Imperial Guard it is not unlikely that George would have accompanied Constantius Chlorus to Britain. The legend of George's friendship with Constantine has some circumstantial evidence in its favour. Constantine either erected or enlarged the church over George's grave at Lydda, built a church on the site of his martyrdom, and dedicated a church to him in Constantinople. That is surely a lavish remembrance on the part of a stranger?

One legend which cannot be ignored is that of the dragon. It arrives late on the scene and is generally taken to be a parable of Good overcoming Evil, of much the same sort as the legend of St. Francis and the Wolf of Gubbio. This, however, does not explain why it was universally attached to St. George.

It is suggested that it has earlier, symbolic, roots. Constantine was depicted, on a bas relief in the Church at Lydda, standing triumphantly upon a dragon. He also issued a coin bearing, on the obverse, the image of a dragon, prone beneath the *chi-rho* banner under which he had won the Empire. Galerius is several times referred to as "the Dragon". Symbolically then, the legend celebrates the fact that George, by his martyrdom, overcame the Pagan Empire and brought it into the service of the Church, symbolized by the Maiden.

An historical novel is not history and it is not constrained by the disciplines of history. The novelist can use his imagination in a way denied to the historian; he can draw upon legend as well as upon treatise. According to the Greek "Acta", George was born in Melitene where his father was martyred, and his mother fled with him to her family's estates in Lydda. Other sources say that he was born in Lydda. The historian cannot resolve this dispute, but the novelist can suggest that he was born on the journey between Melitene and Lydda. The seventh-century *Chronicon Pascali* lists among those martyred under Decius a certain "Holy George", and it is argued by some, though against all the other evidence, that this was the "real" St. George. Again, the dispute is beyond solution for the historian, but the novelist can resolve the problem by identifying "Holy George" with the great-grandfather of "our" St. George.

All the main characters in the book are historic persons with the following caveats. I have, for dramatic purposes – his lifelong animosity, among others – represented Galerius as older than he was. The name of Justus' daughter to whom George was betrothed is unknown, and I have called her "Justina". The marriage never took place, and this could only have been for a serious reason. Nothing is known of the lives of Martha and Katherine other than their being named as George's sisters.

Nothing is known of the parentage of Lucius and Cyrennius, nor of their life, except that they recovered George's body and brought it to Lydda. Nothing is known of Andrew except that he was George's uncle, received his remains, and built the first church at Lydda, allegedly with a recovered treasure. "Grananna" is an invention, except in the sense that George would certainly have had a "Nanny", who would have had a great influence on his upbringing.

Mansour and Claudia are a special case. They were introduced merely to relay to the reader essential information about the journey to Lydda, and were intended to be nothing more than "spear carriers". Both took on an independent existence, running away from their author. In defence, Mansour is typical of the freedman factotum who managed villas, cities, and at times even the Empire. I have made him a Samaritan, because Samaritans held such posts, but also because St. George is associated with the conversion of Samaritans.

A plainly Arian interpolation in Pasicrates is the smearing of St. Athanasius as a "magician" hired to "poison" George. St. Athanasius would in fact have been a child at the time. But St. Athanasius had grandparents, and I have turned the tables on the "heretic and schismatic" interpolator by having his "Athanasius", the grandfather of St. Athanasius, defeated in his attempt to poison George's faith, and converted instead. Their neo-Platonic dialogue is based upon Kingsley's version of that between Hypatia and the converted Raphael ben-Ezra, a hundred years later, hence again the "grandfather" ploy. In the same way, the Romano-British patricians, and the native kings whom George meets, are the ancestors of those who came to the fore in the fifth century. Anyone whose curiosity is aroused may find a genealogy of the Aurelii and Eutherian houses in Edward Foord's magisterial *The Last Age of Roman Britain*.

The account of St. George's trial is based upon the *Encomium* of Theodore of Jerusalem. The Wallis Budge texts make it plain that George professed the Trinity, the Incarnation, the Real Presence, the intercession of the Blessed Virgin as Theotokos, and the Primacy of Peter. He was no Arian, nor Nestorian, nor Monophysite either.

This is an historical novel, not a history. I have followed Wallis Budge's brief outline of St. George's life, but used the imaginative inference of the novelist to reconstruct from what we do know of the Roman environment, religious, political, social and economic, the part that such a man at such a time would play in it. My first purpose has been to bring our Patron Saint out of the shadows into the world of his day, and present him to our day as a real person who knew bereavement, sorrow and heartache before winning the crown of martyrdom. My second purpose, like that of the authors of the Fourth-Century "Acta", has been to entertain. The reader must judge if the latter has been achieved.

Anthony Cooney,
Liverpool, January 2004

PART ONE
A.D. 270

CHAPTER ONE

Kira threw aside the distaff and spindle with a sigh of boredom. She was engaged, as the ancient frescoes assured her, in the unceasing labour of the Roman matron, before luxury and an abundance of slaves had sapped the stern Roman virtues. She paused for a moment feeling the swaying of the wagon and then arranged herself in a prone position on her couch. The old nurse, seated on a stool against the partition which divided the wagon glanced at her keenly.

"The child will be born before tomorrow", she said.

"Oh don't start that again, Nanny", Kira spoke sharply, "My son will be born in Lydda in the house of his ancestors."

"You always were a stubborn child", the nurse grumbled, "and now a wilful woman. We ought to have stayed in Melitene until the child was born, and travelled to Lydda in the late spring."

Kira answered impatiently, "How was I to know there would be late snows to delay us? By now we ought to have been at Antioch, boarding a fast galley to Joppa."

She took up the distaff again, an indication that, as far as she was concerned, the conversation was finished, and idly twirled the spindle a few times before the thread broke. With an impatient gesture she again flung the distaff aside.

Kira Theognosta's Greek lineage, inherited from those who had conquered with Alexander, was evident in her grey eyes, the luminous skin and the perfect proportions of her features. It was not mere flattery of her parents that had caused men to call her "The Rose of Sharon". Nevertheless, Greek though she was, the mass and ripple of her hair was caught up and braided in the old Roman style, the gold of the hair matching that of the braid, for it was a fad or fancy of her pregnancy to see herself as a Roman Matron of the noble days of the Republic. The enthusiasm of youth, fired by her new status of *Domina*, found its models in the faded frescoes of the Roman past. The patrician woman suckling an infant held in the crook of one arm whilst spinning with the other, the domina of a great household sitting among her slave girls at the loom – these were the Roman virtues of industry and thrift which she wished to emulate. Had not the great Augustus himself refused to wear any garment not spun and woven by his wife, Livia, and daughter, Julia? It was true that she had not herself set to work cutting and sewing gowns copied from the women in the frescoes, but she had instructed her maids to do so, interfering and fussing in their work, convinced she knew the craft better than they did.

Now Kira lay back on her couch gowned in a pure white robe, without ornament or decoration other than the two narrow purple stripes down the front which proclaimed her a Roman citizen. The absence of ornament was deliberate, for in her mind's eye she saw herself in the role of Cornelia, daughter of great Scipio Africanus, and famous as the mother of the Gracchi. Kira knew the story well, and lying there she saw it all again in her mind's eye. When the rich women whom the plainly-gowned Cornelia was entertaining had asked her patronizingly, "Where are your jewels?" she had called her two sons, and holding them before her, had replied, "These are my jewels." The story was a foundation legend of Rome, the female obverse to the oath of the Horatii to hold the Tiber bridge against Tarquin until it was cut down behind them. Kira, as she felt the baby kick, could hardly wait for such an opportunity for noble sentiment to befall her.

This pleasant reverie was interrupted by the old nurse, "What if the child be a girl?"

"It will be a boy!" Kira answered impatiently, "I know it will, I have – " she paused, hesitatingly.

"You've been to the soothsayers!" exclaimed the old woman with a sudden flash of insight, "You foolish girl, dabbling in pagan wickedness, and you – your family descended from the Saints at Sharon and Lydda visited by the Blessed Peter himself. How could you be so wicked after all we've suffered. If your mother knew of this! And of course she would blame me, though what authority I can have over a married woman I don't know."

"Oh rubbish, Nanny", Kira was plainly uncomfortable, "It was just for fun, my maids told me of this soothsayer, who really can see the future, and we went together but only to giggle."

"Giggle!" exploded the old woman, "I'd give them a good whipping and let them giggle at that! The Dominus is too lenient with them, and so are you! A patrician lady should keep some distance between herself and her slaves, and not go gallivanting off with them. You mustn't be too familiar with these girls. You're too young to know, I always said so, that's the whole trouble – if the bishop heard of this – after all we've suffered, and the Dominus' grandfather, Holy Giorgios, thrown to wild swine under that fiend, Decius, and you! To consort with them and their devils." The old woman's disjointed sentences trailed off.

Kira looked downcast, but rallied.

"Those days are over now Nanny, Decius is dead, slain by the Goths as a punishment from God, and the new Emperor knows that Christians are as Roman as everyone else. We mustn't be so prickly in future and we must join in things more, if we want the Pagans to understand us better. It was just fun to have my fortune told."

Her voice also trailed off. She was telling herself that, after all, the household maids were the only girls of her own age in the stuffy society of Melitene, which she had hated, so who else was she to laugh and gossip with? The old nurse was too narrow-minded and bigoted to understand, and what else could one expect from the old anyway?

"So! And what did this charlatan tell you?" Nanny was curious in spite of herself.

"Why! That I would bear a son and that his name would be great. He would do something which would renew the Empire, though what it was was hidden from her. He would overthrow the dragon, she was very particular about that, and he would be famous throughout the Church, East and West, Latin, Greek, Syrian and Coptic, and in faraway lands, and held in honour next to Peter and the Apostles".

The old woman's squawk of anger and indignation at this impiety, as she deemed it, interrupted the excited babble.

"Not another word, not a word. The demons are liars and tell you lies to trap you into vanity and pride. You foolish, foolish child. How many years' penance will the bishop give you for this? Have you thought of that?"

"Not many", Kira answered airily, "He is a friend of my father and besides which he depends upon our family for his villa."

Gratified by this consoling thought, Kira picked up the distaff and spindle, mended the break and began to spin again. If she thought that her old nurse had been crushed she was mistaken, for Nanny immediately took up another grudge.

"Romans", she nagged, "sons of the She-Wolf. Barbarians with solid bone skulls! What right have they to rule Greeks? Why must you dress like a Roman?"

"We are all Romans now", Kira replied, deliberately in Latin to vex the old woman the more, "The whole world is Roman, Nanny", and having at last silenced her, began to spin again.

CHAPTER TWO

The Cappadocian plateau is neither an hospitable nor an attractive place. The paved way had zig-zagged up from Melitene, leaving behind the cultivated land, the vine-yards and the orchards of plum and olive and almond. Reaching the ridge of the plateau it struck out, ruler-straight between bare peaks, toward the distant pass which would take them to the road to Antioch. Two riders breasted the last steep incline of the ascent and paused to take in the scene. Nothing moved upon the paved way, and upon the plateau there was no sign of human habitation. There had been a late snowstorm here on the high ground which had delayed the caravan for two weeks, but at last there had been a thaw. The road was covered by a thin and miserable slush. The channels on either side, washed out by a hundred winters, ran gurgling with melt water upon which slivers of ice still floated. There was a smell of cold and winter on the air. The waste spread out from the road, stretching to the bare rock of the peaks which rose on all sides. The land was dotted with marsh, identi-fied by the bull-rushes and the croaking of innumerable frogs, busy about the tasks of mating and spawning. Between the marshes was a waste of thorn bushes, rather like a stubby gorse, interspersed with sage. There seemed hardly pasture for goats, let alone sheep. The plateau was dissected by ravines, bridged in the Roman style of close-set piers and massive slabs.

Life here was harsh, harsher than the life which the army offered. The peasants of the Cappadocian plateau were the best soldiers in the world, and it was from them that the Empire recruited its auxiliary forces, and with increasing admission to citizenship and the slow degeneration of the Roman stock, even its legions. The down-side was that the peasants made tough, hardened soldiers because they were thieves and cut-throats. If there were any brigands about it would be in the ravines near the bridges that they would be lurking.

The taller of the two riders looked back down the way they had come and noted with satisfaction that his caravan was commencing the last slope of the zig-zag road. His mount and his apparel marked him out as a man, not only of wealth, but of authority in the Empire. He was Anastasius, Governor of Melitene, the principal city of Cappadocia. The horse on which he sat was a magnificent, jet-black Arab. He was wearing the breastplate, wrought in one piece, embossed with lions' heads and eagles, of a Military Count of the Empire. He wore the scarlet-crested helmet of old Rome and the voluminous cavalry cloak; scarlet so that no enemy should ever see Roman blood. His only conces-sion to modernity was a long cavalry sabre, which hung at his belt instead of the broad bladed stabbing sword by which Rome had dominated the battle-field for centuries. For all his Roman dress, Anastasius was indisputably Greek. He had the red-gold hair and grey eyes of the Achaeans, and might have walked with Solon, or stood at Marathon. His companion was decidedly a civilian. Riding a mule, he carried no weapons. Purple black locks escaped from his hood. His complexion was the olive brown of the Levant, his eyes a darker brown still, his face long and sensitive. He combined expertly the offices of Secretary, Treasurer and Lawyer, to Anastasius.

"The road is long, Domine", he said gravely, "and we are late."

"I know, I know, Mansour. It has been one thing after another, but we'll make better time now."

Mansour merely nodded. After a few moments' silence, Anastasius went on.

"What do the maps show?"

"They are very inaccurate, Domine", Mansour replied, "The map makers are fanciful. They show a tree as though it were a forest and a bare peak as though it were a mole-hill, but there is something which might be a ravine crossed by a bridge, twenty miles on."

Anastasius made rapid calculations, "We will need at least an hour to rest, water and feed the horses; inadequate, but all we can afford. Another three hours should see us to the ravine just before dark. It may not be much, but it's a lot better than spending the night on the open plateau. I can feel knives in my back at the thought of it."

"It may already be occupied", suggested Mansour quietly.

"Then we'll have to rely on the Dacians to chase them out, but what I wouldn't give to feel a wall around me!"

As if at the word 'Dacian,' the first of their escort crested the rim and the optio saluted.

"Carry on", responded Anastasius, "we must get the whole caravan up here as quickly as possible."

Twelve cavalrymen, two by two, followed. They were impressive, in coats of scale-armour painted white, their long spears pointed to the sky. The two men watched them pass.

"It is ironic", Mansour began, "that Dacia, the last province added to the Empire, should be the first to be abandoned."

"A mistake", Anastasius promptly retorted. "The Dacians were Romanized and Latin-speaking within a generation."

A spasm of distaste crossed Mansour's face, "Latin?" he queried. "Well yes, of a sort."

Anastasius laughed, "You are a pedant, Mansour, and you don't think much of Dacians."

"Dacia is a land full of dragon lore", the scribe replied, "but for all that I've never met a Dacian who'd seen a real live dragon himself, though they all know any number of others who have."

"They are boasters, I'll grant you, but they're first-rate cavalrymen, and they still fight for Rome, abandoned or independent, however you put it. Odd though, their Tribune was most reluctant to let me have even a dozen of his men for escort."

"Galerius Valerius Maximianus", mused Mansour, "It does not surprise me. He hates Christians even more than Samaritans and Jews."

13

"I didn't notice that. He was civil enough, just very reluctant."

"We Samaritans can smell hatred", Mansour said, without rancour, "Everyone hates us."

"The Jews say that you're not true descendants of Abraham and that you don't accept the prophets", Anastasius pointed out.

"The Christians", Mansour parried, "say that the Jews plot against them, and the Pagans say that the Christians practice human sacrifice and cannibalism, you both deny the accusations."

Anastasius laughed again, "And what do you Samaritans think of Jews and Christians?" he asked.

"Why, we think you're both a very good thing, since you get all the kicks that would otherwise be aimed at us."

Anastasius laughed again, "You're a cynical rogue, Mansour."

"I serve you, Domine."

From any other freedman this would have been insolence, but Mansour had served Anastasius for many years, and the latter accepted it with a roar of laughter.

"Here comes the Domina's wagon", was all he said.

Four straining horses crested the rim, hauling the house on wheels where Kira impatiently spun and her old nurse dozed. Not for a moment did Anastasius think of leaving his post supervising the sharp turn onto the straight road, to see or speak to his wife. That was not the Roman way. He calmly called orders to the wagoners until they successfully negotiated the corner, the horses gratefully slackening their effort. The wagon passed, he turned to Mansour.

"What is the difference between the Samaritans and the Jews?" he asked.

"They say we are heretics and we say they are heretics", Mansour's voice was serious.

"That is not a difference, that is a similarity."

"Also, our numbers diminish."

"Perhaps Samaritans are becoming Christians", Anastasius said, getting his own back for Mansour's earlier sally.

"That would be to become a man with a chip on both shoulders", Mansour countered.

"But come, Mansour", Anastasius pursued the point, "Samaritans must have become Christians in early times, for there are Christians in Samaria now."

Mansour was quick to meet the challenge, "Why yes, and there are Christians in Galilee, there are Jews still in Galilee in spite of Titus, there are even Samaritans in Galilee, and there are Gentiles everywhere."

"And all under the hand of Rome, Mansour", Anastasius' voice took on a serious tone, "which means that we can all get on with our business without throats being cut in the streets. But here is the next wagon."

This wagon carried half a dozen maids, without whom Kira insisted it was impossible for her to travel. They were giggling and chatting to the wagoners, the merriest among them a Spanish girl, Claudia. "A forward young madam", Anastasius

14

remarked to himself. They fell silent at the sight of Anastasius, but Claudia's dark eyes flashed a glad smile at Mansour.

"Watch your business on the bend", Anastasius called to the wagoners, "and you women keep silent."

The wagon passed and he turned again to Mansour.

"What did you make of Galerius?" he asked.

"He is a cold man, ambitious, and intends to climb high, higher than Tribune of a cohort of auxiliaries. His soldiers call him 'The Dragon', and his slaves something else."

"There is more", said Anastasius, "I know you well enough to know that."

"I spoke to a brother Samaritan on his staff whilst you were conferring. I persuaded him, brother to brother, of my need to know certain things." Mansour was hesitant.

"And?"

"Galerius spends. Spends a great deal more than a Tribune's pay."

"On subversion?"

"No! At least not in the usual way. He subverts and entraps with orgies. The female slaves are pressed into this, and he himself is insatiable."

Angry spots appeared on Anastasius' cheeks, "The Law of Rome forbids ravishing a female slave, or forcing her into such service."

Mansour laughed softly, "Domine, the Law of Rome extends only as far as the swords of Rome. Do you think they", he jerked his head after the Dacians, "are going to burst into his villa and arrest their Tribune?"

Anastasius was lost for a reply for a moment, "Nevertheless, such a man is not worthy of authority."

"And who will take it from him? Domine, Rome is dying. Look at this road. Where are the patrols which kept it safe? Where are the inns where the traveller might shelter each night? Gone, all gone in a century of civil war and rival emperors. The blond giants with the cold eyes are massing beyond the great rivers, the horsemen gather in the east, and men like Galerius rob the taxes and prosper."

"We have no evidence of that", Anastasius replied, "and very little chance of getting any. But for the rest, Rome will recover, Rome must recover, if the world is not to sink into savagery."

He was interrupted as another wagon, mule-drawn, crested the hill. This one was empty, for it was the wagoners' sleeping quarters. Others, also drawn by mule teams, followed at more frequent intervals, carrying fodder for the horses and mules, corn, oil, wine and dried fruit, olives and cheeses for the party, the field kitchen, sleeping quarters for the escort and rear-guard, a string of spare horses and mules, and finally the rearguard itself. There were twelve of them and their captain, riding sturdy, rough-coated ponies. They wore thick felt trousers and leather coats and leather helmets banded and studded with iron. Felt gauntlets covered their hands, their eyes were slanted against the sun, wind and snows of the endless steppes. Each had slung across his back a mighty bow of horn.

"And what do you think of Huns, Mansour", Anastasius asked, switching to Latin and lowering his voice, lest the objects of his question understood Greek.

"I think they do not wash often enough, if at all", Mansour replied, "also that Rome is casting her net ever farther afield."

"I agree with you there, yet they're good fighters. They can ride and shoot from the saddle, to the front or the rear as they lure an enemy in pursuit."

"Well let us hope they don't decide to shoot us", Mansour replied drily. "They never seem to leave their horses; they eat and sleep on them. I wish they would wash on them if that made the practice more frequent."

"But you don't think it wise to recruit them, even if they did wash?"

"I think", replied Mansour, "that a great host of them moving westward may be the reason why the Allemans and Goths burst so desperately across the frontiers. If these are the advance guard, how far behind is the main body?"

Even as he spoke the Hun Captain barked a command in an incomprehensible tongue and his men split into two files, moving off the hard surface of the road to gallop on either side of the caravan, spreading out in skirmishing order.

"Well you see, my mournful Mansour", Anastasius said, watching the manoeuvre with the appreciative eye of the cavalryman, "they know their business; now let us see to ours and get up with the van."

CHAPTER THREE

Anastasius passed Kira's wagon without slackening pace.

Drawing alongside the optio of the escort, he ordered, "An hour's halt to feed the horses and mules, the wagons to remain in column of route. After the beasts are watered and fed, cold rations for the men."

The column reacted to the order with the precision which had carried the legions from the Clyde to the Euphrates, halting from rear to van without any confusion. No moment was lost; as each wagon halted the wagoners draped blankets over their horses and mules and then hastened with leather buckets and nosebags to water and feed them.

Shrieking and giggling, Kira's maids leapt from their wagon and ran for the lead wagon. The old nurse was waiting for them at the top of its steps.

"Be off, you hussies", she shouted. "The Domina has no need of you and no time for foolishness."

The girls halted, crestfallen; they were thinking of the gossip and the sweetmeats they had hoped to share with Kira.

"Be off!" the Nurse shouted again, "Get back to your spinning, you idle hussies."

They turned reluctantly, Claudia, the bright-eyed Spanish girl remarking in a voice loud enough for the old woman to hear, "Who does she think she is? She's just a servant like the rest of us." The old woman's face flushed with anger, and she reached up to take a switch from over the door. The girls shrieked again and ran back to their wagon.

Anastasius had not missed any of this, but he had other things to attend to. By this time the beasts had been watered and given their nose-bags. Soldiers and wagoners were drinking watered wine and chewing dried figs and bread softened in olive oil. The Huns, contrary to Mansour's belief that they never dismounted, were standing by their horses drinking fermented mare's milk from skin bottles and chewing on dried horse meat.

Having satisfied himself that all was in order, Anastasius mounted the steps of the wagon. The first section was arranged as a dining room in the old Roman manner, a low table with couches on each side. The nurse was waiting for him.

"Domine", she bowed briefly, and went on hurriedly. "The child will be born tonight. The weather will freeze again and we must have more shelter and warmth than this, and I must have help; those silly girls are useless."

"You are certain of this?" Anastasius asked.

"Did I not bring the Domina into the world? Have I not brought a hundred others into the world? She is carrying the infant low, and it will be a difficult birth. You must do something!"

Anastasius felt desperate. This was a situation altogether outside the experience of a cavalryman of twenty-five.

"I will speak to Mansour. He says there is a ravine about twenty miles from here. At least we can get out of the wind and have fire."

He did not wait for the nurse's reply, since he knew it would not be complimentary about men in general and her little girl's blockhead of a husband in particular.

As he entered the second room, Kira sprang up from the couch and hastened to him. A Roman girl of seventeen might usually be regarded as fully adult. Kira's childhood had been prolonged by doting parents, particularly her father, Dionysius, Count of Lydda. Now she met Anastasius with a string of complaints.

"The journey is so long! Nanny is horrid, she won't let my maids in to see me. How am I supposed to spend the time? And all this nonsense about the baby being born a week early, when I know that he will be born in Lydda."

Anastasius thought ruefully that it was his own weakness before Kira's determination to reach Lydda for the birth which had resulted in their starting this perilous winter journey, rather than wait another few weeks. Nevertheless he said nothing of this, but led her gently back to the couch.

"My dearest", he said, stroking her hand, "Nanny is quite right not to let the spinsters in, they would only excite you. They are foolish, frivolous girls, and you mustn't be so familiar with them, even if they are your own age. Remember that one day it will be your duty to choose husbands for them. How can you do that if they don't look up to you as a wise and careful mistress?"

Kira, far from becoming serious at this prospect, was delighted.

"Why! I will choose for them husbands whom they want",

Anastasius smiled, "Well that's what it usually comes down to", he said, "but nevertheless it's your duty to see they don't give their affections unwisely. It wouldn't do for a lady's maid to become enamoured of a goatherd, and you must see to it that such mismatches don't occur."

Kira was silent for a few moments, and then with great determination said, "Well then! I'll make my first choice now. I'll marry Claudia to Mansour!"

Anastasius could not prevent himself exploding with laughter.

"Claudia! That little minx with the glad eye who thrusts her bosom out and sways her hips every time she passes a man, even if it's a smelly muleteer? And poor Mansour! Why, she'd frighten him out of his five wits!"

Kira pouted, "Claudia's a very nice girl; she makes me laugh and she talks of no one else but Mansour. She thinks he's the cleverest and handsomest of men, and so he is really, so Claudia will have Mansour, and you must speak to him about it."

Anastasius tried to look serious.

"You forget", he said, "That Mansour is a freedman, and might have something to say in the matter. Beside which, a freedman couldn't marry a slave."

"That's very simply settled: you must emancipate Claudia as soon as we reach Antioch, and then they can be married."

"If I emancipate Claudia in Antioch", Anastasius answered in a teasing voice, "she'll not be a slave any more and you'll not be able to choose her husband."

"Don't make difficulties", Kira stamped her foot, "I tell you that Claudia is crazy about Mansour and will marry him straight away. You can talk to him about it."

"Choosing husbands for her maids is the Domina's province", Anastasius said, becoming firm. "I certainly can't interfere. It would be very humiliating for you if I did; the gossips would say that you couldn't manage your household."

"Oh don't be so stuffy", Kira cried, "There is no rule against you asking Mansour why he's never married and dropping hints about Claudia."

"Well, I will", promised her husband, "but I think the poor man will desert us at Antioch. Mansour married to a little minx like Claudia! Still it might make him laugh once in a while."

"Claudia can make anyone laugh", Kira asserted, "and Mansour will be a very happy man."

"I'll bring the subject up", Anastasius promised, "but I can't say it will be easy. Now I have to get the caravan moving."

He kissed his wife on the forehead and left, still chuckling to himself.

CHAPTER FOUR

The skies had cleared and there was now warmth in the April sun. There were even dry patches appearing on the paved way, but the clear skies threatened another freezing night. The column was on the move precisely on the hour. Anastasius called the optio to him.

"Send two men on fresh horses to reconnoitre the ravine about twenty miles ahead. I need to know if it's occupied by any hostiles, if there are any buildings, even ruins, and the state they are in. Send one of the Huns with them and tell him to keep his bow ready."

"Will he understand Latin?" the optio's reply had a note of surliness in it, and Anastasius looked at him sharply.

"As well as you understand Greek I imagine, and probably orders a lot better! Send the man to me first and I will see that he understands what he is to do."

The Captain saluted. "Dacians!" Anastasius mused, "what was that phrase Mansour had used about a Samaritan who became a Christian – 'A man with a chip on both shoulders'. Well, that certainly fitted Dacians with their love-hate relationship with Rome." A Hun was brought to him.

"You understand Greek?" he asked.

"Yes, Tsar", the man answered, "a little."

"You are to go with these two", he gestured to the waiting cavalrymen, "They are going to scout ahead. You are to have your bow strung and ready, but you are not to shoot at anyone unless they are armed and pursuing you. Do you understand?" The man indicated that he did. "Then repeat your orders to me." The man gave a satisfactory, if hesitant, reply and Anastasius sent the party off.

"Let's ride ahead a little, Mansour", Anastasius said, "and tell me what you dislike about Huns so much. I was watching your face as I spoke to that one."

"This is a different kind of barbarian, Domine. The Goths, Allemans, Franks, Burgundians, all of these are farmers, shepherds, fishermen or craftsmen in iron and wood. They see the Empire and envy its security and prosperity. First they think they can come and loot what they want, but when they are chastised by the army and find raiding not so easy as they thought, they think again and ask to settle. If they are settled within the Empire they remain farmers or craftsmen. If there is no spare land or trade they join the army and fight for Rome."

"And the Huns?" prompted Anastasius.

"The Huns are nomads. They do not sow or reap, but feed upon the horse and follow the grazing. When the Hun sees the Empire he sees a blasphemy, a sacrilege against his gods of wind and thunder, and his horse gods."

Anastasius was a soldier, in all else a simple man, and he was slow to grasp such subtleties.

"Why a blasphemy?"

Mansour smiled his scholar's smile.

"The Hun sees grassland ploughed up, and that is blasphemy to him. He sees the land divided by walls and hedges, carved up by roads, and that is an abomination. He sees villas surrounded by rich land, and is told to keep his horses out. That is a threat to his way of life, to all he knows. He sees cities with stone walls which bar his way. 'Where', he asks himself, 'will our horses graze if all the world becomes like this? Who will honour the horse gods and the gods of wind and thunder when all the world is paved or ploughed?' " Mansour's voice became urgent, "Domine, the barbarian who wants to share in the Empire is only a temporary problem; the Empire teaches him to aspire to what he desires. The barbarian who hates what the Empire is will destroy it. He will see it as a holy deed to batter down the walls and slaughter the sacrilegious who every spring rape the earth with sharp iron. It has all happened before to ancient civilizations beyond the two rivers."

"I had not thought of it like that, Mansour, only of good horse soldiers. We will write of this in our next dispatch to the Emperor."

Mansour smiled again, "If the Emperor ever sees our dispatch, I have no doubt he will hit upon the excellent plan of paying the Huns to go and plunder the Persians! That will seem to him cheaper than two or three new legions."

"Well it might be, at that", Anastasius exclaimed.

"Those who are paid to go away always come back for more. Bribes cannot save the Empire; only a new spirit, a new faith, can do that."

"And from where, Mansour, shall we get that?"

"From one who will make the kingly sacrifice for the life of the People", Mansour answered simply.

"You are a gloomy fellow Mansour" Anastasius said, seeing the opportunity to turn the conversation to the matter Kira had charged him with, "no wonder you never married."

"Domine?"

"I said 'no wonder you never married'. Now come, there is time to do so even in a scholar's life."

"It is a difficult matter, Domine", Mansour replied after a short pause. "A Freedman cannot marry a servile woman without loss of caste, and there are few free families who are willing that their daughter should marry a Freedman, unless of course he is rich."

"So! You would like an increase in your salary! Well it shall be so, but why not marry a freedwoman?"

"Freedwomen tend to be", Mansour paused to add some delicacy to the word, "elderly."

"Why if this be the case, the more emancipations, the fewer marriages we shall have", Anastasius exclaimed, slapping his thigh. "But Mansour, you would not want some flibbertigibbet for a wife surely? I'd have thought a mature, serious woman more to a scholar's taste."

The conversation was not as difficult as Anastasius had anticipated, indeed he was beginning to enjoy his banter at Mansour's expense. The latter gave a little laugh.

"I often wonder why men always think that a scholar dreams of ugly women with thin lips and thin tempers, and not of willing girls with long legs, soft arms and pretty faces?"

Anastasius exploded with mirth, "Why, you dirty old man, Mansour!" he cried, "You've been ogling the Domina's maids in secret. What a seething cauldron of passion is now exposed. Be glad you are not a Christian, Mansour, obliged to confess such thoughts. I tremble to think of the penances the bishop would heap upon you; a barefoot pilgrimage would be the first and least of them I should say."

"Under your pardon, Domine, "Mansour answered with dignity, "I am only two years older than yourself, but I will confess that there is one of the maids I can't help admiring every time I see her."

"Which one?" chortled Anastasius, "Tell me, which one has taken your fancy? I demand to know."

The next moment Anastasius jerked his horse to an astonished halt as Mansour replied, "The girl with the merry eyes, Claudia."

"Claudia!" exploded Anastasius, "but she's illiterate Mansour, how could she make a scholar happy? She'd be continually interrupting your studies with demands for attention, endlessly wanting flattery and fripperies."

"There would be great satisfaction in teaching her to read", Mansour replied with a sly smile.

"There would be great satisfaction in teaching her a few other things", laughed Anastasius, "and I suggest being less pert for a start. But Mansour, are you serious? Would you marry Claudia if the Domina were to offer her?"

"With pleasure, Domine", the scribe answered.

"Well you must state your case to the Domina, not to me; but I can tell you this without any impropriety on my part, the girl is willing, and as soon as we reach Antioch I will search out a magistrate and emancipate her, and you will be married next day before you can escape." He turned serious, "You *will* continue to serve me, won't you Mansour? There's a house and garden at Lydda for you if you do."

"I had never thought of anything else, Domine", Mansour replied.

"Good! Good! Now I must ride back and see all's well. You keep ahead for the first sight of the scouts returning. I want to know every detail."

"I will ensure that I speak to them before our Dacian optio does", Mansour replied enigmatically.

Anastasius wheeled his horse around and rode back past the escort. Halfway down he turned in the saddle to look back. Either Mansour or the mule, one or the other, was performing a merry little dance down the road. Laughing, Anastasius came level with the Domina's wagon. He was surprised to see the head of Claudia thrust out of one of the windows.

"She must have got past Nanny somehow", he thought to himself.

Claudia did not at first see him because she was staring hard down the road to where Mansour was cavorting about. Catching sight of him she ducked her head in quickly, but not before he had caught the gleeful expression on her face. The sound of laughter came from the wagon and Anastasius rode on down the column shaking his head in bewilderment. He had the feeling that somehow, though he could not imagine how, he had been bamboozled.

CHAPTER FIVE

Anastasius cantered down the column, noting the condition of the horses and mules. Another stop would be necessary. He glanced at the sun. But no more than half an hour if they were to reach the shelter of the ravine before dark. He was intrigued by the Hun cavalry. They did not appear to need to rest their horses as often. The Huns hovered and darted like hawks and at first it all appeared random. Anastasius, however, soon discerned the pattern.

The Huns rode in pairs, the horseman on the outside leading, the inside man trailing at a slower pace. Then the inside man would urge his horse forward at a gallop, to take the lead, whilst the outside man would rest his horse, before trailing. The Huns' bows, Anastasius estimated, pulled twice the poundage of the Roman bow. He was witnessing, he realized, a new kind of warfare. Given that horsemanship and given that bow, they could raid a column or attack a battle line whilst keeping out of bowshot. He recalled Mansour's anxiety – how many Huns were there moving across the endless Steppes? How was it that Roman horses had to be either changed or rested so often? *Mutationes*, where horses could be changed, were situated every twelve miles on the *Cursus Publicus*, the official network of roads, and *Mansiones*, inns providing a night's lodging as well as a change of horses, every forty miles apart. When you saw the Huns riding, it was obvious that something was wrong, and that something was plainly the Roman harness which restricted the animal's breathing and circulation – but was there an alternative design? Reaching the end of the column, Anastasius turned to canter back and thought again of Mansour married to Claudia. He had to smile!

"It must be providence", he told himself; and after all, his own marriage had all the marks of providence. Anastasius' family, like Kira's, was Greek, part of the widespread Greek diaspora. They had acquired estates between Mount Lebanon and Sidon. Like Kira's family they had become Christians in Apostolic times, and claimed, like hers, to be among "The saints at Lydda and Sharon" visited by the Apostle Peter. Anastasius' grandfather, Giorgios, had married the heiress of a Bithynian estate and moved to the Euxine coast, leaving his Lebanon estates in the care of factors. He had been put to death in the most horrible way in the persecution under Decius, and in the family was called "Holy Giorgios, the Martyr". His son, John, had, after Decius' death, entered the Imperial Service and risen to be Governor of Cappadocia. Anastasius had followed his father into the Imperial service, and having made a good impression with his skill as a cavalry commander, had been appointed, at the age of twenty-three, military commander to Dionysius, Count of Lydda.

Welcomed home by his kinsmen, they had urged him to marry within his clan and remain in the land of his fathers. He was persuaded to do so the day that he met Kira. Entering Dionysius' villa to take up his duties, he saw her in the atrium. She was standing by the pool in the subdued light that fell through the open square in the roof. At sixteen, on the threshold of womanhood, her beauty was ethereal, every movement of head and slender body was entrancing, her hair shone about her like a halo. Anastasius was smitten for life. What Kira saw stepping out of the bright sunlight was a Roman officer, tall, broad-shouldered, handsome and youthful, his helmet adorned by the red ostrich-feather crest of a Tribune. She had almost swooned with delight.

His courtship had been conducted, as was proper, by his Lydian cousins. Dionysius had been impressed by the young tribune and by his prospects, but more importantly, he was a Christian and kinsman.

"My family have never worshipped false gods or idols", Dionysius had told Anastasius, with a justifiable pride.

"Nor, Sir, has mine", he had replied, "for we also welcomed the blessed Peter to Lydda."

The marriage was hastened forward by an Imperial summons for Anastasius to return to Cappadocia as Governor of Melitene.

Anastasius and his young bride took up residence in that city, where Kira conceived and became homesick. She had despaired of seeing her beloved Lydda again for many years, if at all, when everything unexpectedly changed. The Emperor, Claudius II, surnamed "Gothicus" after his great victory over the barbarians, died of plague after a brief three-year reign. He was succeeded by his right-hand man, the brilliant general and administrator, Aurelian, who began a thorough shake up of the Empire. Within weeks Anastasius had been appointed Governor of Galilee and he and Kira could return home.

Reaching Kira's wagon, Anastasius flung the reins to the driver and swung on to the steps. The old nurse was waiting anxiously.

"Have you found a safe place to stop?" she demanded.

"I've sent scouts ahead", he told her, "Now I'll see the Domina."

"She has that foolish Claudia with her. They think I'm too old and too stupid to know about the wicket gate in the back of the wagon."

"She must be a spirited girl to have jumped down from her own wagon, sprinted here and swung herself up to the gate. I wonder you didn't make her leave the same way."

"Ach! She's doing no harm by herself, it's the noise and chatter of the whole gang together that excites the Domina. I'll throw her off at the next stop." Anastasius smiled to himself as he entered the rear room. The old nurse was not as hard as she liked to pretend.

Kira and Claudia, as it happened, were doing nothing more exciting than spinning – Claudia far more expertly, the spindle seeming to dance in her fingers. Rome's demand for textiles was insatiable. The Roman obsession with daily bathing and fresh linen had spread to every city of the Empire. No Roman, however humble his rank, would deign to wear animal skins; even a slave would snigger, "Fur-clad barbarian", behind his hand at the sight of a German emissary sweltering in his fur cloak in the Mediterranean sun. The wealthy wore silk, the import of which from the legendary Cathay was bleeding the Imperial Treasury of its silver and gold reserves. The imported silk cloth would be unwoven by an army of slaves working in factories, and then rewoven with wool for winter garments. The less rich wore linen in the summer and wool in the winter. The poor wore what they could, provided only that it was cloth and not fur. In wealthy households, with the surplus of slaves which their status required them to maintain, linen and wool were still spun and woven in the villa, though it was now rare indeed for a great lady to sit, as in the days of the Republic, with her maids, spinning and weaving and patching and darning.

Claudia gave a little gasp as Anastasius entered. She was a pretty girl, he thought to himself, with her jet black hair, coal black eyes and oval Spanish face. Kira leapt to her feet and ran to him.

"Oh Anastasius, this awful journey is my fault, but I did so want for my son to be born in Lydda." Anastasius led her to the couch and sat her down again.

"Don't worry", he reassured her, "After tomorrow, when we reach the pass and the great road to Antioch, there will be inns at the end of each day's journey where we can stay the night in comfort and safety, and we'll be able to change the horses frequently, instead of resting them. Soon we'll be passing through towns and villages all the way to Antioch."

Kira still wanted to justify herself.

"I did so want to be home, and for our son to be born in his own land. He will be great and his name will live."

"Then", said Anastasius, smiling at her fancy, "he will be great wherever he is born, whether in Cappadocia or in Lydda."

He turned his attention to Claudia, who had been trying, without much success, to melt into the wall of the wagon. This amused Anastasius so much that he could not be angry with her. Instead he put on an expression of mock severity and said, "So, I hear you are to be wed, Claudia?"

Flustered and blushing the girl replied, "I hope so, Domine."

"So do I, young woman, since it will stop you disrupting my household."

Claudia's blush deepened beneath the olive skin, "I'm sorry, Domine, I crave pardon."

Anastasius could keep his face straight no longer and laughed aloud, "How long have you been in the Domina's service, Claudia?"

"Since we both were ten", Kira interrupted, coming to her friend's aid, "My father bought her. She was alone in the slave market with no one to protect her – I heard my father tell my mother so – and that he bought her to save her from evil men who would put her in a brothel."

At this Claudia burst into tears and hugged Kira who began to weep in sympathy. Anastasius was nonplussed. Horses he could handle; men, most of them rough and battle-hardened, he could handle; but young women in tears left him helpless.

"Now, stop crying", he ordered sternly, "I only wanted to be certain of your length of service, because when we reach Antioch you will be emancipated and then married. As a freedwoman you must have a dowry. It would be a disgrace to me if it were too little, and a source of gossip and slander for idle tongues if it were too large."

Kira let out a little cry of delight and, jumping up, flung her arms around his neck in gratitude for his generosity and forethought. Gently he pressed her back down on the couch. A sudden thought struck him.

"Do you remember your father and mother, Claudia." he asked gently. The girl suppressed her sobs and looked up proudly.

"My father was a soldier. He was killed in battle beyond the great river."

Anastasius' eyes widened in surprise, "A soldier! A legionary?"

Claudia caught the question in his voice, "Oh yes, he was a standard-bearer."

"Which legion?" For a soldier the question was automatic.

"Why, the Hispana, the IXth."

"A legion of ill-omen", Anastasius interrupted.

"I still have one of his medallions with the number on it. I hid it when they took me away to the slave market."

Angry red spots had appeared on Anastasius' cheeks, "Who?" his voice frightened the two women, "Who committed this outrage, a daughter of the legions sold into slavery?" His voice grew so fierce that Claudia began to cry again, and Kira's lip was trembling.

"There, there, my child, I'm not shouting at you, we'll say no more if it frightens you, but if you can, tell me what you remember."

Claudia frowned in concentration, "Some of it I can never forget, I was so frightened. There was a centurion. He said that he would marry my mother and look after her, but not me. He said my father owed money and that I must be sold to pay the debt, otherwise my mother would be sold. I heard him telling my mother that he and all the centurions owed money, but the others had prisoners and he hadn't, and selling me would pay his and my father's debts. My mother kept saying 'No! No!' so he began to beat her with his fists. Then an officer with red ostrich feathers came".

"A Tribune!" interrupted Anastasius in wonder.

"I think so, and he took me away. I was put in a wagon with barbarians who were being sold. They frightened me. and I still remember how they smelt in their dirty fur. I couldn't understand anything they said, and that made them laugh, but they were kind to me and gave me bread and honey. We were in the wagons a long time till we came to the sea, and then we were put on ships. Some bullymen put chains on the barbarians who yelled and shouted and hit out with their fists. Some of the barbarians were beaten down with clubs, and one leapt into the sea, but they didn't bother putting chains on me. It was a long time and I was very sick, but we came to a city – I know now that it was Sidon – and I was put on a platform and a man came and bought me and gave me honey cake, and took me home to Kira, and the first thing that Nanny did was bathe me and dress me in clean clothes, and I heard her say, 'Burn those,' and I screamed and ran over to my old clothes and got my medallion out."

Anastasius' expression had grown more angry as he listened to Claudia's story.

27

"It is unlawful", he almost bellowed. "The law forbids a man to sell himself into slavery, and that must mean his children too. Mansour would know for certain, but I think you were never legally a slave. That a Roman soldier should do such a thing – betray a comrade and sell his child! It is beyond belief, scandalous, an outrage!" He paused for breath, "Still, it will do no harm to go through with the manumission. Do you remember the name of the tribune?"

"Oh yes!" replied Claudia, "I learned that on the journey, I can never, ever forget it. His name was Galerius."

CHAPTER SIX

Three horsemen were riding back along the road at a gallop.

Mansour urged his mule forward and turned across the road to intercept them. Anastasius also urged his horse into a gallop as the Dacian optio left his place at the head of the column. Anastasius, in a sore temper at what Claudia had told him, was not in the mood for a subordinate to ride ahead of him.

"Back!" he shouted, "Hold your station."

By this time the three horsemen had drawn up by Mansour and were engaged in excited conversation. Anastasius reined up beside them.

"What news?" he asked abruptly.

Mansour turned to him, "They say, Domine, that a bridge crosses a river and below the bridge the ravine opens out, behind that hill before us, and that beside the river there is an inn, a *mansio* no less, with stabling, dormitories and an inn yard large enough to take all our wagons."

Astounded, Anastasius asked, "Your map shows nothing of this?"

"No, Domine."

"It must be out of date!"

"It is the latest tax map, Domine."

"Then the inn must have been built since?"

"I hardly think so, Domine."

"Well, never mind. It's good luck for us."

By this time the Dacian cavalry had caught up with them and they moved off the road, letting them go by.

"You are certain that the inn is open, not a ruin?" – the question was addressed to the Dacians.

"Certainly Domine, we spoke to the *patrona*."

"The patrona?"

"The patron was out, fishing."

"And what did the patrona say?"

The Dacian shrugged, "She said that they were ready for travellers, even caravans."

Anastasius pondered this, "No chance of their being brigands in disguise?"

The Dacian looked startled at the thought.

"No, Domine! The place was too orderly; there were slaves working in the stables, bread baking in the ovens; brigands do not live like that."

"Very well, then, return to your posts. What do you make of all this Mansour?"

"It is extremely puzzling. A new inn could not have been built since the last tax map. Possibly it is an old one restored."

"Well, it still seems like good fortune to me, Mansour; but, in the circumstances, we must be cautious. First, the horses must be watered and rested for half an hour."

"But it is little more than two miles to the bridge, Domine, is that necessary?"

"Yes, I'll not push the horses beyond their strength, even a mile. Besides the road is now steadily uphill; that takes it out of tired horses. They may refuse halfway up and not move for an hour. Whilst we rest the horses, ride ahead and find this patrona, or better still the patron. Tell him we require shelter for the night, for men and beasts, but say that we'll not eat him out of house and home if their supplies are low after the winter. Tell him we have our own fodder and food; what we require is shelter. More important is that they prepare a lying-in room, and ask if there's a skilly-woman who can be called. If not, is there some woman who can assist Nanny at a birth if Nanny proves to be right. Pay something in advance, in gold, and then meet us at the bridge. Take two of the Dacians with you."

"I'd prefer, Domine, to take two of our own drovers with me. They can all use a spear."

"As you wish, Mansour, and here they are abreast of us; pick two out and let them get horses saddled." Anastasius galloped down the caravan.

The land was now definitely rising toward a rounded hill, itself little more than a roll in the land, and the horses and mules were lathering as they took the strain. Anastasius slowed down beside the Dacian optio.

"Half-an-hour halt to water the horses."

The Captain nodded, flag-signalled the column, and the caravan came to a smooth halt. Mansour and two drovers came galloping along the side of the road and headed for the bridge.

Anastasius gave the good news of warmth and shelter to Nanny. She was happy to hear it, but deterred him from disturbing Kira.

"The Domina is sleeping at last. That young hussy Claudia is sitting with her. She has some sense after all, but it's better you don't go in and wake her."

Anastasius meekly submitted and remounted his horse.

Mansour reached the crest of the long incline and pulled up at the bridge. The torrent plunged steeply down into a ravine, one side of which was formed by the escarpment of the low hill to which they had been heading. A side road led off before the bridge, descending the escarpment for about a quarter of a mile to where the gorge opened into a dale sufficiently wide to accommodate the substantial building and outhouses now revealed.

Directly opposite, across the bridge, was a row of twelve crosses from which hung decomposing corpses.

"I see that we are back among civilized men", Mansour remarked to the wagoners, who hastily crossed themselves.

The far side of the ravine, above the inn, had been extensively terraced, perhaps over centuries. The terraces, however, appeared newly cultivated; green with shoots of barley, cabbages and broccoli, and dotted with plum and almond trees. Mansour noted that the side road did not end at the inn, but continued down the dale until it disappeared behind the shoulder of a hill. The road was newly paved. The inn itself was now the subject of his scrutiny. It had been re-roofed, though not so recently that discs of moss had not taken hold on the tiles – perhaps two or three years before the latest tax map. The stables and dormitories had also been re-roofed and repaired with new doors and window frames. Some walls still showed black patches where the buildings had been fired. He studied the scene intently. It was one of good order. A broad, well-set man with red hair and beard and the straight back of a soldier was crossing the inn yard, carrying a net and wicker basket. This, Mansour guessed, was the Patron. The road down the escarpment was not over-steep and should not prove difficult for the wagons.

Mansour and his companions started down the road. They were met at the gateway by armed retainers, who, satisfied at the name of Count Anastasius, admitted them. Mansour rode across to the atrium. A middle-aged woman with iron-grey hair met him. He dismounted before addressing her, and noticed the quick flicker of appreciation in her eyes for this courtesy. "A Dacian", he concluded, and addressed her in Latin, "Madam, the Count Anastasius and a large caravan will require lodging for the night."

"I can speak Greek", she answered, a little tartly, "But you will have to speak to the Patron. He is in his cabinet."

"There is one matter I would speak of to you", he replied. "The Domina is with child and may give birth tonight. A lying-in room will be required, but also a midwife."

The woman smiled, "It is hardly likely that there will be one here, but I will serve."

Mansour chose his words carefully, "There is a nurse, Nanny to the Domina since her birth. She will expect to be in charge."

The woman laughed, "I know all about nannies", she said, "Have no fears on that account."

"Perhaps, then, you will be kind enough to lead me to the Patron?" She motioned him to follow and led the way into the atrium. Mansour swept the room with a glance. There was the *impluvium*, or central pool, of course, which kept the atrium cool, but he was more interested in the mosaics of the floor.

The principal design was a bleeding bull. Through the opposite door he could see the herb and flower garden which occupied the peristyle. This was ostentatiously a Roman villa! The woman pointed to a door and he crossed over to it and knocked. A strong voice bade him enter. His eyes flickered as he took in the room. Its length was twice its width, with a row of four windows down one side. It was empty except for a table in the centre, behind which sat the red-bearded man he had seen with the fishing net. The latter stood up and announced himself in good Latin, "Rufio, ex-centurion of Cohort V of the IXth Hispana, at your service."

Mansour's start at the words was involuntary. Mentally he kicked himself for showing surprise. Rufio looked at him keenly.

"No!" he exclaimed, "The Legion was not cashiered for cowardice, as the slander goes. The Legion was under strength, there was not a cohort up to establishment when we crossed the Danube. We marched into a trap and were cut to pieces. What many forget is that we still won that battle. The IXth was stood down because there were too few of us left to rebuild it."

"Your pardon", Mansour bowed slightly, replying in Latin, "I had not thought it otherwise."

Then, appearing to change the subject, he crossed the room to the far window, carefully leaving the door open.

"How pleasant this room is, Centurion, with the cool air from the atrium." He looked out of the window and his glance swept the path that ran along the outside wall. "And what a splendid view of the river. Happily the, ahem, 'unfortunates', by the bridge are out of sight."

Rufio showed his pleasure at being addressed by his old rank, and, smiling, spread his hands, "Not unfortunates, sir. Brigands! Brigands getting their just deserts. The Tribune Galerius will not abide them. They are hunted down and any taken alive are crucified along the road as a warning to others. The women and children are sold into slavery and the Tribune shares the price between us old centurions of the IXth. You can feel perfectly safe travelling along the roads from this point on, be assured of that."

"It is reassuring to hear that, Centurion, for we have a large caravan and will require lodging and stabling for the night. No! Have no fear we will not devour your stores, we have fodder and food of our own."

Rufio, who had been about to protest that his storerooms were all but empty, smiled with relief. His smile became broader as Mansour placed three gold coins on the table.

"A deposit", he explained, "We can settle up the difference when we leave. One thing more, I have already spoken to your wife about it; there may well be a birth tonight and a lying-in room is required."

"You will have our best room." Rufio replied expansively. "Have you a list of your people and animals? The Count and yourself will of course require rooms, the rest can be accommodated in dormitories."

Mansour placed a list on the table.

CHAPTER SEVEN

Kira had dozed fitfully for an hour or more when she was disturbed by voices outside the wagon. At first she fitted them into a dream of home, for, whoever it was outside, they were talking in Aramaic. Waking fully, she realized that they were two of the wagoners they had taken with them to Melitene. Greek was her mother tongue, and at first the Aramaic was hard to follow. The wagoners, their mules watered, were snatching a brief rest, sitting on the back steps of the wagon. Their voices carried through the thin walls.

"Where are we? Tell me that! In the middle of nowhere, surrounded by cut-throats. We'll all be murdered in our sleep", one was saying.

"What about the escort?" a second voice replied. "The Dacians will be on guard."

"A dozen men", scoffed the other, "What if a hundred brigands make a rush at us, how'll a dozen hold 'em off?"

"There's the Huns", the second man countered.

"The Huns!" the first man exclaimed, incredulity in his voice. "They'll most likely cut our throats before the brigands do. They can see in the dark, so it's said, creep between the wagon wheels and cut our throats before we wake up. Except the wimmin, they'll take 'em back for their chiefs. Their chiefs is 'alf man an' 'alf 'orse, 'orses with mens' 'eads an' arms, an' they 'ave bows made of young birch trees that only they're strong enough to draw. Their own mares only give birth to 'orses, so they need 'uman wimmin to keep the stock goin'."

Kira, listening to this conversation with growing panic, shrieked in terror at these last words. Claudia rushed over to her, Nanny came bustling in.

"We're going to be murdered during the night and carried off to be raped by monsters", she cried, as they tried to calm her, "and it's all my fault." Suddenly she stopped and clutched her belly.

"My baby", she cried, "My baby. It's beginning."

$$*\qquad*\qquad*$$

Anastasius resisted the impulse to order the wagoners to gallop. The horses would have been winded before they reached the crest of the incline – but he did urge them forward at a quickened pace, leaving the rest of the caravan behind. Mansour was waiting at the bridge; he sensed the urgency of the situation. Pausing only to guide the wagon onto the side road, he galloped back to the inn. By the time the wagon had reached the inn yard, a litter was waiting to carry Kira to her lying-in room, warmed by a charcoal brazier.

Anastasius followed the litter to the door, which was firmly shut in his face, "No men here!" ordered Nanny. "Go away, it will be a good while before you're needed."

Returning to the inn yard, he was in time to see the rest of the wagons arrive. Blankets were thrown over the horses and mules. They were unhitched and led away to the stables for watering, feeding and grooming. It was all very efficient, trained men moving purposefully in a well-drilled operation, military in its precision – a fact not lost upon Mansour. The only hitch occurred when the escort came clattering in. The Huns refused to sleep under a barracks' roof, opting instead to sleep under the wagons, as they had done previously, wrapped in the thick felt blanket every man carried, but accepting the luxury of palliasses from the dormitories.

Everything being settled, Anastasius began to take an interest in his surroundings. The sun was setting beyond the ridge and the dale was golden in the afterglow. Anastasius saw the terraced fields and the springing barley and thought, "So, my son is to be born in cultivated land after all, and not in a desolate waste." He returned to the atrium to await events.

Mansour meanwhile had collected his saddle-bag. He took out the scroll which was the record of their journey, and joined Anastasius. Neither spoke, Anastasius having his eyes fixed on the corridor which led to the lying-in room. It seemed long hours before there was a piercing howl and the tough soldier turned pale.

"Have no fear, Domine, all is well", Mansour said in a low voice.

"And just how the hell does a bachelor like you know that?" demanded a nervous and irritated Imperial Count.

"I only tell you what the old wives say, Domine", replied Mansour softly.

"I'm sorry, Mansour, but this is worse than waiting for the first charge in battle."

The door at the end of the corridor opened and Nanny appeared carrying a naked infant, lying on a linen cloth. She approached Anastasius and with profound dignity and reverence held out the child to him.

"Praise God, you have a son, Domine", she said. Anastasius took the infant in his arms and held him. He noted, almost as if standing outside the event, that the infant had a pugnacious expression on his face and a fuzz of golden hair. His voiceless contemplation of the wonder he held in his arms was interrupted by Nanny.

"How is he to be named, Domine?"

Anastasius saw again the cultivated fields about the inn, springing green amidst waste and wilderness, the fruit trees bursting into blossom for Eastertide, a perennial resurrection and renewal, and with this came, insistently, the thought of his martyred ancestor, Holy Giorgios. Exaltation filled him and he seemed to grow taller as he held the child in his arms; those in the atrium grew still as they sensed that the spirit of prophecy had fallen on him.

"His name is Giorgios" – Anastasius was startled to hear his own voice, strangely resonant. "And it will be great throughout the Empire, beyond the Euphrates and beyond the Nile. He will be known as 'Husbandman of God', 'Knight of Christ', 'Mighty Man of the Galileans'. The ships of a nation yet unborn will carry his banner across the seas of the world, a sign of hope to those in despair, of deliverance to the captive, of liberty to the conquered and freedom to the oppressed. He will suffer in the flesh, knowing sorrow, mourning greatly, but he will do a deed by which another shall restore Rome." Anastasius ceased speaking and, a little bewildered, handed the infant to the nurse. Everyone, including Anastasius himself, remained silent, awestruck.

Mansour looked up from his writing.

"I have recorded the name and the prophecy, Domine", he said, "How shall I record the place of birth?"

"Why, we're still in Cappadocia, though exactly where I don't know", Anastasius replied, "but 'Cappadocia' will be sufficient."

"The Domina desired so much that he be born in Lydda – " Mansour left the statement hanging in the air. Anastasius looked hard at him.

"No, Mansour, I will not falsify records, even to please the Domina. Cappadocia it must be."

"As you wish, Domine", Mansour replied, as with great care he wrote, "Lydda, via Cappadocia."

CHAPTER EIGHT

Mansour retired to his cubicle and took the map of the area out of his saddle bag. The scale was fairly reliable. Roads and rivers were marked but mountains were shown by pictures, the peaks invariably ending in a point. Mansour traced the way they had come; the torrent was marked and a dotted line, indicating a trackway, followed it some distance before petering out. No inn was shown on the map. Thoughtfully, Mansour rolled up the scroll and took out another labelled Legio IX Hispana. He unrolled it and began to read, mentally converting the complex Roman system of dating:

Legio IX Hispana

27 B.C. Raised in Hispania by Augustus.

9 A.D. Deployed in conquest of Pannonia and stationed there.

43 A.D. Deployed with the II Augusta, XIV Gemina and XX Valeria Victrix for invasion and conquest of Britannia. Soldiers of the Hispana refused to embark as a rumour swept the camp that they were being sent to the edge of the world. Mutiny spread to the other legions and had to be contained by diplomacy until the arrival of a commissioner from Rome who successfully appealed to the soldiers' self-respect and brought them back to their duty.

50 A.D. Severely mauled at commencement of Boudicca's revolt, losing 2000 men. Agricola reported to the Senate that it was the arrogant and abusive attitude and the corrupt practices of the Legion's officers, including the rape of the Queen and her two daughters, which was largely responsible for the rebellion.

69-70 A.D. Deployed in conquest of North Britain with headquarters at Eboracum.

117 A.D. Deployed for the conquest of Caledonia. Four cohorts of the Legion were totally destroyed and the sacred eagles lost.

122 A.D. Replaced at York by VI Victrix. Three cohorts of the Legion stationed in Nijmegen, Lower Germany, retained the name of the Legion.

130 A.D. Returned to Pannonia on garrison duties.

161 A.D. Routed by Parthians on Armenian frontier

A.D.170 Frontier duties on Danube.

250 A.D. Recruitment drive in Hispania marginally successful.

263 A.D. Legion at half strength deployed across the Danube. Surprised by Gothic cavalry with heavy losses. Rescued by Dacian auxiliary cavalry. Joined in pursuit of enemy and taking of prisoners.

264 A.D. Legion finally stood down.

Mansour's informant, who had access to the *Notitia Dignitatum*, the official list of the legions and their postings, had done well in supplying him with the gist of the Hispana's record, but it was the note which followed that riveted his attention. He read it several times and then put the scroll away.

The following morning, Anastasius decided that they would rest at the mansio for three days, though even that, he felt, was the minimum before Kira should travel again. Mansour joined him in the inn-yard.

"Our centurion tells me that from here on the roads are safe, Domine."

"Maybe so", replied Anastasius, "but I find it difficult to believe that even our friend Galerius and the terror of his *lex talonica* could clean up so quickly after a century of mutinies and secessions. We'll take a ride down this by-road with a couple of the Hun bowmen behind us."

Rounding the shoulder of the hill which had hidden the rest of the dale from view, they were astonished. The terracing they had seen from the inn continued down the dale. Apple, plum, almond and olive trees were dotted around, as were frames for vines. All the terraces were green with barley and wheat shoots; there was a number of farmhouses – long, low half-timbered affairs. Men and women were working, tying in the vine shoots and hoeing the crops.

"And the map shows nothing of this?" Anastasius enquired.

"Nothing, Domine. The terraces are very ancient, the work of generations, but the cottages are new, so the terraces have been restored. This road we are following was shown, but as a trackway, and now it is paved."

"Who could have used the trackway? Who could have built the terraces?"

"The Hittites, I think."

"Who were they?"

"An ancient people. They had an Empire in Asia Minor before the Romans, before the Greeks even. They are mentioned in the Hebrew Scriptures, and there are some scholars who think that the Troy of Greek legend was a Hittite city whose ships raided the Aegean for women slaves to work the Trojan looms."

"You're a store of fascinating information, Mansour", Anastasius said smiling, "but more to the point, who can have restored it?"

"Who indeed, and why?" Mansour countered.

"The harvest from these terraces would commission a Legion."

"Or four ala of cavalry", Mansour mused.

A mile along the road the terracing became rarer and eventually gave way to slopes of goat-cropped pasture. The paved way continued ahead of them.

"I think we've seen enough, Mansour", Anastasius said, "If there were brigands or deserters around here those farmhouses would be burnt and looted. We'll turn back now."

They had ridden in silence for some time when they saw a man plodding along the road toward them. His garb showed him to be a farmer. Seeing the party on horseback he drew to the side of the road. Old habits die hard and as Anastasius drew level he sprang to attention, smiting his left shoulder with his right fist in the legionary salute.

Anastasius drew rein and looked at the man, "A retired legionary I see. Of what Legion?"

"Trooper of the 1st Cohort, the IX Hispana, Sir".

"Indeed! And are there many veterans of the IXth settled here?"

"Why, everyone, Sir, all the *coloni* are old comrades of the IXth."

"Who do you pay your rent to?" Mansour interposed. The man looked uneasy at the question.

"Why, to Rufio at the inn, he's the agent."

"And your taxes, you do pay taxes don't you?"

The man laughed harshly, "Is there anyone who doesn't?" he asked. "Rufio collects them for the Publican."

"Who is . . . ?" Mansour pressed the point.

"That I don't know, I'm content to let Rufio deal with him."

"Do you pay in cash or in kind?"

"Why, in kind", replied the man, clearly beginning to resent this interrogation. "Where would farmers get cash from? We pay the rent in kind and the tax in kind."

"Don't press the poor man so, Mansour", Anastasius intervened, "You'll have him thinking we're imperial spies looking for more tax. Give him some silver for a jug of wine at the inn, and let's be on our way."

Mansour fished out of his purse five or six denarii and handed them down to the man, who was pleased enough to take them.

CHAPTER NINE

After the mid-day meal, Mansour wandered away from the inn until he found a vantage point from which he could observe all arrivals and departures. He did not have to wait long before Rufio emerged, fishing net over his shoulder, and set off down the bank of the river. Mansour followed at a discreet distance, and when Rufio selected a spot on the bank of a large pool, Mansour emerged from cover and wandered over to him.

"Ah, Centurion", he began as he seated himself beside him, "a very pleasant pastime." Rufio, still pleased at being addressed by his old rank, smiled broadly.

"My wife has a liking for trout, and I've a liking for peace and quiet."

"Ah yes, our Patrona. Have you been married long, Rufio?"

"Since five years after the IXth was stood down."

"And you opened this inn with your bounty?"

Rufio's face clouded, "We received no bounty. We were treated unjustly. If it hadn't been for the Tribune Galerius the veterans would have been reduced to beggary."

"I've heard of his generosity", Mansour smiled, "and of his open-handed hospitality."

"Indeed!" exclaimed Rufio, becoming enthusiastic. "Galerius restored this inn, made me tenant, and appointed me agent for the coloni. That's how I came to marry; my wife was a maid in his household."

"And he gave all the veterans land holdings for their own?"

Rufio laughed, "That would indeed be generosity, more than most could afford. No! Galerius is the landlord and shares the crop."

"Is Galerius also the tax-farmer?"

Rufio looked sharply at Mansour and had the uneasy feeling that he had said too much.

"Yes", he answered shortly.

"The tax of course is paid in kind?" Rufio's expression became hostile.

"You ask a lot of questions, Samaritan."

If the intention was to be offensive, it completely failed. Mansour merely smiled and said, "I must ask more, Dacian."

"I'm no Dacian", Rufio exclaimed, bridling, "I'm a Roman."

"Then let us talk like Romans. You, Rufio, are guilty of the worst crime a Roman soldier can commit: you betrayed a comrade and sold his child, a daughter of the legions, into slavery. My Master, the Count Anastasius, is a just man, more than that he is a lenient man, but if he learned who you are he'd hang you from your own inn sign, and only his Christian sensitivities would prevent him from crucifying you with the brigands on the hilltop."

Rufio paled, but he drew himself together.

"I am under the protection of Galerius", he almost snarled.

"Galerius is not here; Anastasius is", Mansour replied calmly. "But you have the opportunity to make some amends."

"What do you want?" Rufio asked sullenly.

"Only a little information. This inn: it's very large, some storehouses are new." Rufio answered in clipped accents.

"Galerius believes the new emperor will carry on the work of Claudius Gothicus and restore order and that there'll be a great increase in travel and trade."

"Hmm. And meanwhile the inn is large enough to encamp four *alae* of cavalry. Tell me, what became of the child's mother, the woman whom you offered to protect?"

"She died", Rufio replied shortly, and seeing that Mansour was not satisfied with this, went on. "After the girl was taken away she hardly ate, and what she did eat she brought back. There was nothing I could do to console her. I didn't want to sell the child, but it was her or her mother. We were all in debt to Galerius and he was a very hard man in those days."

"Yes! I've read the story. It's true that the IXth wasn't cashiered. Gothicus' nephew, Constantius Chlorus, urged against it for the sake of the army's honour; but the IXth was stood down because the Imperial Commissioner concluded that it couldn't be reconstructed. The legion, according to his report, was corrupt from top to bottom: the centurions and decurions stole from the soldiers; the soldiers stole from the storehouses and openly talked of murdering their centurions when the next battle offered them the opportunity. You were stood down without bounties or donations and with bare pensions. Unfortunately, that put you all in the hand of someone like Galerius, who suddenly became generous. Tell me about it."

"Tell you what?"

"You can begin with the tenancy contracts, what are the terms?"

"Why that the tenants and their children and their children's children remain bound to the farms and share the crop."

Mansour's eyes widened.

"The man's cleverer than I thought. He's invented a new kind of slavery. And what of the rents-in-kind? Even a glutton like Galerius couldn't eat all the corn that's grown here."

Rufio permitted himself a gruff laugh, "The rent's collected in corn. Galerius leaves the fruit and vegetables, and a share of the corn and wine, to the tenants."

"And what becomes of the corn?"

"It's stored here at the inn. When the new harvest is gathered, last year's corn is sold at Antioch and the new lot stored in its place."

Mansour nodded, "So there's always a supply at the depot? I see, and this new road, where does it go?"

Rufio made an effort to assert himself, "Find out!" he snarled, "Walk down it and see!"

"Fortunately, I don't have to walk that far, only to the women's quarters where there is one who can identify you as the villain who illegally sold her into slavery."

Mansour placed his hand under his chin and gave a passable imitation of a man hanging.

Rufio's brief defiance collapsed, "It meets the Antioch road, and, if that's what you want to know, it'll take a week off your journey."

Mansour was silent for a while.

"Galerius collects the rent for the land, and that is legal, but this inn and these coloni are not on the tax map, even though Galerius is the tax-farmer. What of that?"

"I know nothing of that!" snapped Rufio, his temper rising again. "I do my duty. The tax is collected in wine and oil and I hand it over to Galerius, that's all I know."

"Very well, I accept that", Mansour said.

Rufio bristled again, spoke rapidly, his breathing hard.

"Oh! So you accept my word d'you? And 'oo are you to question me? You, easy-livin' scribe to a Count 'oo doesn't even need to draw 'is army pay to live in luxury, with estates 'ere, there an' everywhere, an' slaves to do the work! What d'you know of the legions? They pay us once a quarter in coinage which is lead trash dipped in silver. Money which'll only buy 'alf of what it would before a month is out. 'Ow d'you think the women and children of the legions eat if their men don't steal rations from the mess? 'Ow d'you think a centurion lives on 'is pay without goin' into debt? 'Ow d'you think 'ee pays the debts if 'ee doesn't take a share of the soldiers' prize money? Yes! I sold the child an' that was better than watchin' her waste away with 'unger. You think Galerius is pilfering the taxes an' makin' 'imself rich? Well maybe 'ee is, but 'ee's been good to us veterans of the IXth. 'Ee takes a share of the corn an' wine an' oil, but 'ee leaves everyone enough to eat well everyday an' keep the Satur-nalia with hospitality to friends and neighbours. If you want to look for criminals, go an' snoop around the contractors 'oo rip us off an' raise their prices after every pay day. Y'think y'know everythin' don't you, an' you'd like to know about the new road? Well any old soldier could tell y'what that road means. It means that if the Eastern frontier is broken again an' the Persians drive for Antioch, Galerius can 'av four ala of cavalry, followed up by the infantry, in place before Antioch within a week, while the other generals are still sittin' on their backsides in Rome, an' if ever Galerius is 'ailed as emperor, the old sweats of the IXth will be shoutin' loudest an' marchin' with 'im."

Mansour remained silent after this outburst. Much of what Rufio had said was true, but he also knew that Galerius could still have an army down that road and in Antioch within a week whether the frontier was threatened or not. And the man who held Antioch, held Syria and controlled the Eastern Mediterranean as far as Egypt, and he who controlled all that was an Emperor only waiting to be proclaimed.

Rufio also remained silent, savouring the feeling that he had justified himself and crushed the man beside him. At length Mansour broke the silence.

"Perhaps I have judged you too harshly. Perhaps even Galerius has his eyes on the Persians and not on the Purple. For my own part I can't save the Empire, however much I would like to. The point of balance has been passed and the scale is inexorably tilting. I can only do what I can to save my people from the ruin which will follow."

Rufio looked rather blank as he heard this, and was again feeling uneasy at the thought of having said too much.

"Don't worry, Rufio, I'm not about to send a report post haste to Rome. As I said, I cannot save the Empire, I can't stop Galerius. I cannot even give a full report to Count Anastasius without putting him and his household in peril. What I've learned may help me save my own people and my friends, that is all. But I have some advice for you. Don't hasten to Galerius to report to him. You have said much, probably more than you know, but he will know and would undoubtedly have you murdered, and painfully. There is also one other piece of advice I can give you. Endeavour to stay out of sight, for I cannot answer for it if the one here who can identify you should recognise and denounce you."

He stood up and, leaving a discomforted Rufio staring dismally at the river, walked back to the inn.

CHAPTER TEN

The infant Giorgios was both healthy and strong, and by the third day Kira was up and about, exploring the river bank with her maids. On the fourth morning the caravan resumed its journey, but taking the new road. No one was so relieved to see them go as Rufio. The whole atmosphere of the journey became light-hearted. The sense of urgency and gloom had gone, perhaps because the gradient was steadily downhill, or because Spring had really arrived. Crocus, hyacinths and lily-of-the-valley sprang to life along the roadside almost, it seemed, as they passed.

Several nights of camping were necessary before they joined the great highway to Antioch, but the fear and anxiety felt at the idea of spending the night on the open plateau was gone. The road ended in the courtyard of a large mansio, well supplied with stables and storehouses.

"I don't think we need rack our brains as to who is the owner of this place", Anastasius remarked drily to Mansour.

"No!" replied Mansour, "and this one *is* on the tax map!"

The following morning their escort, no longer required now that they were on the cursus publicus, left them to return to Melitene, well pleased with the donation Anastasius had made them. They took their supply wagons and spare horses and mules, and the much-reduced caravan set off for Antioch, everyone happy in the knowledge that they could now change horses at the frequent mutationes and look forward to comfortable lodgings each night. Progress was now measured by the cylindrical milestones of the cursus publicus, each carved with the name and year of the Emperor in whose reign it had been erected. The tedium was relieved by the exchange of news with passing patrols of the *beneficiarii*, experienced veterans of the legions, who policed the roads.

Anastasius broached what he felt might be a delicate subject with Mansour as they rode at the head of the caravan.

"Claudia", he said, "is not a Christian."

"Neither is she a Samaritan", replied Mansour, unhelpfully.

"I know that!"

Anastasius was a little testy; Mansour's verbal games were all very well, but could be annoying where directness was called for.

"When I say that she is not a Christian, I mean that she is a pagan, or at least her parents were. They honoured the gods of the City, and her father, like many soldiers, was initiated into the mysteries of Mithras."

"Of all this I am aware, Domine", Mansour replied, "and of the policy of your house that slaves and freedmen are not pressured to ask for baptism."

"Exactly!" Anastasius said with emphasis, "that's the point. Claudia is not an irreligious girl, she's simply not serious. She no more believes in the gods of the City than you or I, but she has a foolish fancy for soothsayers and fortune-tellers. Apart from that she just doesn't think about religion."

"I know that Christians regard marriage to the non-baptized as deplorable, even though permissible", Mansour said seriously. "Your apostle Paul has even granted in such a case the privilege of divorce, which I understand is the only one in your Faith; but as Claudia is not baptized, our marriage should pose no problem."

"You mistake me, Mansour", Anastasius said, "it is of you that I'm thinking. Can a Samaritan marry a pagan, or indeed a Christian? If the answer is 'No', you must not feel bound."

Mansour chuckled, "Thank you, Domine, for your concern, but we Samaritans are not as strict as you in this matter. You forget our origins. There are Samaritans only because of inter-marriage between the remnant of Israel, left behind when most were taken into captivity, and the Assyrians who were planted in their place."

Anastasius relaxed, "Well, all is well then!"

"All is well indeed, Domine", Mansour replied.

Antioch was a place of wonder. Anastasius had wisely stopped at the last inn, only a few miles from the city so that they might enter it early the following morning. Even so the streets were crowded with vehicles of every kind. Kira and her maids gazed in awe at a thousand new sights. Slaves padded along carrying the litters of wealthy women overloaded with gold and jewels and clothed in rainbow-coloured sheer silk. Nanny clucked in disapproval at certain women, gold gleaming at wrists and neck, walking unaccompanied except for a slave following at a respectful distance.

"Roman strumpets!" she squawked, at the sight of women wearing gold about their ankles, with painted toe-nails peeping through gilded sandals. "Shameless! What Greek woman would flaunt herself like that?"

Men affecting the old-fashioned Roman toga hastened about mysterious business followed by slaves with arms full of scrolls. In the main Forum, porters and stall-holders cursed and swore and came to blows in a dozen tongues. Whenever a fracas threatened to get out of hand, the city police and the lictors waded in beating indiscriminately with their rods in complete disregard of who might be in the right and who might be in the wrong. Indeed, any such enquiry would have exacerbated the situation since it seemed that everyone was the aggrieved party.

Shops and stalls displayed the tribute of the world, for this was the third city of the Empire, the meeting place of land and sea trade routes which spanned the known world, wealthy beyond imagining. The sellers of silks and spices, gold, silver, jewels, gauze, and muslin so fine that a scroll could be read through it; carpets from Persia, perfumes from India, papyrus from Egypt, ointments and incense from Arabia, all jostled together for attention. Moneychangers shouted their rates amidst the Babel of other cries seeking customers for wine-shops, restaurants and brothels. The great basilica was a splendour of polished marble, glowing in the sunlight. Statues of gods and heroes stood on plinths before it or in niches in the walls. A magistrate was making his way toward the porticoed entrance, preceded by the lictors bearing the rods and axe of justice, the crowds making way before them. The odours of burning flesh and incense mingled on the stoas of temples from which blood-spattered flamens uttered their prophecies, and philosophers and sophists endeavoured to lecture their mocking audiences. The caravan inched and fought its way through to the harbour before seeking refuge in a mansio of some splendour, entered through a portico of Ionian columns and enclosing a courtyard of gardens and fountains. Four tiers of balconies ran around three sides, giving access to the rooms.

The harbour itself left the maids delirious with delight. It seemed that the whole of humanity was there. The quays were thronged with sailors and merchants. There were huge men, as they seemed, from Nubia beyond the upper reaches of the Nile, Ethiopians with long, wedge-shaped faces and high, perfectly straight noses, giant yellow-bearded men in bear skins from the far North, coal-black men from far down the Atlantic coast of Africa, beyond the great desert, small, wiry Spaniards, red-haired Britons, Copts and Libyans, quick-spoken and quick-witted Greeks, brown, black, white and yellow, it seemed like paradise to the man-mad girls.

Vessels of every kind, Arab dhows with triangular sails, Roman galleys, Greek and Syrian merchantmen, long ships with dragon figure-heads, which had made the endless voyage down the Volga, and across the Euxine Sea, lay alongside the quays, loading and unloading. Cotton, linen, corn from Egypt, copper and tin from Britannia, amber and tallow and live bears from the Volga lands, live ostriches and lions from Africa, silk from China, dried fish from the Aegean, marble from Sicily, amphorae of wine and olive oil, fine pottery and bronze-ware from Greece; cedar from Lebanon; the sights and smells were endless, whilst the air was filled with the shrieks of scavenging sea-birds and the cacophony of sailors and porters, merchants and agents, speaking and shouting in a dozen languages.

Kira insisted upon climbing a tower at the corner of the mansio, from which the entire city could be viewed; its palaces and temples, public gardens and artificial lakes. Later, when dusk had fallen, they climbed the tower again to see the city at night. The forums and main thoroughfares were lit by the soft, glowing light of a thousand street lamps burning olive oil.

As the early sun slanted down over the roof tops into the streets and thorough-fares, they were awakened by a cascade of sound. Bells from every quarter of the city began to ring; first one and then another, until all were chiming together. There was fierce rivalry between the public bath houses to be the first to ring the bell which announced that its hot baths had reached the right temperature. The result of that rivalry was a city awakened every morning by a hundred bells to sun-glowing colonnades and tree-shaded squares, a sublime experience of sight and sound.

Anastasius ordered litters for Kira and Claudia and, leaving the infant Giorgios in the jealous care of the old nurse, he and Mansour accompanied them to the Basilica. A notary was found to write in duplicate the scroll for Claudia's manumission. Armed with this and accompanied by the notary, they went before a magistrate in the praetorium. There, before a statue of the she-wolf suckling the infant Romulus and Remus, copied from the sacred icon on the Capitoline Hill, the ceremony of manumission was performed. The scroll was read out, Anastasius signed it, and the copy, Mansour and the notary signed as witnesses; the magistrate then signed and impressed a wax seal upon both copies.

One he gave to a scribe for the archives. Holding the other, he struck a bell three times and said to Claudia, "Thou art now a freedwoman." He handed her the scroll and Claudia, weeping with joy, kissed it and hugged it to her bosom.

Anastasius paid the notary and the magistrate their fees and the party left.

CHAPTER ELEVEN

Mansour was busy in the afternoon. Armed with the Imperial Commission appointing Anastasius Governor of Galilee and authorizing his journey, he was able to find the party a passage to Joppa after several hours of enquiry. The ship would sail in three days' time.

The following afternoon a larger party set out again for the Forum and the basilica. Claudia, in a new white tunic, her hair wreathed in flowers, was carried in a litter, followed by the other maids who tripped along in great delight carrying bouquets of flowers. Kira followed in another litter, with Anastasius riding beside her. Mansour and the foreman wagoner, pressed into service as "Best man", had gone ahead to await them at the basilica.

Before a presiding Magistrate and with due ceremony, Anastasius gave Claudia to Mansour in marriage. Claudia and Mansour exchanged vows before the witnesses. Mansour bestowed gold and silver upon his bride and tears flowed down Kira's cheeks as Claudia uttered the ancient words of the Roman marriage vow: "Whither thou goest, Mansour, thither go I, Mansoura."

The party returned to the inn for the wedding banquet and Kira and her maids prepared the marriage chamber, spreading new sheets upon the bed, scattering herbs and flowers upon it and sprinkling the room with rose-water. Then, giggling with delight, dancing and singing a wedding hymn, they escorted the blushing Claudia thither to await Mansour. Later, her eyes glowing softly in the moonlight which spilled into the room through windows open to the perfumed night, she breathed, "My wonderful, wonderful husband." And Mansour, the dry scholar whose passion had been learning, and the things of the intellect, was flooded with a new tenderness and knew a new truth.

*   *   *

The following day Mansour negotiated the sale of the draught horses, mules and supply wagons to a villainous looking, one-eyed Arab horse trader who offered the lowest possible prices to those about to embark, on the assumption that they were in a hurry and had no choice but to accept. The rascal however found that he had met his match in Mansour, and with many imprecations calling down vengeance from heaven, interspersed with laments for his imminent impoverishment, agreed a fair price. Anastasius' own horse and the furnishings of Kira's wagon were to be transported with them.

The rest of the day was spent in further exploration of the wonders of Antioch. Behind the quays were the workshops of those who made sails and ropes. In another quarter, along a narrow street, were the premises of sculptors, fresco painters, mosaic artists and marble polishers. Another quarter was the home of the metal workers, offering among other things bronze lustral bowls, ink-horns, jugs and tripods.

A long, sawdust-strewn street held the premises of carpenters, cabinet makers and woodcarvers. Streets of glass-blowers, potters and tile-makers ran down to the harbour. An imposing synagogue with porticoed entrance formed one side of a pleasant square, and a little further on they came to a Byzantine church, distinguish-able by its shallow domes, faced with polished marble slabs. There were smaller, but no less ornate, Christian churches which announced that their liturgies were in Latin, Syro-Chaldaic or Coptic.

There were temples of strange eastern gods as well as those of Egypt and Greece. Antioch was, beyond all doubt, a fabulously wealthy city, and all its communities prosperous.

Returning, they passed through another large forum. The far end was occupied by a great porticoed building with a wide stoa before it. The stoa was crowded with men and women, shouting and waving pieces of papyrus. Other men and women were hastening across the forum to the stoa in what seemed to Kira a belligerent manner, and she noticed that many of the women were ornamented, like those of whom Nanny had been so disapproving, with gold at ankles and toes.

Both Kira and Claudia became frightened as the shouting and gesticulating grew louder.

"What's happening?" she asked fearfully, "Is it a riot?"

"Nothing as harmless", answered Mansour, drily, "it is the Bourse. Everyone is anxious to buy shares in the next harvest."

"Whatever for?" asked Kira, frowning in puzzlement.

"If the harvest is poor and there is a shortage of corn and oil, the prices will go up, and those who have a share will make a good profit", Mansour said with a wry smile.

"That seems very foolish to me", Kira exclaimed. "The harvest might be good and prices fall, so they will lose their money."

"Not so!" Mansour replied, "Those who buy shares in advance are usually members of the City Curia, or the patrons of members, so if there is an abundant harvest they vote that the city buy the surplus and store it. That causes the price to rise, but when winter comes and supplies begin to dwindle, they vote that the City sell the corn back to the merchants, with whom they hold shares, at the low price the city paid for it, and so they profit twice."

Kira frowned, "But that's dreadful! Don't they have any thought for all the people without bread?"

"Certainly!" replied Mansour. "It would seem that they never think of anything else, for the plight of the poor is never off their lips in the Curia."

"But what do they do about it?" Claudia, who was now taking an interest, wanted to know.

"Why, they vote in the Curia for the City to buy the surplus corn from the merchants to whom they have just sold it – at, of course, the new price increased by shortage – and issue it as a daily dole to the poor, many of whom are poor because of the taxes they have to pay to the City for the purchase of corn."

Kira's mind was in a whirl as she tried to follow this. At last she dismissed it determinedly.

"It is either very stupid or very wicked. My father stores the surplus corn and oil and wine from our estates so that none of his people will go hungry in the middle of the year, and I am certain that that is what Anastasius will do."

"I am certain that he will do so, Domina", Mansour said softly.

"My father is a river to his people!" Kira continued firmly.

"Indeed, Domina, he is so", replied Mansour.

The following morning they boarded the ship which was to take them home. Claudia, as befitted a matron, put on airs to the resentment of the other maids.

"It's alright for her", they muttered, "but when are we going to get husbands?"

"Did you see that sailor on the quay?"

"No! I'm looking at the one up there at the front of the ship."

"He's the Captain, silly, you won't get him!"

"He's probably got a wife in Antioch already."

"And in Alexandria too."

"Don't be spiteful."

"And don't you be stupid!"

"And all of you stop chattering like monkeys", came Nanny's stern voice; and so, with the wind set fair and the ship riding high on the waves, they bowled down the coast of Syria. Dolphins joined them, sometimes leaping ahead as if to show the way, and sometimes taking up position on port and starboard like an escort.

"The wine-dark sea", Mansour murmured to Claudia, remembering Homer's evocative phrase, "and he got it right, just exactly right."

"Who did?" asked Claudia, her beautiful brow creased in a frown.

"Oh! A poet of long ago", Mansour replied and Claudia wrapped her arm through his.

"My clever, clever husband", she murmured, looking up at him with adoring eyes.

*　　　*　　　*

The mass of Mount Lebanon, clothed in its cedar forests which were both its glory and its wealth, rose over the horizon announcing that they were near their journey's end; and the ship seemed to sense this, bounding forward, skimming the waves.

Then, almost before they knew it, they were tying up to the quay at Joppa. A short ride brought them to Lydda, where Dionysius, his household, the two city magistrates and the members of the curia were waiting at the gates to welcome the new governor.

In this way the infant Giorgios came for the first time to Lydda, the land of his fathers, of his happy infancy and of his boyhood, in which began the sorrows foretold by his father.

CHAPTER TWELVE

Caius Galerius Valerius Maximianus woke pleased with life. The scroll beside his couch had been delivered, under the Emperor's seal and by Imperial Courier, the night before. There was a scratching at the door and he bellowed a "Come in!"

A new girl of about fourteen entered – "Egyptian", he noted – bearing a salver with a bowl of scented water and a towel. Kneeling beside the couch, she began to bathe his face and hands.

The contents of the scroll among other things absorbed his thoughts, but he idly fondled her as she sponged his face. He was not greatly interested in the girl – his fondling was more a small but gratifying exercise of power; also, he never passed an opportunity to gather information which might be relevant to a scheme in hand.

"Where are you from?" he asked.

"Alexandria, Sir."

"What gods do your people worship?"

"Zeus All-Father and Isis, Sir", the girl answered, puzzled. She had not expected from her brief preparation to discuss religion with the Tribune.

"Ah! Are there many Christians in Alexandria? Do they have many temples?"

"One large temple, Sir."

"And Jews? Are there many Jews in Alexandria?"

"I think so, Sir, they have a big temple."

"And Samaritans?"

The girl looked blank.

"Samaritans, Sir?"

"Yes Samaritans. Do they have a temple in Alexandria?"

"I do not know, Sir, I don't think so."

"But there were Samaritans there ten years ago?"

"I don't know, Sir."

Galerius was fully aware of the limitations of anecdotal evidence, but he had an instinct for that 'on the spot' knowledge which people unconsciously absorb. Satisfied, he pushed the girl away with his foot and called for his dresser; and then, upon second thoughts, turned to her and said, "Wait here until I return."

Today of all days he would wear his ceremonial armour, the gilded breastplate, the gilded greaves, and a gilded bronze capulet instead of the helmet.

After a brief breakfast he entered the praetorium where he was joined by his prefect, Licinius. He seated himself on the solitary chair and Licinius took his place, standing at his right. Galerius unrolled the scroll to enjoy the delayed pleasure of reading it again.

"Know that our good and faithful friend and true Roman, Caius Galerius Valerius Maximianus, Tribune of the Dacians, is invested by us in the Patrician Order as a Military Count of the Roman Empire, and is appointed as Governor of Cappadocia."

Galerius passed the scroll to Licinius.

"You see, I have come far, for a Dacian."

"And further yet, Domine", Licinius replied, quick to use the new style.

"And you with me, Licinius, you shall be the new Tribune and, one day, Praetorian Prefect."

Galerius, as his name indicated, was in fact a "Roman" Dacian, descended from those settled by Nero within the Empire two centuries before. Nevertheless, with his dark saturnine features and jet-black hair he was typically Dacian. He turned to Licinius.

"Now let us have Qassem in"; and then, to the two scribes at a side table, "This interview is not to be recorded."

Licinius struck a gong and the door opened and two soldiers marched in a man who was plainly terrified. Galerius drummed his fingers on the arm of his chair.

"Qassem, how long have you been in my service?" The voice was friendly but carried a tone of hurt and disappointment.

"Ten years, Sir", the man replied, his mouth dry.

"Address the Count as 'Domine' ", Licinius barked.

The man gulped, "I'm sorry, Domine. I didn't know, I hadn't heard."

"There, there", Galerius soothed, "Do not be so hasty, Tribune. Qassem could hardly know what we have only just learned ourselves. But ten years, Qassem, ten years, and now I find that you have been talking."

"Talking, Your Excellency?" Qassem appeared genuinely puzzled.

"Yes, talking, Qassem. Idle gossip, no doubt; but talking, to be precise, to one Mansour, secretary to the Count Anastasius. I am informed that you told him that my troops call me 'The Little Dragon'."

Qassem almost sighed with relief, "That is true, Domine. It was when he came with his master to request an escort, we fell to talking. I mentioned it to persuade him of the esteem and admiration the troops hold you in."

"Of course you did", Galerius said, stepping down from his chair.

"There, I told you, Licinius, this was nothing." He patted Qassem on the cheek in a friendly manner. "But you know that only the Emperor carries the dragon banner." Qassem's lip trembled and Galerius' voice took on a tone of menace. "Why did you give my enemies in Rome a weapon against me?"

Qassem shook with fright, "Domine, I did not mean to do any such thing. I didn't think."

Galerius' right hand swung in a savage back-handed arc, smashing across Qassem's face and sending him sprawling. The guards dragged him to his feet with nose and lips bleeding.

"You are a liar, Qassem!" Galerius spat. "I have eyes and ears everywhere. I can know what the Emperor had for breakfast this morning if such knowledge were necessary. You did not 'fall to talking' with Mansour. The Samaritan pig sought you out because you also are a Samaritan pig, aren't you?"

Qassem's face reddened at the insult. Terrified as he was, he protested: "Domine!"

The two guards at the flick of an eye from Licinius seized his arms and twisted them up his back.

"Answer the Count!" Licinius shouted.

"You are a Samaritan pig?" Galerius repeated the insult. The guards twisted the man's arms more savagely.

"Yes, Domine", Qassem gasped.

"Say it!" The guards twisted his arms again.

"I am a Samaritan pig", Qassem croaked.

"There, there", Galerius' voice became gentle. "You see how easy it is to admit the truth? And how much better you feel after?"

He brought out a linen handkerchief and dabbed the blood away from Qassem's face.

"Now what else did you tell Mansour?"

"I, I can't think. He had a way of asking questions; whatever I answered, he used it to ask another question which I could not back out of. I swear I did not mean to tell him anything."

Galerius said nothing for a while, then he looked at Licinius, "Yes! This Mansour and his little tricks have come to our attention before." He turned back to Qassem, "And you told him nothing more?"

"Not that I can think of, it was some time ago, I thought nothing of it afterwards."

Hope was returning to Qassem. Galerius shook his head sadly.

"I did warn you about my eyes and ears. My information is that you told him of our entertainments here, repeated slaves' insolent complaints and that my expenditure on hospitality was greater than my income."

Qassem's legs buckled; "Mercy, Domine", he croaked, "Mansour tricked these things out of me. I thought I was persuading him of your generosity. I didn't see it as you put it now."

Galerius returned to his chair and began leisurely to draw on a studded leather gauntlet, gesturing to the guards to drag Qassem up onto his feet.

"And what did you tell this filthy spy of the sources of my treasury?" The voice was very even.

"Nothing, Excellency, nothing, I swear."

"Well, that at least is the truth, for fortunately you know nothing of them."

Qassem looked almost relieved, but only for a moment.

"Now, Qassem, because you have not told the truth, or forgotten it, I am sending you to the interrogation room where your memory will be restored. You know the interrogators there and the pleasure they take in their work. The scribes will record every word which passed between you and Mansour, every word, mind, for I must know everything. You will also tell of all your previous meetings with this Mansour."

Qassem gasped, "I swear, Domine, I never met him before, never, never."

"It is foolish to lie, Qassem, for we will discover the truth in any case. You will be questioned three times and if there is any discrepancy in your answers the questioning will begin again."

Qassem was now white as death.

"Mercy!" he screamed, "I swear I'll tell you everything I can remember!"

"Of course you will. Of course you will", Galerius said pleasantly, getting up from the chair and stepping toward the man. He raised his gauntleted hand high and Qassem instinctively bent back from it. Galerius jerked his right knee up and drove the curve of the greave into the pit of Qassem's stomach. The man jack-knifed onto the floor in agony, his face purple as he frantically fought for breath.

"Take him to the interrogators", Galerius ordered as he turned to resume his seat.

"And after?" the senior guard asked. Galerius looked back over his shoulder.

"Sell him to the galleys at Trebizon. Share the price between you."

The guards dragged the gasping twisting body from the room.

CHAPTER THIRTEEN

"What next, Licinius?"

"There is the question of the inn-keeper."

"Ah yes, Rufio, sometime centurion in Cohort V of the IXth Hispana, as he tells everybody. Did he do any talking?"

"There is no evidence of it."

"Anastasius used the new road to cut his journey to Antioch."

"The road could hardly be hidden; the caravan was at the inn three days after the birth of the infant." Galerius arched an eyebrow. "A son", Licinius said, "named Giorgios, after his great-grandfather, a Christian criminal they call 'Holy Giorgios', because he was executed under Decius."

"Which shows they are still subversives, but go on, Licinius."

"During that time Mansour made several leisurely excursions in the area. He seems to have found the road for himself and scouted it."

"Did he take an escort?"

"Yes, two of their own wagoners."

"Not the Dacian cavalrymen, nor even the Huns?"

"No!" Galerius drummed his fingers on the arm of his chair.

"Go on."

"Mansour was with Rufio only twice. Once, at the beginning, to make arrangements for stabling and for the lying-in, and once at the end, to settle the bill."

"Was everything which passed between them heard?"

"Unfortunately, no! Mansour went into the cabinet leaving the door wide open, with a pleasant remark about enjoying the breeze. He stood at the side of the desk where he had a good view of the doorway and of any movement near the windows. Our agent could not get close enough to hear without discovery."

"How careful this fellow is", Galerius mused. "What is he, do you think? An Imperial spy?"

"I doubt it, Domine, he's too clever for Rome to waste on such as Anastasius; but what of Rufio, should he be questioned?"

Galerius held his chin in his hand for a longish interval.

"No! He may be garrulous but he knows nothing and he may be useful later. Now! What do we know of Anastasius?"

"An honest soldier, a simple man."

"Is he political?"

"No! He will serve the Emperor legally succeeding."

"The operative word there, Licinius, is 'legally'. That is where politics comes in and honest soldiers stick to their principles – but I take your point. Now, this Mansour, what of him?"

"A fox, Domine."

"A fox with a twitching nose, Licinius." Galerius put his finger tips together. "But who does he serve? I agree with you, he's not an Imperial spy."

"He serves Anastasius."

"I don't doubt it, but what or who else?" Galerius sat thinking and Licinius did not interrupt. At length Galerius turned to one of the scribes, "The last census!" The man hastened to fetch a scroll. "What is the Samaritan population of the Empire?"

"Four hundred thousand, Domine, the main concentration being in Samaria as you would expect."

Galerius' fingers drummed on the arm of his chair.

"A sharp decline. The Jewish and Christian populations increased, I noted it at the time. Now why should the Samaritans decline? It can only be because significant numbers are leaving the Empire, probably crossing the frontier into Persia."

Licinius shifted uncomfortably. He felt a remark was expected of him.

"Is that a bad thing, Domine?"

"It is if they take their gold with them."

Licinius' face brightened, "Before we get it?"

"Exactly! Before we get it. It takes a lot of gold to win the Imperial throne, and a lot more to stay there. But why are the Samaritans leaving the Empire?"

Galerius' finger tips came together again. Licinius, though he felt an answer was expected, could think of nothing to say.

"Licinius!" Galerius' voice became brisk, "The Plebs believe that all religions are equally true. The philosophers assert that all religions are equally false. I consider that all religions are equally useful; useful that is for bringing together in a few places, where they can be most easily confiscated, gold, silver, ivory and precious stones. I regard prophecies and the foretelling of the future as so much nonsense, but I do think that an intelligent man, well-informed about the past, can read the present and discern the trends which will make the future. Take the Samaritans. They do not have the organization which the Jews and the Christians have, no synagogues or churches, no rabbis or bishops, yet here they are acting in concert as though forewarned. That tells me that someone is gathering information, perhaps only a little, but sufficient for him to perceive what our future policy will be. This Samaritan business and the leaking away of gold has puzzled me for some time, until this sly fox, Mansour, left his covert. I asked you whom he served. He serves his people!"

He turned to the scribes. "Take a new scroll and label it 'Mansour'. Make an entry: 'Mansour, freedman and secretary of Count Anastasius. Married at Antioch to Claudia, handmaid to Countess Kira, daughter of Dionysius, Shaikh of – "

Galerius stopped abruptly.

"Of course! of course!" He turned to the scribes, "Do not write this." He drummed the arm of the chair for a few moments, and turned to Licinius, "What a pretty little scheme we have here, and right under our noses too! We have been so busy watching your 'simple soldier', Anastasius, that we forgot about the other sly fox hiding behind his Roman rank."

"You mean Count Dionysius?" Licinius asked, a trifle uneasily, since he suspected that he was about to be blamed for something.

"*Shaikh* Dionysius!" Galerius said emphatically, "but we have always thought of him as 'Count of Lydda'."

Licinius remained silent, deeming it best to say nothing.

Galerius spoke again, "Lydda, a small city, but a meeting-place of caravan routes. It also has a Rabbinical school and a Christian college. A very pretty scheme; the place is full of merchants, camel drivers, sailors, students, strangers coming and going. Who would notice a few Samaritans with heavy bags joining the caravans?"

Licinius pursed his lips.

"But this Dionysius is a Christian; these sects, Christians, Jews, Samaritans, are all at each others' throats. Why would he help Samaritans to leave the Empire?"

"Because he is their Shaikh!" exclaimed Galerius, "That's what we overlooked. A Shaikh is a river to his people, his honour requires it, whatever their religion might be." Galerius fell silent again, thinking. At length he spoke. "But how does he, or this Mansour, know that the Samaritan gold is first on our list? How, for that matter, do the Samaritans know? There has been a leak somewhere, Licinius, and I think I know where. Qassem is not the idle gossiper he pretends to be. Send to the interrogation chamber; I want him kept alive for more subtle questioning."

Licinius called a messenger, but he was still puzzled.

"But if there is a leak, why aren't the Christians and the Jews leaving, or at least hiding their wealth?"

Galerius smirked, "They have nowhere to go, Licinius. They are tied to the Empire by their temples and colleges, and by their estates and trade. Their property and wealth binds them fast to the Empire, so they tell themselves that it will not happen, or only to the other lot. The Samaritans on the other hand don't have temples or colleges, I confirmed that myself only this morning."

Licinius nodded. "I see", he said.

It was an unfortunate interruption, for it led Galerius into another train of thought.

"You have rather outsmarted yourself, Licinius, suggesting that I ask Diocletian to persuade the Emperor to transfer Anastasius from Cappadocia to Lydda."

Licinius knew better than to protest that it had been Galerius' idea, so he merely murmured, "I thought it the best way to get rid of this Mansour fellow."

"Quite so! Quite so!" Galerius smiled tolerantly, "but from now on you must keep a close watch on this Mansour and record everything he does, everyone he meets, everywhere he goes, until we establish his connection with Dionysius, and this time don't let your obsession with Anastasius blind you to the identity of the real fox, Dionysius."

Licinius remained silent, and at that point there came an interruption as the messenger returned.

"Well?" demanded Licinius. The messenger looked plainly uneasy.

"The prisoner, Domine – "

"Well?"

"He has expired."

Galerius gave an expression of annoyance, but shrugged. "These things happen", he said, and stood up and walked to the door. He turned and spoke to Licinius, "I have something to attend to. Go and see what the prisoner said before he expired."

Galerius strode down the corridor humming a little tune; he even gave the *optio* of the guard on duty outside his chamber a crooked smile. The Egyptian girl, sitting obediently on the couch looked up, doe-eyed, as he entered. The door closed behind him. One of the guards winked at the other and hissed softly, "The dragon's going to devour another maiden."

"I hope there's some leavings", replied the other with a leer.

"Enough of that!" snapped the optio. "The Tribune won't abide dirty talk. He won't tolerate it. He won't."

CHAPTER FOURTEEN

Spring turned to summer and the infant Giorgios learned to sit up in his cradle and to throw things out of it, to the annoyance of his nurse. The downy hair of birth had given way to a mop of fair curls, and his limbs were straight and strong.

His parents were amused by his slightly puzzled expression and the little frown he wore.

"He thinks a lot", Kira would tell Anastasius, with pride.

The Empire prepared to celebrate the "Augustalia." Dining clubs considered menus; the guilds planned their processions and pageants; athletes, gladiators and charioteers stepped up their training; and wine merchants laid in extra stocks.

Dissatisfaction with Christians, Jews and Samaritans began to be expressed because they absented themselves from the ceremonies honouring the gods of the City with which the holiday began.

Indignation grew among the people and suspicion among the authorities. Worshippers of other strange gods from the east made no difficulty about sacrificing to the gods of Rome, why should these sectarians?

"They're glad enough to join in the feasting and drinking", was a commonly expressed complaint.

It was in the midst of these preparations that the Empire was struck a blow totally unexpected and unprepared for. Zenobia, Queen of Palmyra, a desert kingdom between the Mediterranean coast and the Euphrates and an important buffer state between Rome and Persia, repudiated her late husband's treaty of alliance. Her heavily-mailed cavalry swept across Syria and took Antioch whilst Galerius, back in Cappadocia, floundered.

*   *   *

With Antioch captured, Zenobia divided her forces. One army swept south, through Lebanon, Galilee and Judea into Egypt, to take the prize of Alexandria, wealthiest city of the Empire. Another army drove north, across Cappadocia, Galatia and Cilicia.

Their rapid advance was facilitated by Galerius' new road and his secret stores of corn and fodder. Rufio had barely time to tip the contents of the cash chest into his saddle bags and gallop off, deserting alike his wife and his old comrades, before the Palmyran cavalry came clattering up the road. Galerius, in full retreat, watched thunderstruck as all his grand schemes tumbled into ruin. With Antioch forever beyond his grasp, he began to plan anew.

There is little doubt that Zenobia could have carried her frontier to the Aegean, if Persia had accepted her offer of an alliance. Unaccountably, Persia rejected the offer in the coldest terms. Reading this as a threat, Zenobia withdrew troops to guard Palmyra and her Euphrates frontier. Galerius gathering his Dacian cavalry was able to check her at Ancyra, holding on to the province of Asia and the Bosphorus by his fingertips.

Zenobia in her advance to Egypt had bypassed the coastal cities which she believed, wrongly, to be strongly garrisoned.

Learning in Alexandria that such garrisons as there were had been withdrawn by sea to Asia, she directed troops back north to seize the coastal ports. She had also avoided contact with the four legions stationed across hundreds of miles of desert along the Euphrates. They in turn, their prime duty being to hold the Persian frontier, made no effort to cross the desert westward and fight. The Xth legion in Judea deemed it prudent to follow this example, retreating into the desert beyond the Jordan and falling back upon the Euphrates to join the Syrian legions.

The infant Giorgios knew nothing of this historic drama, but not so his father and grandfather. They were in an all but impossible position. The field army was out of their jurisdiction, and in any case was out of reach. Galerius had stripped the coast of garrison troops and they had nothing with which to defend Lydda except the city police. The approach of Zenobia's mopping-up force was heralded by a rider of the postal service. He came galloping up to Dionysius' villa to shout "The Palmyrans are coming", and then rode on with the eagerness of someone carrying dramatic news.

Dionysius, his son, Andrew and Anastasius set out for the city. On the way they stopped at Mansour's house. "If I don't return", Anastasius said to him, "I leave you in trust my son and my wife", They continued their way to the city in silence.

Reaching Lydda, they found panic beginning in the streets. Dionysius mustered the city police to control the situation, though it was probably saved by a cry from the watchtower of "Here they come!" Everyone seemed to freeze and grow oddly calm.

The citizens stood by as the three horsemen led the city police, followed by the two magistrates and the curia, out of the city. They lined up before the gates.

Anastasius studied the approaching enemy carefully. They came on in column of route and not as a mob; this at least was reassuring. A young captain led the column, and when they were within fifty yards of the gates he called his troops to a halt.

He rode forward alone. Andrew half drew his sword, but at an angry word from his father sheathed it. The Captain halted and, in Greek, demanded, "Who stands in my path?"

"I am Dionysius, Count of Lydda", replied the older man, "and this is Count Anastasius, Governor of Galilee, and this is my son, Andrew."

The Captain smiled. "And these", he cast a look over the city police, who one by one were melting away, "are your army?"

"They are a Roman army", Dionysius replied with dignity.

"I do not come to fight you, Count", the Captain replied, pleasantly enough, "but to take this city in the name of the Augusta Zenobia, if possible without damage or bloodshed."

Anastasius noted the title "Augusta". It might mean nothing, or it might mean that Zenobia was not setting herself up as an independent sovereign, but as Imperatrix of the Eastern Empire – Roman still, but not ruled from Rome. "In that case", he thought wryly, "Mansour's gloomiest forebodings are coming true."

With Gaul, Hispania and Britannia in the hands of the pretender, Victorinus and the Eastern provinces now in the hands of Zenobia, the legal government would control little more than Italy and the Balkans. "The Empire is fragmenting", he said, half aloud, and then realized that Dionysius was speaking.

"I know of Queen Zenobia, but not of Zenobia Augusta."

The Captain, who until now had been smiling, frowned darkly.

"Then beware lest you hear of her in future. The Augusta was proclaimed by the army, as so many of your pretenders are, but she is the true Augusta, descendant of the Divine Alexander and re-incarnation of Cleopatra."

Anastasius thought it wise to intervene at this point.

"If you do not come for bloodshed, what are your terms?"

The Captain searched him with his eyes and, evidently satisfied, replied, "First, that the city and the city treasury be surrendered to the Augusta, intact, acknowledging me as her Governor.

"Second, that you, Count Anastasius, and you, Count Dionysius, surrender your offices and titles to me and retire into private life. Your estates will not be sequestered so long as you pay the Augusta's taxes.

"Third, that the City Police be placed under my command.

"Fourth, that the magistrates and curia perform their functions under my direction and the law of the Augusta Zenobia."

Anastasius was aware, though he did not give so much as a glance behind him, that the city police were deserting now in threes and fours. He mused for a moment and then replied,

"These are generous terms indeed, Captain, especially as we have no means to resist them."

Turning to Dionysius he said urgently, "We must accept."

Dionysius nodded gloomily, replying in a low voice, "His troops are disciplined and he is clearly a cultivated man. We must wait for better times and the return of the Eagles."

Anastasius turned to the Palmyran. "We accept."

They escorted the new governor through the forum, lined by curious citizens, silent until one shouted, "Better the barbarian than the tax gatherer", and a murmur of agreement ran through the crowd. They watched the Palmyran take possession of the basilica and dispose his troops about the forum, and then, with the dread that the shout and murmur signalled the fall of Rome and the end of civilization, rode silently home.

*   *   *

Rome, with the Empire split into three hostile fragments, seemed at the nadir of its fortunes, but another blow was to fall. Claudius Gothicus, Emperor for barely two years, died of plague in August 270 A.D., and the final disintegration seemed imminent.

Once before, when Hannibal had marched through Italy, annihilating legions to his right and to his left with none daring to face him, all had seemed lost. Then great Scipio had risen in the Senate to stamp his foot, and at his stamping new armies had sprung from the very earth. Now a second Scipio arose, Aurelian, Cavalry Commander to Claudius Gothicus, who was proclaimed Emperor by the Danube legions. He also stamped his foot, and throughout Italy, Illyria, the Balkans and Africa, Rome lifted up her eagles. Aurelian set his face toward the frontiers and began four long, weary years of marching and fighting from the Ebro to the Euphrates. At the end of those years the Empire united and secure, the Senate proclaimed him, "Aurelian Augustus, *Restitutor Orbis*" – "Restorer of the World".

PART TWO
272 – 286 A.D.

CHAPTER FIFTEEN

Giorgios' earliest memory was of sitting in the spring sunshine on the warm flag-stones of the peristyle, playing with pebbles. At the age of two his horizons were filled by his father and mother, Iris (promoted from among his mother's maids to be his nurse,) and "Uncle" Mansour and "Auntie" Claudia. More distant figures were his grandfather, his mother's elder brother, Uncle Andrew and "Old Nanny". That redoubtable woman had turned a deaf ear to all attempts to persuade her that she had retired from active life. She still kept a watchful eye, on Iris in particular and the rest of the household in general.

Giorgios' father, grandfather and uncle were sitting at a table, enjoying the sun-shine, a jug of wine and earnest conversation. In their lowered voices and serious tone, Giorgios sensed anxiety and it frightened him. He began to howl and Iris rushed over, picking him up and comforting him. That was his short, vivid memory of the event. Before and after were a blank.

The three men were in fact discussing some momentous but incomplete news, related by Dionysius.

"Aurelian has moved at last."

"Impossible", Anastasius said. "He has to plan the movement of an army from Rome to the Bosphorus; just think of the commissariat problems."

"You forget Diocletian!" Dionysius exclaimed. "That man is a genius. The army has crossed the Bosphorus and joined Galerius at Ancyra. Aurelian's cavalry brushed aside the Palmyrans and advanced right into the heart of Galatia before Zenobia challenged him. There has been a battle, at Tyana."

"Who was the cavalry commander – Galerius?" Anastasius asked, professionally curious.

"No! Apparently, Aurelian brought his own man, Constantius."

"Constantius Chlorus!" exclaimed Anastasius, "Claudius Gothicus' nephew?"

"The same."

"I've heard a lot about him, and all to the good, but Galerius won't like his nose being put out of joint like that. Still, it shows Aurelian knows his man". Anastasius could not keep a note of satisfaction out of his voice.

"Credit where credit's due, Anastasius", Andrew interrupted, "Galerius did hold the line at Ancyra. If Zenobia had reached the Bosphorus, Aurelian couldn't have landed his army unopposed."

Anastasius grimaced.

"Well yes", he said at length, I'll grant you that, but to do it he stripped the coast of garrison troops, right down to Gaza. I don't deny he's a first-class cavalry commander, it's just that he spoils it all by being a first-class copper-bottomed bastard."

"Are you certain of all this, father?" Andrew asked.

"Yes! The news came in dispatches from a reliable source."

They were interrupted by a slave approaching to refill the wine jug, so saving Dionysius from further questioning on that subject.

"It will still be a long time before we see the Eagles again", Anastasius remarked, "and I must say I've found our eighteen months' rustication rather pleasant. It's a relief not waiting to be stabbed in the back."

Dionysius laughed but Andrew pursed his lips. He did not like to hear criticism of the Empire. At this point Iris interrupted them, bringing Giorgios back, his tears and his anxiety wiped away. Set down, he came tottering toward them, mouthing "Dadda, Dadda", and the three gave him all their attention.

Another of Giorgios' early memories, though it was only with hindsight that he placed it after the first, was of his mother taking his hand, with Iris in attendance to carry him when he grew tired, and leading him through the gardens and orchards which surrounded the villa. They came at last to the foot of a gentle slope, the grass cropped short by several goats. It was separated from the path by a low hedge and wicket gate. His mother pointed, saying, "Aunt Claudia's goats."

"Why?" demanded Giorgios.

"They give her milk, and fine wool to spin."

Along the brow of the slope there was a thick hedge of Rose of Sharon, now covered in golden blooms. Giorgios pointed to them, chuckling with delight. The hedge marked the boundary between their own gardens and those of the Governor's official villa which they had been obliged to vacate when the Palmyrans came. Kira's mother had died shortly after their return to Lydda, happy to have held her first grandchild in her arms. This was one reason why they chose to live with Dionysius rather than in Anastasius' own family villa. Another reason was, as Anastasius put it, "to keep an eye on that young hot-head, Andrew".

Kira took a path along the hedge at the foot of the slope and they came to another gate which gave onto an orchard and garden and a half-timbered cottage. Giorgios' curiosity was caught by a strange little building attached to the side of the cottage. It was a white tower, with small round holes in its sides, through which pigeons were entering and leaving.

"Birdies", he cried, pointing, "Birdies!"

"Yes", his mother answered absently, "Uncle Mansour's pigeons."

To Giorgios' delighted astonishment, a pigeon came fluttering over the hedge, and, exhausted, tumbled on to the grass.

"Sore foot", Giorgios said, pointing to a band of white linen around its leg, "Uncle Mansour make it better?"

A maid, a local girl paid a salary – for Mansour would have no slaves in his little domain – admitted them to the cottage.

They entered a small square atrium. The floor was tessellated in a black-and-white mosaic of geometric patterns; it was entirely innocent of images of men or beasts. They crossed the atrium, skirting the pool, and entered a cool, pleasant room, its white walls relieved by terra cotta panels. A large window faced south, admitting golden sunlight. Auntie Claudia was lying on a low Roman-style couch, and beside her was a cradle. Intensely curious, as only an infant can be, Giorgios toddled over to it and peered inside. And there, in the cradle, was a tiny baby making strange noises. Giorgios began to chuckle. "Baba, Baba", he cried, and then began to roll about on the floor in happiness.

"This is Auntie Claudia's little baby", his mother said. "His name is Lucius."

"Play, play", Giorgios chortled. Memory closed at that point, but the scene often came back to him, unbidden.

It was shortly after this incident that Dionysius had more news for Anastasius and Andrew.

"Zenobia has been defeated at Tyana and is in full flight toward Antioch. I don't know anything more, except that Galerius is leading the pursuit."

Galerius in fact moved his Dacian cavalry at great speed down his new road to the coastal Cursus Publicus and reached Antioch ahead of the retreating Palmyran army. He did not attempt to take the city, but placed his forces between it and the enemy. Prevented from falling back on Antioch, the Palmyrans retreated east to Immae, where the main Roman army advancing from Tyana caught up with them. Forced to make a stand, Zenobia's forces suffered another defeat, but were able to extricate themselves and retreat in good order to Emesa, the last city before Palmyra itself. The next day, Galerius entered Antioch in triumph, but not, as he had long hoped, as Emperor. Swallowing his frustrations, he handed the city over to Aurelian with all due deference. Aurelian in return raised him to Senatorial rank.

"So, the scoundrel is back in favour", Dionysius growled when this news reached them, "and all by good luck."

"He's a good cavalryman", Anastasius remarked, though without enthusiasm, "and that manoeuvre was brilliantly executed. If Zenobia had been able to fall back on Antioch there would have been a long siege. Now, with Antioch in his hands, Aurelian can bring in reinforcements and supplies by sea."

"Well, what does it matter if this Galerius is a bit of a scoundrel", Andrew demanded impatiently, "We're winning the war aren't we, and Galerius is doing it for us. Why don't we collect all our tenants, arm them and liberate Lydda right now?"

Dionysius shook his head. "All that that would achieve would be a lot of destruction and bloodshed. Untrained peasants and farm workers can't fight armoured cavalry. We must wait for the eagles, and let's hope that the Palmyran Captain has the good sense either to leave or surrender when they arrive."

Andrew snorted in disgust, "When are we going to fight?" he demanded.

Much to Anastasius' satisfaction, the Palmyran forces did leave, not only Lydda but Egypt and Judea also, recalled by a now desperate Zenobia to defend Palmyra itself. In Alexandria the Prefect of Egypt resumed his office. The Xth Legion, in makeshift camps along the Euphrates, deemed that the time was right to reoccupy its more comfortable headquarters at Caesarea.

From Lydda the chief of the city police rode out to Dionysius' villa with the news that the Palmyran garrison had disappeared overnight, leaving the city threatened by turmoil. Without delay Dionysius set out with Anastasius and Andrew to reclaim the basilica and re-establish Roman rule.

They found Lydda tense; the market stalls in the Forum were empty and the shops boarded up. The city police had kept the criminal element subdued and there had been no looting. They dismounted at the city gates and strode across the Forum to the basilica where they were met by the magistrates and curia.

Dionysius mounted the steps of the stoa, a semi-circular stone platform before the basilica's porticoed entrance, flanked by Anastasius and Andrew. At the sight of the red cloaks and horse-hair crests the crowd pushed forward and fell silent.

"Citizens of Lydda, you know me", Dionysius' voice carried across the Forum, "I am Dionysius, Count of Lydda, the military authority for this city. The armies of Zenobia have been defeated in two great battles. Zenobia has withdrawn her forces from Egypt, Galilee, Judea and Syria. The Xth Legion is on its way from Caesarea to punish by decimation", a horrified groan shuddered through the crowd and Dionysius waited for it to subside, "to punish by decimation", he repeated, "any city which has not immediately submitted to the Augustus Aurelian and maintained the Roman Peace. Your magistrates, curia and I myself, are determined that this will not be the fate of Lydda. Everyone will now disperse and go about his business. Looters and rioters will be subject to summary execution."

He turned on his heel and entered the basilica, followed by the magistrates and curia. "Have the criers go about the city repeating the Edict", he said to the First Magistrate. The man, overawed, gave the necessary order.

Dionysius led the way to the dais at the far end of the basilica. He stopped and, turning to the magistrates, bowed and said, "This is your place, not mine", waving toward the two seats, one higher than the other; then to the members of the curia, he said, "Pray, go to your places." They, still bewildered, moved to the stone benches which made a semi-circle before the dais and sat down. Dionysius remained standing, not upon the dais but to one side and below it. The members of the curia were won immediately by this deference to Republican legality.

"What of the Treasury?" Dionysius asked the First Magistrate.

"Empty", the man replied gloomily. "The Palmyrans used it to pay merchants for their supplies, and what was left they took with them."

"What is the most immediate need for money?" Dionysius asked.

"The wages of the police, the fire brigade and the watermen", the First Magistrate answered without hesitation, "but the city tax has been collected for this year. To attempt to collect it again would provoke a riot."

Dionysius waited a few moments and then said, "Very well, as Count of Lydda I will make a donation to the city treasury."

He mentioned a sum which made the curials gasp, and then turned to Anastasius who, speaking without hesitation, said, "And I will make a similar donation."

Dionysius looked hard at the First Magistrate, who, like most of his kind, was of the Equestrian Order and a rich merchant. The man gulped, but saw that he had no choice.

"And I", was all he could manage.

Dionysius turned his gaze upon the Second Magistrate, who began to make excuses, "Trade has been very bad, we have lost much. . ."

"And will lose a lot more without police, firemen and watermen", Dionysius interrupted him.

The man flapped his hands helplessly and pledged his donation. Dionysius turned his gaze upon the curials, looking hard at each in turn, and each in turn rose to announce his donation.

"I will return tomorrow", Dionysius announced, "with my own donation, and to see that each of you brings what he has pledged. Now we will leave you to conduct your business, which you know better than we."

The three strode from the basilica, out on to the stoa, where they were greeted by cheers from the crowd to whom a crier had been announcing the donations. Dionysius held up his hand, "To your homes and your businesses my friends", he called. "How can you buy your bread and your oil and wine if nobody opens his shop?" Turning to Anastasius, he said, "Let's hope the Xth gets here soon."

CHAPTER SIXTEEN

It was not the Xth which came to the relief of the city.

The next day there was a shout from the watch tower, and hastening to the roof, Dionysius, Anastasius and Andrew saw a column of dust in the distance and the glint of sunlight on spears. They watched as the column drew nearer.

"Who is it", Dionysius asked his son. "Your eyes are keener than mine."

"I can't make out the banners yet", Andrew replied, "but it's cavalry, so it's not the Xth."

Mansour appeared on the tower, and Dionysius, catching his eye, wandered over to him. Mansour slipped him a strip of linen, which Dionysius palmed and glanced at. His eyes widened in surprise and he hastened over to the parapet to gaze fixedly at the approaching column.

"Who is it?" Anastasius asked, "Can you see yet?"

"Diocletian", Dionysius replied. "It's Diocletian. He can only have come from Aurelian himself, but why does Lydda merit such attention?"

Diocletian rode up to the open gates of the city. His standard-bearer rode to his right and several paces behind. A tribune of Auxiliaries led two *turmae* of Gallic cavalry, sixty-four troopers, plus their decurions and standard-bearers.

Diocletian did not dismount to enter the city, a fact not lost upon the magistrates and curials. Hastily mustered to greet him, quaking at the knees, they lined both sides of the gateway, a nervous welcoming committee, for this was the man who might have been Emperor; and, more fearful thought, might be Emperor yet. They bowed as he passed, but a curt nod of the head was his only acknowledgement.

Anastasius, Dionysius and Andrew were lined up beyond the gateway. Anastasius studied Diocletian with interest. He knew that he was twenty-seven, an Illyrian, born at Spalato in Dalmatia, the son of a freedman who had been the scribe of a wealthy senator. Like everyone in the army, he knew of Diocletian's sensational rise through the ranks to the Imperial Staff. The son of the freedman now had the ear of Emperors and was one of the most powerful men in the Empire. What Anastasius saw was a tall, well-set man, with a round, clerkly face, broad nose, wide mouth and large eye sockets, already wrinkled. His hair, cut short in the Roman fashion, nevertheless stubbornly curled, as did his beard. His face seemed set in stone, expressionless. He sat his horse straight-backed, the left arm hanging by his side, the right hand loosely holding the reins which rested on the horse's neck. His eyes missed nothing. They did not dart about, but moved slowly and calmly. There was about them the quality of glass. Diocletian stopped and the three men saluted him; he returned the salute with a brief nod and looked at Anastasius.

"You are Count Anastasius?" It was a statement rather than a question.

Anastasius bowed, "I am, Domine."

"And you are Count Dionysius?"

"Yes, Domine", the older man replied with a brief bow of the head.

"And who is this?" Diocletian nodded toward Andrew who promptly became tongue-tied.

"My son, Andrew, Domine", Dionysius replied for him.

"Then let him go about his business. I wish to speak with you both. Follow me to the basilica."

Diocletian rode on without a backward glance, into the Forum. A great crowd had gathered. They stood silent and nervous as the lictors cleared a way.

"Has Diocletian come to decimate the city for collaboration with the enemy?" That was the question in more minds than one. The fact that he was accompanied by only two turmae was reassuring. Surely more would be necessary for a decimation?

Diocletian rode on, his eyes moving slowly across the Forum. He noted the open bakers', butchers' and wine shops, the stalls piled high with fruit, vegetables and fish. His eyes swept the portico of the Temple of Apollo – no sign of damage or looting. Across the forum he studied the basilica, all was quiet and orderly. He scanned the crowd, suitably cowed, no slogans, no impudent shouts, no disorder.

Suddenly a man in the crowd shouted, "Hail Diocletian!" Immediately a forest of hands rose in salute and the crowd gave vent to a great shout, "Hail Diocletian! Hail Diocletian Invictus!" He gave no sign of being either pleased or displeased. No one wanted to be the last to salute this terrifying man in his gilded armour, scarlet cloak and ostrich feather-crest, nor to be the first to cease the cry.

If there were any not sharing the sentiment, they nevertheless joined in the ovation, each fearful that the man next to him would denounce him if he did not. Diocletian continued on his way, riding to the basilica, his face set. Coming to the stoa he glanced up at the portico supported by Corinthian columns, dismounted and strode in past the salutes of the city police. His cavalry immediately spread out, fencing off the stoa.

Diocletian strode the length of the basilica, his boots ringing on the marble floor, tessellated with a black border.

Following him at a discreet distance, Anastasius found himself thinking, absurdly, "I hope he doesn't notice the cracks in the marble flags." Diocletian, having reached the end of the hall paused at the icon of the Capitoline wolf. He bowed briefly and passed on into the apse. Without hesitation, he mounted the steps and sat upon the seat of the First Magistrate of the City.

Anastasius and Dionysius came to a halt and stood before him. He did not invite them to sit, but studied them closely. At length he spoke.

"You have kept good order here. In other cities there has been rioting, looting and arson. That was because Roman authority was not immediately re-imposed after the flight of the rebel garrison. It is apparent that you, Count Dionysius, acted promptly." He paused and the two bowed in acknowledgement. Diocletian went on, "However, you surrendered the city to Zenobia without a sword being drawn. Was this the act of Romans?"

Anastasius and Dionysius looked at each other in consternation. Anastasius spoke first.

"With respect, Domine, we had no troops, Count Galerius withdrew all garrisons from the coast when Zenobia took Alexandria."

"I am aware of that", Diocletian said coldly, "I signed the order for the withdrawal myself. It was more important to hold the Bosphorus than to hold Syria. The counts and procurators who remained were expected to organize the defence of their cities. You did not."

Confusion gripped Dionysius; whatever he said would appear either a weak excuse, or impudence. He decided to risk impudence.

"With what could we defend Lydda, Domine?"

"You could have closed the gates, armed the citizens and manned the walls."

Anastasius risked interrupting, "Domine, the walls are not built of stone, as in Europe. They are sun-baked brick. They would have crumbled in a day before battering rams, or even in some parts, at the blast of trumpets."

Dionysius looked at him for several seconds, then spoke.

"What of that? A determined resistance would have forced Zenobia to send more troops, so weakening her advance."

"The citizens, Domine, are not trained in arms. There would have been great bloodshed and to no avail. The city would have been taken in days rather than weeks. Once the walls were breached the citizens would have been slaughtered as a punishment for resistance."

A sardonic smile played on Diocletian's lips.

"You Christians", he said at length, "You never seem to understand that blood is plentiful, that life is cheap. Every week gladiators gamble their lives in the arena for glory. Your beliefs, I have long thought, threaten the safety of the Empire. They encourage clemency where there should be ruthlessness; weakness where men should be hard. I have to ask myself, when the moment comes, will you fight for the Empire or preach sermons about violence?" He stopped, evidently awaiting a reply.

Anastasius searched his mind for what he had heard of this man. Diocletian's enemies, those jealous of his rapid rise, and those contemptuous of his servile origins, sneered when they spoke of him, "Not a real soldier, y'know; an administrator really, he's really a tax collector, no doubt he'd make a good Treasury man, but not a real fighting man."

Taking a deep breath he said, "Under your pardon, Domine, if we had defied the Palmyrans the city would now be a deserted ruin. As it is we waited, confident that the eagles would return, so you reclaim for the Empire a thriving city, not a desolation which yields no revenue to the Imperial Treasury. There is also the harbour at Joppa, undamaged and unblocked. Perhaps we Christians are more practical in the long run? As for loyalty, Christian soldiers have proven often enough that they will fight for the Empire."

Diocletian's face remained expressionless, but what he said next took them completely by surprise.

"What you say is true. This enquiry is concluded." He paused, "But I have other business with you. Zenobia is making a stand at Emesa and the Emperor is determined to crush her there rather than face a long siege of Palmyra itself. He is taking personal command of the battle. Constantius Chlorus will command the left wing and Count Galerius will command his light cavalry. I will command the right wing. I need a commander for my light cavalry, and you, Count Anastasius, have been recommended to me." He took a scroll out of his tunic.

"Here is the Imperial Commission. Be ready to start for Emesa tomorrow."

Dumbfounded, Anastasius took the scroll. Diocletian waited a moment before speaking again.

"Count Dionysius, I will dine at your house tonight. I do not favour the Roman custom of lying on couches to eat. It has always seemed most uncomfortable to me, apart from which it gives me indigestion. I prefer to sit, and for those who dine with me to do likewise. I also favour plain food and weak wine. We will meet again this evening."

Realizing that this was a dismissal, the two saluted and walked out, not knowing if they should feel relief or trepidation. Mansour joined them on the stoa. He turned to Dionysius.

"He is, I understand, Domine, very partial to cabbage."

CHAPTER SEVENTEEN

At two years old, Giorgios, like most children, was more sensitive to atmosphere than adults realize. He felt both the excitement and the anxiety that gripped the household. He gazed in wonder at his father, magnificent in gilded breastplate, helmet, greaves and enveloping scarlet cloak. He was fascinated by the cavalry sabre. When Anastasius took him in his arms he traced the outline of the eagle and the lion-heads embossed on the breast plate, and perhaps it was then that he decided that he too would be a soldier and wear such splendid armour. His mother was weeping softly, Auntie Claudia was uttering soothing sounds, Uncle Mansour was standing silently by Dionysius, who was looking grave. He sensed that his Uncle Andrew was cross.

"Why am I not going?" the latter demanded.

"Because you were neither asked nor ordered to", Dionysius told him sharply. "Besides you are needed here. Diocletian has laid on me the duty of raising and training a defence force to support the turmae of cavalry he's leaving us. I will need your help. Diocletian has made it very plain that Lydda must be held against any attack, even down to the last man."

Andrew scowled, "What chance of that when the Emperor has crushed Zenobia? We'll just be kicking our heels here whilst everything is happening out there."

"Andrew", Anastasius interrupted, "if you knew anything of battles you would be glad to be back here, best of all with no enemy in sight. The soldier's enemy isn't the army opposite, the soldier's enemy is war itself."

He turned away, lowering Giorgios to the ground, and took Kira in his arms, a signal for her to burst into tears.

"You'll frighten the boy", he whispered in her ear. "Be brave."

Kira recalled her role as Roman Matron, another Cornelia, Mother of the Gracchi, and suppressed her sobs.

"You'll bake in the desert in that armour", she scolded him.

Anastasius laughed, "I'll take it off at the mid-day meal; but it's fitting that I should meet Diocletian in armour. I have arranged everything about the estates with Mansour. When Giorgios is three, Mansour is to start teaching him Latin, not to mention decent Greek. I've arranged with your father to increase Mansour's salary."

"But you'll be home before then?" It was a question and a plea.

"I hope so; now, a Roman parting, no tears." He kissed her and bent down to kiss Giorgios' cheek, saying, "Remember, you're the man of the house now", and strode over to his horse.

The early morning air was still cool, and a light breeze from the coast carried the scents of spring from the orchards and vineyards. Already the field workers were out, singing some ancient Aramaic work-song. Anastasius wondered if he would ever see the place again as he raised his arm and let it drop, and his little cavalcade started forward. Men of equestrian rank and above were required to provide their own horses and supporting train, so behind him were three war-horses and a dozen mules carrying fodder, water, corn and wine, tended by four muleteers and a farrier. Anastasius set his features in the expression of Roman gravitas and did not look back.

Kira took Giorgios by the hand and led him indoors.

"You must pray for Dadda", she told him, "pray that he will come safely home. We will pray to Mary Theotokos, mother of Jesus, and our mother in heaven. Our Lady will bring your dada safely home."

In the quiet of the atrium, Giorgios prayed fervently, especially to the Mother of God, though in his childish way he felt it more proper to ask for the safe return of his "father", rather than his "dada".

When he had finished he turned to his mother and, with complete assurance, said, "It's all right now. Jesus' mummy has told me she will bring Dadda back safe and well."

Kira, at first astonished, looked at her son, standing there so innocently and so calmly certain. A light seemed to be about him, and she felt the same calmness of spirit.

"Yes", she said, "God and his Blessed Mother will bring him back to us."

* * *

The green freshness of the coastal plain gave way to the desert that lay between them and the oasis of Palmyra. Gradually agriculture turned to pasture; crops, to herds of goats and camels; Greek attire, to the enveloping robes of the desert. The long column of Diocletian's cavalry turma and its baggage train, which Anastasius had joined at Lydda, followed roads which became more and more uneven, sometimes covered in drifting sand, and everyone was glad when the light began to fade and the evening breeze sprang up.

Anastasius dined in Diocletian's tent with the Tribune and Decurion of the cavalry. Little was said at the table, for Diocletian was a man of few words. Toward the end of the meal he suddenly spoke to Anastasius.

"Aren't you curious about who commended you to me?"

Taken by surprise, Anastasius could only reply weakly, "I had wondered."

"Are you a friend of Count Galerius?"

Even more surprised, Anastasius said, "I would not have thought so."

"Ha!" Diocletian's brief laugh seemed to hurt him. "Then perhaps he hopes you'll be killed."

They sat eating without further words for some time, while Anastasius digested the fact that he owed his commission to Galerius. He could only agree with Diocletian's conclusion.

Suddenly Diocletian spoke again, "Why do you think Aurelian sent me to Lydda?"

"We were puzzled, but the Emperor knows best."

"Ha! A diplomatic answer. But don't be flattered. My chief mission was to Caesarea. Aurelian sent me to impress upon the Legate of the Xth that this time they are to march toward the sound of battle, and not away from it. Five cohorts should be on the road by now."

Silence descended again. They finished the wine and Diocletian declared that he kept early hours. Taking this as an order, Anastasius and the other two rose, bowed and left the tent. The cooking fires were still smouldering, giving off an unpleasant odour of dried camel dung. Groups of cavalrymen squatted about them, drinking watered wine and talking in low voices. Apparently they knew better than to disturb Diocletian's repose with shouts and laughter.

Anastasius looked up at the splendour of the desert sky, the great cloud of the Milky Way, a cascade of light behind brilliant stars. He picked out the Plough, pointing directly to the Pole Star. He had told Kira that he would do this each night and think of her. He turned to the Tribune and Decurion, "I will take the first duty watch. It falls to you Tribune to take the second, and you, Decurion, the last."

"As you wish, Domine", the Tribune replied.

The journey across the desert was tedious. Sand there was, but the more usual landscape was flat, cracked mud or bare brown hills between which the road wound. Occasionally they saw in the distance a caravan. Trade went on in spite of the war, but the caravans gave them a wide berth.

The second evening was much the same as the first. Diocletian ate and drank both sparingly and silently, until suddenly he turned to Anastasius and asked, "Why do you think Zenobia is massing her forces at Emesa, instead of holing up in Palmyra itself?"

Anastasius sensed that he was being tested.

"Emesa guards the oasis. If she can hold us there we run out of water and she doesn't."

"Good! Good!" Diocletian exclaimed.

"If we defeat her at Emesa she can still fall back on Palmyra", Anastasius added.

"Yes!" Diocletian said, "but what if *she* defeats us?"

Anastasius looked back at him blankly. Defeat was not a Roman word.

"You have no plan of retreat, Count?" Diocletian pressed the point.

"We would fall back on Antioch."

"Yes, that's if we were pushed north, but what if we were pushed south?"

Light dawned on Anastasius, "We'd fall back on Lydda and be supplied by sea through the port of Joppa."

"Ha! Now you understand why Lydda was important enough for me to interrupt my journey from Caesarea. But we would not be supplied by sea, we would be withdrawn by sea, or what was left of us."

Anastasius' face registered astonishment.

"But Zenobia would recover all she had before. It would be another year before Rome could mount a reconquest."

"There would be no reconquest", Diocletian said evenly.

"No reconquest?" Anastasius repeated, stunned.

"There are no more legions available", Diocletian replied. "Rome has never had enough legions nor enough auxiliaries. A legion is a huge capital investment, and it's one which pays no dividends while still piling up running costs. It has always been Roman policy to have too few legions rather than too many. Now the legions and their auxiliaries are strung out along a frontier from the Clyde to the Euphrates Delta. They are spread too thin for any to be withdrawn for a second attempt here. Now you understand how critical this battle will be?"

Anastasius nodded. He remembered Mansour's gloomy forecasts, and for the first time felt dismay.

CHAPTER EIGHTEEN

Emesa was a small, unimportant city. There was a forum, a basilica, a few small temples and a number of town houses; the majority of citizens lived and farmed outside. Beyond the city, however, were groves of date palms, fig and olive trees, vines and patches of corn and vegetables. The sluggish water of a network of irrigation channels gleamed in the hot sun. Emesa stood on the fringe of the oasis of Palmyra. Before the town there was a last roll in the desert which dipped down into a shallow valley to rise again a little higher on the city side.

Zenobia's forces were deployed along this higher slope. Aurelian had advanced to the crest of the lower. The coming battle would be decided in favour of whoever could cross the dip and take the line the enemy stood upon, sending him into flight.

Aurelian sat on his horse beneath the draconarius, the Imperial standard of the purple dragon. About him were his staff, trumpeters and signallers. He surveyed the opposite slope through a hollow tube. Turning to Constantius Chlorus, he said, "I see no sign of Zenobia, no banner, no war-horse."

"Let's hope she's taken refuge in Palmyra", Constantius replied. "Her presence is worth several cohorts to them."

"I would rather, Constantius", Aurelian remarked, "woo men back into the Empire than coerce them into it, but she has refused all peace offers, and by the look of their line we're in for a bloody day."

Anastasius had had his first sight of Lucius Domitius Aurelianus Augustus the previous afternoon. On the last morning of their journey, the Tribune and Decurion had become suddenly communicative in their praise of the Emperor.

"A stern man", the Decurion had said, "Ee won't abide slackin'. I can tell you, the Xth are for it once this Zenobia woman's put in 'er place. They'll be drillin' and marchin' till they're worn down to their knees an' doin' night duties till they've got cats' eyes. I wouldn't be surprised if the Legate and his Tribunes are sent to Rome in disgrace once this lot is over."

"Aurelian ranks with Julius and Augustus", the Tribune had volunteered. "We haven't lost Claudius Gothicus while we have Aurelian. Last year we fought the Vandals and drove them back across the Danube and they were glad to sue for peace. Then behind our backs the Juthungi and Marcomanni invaded Italy. Aurelian marched us back from the Danube at forty miles a day, defeated the barbarians in two battles and showed no mercy. He let a few get back to Germania to warn the rest against invading Roman territory again."

Anastasius was astonished that so much had been done in little more than a year, but he had not heard all.

"We were on our way to Byzantium for crossing the Bosphorus when the Goths erupted across the Danube ahead of us. They hadn't realized a Roman army was on its way and we hit 'em hard; they were glad enough to sue for peace. Aurelian granted them Dacia. They're settled there as Federates, allies of Rome, holding the

Carpathians against barbarians from further east. That done, Aurelian knew it was safe to bring along the Dacian cavalry. They've already proved they're a match for the Palmyrans."

Anastasius was more than ever curious to see this Emperor who achieved so much and aroused so much admiration in his men. Now he was able to watch him as he sat on his horse and surveyed the enemy line. He was of medium height with a thick-set neck and stubbly jowl. The nose was the most prominent feature of his face, large and high-bridged. The eyes were deep-set, a cavalryman's eyes, used to scanning far distances, and alert with a high intelligence. He could not be called handsome, but his face was full of character. His hair was cropped short, combed forward and rolled under along the forehead in a very old-fashioned style. Anastasius wondered if Aurelian saw himself as the great Julius?

The object of Anastasius' study had returned to his scanning of the enemy line. The centre was held by infantry, drawn up Greek fashion, in phalanxes; a formation inherited from Alexander, centuries ago. Shoulder to shoulder and shield to shield, the phalanx presented a porcupine front of spears.

Aurelian turned to Diocletian, "I think their arms will ache before the day is out. We'll give them time to get tired before we attack the centre."

He returned to his scanning. On each wing were heavy cavalry, both men and horses protected by coats of scale armour, whitened to reflect the sun. Their helmets, covering the face to the mouth, were made fearsome by eye slits.

"There's our main danger", Aurelian said, speaking to both Diocletian and Constantius at once. "Can our Dacians match them?"

"The odds are even, Augustus", Constantius replied, "except that we have the Judean clubmen to hammer those helmets down to their chins as they did at Immae."

Aurelian gave a brief laugh, "It's the old argument about how to eat an egg", he said, "tap it or slice it!"

He turned his attention to the light cavalry, two *alae* on the extremes of each wing. They were armoured with a round helmet, a shirt of chain mail and an oval shield. Their weapons were two javelins or a bow and a long slashing sword. Their function was to break up a defensive line or phalanx of infantry in preparation for an infantry attack.

"I think our Gallic cavalry can match them", Aurelian said aloud.

The Roman centre was held by auxiliary infantry, not legionaries, for a legion, with its engineers, surveyors and road-builders, was much too valuable to be committed to battle until the outcome was certain. At that point the "Roman mincing machine" would be deployed to finish off the enemy. Only Roman citizens were accepted by the legions, but with Caracalla's extension of citizenship to the entire Empire sixty years before, the distinction between legion and auxiliary cohort was becoming blurred. Apart from a small force of horsemen in each legion, the Roman army's cavalry strength was supplied by Auxiliaries.

The basic unit was the ala, a force of about 500 men commanded by a tribune and divided into sixteen turmae. The turma or "troop" consisted of thirty-two men under the command of a decurion. The auxiliary infantry units were modelled on the legions. The basic unit was the cohort, commanded by a tribune, and, like a legion cohort, divided into six centuries. Originally a century may have numbered a hundred men, but by this time its paper strength was eighty, plus the Centurion and decurions, giving the cohort a total strength of about five-hundred. Auxiliary cohorts, unlike the legions, were armed with a variety of weapons – spears, long swords, bows, slings, and clubs. Aurelian had also placed his heavy cavalry on each wing, with the light cavalry covering their flanks. Behind the centre, in reserve, were three cohorts of the Praetorian Guard, the Emperor's "household" troops.

CHAPTER NINETEEN

"They are a long time doing nothing", Aurelian remarked. An hour had passed and the sun was growing strong.

"They are sitting on the wells, Augustus, we are not", Diocletian pointed out.

"Then we must shift them off them", Aurelian replied.

He passed an order to the signallers, and the infantry moved with precision to open up a score of avenues in their ranks. Sappers from the Praetorian Guard ran out ballistae, each armed and ready with a deadly iron-tipped bolt. At the sound of a trumpet the bolts were sent across the dip to crash through the shields and armour of the phalanxes opposite. In the expert hands of the Praetorians each ballista hurled three bolts a minute into the enemy centre. The Palmyran generals had but one choice – withdraw or counter-attack. There was a rapid signalling with flags on the Palmyran side, and to the sounding of trumpets an ala of heavy cavalry from both wings of the Palmyran front began to move down the slope in a curving charge which would bring them together at the bottom of the dip.

"They're going to attack our centre, and without infantry support!" Aurelian exclaimed incredulously. "They must be after me!"

"Order the heavy cavalry to charge their flanks as they begin the ascent", Diocletian suggested eagerly.

"That's obviously what they want us to do", Aurelian replied, "No! We wait. They have something up their sleeve and I want to know what it is."

The Palmyran squadrons had now joined and began the uphill gallop at the Roman centre. Aurelian watched them till the front riders were half-way up the slope.

"Now!" he cried, and the trumpeters sounded a signal which sent half the Roman heavy cavalry on both wings in a diagonal charge at the mass of Palmyran horse. There was a flurry of flags on the Palmyran side and on both wings a troop of camels mounted by bowmen appeared from behind the hill. They charged down the slope at the gallop and Aurelian gave a satisfied grunt, "So! A variation on the 'concealed flank'." The speed of the camels was intended to take them round the flanks of the charging Roman cavalry before they had clashed with the Palmyrans, cutting down the Romans with a devastating hail of arrows from their heavy horn bows. The camel squadrons, however, were too late; Aurelian had delayed his counter-attack just long enough to ensure that it would hit the enemy flanks before it could be countered. With the Roman cavalry carving through the mass of Palmyrans, arrows were as likely to strike friend as foe. The two lines of camels were reduced to riding around the mass of fighting cavalry, choosing targets with care. Nevertheless, they were inflicting casualties on the Roman heavy cavalry.

Back at the Roman centre, the Palmyran cavalry had recoiled from the Roman shields, regrouped and charged again. Trumpet signals rang out and Cretan archers, moving in behind the front rank of infantry, loosed a barrage of arrows. Horses and men went down and the charge was thrown back in confusion. Aurelian turned to Diocletian and Constantius, "Get rid of those camels for me. Send in your light cavalry."

Anastasius read the signal, ordered his first ala to readiness, drew his sword and charged. He hoped that Galerius would be doing the same on the other wing. They thundered down the slope toward the camel squadron, bows sang, and behind him Anastasius was aware of men falling from their saddles. Getting the scent of the camels, the horses became nervous and tried to swerve, but the Gallic horsemen forced them on. Anastasius saw a face before him and an eye squinting along an arrow. He flung up his shield and the shaft pierced it but failed to penetrate his armour. By reflex action his sabre swept down and the face disappeared, a body was somehow on the ground beneath the camel's hooves. He slashed again, cutting the beast's neck.

Pausing to glance about, he saw the fighting raging all round him. His troops were now at close quarters with the camel squadron, too close for the Palmyrans to use their bows, but these they were swinging round as clubs, with deadly effect. A blow from the heavy horn bow could break a neck or cave in ribs. He saw the rear of a camel and bent across his saddle to slash at its hamstrings; the squealing animal went down. As he straightened up he felt the wind of a bow missing his head by a hairsbreadth.

He swung his sword, point upward, and caught his assailant in the thigh. The man fell from his camel, blood pumping from his groin. Anastasius looked around; his men seemed to be getting the better of the fray. Suddenly it was all over; half a dozen riderless camels were loping back up the hill and trumpets were sounding the recall. Somehow, Palmyrans and Romans separated themselves, retreating to their own lines, leaving behind an appalling spectacle of dead and wounded men and beasts, with screams and shouts rending the air.

"I think we had the edge there", Constantius remarked. "They seem to have left more behind than we have."

Aurelian waited, pondering his next move in this deadly positional game. From across the shallow valley came the sound of trumpets and the Palmyran light cavalry came on in a curving charge which would bring it onto the flanks of the Roman line. At the same time their heavy cavalry on both wings charged directly at the Roman heavy cavalry. The intention was clear, to roll up the Roman wings and attack the centre on both flanks.

"But why", Aurelian asked aloud, "are their phalanxes not advancing in a frontal assault? Can it really be incompetence?"

Anastasius thought quickly. He had no intention of waiting for moving horses to crash against his standing horses. Shouting orders to his second ala, he led a curving charge as the enemy started the climb uphill. The two forces met halfway down the slope, and the impetus of the Roman charge carried the Palmyrans with it. Aurelian, watching, turned his gaze to the left flank where Galerius was standing waiting for the enemy. He flagged an order to charge, which Galerius did, too late to be effective.

There was a melee of squealing horses and slashing swords, and the Palmyrans gained the brow of the slope, driving back the Roman line. Some broke through to find themselves faced by two centuries of the Praetorian Guard. They hurled their javelins with deadly effect and then withdrew.

The clash of the heavy cavalry was awful. The Romans held their line until the enemy had lost their impetus, and then opened ranks to allow through the mounted Judean clubmen. Swords or spears, baffled by the shield, might not pierce the scale armour, but the heavy clubs could inflict terrible damage on heads, shoulders, ribs and knees. Slowly, the Palmyrans were forced back down hill, giving even greater advantage to the clubmen. Reluctantly, the Palmyran trumpets sounded the recall.

Anastasius led his depleted ala back uphill to where the first ala had been holding the line. The Roman heavy cavalry pulled back into position, and over on the left wing Galerius ruefully surveyed the mauled remnants of his two alae of light cavalry.

"Our round, I think, Augustus", Constantius said.

Aurelian looked at him, "With our left flank in tatters?" he asked.

There was a shout from a signaller, and Aurelian turned to look where the man was pointing. Approaching was a cloud of dust. It was undoubtedly a column of troops, and their line of march would bring them along the top of the opposite slope.

"Who are they?" he asked.

"Persians!" Diocletian exclaimed.

The same question was asked by the Palmyran commander, "Romans!" replied his adjutant.

Constantius put a hollow tube to his eye, "The Xth!" he shouted exultantly.

"The Xth it is!" exclaimed Aurelian. "Signal to Count Anastasius, 'Be prepared to support advancing column'."

On the opposite slope the Palmyran commander scanned the column.

"Romans?" he muttered. "And on our flank."

"The Xth Legion", his adjutant confirmed. "What now?"

"One final effort. Order the heavy cavalry on the right to change position with the light cavalry, the phalanxes to advance and attack the centre, supported by heavy cavalry on their left and light cavalry on their right. The light cavalry on the left to advance against the Xth and hold them back, the heavy cavalry on the right to attack the enemy light cavalry and break through to the rear." Trumpets and flags began to signal the orders.

Aurelian watched the light and heavy cavalry on the Palmyran right switch places in a neat manoeuvre and outguessed his enemy.

"Confirm order to Count Anastasius to support the Xth. Order the First Praetorian Cohort to reinforce Count Galerius. Order both wings of heavy cavalry to attack advancing enemy centre."

The Palmyran phalanxes were now moving downhill at the charge, their supporting cavalry moving at a hand-pace. The clash came at the bottom of the dip, the

Roman cavalry fighting desperately to break through. The phalanxes began their uphill run to be met by a storm of arrows and ballistae bolts. They faltered, broke and began streaming back.

"They no longer believe they can win", Aurelian remarked. "Order the Praetorians to advance." Charging downhill, the Roman Mincing Machine went into action.

Meanwhile, the Palmyran heavy cavalry had made short work of the tattered remnants of Galerius' light horse, only to be met by a solid wall of Praetorians and a barrage of *pila*, the Roman javelin. Checked, they turned and fled. Far out on the Palmyran left, the Xth legion had formed up into a defensive rectangle and met the charge of the Palmyran light horse with a shower of pila.

The Palmyrans took the punishment and regrouped for a second charge when they were struck in the flank by Anastasius' forces. They made a fighting retreat and several hundred heavy cavalry were able to regain their position on the crest from where they began an ordered retreat to Palmyra.

"No use pursuing them", Aurelian said regretfully, "they've too far a lead. We'll mop up here. Accept surrenders!" He turned to Diocletian, "A great victory, but unfortunately enough got away to give us trouble. I think we are in for a long siege."

CHAPTER TWENTY

"Old Nanna", as she was now called behind her back, though to her face it was "Grananna", crossed the atrium and entered the peristyle. A shady colonnade ran round all four sides and the centre was occupied by a large pool stocked with golden carp. Beds of herbs, flowers, shrubs of the Rose of Sharon and a knotwork of paths, surrounded the pool, save for a small paved area at one end on which stood a lichen-stained stone bench.

Summer had turned to autumn since Anastasius had ridden off to war. It was upon this bench, engrossed by the golden carp, that Giorgios was sitting, a frown of concentration giving him a serious countenance. Seeing him there, unattended by Iris, Grananna gave a sharp intake of breath. Even though the pool was now covered by a strong net, well pegged-down at the edges, it was unthinkable that Iris could have let the boy wander out of her sight. Grananna was about to rush across the garden and haul him away from the pool when a white fan-tailed dove fluttered down and settled on his head. The boy made no movement, sitting contentedly whilst the dove cooed. Grananna stood silent, remembering the prophecy his father had uttered when the newborn babe was placed in his arms.

"His name shall be great from the East to the West. He will overthrow the dragon", and here indeed was a sign to the faithful. She crossed herself.

The next moment, Iris, bad tempered and shouting, rushed out from the colonnade.

"You naughty boy! You naughty boy! Why did you slip away like that?"

The dove flew off to take sanctuary on the roof and Giorgios looked up mildly at his irate nurse. Iris seized him by the shoulder and began to haul him away from the bench. Grananna stepped out from the shadow of the colonnade and called sharply, "Where have you been? How did he slip away from you, you lazy girl?"

At the sight of the old woman, Iris burst into tears.

Iris had in fact been keeping a tryst, and had been so engrossed in what her lover, Gregorius, a market trader, had to say, that she had not noticed Giorgios' absence until, with a final kiss, they had parted. Only then did she realize that Giorgios had gone, but where she could not guess.

Giorgios had become bored, and, as his tugging at Iris' skirts was first ignored and then met with an angry rebuke to "be quiet", he had slipped away to find more interesting things. Now everything, Iris told herself, was ruined. Old Nanna would go post haste to the Domina with her tale and the Domina would be too angry to even think of giving permission for marriage. She might even dismiss her as Giorgios' nurse and send her off to the other end of the estate to look after sheep or poultry, or anything! This thought brought fresh grief to Iris and her tears came as summer tempests.

Giorgios ran to her, "Don't cry, Nanny Iris", he begged, tugging at her. "Don't cry."

This had the effect of increasing her weeping. Distraught, Giorgios ran to the gaunt figure of the old woman.

"Don't make Nanny Iris cry, Grananna. Don't shout at her", he pleaded, his own tears beginning to well. The old woman looked down at the upturned sensitive face. Surprised, she realized that he had grown from baby to little boy, and she softened, instinctively laying her hand on his golden hair.

"There, there", she said, "don't cry." Turning to Iris she said, "Dry your eyes, you silly girl! But let this be a lesson to you, never ever let a two-year-old out of your sight, not for an instant; you can never tell what mischief they'll get up to."

Iris, hope renewed, began to wipe away her tears.

"Go and wash your face", commanded Grananna, "I'll stay with the boy."

Immensely relieved, Iris ran from the garden, and Grananna sat on the stone bench, beckoning Giorgios to her side.

"Weren't you frightened when the dove landed on your head?" she asked.

Giorgios looked at her, blue eyes wide and searching, "Why?" he asked. For Giorgios, the world he was discovering was an endless delight, filled with surprises, and the most surprising of all were the living things. A small bird landed on the flagstones. It hopped toward them.

"Ahh", Giorgios breathed, his eyes shining, his heart tender.

Grananna sat still, seeing the world anew through the eyes of a child. The bird flew away and on a sudden impulse she said, "Whilst we wait for Iris I'll tell you a story, and this is a true story." She told him the story of Adam and Eve and the garden of Paradise, where there was no pain, no sickness and no cruelty, until Adam and Eve disobeyed God and were driven out of the Garden. Giorgios listened attentively. It became one of his favourites, which he would ask Grananna to tell again and again.

So grew a bond between the child on the threshold of life and the old woman near its end.

*   *   *

The short but severe Mediterranean winter, from early December to late January, brought snow down onto the Galilean hills, and this year, unexpectedly, the snow fell on the coastal plain. Giorgios was entranced by it, as it festooned roofs and trees and lay sparkling on the gardens and orchards. Lucius was now toddling and the two played together, chortling as they made snowballs and saw their breath rise like smoke, or stared in wonder at the golden carp laying motionless on the bottom of the frozen pool. A multitude of small birds, growing bold with hunger, gathered around the door of the atrium each morning to await the crumbs which Giorgios and Lucius would bring them.

One morning, before the Saturnalia, which Christians were beginning to keep as Christ's Nativity, Kira took Giorgios by the hand and, with Grananna and Iris in attendance, made her way along the snowy path through the orchards to the gate which opened into Auntie Claudia's house and garden. Giorgios ran to Lucius who was standing looking up at the dovecote, though all the doves were huddled inside away from the cold. The two, chortling with infant glee, hugged each other until Kira called to Giorgios to come with her to see Auntie Claudia. A brazier of glowing charcoal warmed the room a little, and Auntie Claudia lay upon her couch, muffled up in rugs. Beside her was the cradle and a new baby was lying in it, covered with woollen wraps.

"This is Auntie Claudia's new baby." Kira said, "Another little boy, his name is Cyrennius."

Giorgios gazed, wide-eyed, at the baby.

"Does Auntie Claudia not want Lucius now? Can we have him?"

His mother laughed, "Of course she wants Lucius; Auntie Claudia loves both her little boys, and they will love each other."

"Will Lucius still be my friend?" Kira looked at the serious face, the slight frown upon the forehead.

"Why, yes", she said, not laughing this time, "but now you'll have two friends instead of only one."

Then Giorgios said something which disturbed her greatly, "Lucius has his daddy as well. Why has my Daddy been away so long? Will he come back?"

*   *   *

Winter had come, but the bitter cold of the desert did not prevent the arrival of the supply wagons from Antioch and Lydda. Wine and oil from Greece and corn from Egypt continued to maintain the besieging army. The Xth were made aware of the Emperor's continued displeasure as he added to their endless drilling the task of clearing the snow from the roads.

No supplies, nor hope of supplies, came to the defenders of Palmyra. Aurelian saw the dangers of desperation and a possible appeal to Persia.

"Increase the patrols around the oasis", he ordered Diocletian. "Use the light cavalry. Nothing and no one must pass. Arrange for the siege engines at Alexandria to be shipped to Joppa and brought overland. I want this thing over as soon as possible."

*   *   *

Giorgios and Lucius were fascinated by the siege engines being unloaded onto the quay at Joppa. Uncle Andrew took the boys, sitting in front of him on his horse, to see the convoys arrive from Egypt. The boys were awe-struck by the Legionaries in their silver armour and red cloaks. Detachment by detachment they marched along the quay to come to a stupendous "halt", beside the particular vessel they were to unload, every man's right foot crashing down beside his left with perfect timing. The giant siege engines arrived dismantled, otherwise the massive throwing beams would have stood higher than the ships' masts. Giorgios, nearing three years of age, was particularly fascinated by the wheels and pulleys of the winches, as toiling legionaries strained and heaved at the ropes to hoist the engine parts onto waiting wagons. There were smaller ballistae and these came off the ships fully assembled. A cheerful decurion of sappers ordered his men to give the wheels of a ballista a few turns so that Giorgios and Lucius might see how the cogs worked. Reluctantly, the two boys climbed up in front of Uncle Andrew to return to the villa before dark.

Grananna entertained them, as they ate their supper, with the story of Jesus being born in a stable in not-so-far-away Bethlehem.

"Perhaps", she ended, "It was bitterly cold and snowing then, like it is now."

The following morning, Giorgios was in thoughtful mood. Eventually he came to his mother with a strange tale.

"I saw Jesus last night."

The abruptness of the statement took Kira by surprise. She could think of nothing to say, except, "What was he like?"

"He was all white, like a lamp flame, flickering and shining, and he had a banner in his hand with a cross." Kira felt fear.

"Did he speak?"

Giorgios thought about this, "Yes! He said, 'I have kept a place for you among the greatest of the angels. But first you must take this cross'."

Kira clutched at her heart. She remembered that this was not the first dream or vision her child had had. She had dismissed the first from her mind as childish fancy; could she do the same now?

"You were dreaming."

Giorgios smiled at her, "I don't think so, Mamma, because I was awake."

*   *   *

In far-away Palmyra, Zenobia made a desperate decision. She would leave the city and make a dash for Persia, there to appeal for an alliance and the lifting of the siege. She was captured by a Roman patrol and brought before Aurelian. The Emperor treated her courteously but firmly. If the city surrendered it would be spared. If defiance continued, not one stone would be left upon a stone, and the population would be put to the sword.

Zenobia's defiance collapsed and she ordered the surrender of the city. To Diocletian's annoyance, Aurelian ordered corn and wine to be sent into the starving city. He was determined to pursue his policy of wooing men back into the Empire, not coercing them.

There were those among the powerful and the wealthy who disagreed. Sacked cities meant loot and slaves to be picked up cheaply and traded dearly. Aurelian's enlightened policy was not necessarily making him friends.

CHAPTER TWENTY-ONE

There could be no campaigning in the winter and Anastasius was dismayed at the thought of kicking his heels up in Antioch for the next three months. Although it was unusual, and would not enhance his reputation, he determined to seek an audience with Aurelian and ask for leave. The Emperor had taken up residence in Zenobia's palace and was using an ante-chamber of the throne room as a cabinet. Anastasius was ushered in and found Aurelian seated behind a table covered in scrolls and maps.

Anastasius made his request, emphasizing that he only asked for leave because the war was over and that he would be ready to answer his recall instantly. Aurelian leaned back in his chair.

"But the war is not yet over", he said. Anastasius looked surprised. "There is still the so-called Gallic Empire. They have a new Emperor, Tetricus. He is a capable man; he has chastised the Germans two years on the run, chasing them back across the Rhine with heavy losses. The reconquest of Gaul and Britannia will not be easy."

Anastasius felt dismay, but kept his face impassive. Aurelian studied him keenly.

"You have greatly impressed Diocletian and he wants you to command his cavalry on the left wing when we invade Gaul."

Anastasius managed to mumble something about being greatly honoured.

"You have made a powerful friend, one who will rise far in future years. You would be advised to serve him well and rise with him. Besides which, it gives me the opportunity to move Galerius from his cavalry command onto my staff."

Anastasius was startled; he could but conjecture that this move was, in reality, a demotion for Galerius, and would add fuel to the latter's arbitrary enmity toward himself and his family.

Aurelian was still studying him closely, and Anastasius remained silent. The Emperor rang a bell and a slave entered the room. "Wine", the Emperor said, and the slave moved to a side-table and poured two goblets, serving the Emperor and then Anastasius before bowing himself out. Aurelian stood up and moved around the table.

"However, the war in the West must be delayed. I have to move against the barbarians on the Danube yet again. I will leave Galerius with a garrison at Antioch to cover Syria. Meanwhile, an inspection of the legions on the Euphrates to discover why they did absolutely nothing these past three years is necessary. Diocletian, with a strong escort, will be carrying out that inspection after the Saturnalia. He has asked for you as his prefect and I have agreed that you should go." He crossed to the table, and taking a piece, of papyrus began to write. "Here is your pass; enjoy the Saturnalia, but be ready for prompt recall."

*   *   *

In one of the palace chambers that he had commandeered, Galerius was incandescent with rage. He read again the Imperial warrant transferring him from his command under Diocletian to the Emperor's staff.

"This Theognosta clan dogs my feet everywhere", he snarled at Licinius. The latter felt it prudent to say nothing. "The old man spiriting away Samaritans and their gold, and now the son-in-law, taking my command. We emptied our Treasury, Licinius, to stop Zenobia at Ancyra, and then to get ahead of her at Antioch, and how am I rewarded? I'm transferred from my command of the Dacian cavalry to the command of a Gallic rabble who discredit me in battle, and now I lose even that command to Anastasius."

"It might be more useful to be on the Emperor's staff than to be in a field command", Licinius put in smoothly. "He takes colour from a situation and is influenced by those about him."

Galerius looked keenly at his henchman, but for the moment ignored the interruption, pacing about the room.

"There is someone who knows our every move and perversely sets out to thwart it, and I know who that someone is, that dirty little spy Mansour." He looked hard at Licinius. "Mansour will have to be dealt with".

Crushing the Imperial warrant in his hand, he strode from the room.

*   *   *

It was one of the field hands who spotted the cavalcade first. He ran shouting to the foreman.

"The Dominus! The Dominus!"

The foreman, with an eye to his own advantage, cuffed the man and with a curse ordered him back to his work. Then he set off for the villa at a fast pace. The joyful news was brought to Kira, who hastened to Dionysius, and the whole house exploded into bustle. When Anastasius rode up the drive, Kira was waiting at the door of the Atrium, Giorgios beside her. Anastasius dismounted and strode over to embrace her. Roman custom did not permit any excessive display of affection, but it could not stem Kira's tears of happiness.

Anastasius picked up Giorgios, holding him in the air before cuddling him in his arms.

"What a big boy you have grown. Have you forgotten Dadda?"

Giorgios was shy, hiding his face in his father's shoulder, but now he looked him full in the face, the characteristic slight frown of puzzlement on his brow.

"No, Dadda, Mamma knows you."

Anastasius laughed, "So it must be me! And now what present would you like most of all?"

Again, the slight frown, the searching expression in the blue eyes, and then, mind made up, without further hesitation,

"Can I have a baby brother please?"

Anastasius laughed again and glanced across at Kira saying, "We can manage that can't we? But", turning to Giorgios, "I have something for you now, something for a cavalry soldier." He waved to one of the muleteers who went into a wagon, and to Giorgios' intense delight came out leading a tiny horse with saddle and bridle. "This is a horse from the islands far beyond even Britannia, and small enough for you to ride him."

Giorgios patted and stroked the pony, speaking to it all the time. The pony in turn nuzzled its head against his arm.

"What will you call him?" Anastasius asked.

Giorgios thought hard for a few moments and then announced, "Totti-Totti."

"That's a funny name for a horse. What made you think of that?"

"It's the sound he makes when he walks on the pavement."

"These ponies are usually bad-tempered, until they get to know their master", his father said to Kira, "but just look how this one takes to him."

Giorgios looked up at his father, "May I share him with Lucius?" Then as an afterthought, "And my new baby brother?"

Anastasius laughed aloud; no soldier's homecoming could have been more joyful than this one.

"What if you have a baby sister?"

"She will like to ride him, too", Giorgios replied.

* * *

The days passed quickly. Mansour's management of the estates had been impeccable and Anastasius immediately increased his salary. Everything was in order, and it was spring. The snow had gone from the hills and groups of shepherds were leading their flocks onto the higher slopes where the new grass was springing lush and green. Caravans of camels and mules passed beyond the villa's boundaries, headed for Joppa and the new season's sailings. Iris received her manumission and married Gregorius on the Ides of March and went off with him to his new house in Lydda. Mansour had given the groom a good report and suggested the appropriate dowry for the bride. Giorgios grieved the loss of Iris and Grananna noticed his silence. She took to sitting with him in the afternoon sunshine, telling him stories from the Scriptures. He particularly liked the story of David and Goliath and wondered why Goliath had not worn a Roman helmet, coming down over the brows. Grananna had no solution to this problem, but Giorgios thought one out for himself, "He must have thought he didn't need one, because he didn't know God was on David's side."

"Dadda", Giorgios exclaimed one day as he scrambled down from the pony after trotting a complete circle, "Grananna told me the story of Adam and Eve, and of how the serpent tempted them to disobey God, and they were driven from the garden."

"That's right", replied Anastasius.

"Then why didn't Adam take his sword and cut off the serpent's head?"

Anastasius was nonplussed for a moment, but then hit upon an answer.

"Well, Adam didn't have a sword in the garden, he didn't need one. It was only after they were cast out of the garden that men started to kill each other."

The slight furrow appeared on Giorgios' brow as he thought about this, "Well, I would have stamped on the serpent's head."

"But Giorgios", exclaimed his father, "your mother tells me you love all the animals."

"Not all!" Giorgios said. "Not the cruel ones, not dragons."

The next day he had another question.

"Grananna told me the story of Cain and Abel."

"Oh yes?" His father wondered what would come next.

"How did Cain know that God didn't accept his sacrifice?"

Anastasius thought hard and recalled an opinion he had once heard in a sermon, "Because the smoke of Abel's sacrifice rose into the air, but that of Cain's rolled along the ground."

Giorgios remained looking thoughtful, and the next day, having ridden Totti-Totti three times round the practice ground, slid down from his back and said, "The gardeners were burning things and the smoke was all rolling along the ground. I asked them why, and they said that when the stuff on the fire was damp and soggy the smoke always did that."

"Yes, so it does", Anastasius answered warily.

"Perhaps Cain offered God only the damp and soggy things from the fields and the smoke stayed on the ground and that's why he knew God wasn't pleased with him?"

"That's very clever!" Anastasius exclaimed, paternal pride glowing in his face. He turned to Mansour, who had joined them, "Don't you think so Mansour?"

"He soaks up knowledge like a sponge", Mansour replied. "He is far advanced for his age."

It was at this point that Grananna appeared in order to take Giorgios to his mother and the two men walked slowly back to the house.

"What is your impression of the new Emperor, Domine", Mansour asked.

"He is a great man, Mansour", Anastasius answered without hesitation, "a very great man, and he will certainly be counted among the great Emperors, perhaps even with Augustus himself. The soldiers love him because they know that he will not spend their blood carelessly, he is prudent in all things."

"An Emperor without flaw?" there was a question in Mansour's tone.

"Oh yes! A stern and just Emperor, but he has one quirk."

"What is that, Domine?"

"He's a bit of a dramatist", Anastasius replied. "No! that's not the right word, but I don't know how to put it. He acts and dresses the part the circumstances suggest: Caesar, even down to the hairstyle, the stern but just First Magistrate; the Imperator planning a campaign. It's not play-acting, it's more the circumstances which dictate the role he takes on."

Mansour had listened keenly to this, "Then let us hope that he is always surrounded by good men."

"Odd you should say that, but he's moved Galerius onto his staff." He caught Mansour's quick intake of breath, "But I don't think we need worry about that. Perhaps one has to be a bit of a dramatist to be a good Emperor."

They had come to the path below the goat-cropped slope where the Rose of Sharon was coming into golden bloom, and the two men parted company.

Spring also brought Giorgios' third birthday and the beginning of his formal schooling. He spent the mornings with Mansour, learning to read and write his native Greek, for Roman education, influenced as it was by Quintilian, did not underestimate the abilities of even very young children. After the midday meal he and Lucius sat with Grananna listening to her stories, and Giorgios' questions became searching. The afternoons were spent with his father, grandfather and uncle Andrew, playing with a ball or riding Totti-Totti. In the early evening his mother taught him his prayers and sang him to sleep.

CHAPTER TWENTY-TWO

Easter with its solemnity and its rejoicing had passed and Anastasius awaited daily the Imperial warrant commanding him to join Diocletian at Caesarea. That day came and the summons arrived, delivered by Imperial messenger. Kira wept, the past months had been so happy. Abstract "duty" was still a concept she found hard to understand when it conflicted with concrete personal and domestic duty. Giorgios too was distressed at the idea that Dadda was to leave them once more.

Worse was to follow. On the day before Anastasius' departure, the family was gathered in the peristyle when the Imperial post brought the news that Palmyra had renewed its revolt. Grim-faced, Anastasius read the scroll. The Roman garrison of six hundred archers had been treacherously murdered in the night. A man, previously unknown and calling himself Septimus Antiochus, had proclaimed himself Emperor immediately following the massacre. There could be little doubt that he was the major plotter in that crime, nor could it be doubted that a large number of citizens had taken part in the conspiracy.

"This is the end of Palmyra", Dionysius said, ashen-faced as he thought of the ferocious retribution which must come.

Giorgios who had been playing happily when the messenger arrived, sensed the anxiety of his elders and clung to his mother, frightened, but listening to every word.

"Are your orders countermanded?" Dionysius asked anxiously.

"No! I am to go with Diocletian."

Dionysius drew in a quick breath of relief, and so did Kira, though for a different reason.

"Palmyra will be put to the sword", Dionysius went on: "there'll be no mercy, not for any man, armed or not, and the women – "

"Can you blame the Emperor?" Andrew demanded. "After such treachery, such ingratitude, to murder all those men. They must all have been in it!"

"I would have refused an order to join the army at Palmyra", Anastasius said, slowly, weighing his words.

"Then you would have been executed!" Andrew exclaimed. "An officer cannot disobey an order from the Emperor."

"Then I would have been executed", Anastasius replied. "I am a soldier, not a butcher."

Kira let out a wail of dismay and Anastasius continued speaking. Giorgios, frightened by his mother's terror, and sharing it without understanding, hung on every word his father said; he was to remember them always.

"We all know that one day we must choose between God's law and Caesar's. Thanks to Providence, that day has not yet come for me." He turned to Kira with a smile, "You see, dearest, how good God is, and how glad you should be that I'm going to the Euphrates?"

At this thought Kira burst into tears of relief.

"But what if a countermand arrives before you set off?" Andrew demanded.

"Then I will have to refuse it", Anastasius replied. "I cannot murder or supervise the murder of innocent civilians."

"In a long life", Dionysius said, turning to Anastasius, "I have found that Providence is often helped by Prudence. Is everything ready for your departure tomorrow?"

"Everything is packed and the horses prepared", Anastasius replied.

"Then I suggest an increase in your zeal to obey commands would not go amiss. You must set out now, at once, to join Diocletian, as the Imperial warrant commands, and, providentially, before any change of orders might arrive."

The matter was too grave for laughter, but Anastasius managed a crooked smile.

*   *   *

The news from Palmyra received a rather different reception in Antioch.

"At last", exclaimed Galerius, passing the scroll to Licinius, "an opportunity to replenish our treasury."

"There won't be much in the Palmyran treasury", Licinius pointed out; "Aurelian seized it when the city surrendered."

"No matter, there'll be plenty of gold, silver and ivory in the temples and the houses of the rich. Add to that the profits to be made in the slave market here in Antioch and we will fill our coffers again."

"If the Lex Talonica is issued against the city, and it *will* be after the slaughter of the Roman garrison, all male prisoners will be crucified", Licinius reminded him.

"Tish! With luck we can storm the city before the Lex Talonica goes forth. If not, we can interpret it as 'All male prisoners taken with arms'. At any rate, the female prisoners will fetch a good price, and there's a great many sterile matrons who'll badger their husbands into buying them a child."

Licinius smirked, "It is our plain duty to get to Palmyra first!"

"Exactly!" Galerius said exultantly. "We have the siege engines parked here at Antioch, and a sufficient number of troops to plunder the city once the gates are down, and I want it plundered systematically before it is put to the torch."

Urgency was given to Galerius' plans by the arrival of news that Aurelian, with customary speed, had embarked at Byzantium and was on his way to Antioch by sea. He had also ordered five cohorts of the Xth to march from Caesarea. Galerius received further information from his spies. The majority of citizens of Palmyra were dismayed by the slaughter of the Roman garrison and the renewal of the rebellion. They knew full well what the Roman vengeance would be, and a mass flight from the city had started.

"We must move immediately", Galerius ordered, "before too many have escaped. The city must be taken within days, and the prisoners back here at Antioch and sold, before Aurelian arrives. We mobilize at once."

"In the name of the City and the Emperor?" There was a cynical note in Licinius' question.

"Of course. Of course. In the name of Rome and Augustus", replied Galerius.

Forced marches brought Galerius' army to the walls of Palmyra. They found the farms in the oasis deserted and systematically torched them, cutting down fruit trees and palms for their camp-fires and slaughtering all livestock for meat. It was two days before the siege engines arrived, but within hours the gates of the city were broken and Galerius' Huns were in the streets, driving the inhabitants out into the open.

"Throw down your arms and you will be spared", the centurions shouted. The order was reinforced by the immediate crucifixion of anyone taken prisoner whilst still armed. The citizens threw away swords or spears and surrendered.

Galerius' plundering of the city of valuables was methodical, the great temple of Bel being the main prize. While his troops stripped temples and mansions of everything of value, the prisoners were already being mustered into columns and marched away on the Antioch road. Galerius was anxious to be away before the arrival of the Xth legion.

"Have the sappers smash the sluices and destroy the irrigation canals", he ordered Licinius, I will see to the firing of the city."

"Aren't you going to batter down the walls and sow the ground with salt?" Licinius asked.

"Bah! Superstition! We have no time for that. Destroy the irrigation canals and Palmyra will not rise again."

"The troops think it will bring bad luck to leave anything standing", Licinius pointed out.

Galerius gave an exasperated sigh, "And if Aurelian arrives before we leave and hide half of it, he will confiscate the entire treasure. I don't suppose the troops would like to lose their share. But never mind – bring me a sack of salt."

Galerius strode across the oasis scattering symbolic handfuls of salt in all directions. The following morning, at dawn, the army commenced its march back to Antioch, the wagons of booty bringing up the rear.

*   *   *

Anastasius reached Caesarea and his rendezvous with Diocletian on the day that the Imperial command for five cohorts of the Xth to march to Palmyra was delivered. Both watched the Legion parade at dawn the following day. Century by century, cohort by cohort, the column marched out of the fortress, their standards a proud forest of eagles held aloft by the standard-bearers in their ceremonial leopard skins. It was a splendid sight; the tribunes, helmets plumed with scarlet ostrich feathers, leading each cohort on horseback; the centurions picked out by their horse-hair crests, marching beside the standard-bearers; the blood-red cloaks and glinting points of the pila; the steady, rhythmic, tramp, tramp, tramp of five cohorts marching in step; and the cohort bands of horns, drums and cymbals giving the time.

"A thousand years of greatness", Diocletian said, his voice choked with emotion. "There, marching past, is a thousand years of Rome. What power can withstand her? What power on earth could overcome her?"

Anastasius, sharing the elation of the moment, was unable to think of a reply. Diocletian, the rare moment of candour passed, went on.

"They were an undisciplined rabble before Aurelian took them in hand at the siege of Palmyra. Look at them now, proud, determined, disciplined. We have to do the same with the Syrian legions."

"It will be a long task", Anastasius said.

"We have almost a year before we are needed", Diocletian hesitated, "elsewhere."

Anastasius' heart skipped a beat; so the Gallic campaign was not to begin till next year? Diocletian's "almost a year" suggested the Spring of 274 when Giorgios would be four.

At the evening meal, Diocletian, as usual, ate sparsely, drank sparingly and remained silent. At the end of the meal he turned suddenly to Anastasius.

"This inspection has been fortunate for you." Startled, Anastasius nodded in reply. "You would have been in a very embarrassing position if you had been ordered to Palmyra?"

Anastasius managed to croak a "Yes."

"Have no fear", Diocletian went on, "I was also fortunate to have this in hand when Palmyra revolted a second time. Oh no! Not for the same reasons as you – I'm not becoming a Christian, but Palmyra is, or was, a rich city, the meeting of caravan routes from around the world; it poured gold, a great deal of gold, into the Treasury. How am I to tax a ruin?"

Anastasius felt emboldened to reply, "Perhaps it was the burden of taxation which caused the revolt?"

Diocletian gave one of his short, barking laughs. "An old controversy; reduce the rate of tax and you increase the revenue, because the trouble and expense of tax evasion isn't worth the effort; or increase the rate and risk reducing the revenue, because evasion becomes a profitable business – but the controversy, Count, is purely theoretical. The cart has sunk too deep for it to be extricated."

"I once heard a dreadful shout in the forum at Lydda", Anastasius said quietly, " 'Better the barbarian than the tax gatherer!' "

Diocletian looked at him oddly.

"I will try to remember that. Meanwhile we must be on our way at dawn tomorrow. Our business is to reform the legions. Perhaps then we'll have the time to remind such agitators that the barbarians are tax-gatherers too."

CHAPTER TWENTY-THREE

Anastasius returned from the Euphrates in good time for the Saturnalia, and with a long leave before him. Another Easter came and went, and he bought Giorgios a new pony for his fourth birthday; but inevitably the order came for him to join Aurelian at Arles. He sailed from Joppa but did his leave-taking in the atrium, and rode away with one last long look back to where his wife and son stood, side by side, silently watching his departure. Then he set his face toward Joppa, to the long sea voyage, and to the melancholy prospect of Roman legion fighting Roman legion for the survival of the Roman World.

Three weeks later he joined the army mustered at Arles on the Rhône Estuary, where they were to rendezvous with the XIVth legion coming from Mediolanum. Their landing was unopposed because the city and the east bank of the Rhône had been retaken some years earlier by the Emperor Gallienus. Aurelian camped outside the city and the soldiers took the opportunity to get their land-legs back. Aurelian, however, enforced strict discipline against looting or molesting the citizens and ordered that all food and wine be paid for. Anastasius took the opportunity to write to Kira.

"We are safely landed here at Arles and the curious thing is that Tetricus has done nothing to prevent us, though Nîmes on the opposite bank is still in his hands. I have located the Pole Star, and thought of you."

The XIVth and its auxiliary cohorts, led by Diocletian (who had sailed for Rome when Aurelian began his inspection of the Syrian legions) arrived the next day. In his next letter Anastasius told Kira what had happened.

"The following morning Aurelian sent a strong force under Constantius, across the Rhône. They advanced on Nîmes and, to their astonishment, the gates were open and they were greeted by the city magistrates and curia. There was no sign of Tetricus' troops, and no fighting, so you see you have little to fear for my safety. We will both gaze at the Pole Star tonight, and remember."

Anastasius' next letter to his wife was equally reassuring.

"We have begun our march up the Rhône toward Lugdunum, and I suppose that that is where the fighting will begin. Meanwhile, life is almost pleasant, the river is wide and cool, the hillsides are covered in vines, and I have never seen anywhere so green. It is very strange to hear everyone in the towns and villages speaking Latin, even if, as Mansour would say, 'of a sort.' In fact their Latin is much faster and more melodious than old Mansour's textbook Latin. Please tell him so and describe his expression in your next letter. How is Giorgios coming along with his riding and his grammar? For the grammar we can trust Mansour, but for the riding I hope his grandfather is always with him. I will gaze again at the Pole Star and think of you."

Kira's letters were briefer and the writing somewhat laboured. He received the first one as the army reached Lugdunum: "I look at the Pole Star every night, the sky is so beautiful. Giorgios is growing up fast, quite a little boy now and no longer my baby;

but I have a surprise for you when God brings you safely home. Mansour did pull a face when I told him about the funny way they speak Latin in the West."

"We have taken Lugdunum", Anastasius wrote in his next letter, "And all without a sword being drawn or an arrow loosed. The gates were open and the magistrates and curia welcoming, renewing their allegiance to Rome and Augustus. The sky is overcast tonight – no stars – and it promises rain, but I will think of you and Giorgios and try to guess your surprise."

There was little time for writing in the next few days. Old soldiers began to recall Gallienus' attempt to win back Gaul nine years previously.

"They did the same then", one tough old Centurion would say, "Ran away in front of us, refused to stand and fight, and what did we do? Why we followed 'em of course, further and further into Gaul till we was worn down to our knees with marchin'. Then what did they do? They attacked, of course. We were lucky to get back to the Alps, and Gallienus himself was murdered."

"That's how Claudius Gothicus became Emperor", another barrack-room lawyer would assert. "You wouldn't catch Claudius chasing his tail after this lot. He'd overtake 'em and make 'em fight."

The fear of a trap grew and the malcontents became mutinous. Anastasius strode through the knots of hostile soldiers gathered about the agitators, to where a cart provided a useful platform.

"Has any of you gone hungry?" he demanded. "Has any of you missed your wine and oil ration? No! Because Diocletian has kept the supply wagons from Arles running like a river. If we have to fall back, we have supply dumps all the way to Arles."

The knots broke up, men muttering, "Count Anastasius is alright", and "We can trust Anastasius." The grumblers continued to grumble, but under their breath.

Aurelian decided that the best cure for boredom was forced marching. The army would make forty miles a day, walking and running alternate miles, he decreed, and any drop-outs would be left for the hill tribes. They would come down in the night and add heads to their trophy poles. He also forbade all correspondence with the outside world.

The army marched. It marched up the Saône to Dijon, then north west across the Langres Plateau and down into the valley of the Marne, and still Tetricus retreated before them. Then, one morning, the camp awoke to see the enemy line stretched out, battle banners flying, half a mile away at Chalon, his right flank anchored to the river and his left to the last steep hillside.

"Caught in a young wife's bedroom and the window too small to squeeze through", grumbled the Centurions as they went about whacking any slow-moving soldiers with their rods.

"Get in yer place, never mind yer scoff, I'll tell yer when yers hungry."

"Why aren't the bastards chargin' us before we get our kilts on?" the centurions asked each other. Constantius was asking the same question.

"Why are they standing there doing nothing? They could cover the distance before we were ready for them."

Aurelian merely looked enigmatic.

"Hurry the men up. There'll be time for whys and wherefores after."

The Roman line was ready in a remarkably short space of time, and the commissaries began going down the lines doling out raisins and watered wine to the fasting troops.

"They must be waiting for us to make the first move", Constantius said, sitting his horse next to Aurelian beneath the dragon standard.

"Then they will wait all day", Aurelian replied, "I've no intention of crossing dead ground." He pointed to where the land dipped and rose again.

"Look!" shouted Diocletian, "Movement! What? Half a dozen horsemen cantering out of line."

A ripple went through the ranks; Anastasius ordered the first ala of light cavalry to prepare to charge.

"They're bearing olive branches", Constantius said. "They're asking for a parley."

Aurelian frowned, "Well, let them come up to our front, we will meet them there."

"I know the man at the head", Constantius said suddenly, "It's Tetricus' son, he proclaimed him Caesar and heir."

"Then that makes him a rebel", growled Diocletian.

Aurelian said nothing, but urged his horse forward through the ranks to advance some twenty paces before his front line. There the two groups met, but whether what the Gallicans had to say astonished Aurelian as much as it astonished his staff officers, no change of expression betrayed. That evening Anastasius wrote again to Kira.

"Dearest beloved. The war is over! We were ready for battle, and everyone knew that if we were defeated few of us would get back to Arles. Then Tetricus' son, (he is also named Tetricus) rode out to us with an escort. As soon as the men realized that he was asking for surrender terms, they began to cheer; you never heard such a noise, thousands of soldiers banging their shields and cheering like mad. It was a wonderful sound, even if it did terrify the horses. This is all I can write tonight, there is so much to do, and the sky is clear, the stars are wonderful, but none shines like my Rose of Sharon." Later he wrote again: "We are all still waiting here. It's very mysterious. The Gallic army is disbanding, if one can call it that, for what is really happening is that, cohort by cohort, they are taking the oath to Rome and Augustus and then marching back to their bases. Tetricus, his son, and his high staff officers are all prisoners, but very honoured prisoners; they dine with Aurelian every night.

"Tell Mansour that I have got a sample of the written patois for him. I fell to talking with a Gallic Tribune, a massive fellow about six feet high and six feet broad, with yellow hair and a red face. He turned out to be quite an educated man, able to speak Mansour's sort of Latin as well as his own, and some Greek. He has written out a passage for me. I cannot tell you how impatient I am for that glad day when we sail for home. The Pole Star shines as brightly as ever, as do my thoughts of you."

The next letter he wrote was not so optimistic.

"Well, now we know what we were waiting around for. The Gallic troops were all dispersed, but still Aurelian made no move. The rumour went round that one of the surrender terms was that Tetricus hand over the Channel fleet intact and sea-worthy, and that meant we would march north for an invasion of Britannia. That cast a real damper on the euphoria of victory. Britannia, the old centurions told everybody, was a land of perpetual mist and rain, that the men were all tongue-lashed and brow-beaten by their wives, and that the women were all taller and stronger than men and thought nothing of breaking the arm of any man who annoyed them.

"Just as the camp was seething with discontent there arrived a delegation from Britannia, not just the Legates of the II, XX and VIth, but the magistrates of the chief cities and some of the British 'kings,' as they style themselves. One of them, a tall man with snow-white hair, walrus moustache, a large red face constantly creasing with laughter, and startlingly blue eyes, always twinkling with mirth, seemed to seek me out. His Latin was good, though he spoke with a sing-song accent. He told me that his name in his own tongue was 'Coel Hen,' or 'Old Coel' in Greek, perhaps because of his white hair, though my impression was that he was not so old as he appeared. He wore Brythonic dress, woollen leggings and a great cloak of a curious weave of many coloured squares. He was insistent that he was not a subject but an ally and federate of Rome. since he could put fifteen thousand warriors on the field, led into battle by a hundred 'fiddlers,' as he called them. He had brought three of these fearsome musicians with him. Their instruments turned out to be over-large bagpipes. The pipers' fingers fairly danced, or 'fiddled,' as they played, and I could well imagine men charging into battle behind them. I noticed that Constantius seemed anxious to keep well in with him, so perhaps the fifteen thousand is not an exaggeration.

"Now I will come to the point of all this: we were talking over a cup of 'Methglyn', as he called it, made from honey I would guess, when Coel's eyes went opaque and rolled up in his head in the strangest manner. He began to chant, and this is what he said: 'The name of your son will be great, it will be known throughout the world, even in my own country.' I was told that he had what the Britons call 'second sight', by which they mean that he can foresee the future. So, my dearest, your son will, it seems, be famous as you said. I must however add that this Old Coel told Constantius much the same thing. He said that the son Constantius is hoping for should be named after him – Constantine – and that he would rule over all the land he rode upon. Now the war really is over and the Empire united, with the same frontiers as Augustus established two hundred years ago. It cannot be long before I am back home with you both."

Kira, reading this, danced around the atrium. She read it several times and called Grananna to hear it. Disappointment however was to follow.

The next letter began: "I was counting how long it would take before I held you in my arms again when a very grand delegation arrived from Rome. The Senate has proclaimed Aurelian 'Restitutor Orbis'; that, in Greek, means 'Restorer of the World'. The Senate has voted him the most magnificent Triumph in the history of

Rome, more magnificent even than the Triumphs of Julius and Augustus, which means I must go to Rome before returning home. I would gladly miss Rome just to be with you and Giorgios and see the Rose of Sharon in bloom. You do not tell me what your surprise is: I will try to guess as I gaze once more at the Pole Star in our little evening ritual."

Anastasius also wrote to Mansour.

"As I must go to Rome first, and God alone knows how long we will be detained there, I am sending you a careful copy of the script written in this Gallic Latin, or as you would say, 'Latin of a sort'. All that has happened is most mysterious and you would be fascinated by it. Why did Tetricus surrender after leading us a merry dance across Gaul? Why is Aurelian treating him as an honoured guest when in the past he would have been executed as a rebel and a traitor? Several rumours are going around. A common one is that Tetricus wished to end the secession – after all, his three predecessors, Postumus, Marius and Victorinus, were murdered. He accepted his acclamation as Emperor, so the story goes, to do just that; but he dare not do it until Aurelian arrived. Even after we landed he had to appear to have a strategy to defeat Aurelian, until, at the last minute, he could put himself under Aurelian's protection. Another theory is that Tetricus had been in secret communication with Aurelian even before Aurelian left Rome for the war against Palmyra. Everyone is asking how Aurelian knew that the delegation from Britannia was on its way if there was no secret agreement? Well, Mansour, that's the mystery for you, and for future historians, but I think it's a mystery which will never be solved."

Anastasius' letters home could hardly be described as "love letters", with their eager descriptions of marches and battles, but Kira treasured every word of them, for every word dispelled her fears and anxieties. This latest letter, however, created new anxieties. She wrote a letter which caught up with Anastasius as he arrived in Rome itself.

"Dearest husband, must you really go to Rome? I long for you here. Now I will tell you the surprise I mentioned. Giorgios is to have his little brother! Grananna says the child will be a girl, but you know how she is with her foretellings. If I ask her how she knows, she just gets terribly cross. She keeps telling me that no good can come of your going to Rome, for it is the wickedest city in the world. She says that the Roman women are brazen, going about with their hair unveiled, as no decent woman, let alone a Christian woman, would, and that they paint their toe-nails to entice the Devil. Even the priests, she says, are not as holy as the Greek priests because they do not grow beards as the Blessed Apostles did. They shave their faces and the tops of their heads and go about bare-headed. Rome, she says, is the new Babylon, the scarlet woman sitting on her seven hills, and that God certainly intends to destroy it with fire and brimstone. But she does say that God will give a warning first so that all the Christians can flee the city. You must get through the gates straight away if you feel the ground tremble or smell brimstone in the air. I do wish you were here, safely home, and this Triumph business were over and done with!"

CHAPTER TWENTY-FOUR

Anastasius smiled as he read Kira's letter; he well understood her fears and immediately wrote to her, dispatching the letter by one of the fast galleys of the Imperial post.

"I, too, long to be home with you, but most especially now that I have your good news. Tell Grananna that it is no great matter to us whether the baby is a boy or a girl, we are too happy to think about that. You can also tell her that the seven hills are only seven molehills, and that as yet Rome has no walls or gates, though Aurelian has started to build them, so that anyone may escape at any time. I have met some fellow Christians. They suffered much under Decius and, yes, quite a lot of the priests do shave, but that is the old Roman custom. My new friends took me to the cemetery on the Vatican hill across the Tiber. They showed me the tomb of Blessed Peter and I touched it with a silken kerchief for you, and upon second thoughts did the same for Grananna. An old priest, with a beard, became most interested when I told him that I came from Lydda and that Blessed Peter had visited our ancestors. He hastened away and came back to say that the Patriarch wished to see me. The Patriarch's name – or Pope as they call him in Latin – is Felix, and he seemed very old and venerable, with, assure Grananna, a long white beard! He asked many questions about Lydda and the Vale of Sharon and of the families who had lived there for more than three hundred years, speaking Greek very well. I asked him if all five Patriarchs were equal, and he smiled and said, 'Yes. But not to me, for I am the successor of Blessed Peter.' Then he gave his blessing to you, Giorgios, and to our coming child. Do not fret or be anxious, dearest, for the Pole Star shines above Rome as well as above Lydda."

All men of deep and sensitive nature suffer homesickness, only the shallow and the superficial declare that they are at home in any city and that the world is their inn. Anastasius certainly felt home-sickness for his beloved Kira, Lydda and the Vale of Sharon, but as he was not an exile he was able to enjoy his short stay in Rome, storing up his impressions to relate to Kira when he should arrive home.

Rome was magnificent beyond all imagining. In the old Forum he was conscious that he was walking on ground that Romans had trodden for a thousand years – Kings, Consuls, Senators, Emperors; their feet had worn away the paving stones. Here Peter and Paul had preached and been seized and carried off to die.

Looking up from the Forum he saw the Capitoline Hill with its golden-roofed temples, dominated by the great temple of Jupiter. Flanking the Forum was the Palatine Hill built over now by the Palatium, a city within the city, containing the palaces of Augustus, Tiberius and Domitian, golden-roofed temples, the Latin Library, the Greek Library and the college of the Paedogogium.

He enjoyed strolling through the newer, colonnaded fora, which opened one into another, cooled by fountains fed by water brought from distant hills by seven aqueducts. He ambled through the hastening crowds, senators, scribes, scholars, idlers and merchants, or stopped to watch the many jugglers, conjurors and other entertainers. The little groups of friends sitting at tables outside the wine-shops, engaged in animated conversation about every topic under the sun, seemed to him the very essence of civilized life. All of Rome was here, men and women of every race in the Empire. Little wonder, he thought, that the poets had called her "The Eternal City".

Over all brooded the massive bulk of the Colosseum. He gazed at it with mixed awe and revulsion. One could almost smell the blood that had been shed: human blood and animal blood. Thousands had died to satisfy the bloodlust of the Roman populace. How was it that a people who prided themselves on their civilized virtues, *gravitas, urbanitas, civilitas* and *humanitas*, could be changed into a savage mob seething with blood lust, rejoicing in cruelty, as soon as they entered this place?

He looked out across the city and it was then that he heard, quite distinctly, a voice with a sneer in it, "All this I will give unto thee and thy son – ". He spun round to see who the speaker was, but there was no one there and he felt his blood run cold and his scalp tingle. He felt unclean, as though something vile had touched him. There was something diseased in the city and in the Roman soul which only the Faith could cure.

There was little time after that to see more of the city. The over-riding task was preparing for the Triumph. The procession would be mustered outside the city and proceed along the Sacred Way to the Capitoline Hill, where Aurelian would sacrifice to Jupiter, before going to the Palatium, and it would take nine hours.

The Triumph was led by twenty elephants behind which came four royal chariots. In the first, drawn by four stags, rode Aurelian, robed, not in the dignified tunic and toga of the Roman Magistrate, but in a robe of purple silk and wearing a golden diadem of sun rays. He was followed by the chariot of Odaenathus – Zenobia's father and loyal client of Rome – brilliant with gold and precious stones. The third chariot, covered in gold, was the gift of the Persian Emperor. The fourth was that of Zenobia herself. Tigers, giraffes, elks, bulls and other beasts were led by their tamers, followed by eight hundred pairs of gladiators. Then followed the prisoners of Aurelian's wars. The Germans with their hands bound; Tetricus, in scarlet cloak and Gallic trousers and Zenobia laden with jewels and chained with golden chains carried by slaves, walked behind lictors carrying their crowns. Next came the Roman People, representatives of every guild in the city. Wagons carrying the spoils of war were followed by the Senators, and finally the legions brought up the rear. The city rang with the cries of "Hail Aurelian, Restorer of the World", intermingled with jeers at the prisoners. In the temple of Jupiter, Aurelian sacrificed the stags, and then, his face uplifted to the sun, striking the pose of a god, he proceeded to the palace of Augustus to preside over a banquet.

CHAPTER TWENTY-FIVE

Anastasius was too weary even to search for the Pole Star. He stripped off his armour and collapsed on to his bed, but his sleep was troubled by dreams of Aurelian robed in blood-spattered purple, standing on the steps of the Temple of Jupiter and proclaiming himself a god. He was awakened by his orderly, who informed him that the Emperor required his presence.

He was admitted by a stranger. Aurelian introduced him briefly, "My new secretary, Eros." Anastasius took in the man at a glance; slightly built, black-haired, olive-skinned with deep brown eyes, his face was smooth. "Greek", Anastasius noted to himself; but one of the Old People, probably from Crete. In the remoter valleys the Old People had survived with very little intermarriage with later folk. Anastasius was not given to disliking people, even Galerius (though he disapproved of him), but "smooth" was the word to describe this fellow with his deferential bowing. Insincerity enveloped him in a negative aura.

"I am to address the Senate", Aurelian went on. "Diocletian and Constantius will accompany me, of course, as will the legates Florianus and Probus, and so will you and Galerius."

Eros, bowing as he went, disappeared into a side room.

The cavalcade left the Palatine, Aurelian first; on his right hand, half a pace behind, rode Diocletian; on his left, Constantius. A pace behind them were the legates, Florianus and Probus, and behind them again, Anastasius himself and Galerius.

The two legates were unknown to Anastasius, men from the Danube frontier, and he studied them with interest. Both in early middle age, they appeared solid and dependable; of their admiration for, and attachment to, Aurelian, there could be no doubt. Probus was the more striking, with a long, serious face and a permanent frown – of worry rather than temper, Anastasius concluded. The procession was led by the lictors, carrying the fasces before them and clearing the way with their rods. A file of Praetorian Guards in their gilded armour and scarlet crests marched on either side of the horsemen. The procession passed through the Arch of Titus into the Forum Romanum and here the crowds began to gather in earnest, the city police striving to hold them back. Cries arose on all sides, "Hail Aurelian", "Vivat", "Hail Restitutor Orbis."

Aurelian rode on through the Forum, nodding to right and to left in acknowledgement of the cheers. Anastasius was swept up on the wave of emotion; this was Rome, this was greatness, this was glory! At the Tabularium at the foot of the Capitoline hill, the procession turned right into the Forum of Julius Caesar, and still the crowds gathered to catch a glimpse of Aurelian. Reaching the Senate, he dismounted and began to ascend the steps, the others following him.

Anastasius walked in a dream. Up these very steps Julius Caesar had walked to immortality. Here Mark Antony had delivered Caesar's funeral oration. Here Octavius had come to restore the Republic to the Senate and in return had been proclaimed,

Princeps – "First Citizen". Suddenly, Anastasius realized that he was walking in the shadow of one as great as any of these. If any man could save Rome from the fall gloomily foretold by Mansour, it was this man who climbed the steps ahead of him.

They entered the portico and Anastasius gazed up in awe at the statue of Pompey the Great; here Caesar had fallen, bleeding from the dagger thrusts of lesser, envious men.

The Senate, with its crowded tiers of marble benches sweeping around three quarters of the circular chamber, the marble tiles radiating from the ruby circle where those addressing the Senate took their place; the incredibly ancient icon of the She-Wolf: all these were for Anastasius a source of wonder. Here Cato had stood to declaim, "Carthage must be destroyed", and here Scipio the younger had announced to the Senate that the city of Moloch was, indeed, no more. Here Cicero had exposed the conspiracy of Cataline and thwarted the march of his storm-troopers on the city; here, too, his denunciations of Mark Antony had thundered beyond the Alps.

The First Consul, Marcus Claudius Tacitus, venerable and aged at seventy-four years, was seated in his raised chair, and the whole assembly was waiting, hushed upon the words of Aurelian.

The Emperor spoke, quietly and modestly. He spoke with deference, addressing the Senators as "Fathers of the Roman People and of the Republic". The Senators stirred at these words, a wave of appreciation passing through the packed benches, for it was a long time since an Emperor had spoken so. He, Aurelian went on, was the servant of the Republic and had come to give an account of his stewardship. He did so without any hint of boasting, detailing the wars against the German barbarians, from the Alps to the Danube Delta, the war against Palmyra and that city's rejection of Roman clemency, which had led, tragically, to the second war. He spoke of the Gallic campaign which had completed the unification of the Empire and the restoration of the frontiers. Then he stunned the Senate by announcing a pardon for Queen Zenobia. She would keep her rank and dignity of Queen and be granted a pension and a villa in Tivoli. Their astonishment was even greater when he announced not only a pardon for Tetricus, his son and high officers, but that Tetricus was appointed Governor of Lucania, his son was confirmed in his Senatorial rank, and the officers would be posted to widely scattered parts of the Empire to continue their careers. He ended by reminding the Senators that his policy had always been to woo men back into the Empire rather than coerce them. The Senate rose as one man, the chamber echoing and re-echoing to their cries of "Vivat Aurelian!" "Vivat Aurelian, Restorer of the World!"

Then he held up his hand for silence, for he had not yet finished. He would no longer tolerate, he told the Senators – and he knew that they, the Fathers of the People, would no longer tolerate – the extortion and oppression practised by the tax farmers. Imperial commissioners would supervise the tax collecting firms to ensure that they did not exact more than the tax due, and that they did not retain more than their commission. Offenders would be executed. He would also require the moneyers to maintain the silver content of the coinage, and commissioners would be appointed to see that this was done. Debasement of the coinage would carry the death penalty. Above all, he was determined to stamp out corruption and bribery. "If men's confidence in the Empire", he told the Senate, "is destroyed because they have to work hard and long merely to procure an existence rendered precarious by excessive and unjust exactions, then for them civilization has failed and barbarism holds no terrors." As he finished speaking the Senators rose again to applaud, but, it seemed to Anastasius, with less enthusiasm than before and a number of them looked hostile. Aurelian waited for the acclamations to subside, then bowed to the icon of the She-Wolf, bowed to the Consuls, bowed to the serried ranks of the Senators, and quietly left the chamber.

Returning to the Palatium, the party refreshed themselves with wine and figs, Eros moving like a shadow in and out of the chamber. Aurelian turned to Anastasius.

"You are anxious to return to Lydda." It was more of a statement than a question.

"Indeed, yes, Augustus", Anastasius could not have kept the eagerness out of his voice, even if he had tried.

"Well, you have done your duty, and done it well", Aurelian went on, "though you would have been wise to have stayed here in Rome and served Diocletian. He thinks highly of you; he tells me that he learned a great deal about cavalry training and tactics from you on the Euphrates."

Anastasius stood awkwardly. He was being offered a place at the heart of the Empire, a place of power. He remembered the vile voice he had heard outside the Colosseum – "All this I will give unto thee – ". On the other hand, the last thing that a Count could say was that he had no further ambitions and that all his needs and desires were fulfilled in his home and in his native land. He stood unanswering.

"Very well!" said Aurelian abruptly. "There's a naval galley leaving Ostia tomorrow. Eros will see to your warrant. I'm sorry to lose you, but I never offer a man an office twice."

*   *   *

Later, and in another part of the palatium, Galerius was pacing the floor.

"I wonder what that fellow's up to", he said to Licinius. "What's so pressing back east to make him pass up an opportunity of advancement here, besides incurring the Emperor's displeasure? I could see Aurelian was annoyed."

"Perhaps, after all, he's just a fool", Licinius opined. "But why worry, it means we've got rid of him, he won't be a rival now."

Galerius ignored this; he was busy turning something else over in his mind.

"This Emperor has made powerful enemies in Rome, though being a soldier from the Provinces he doesn't know it. I watched the faces of the crooked Senators – they're all known to me – when he announced that he was going to reform the tax gathering and conserve the coinage. Half of them owe their fortunes to extortion and peculation and the silver which should be in the coinage is on their tables. They're probably plotting against him already. When I'm Emperor I'll reduce the Senate to what it really is, the Curia of Rome, so there'll be no opposition from that quarter."

"What do we do about the Hispana coloni?" Licinius asked. "If this investigation gets underway it's bound to be discovered."

"I hadn't forgotten that", Galerius replied, "and I think that this is a case where honesty is the best policy." Licinius looked at him in wonderment. "We will declare it on the tax returns!"

"But we can't do that", Licinius protested. "They'll discover how long the coloni has been there with no tax paid."

Galerius smiled, "Three years to be exact, Licinius. Three years since the tax was paid." Licinius looked puzzled. Galerius went on, "Three years since the Palmyrans swept over Cappadocia and destroyed all the tax records! Things have been too disorganized since then for me to collect the tax, but, patriot as I am, I will pay the three years' arrears from my own pocket."

"Will it work?" asked Licinius.

"You know Treasury officials. They'll be so delighted at getting three years' back tax without needing to put the screws on, that they won't probe any further into the affairs of such an honest man, especially one on the Emperor's staff."

Licinius laughed, but still had an objection; "This is going to cost you a lot of money."

"Not me, Licinius. Send an order to Rufio to double, no! treble, the rents on the farms. Those veterans have been living on my generosity long enough. They're not needed for my new plans so it's time to start squeezing them."

*   *   *

Anastasius was supervising the packing of his belongings and seeing them loaded onto a wagon. It occurred to him that he might have angered the Emperor by not remaining in Rome, but he could not see why. After all, he was always available at Lydda and ready to serve whenever he might be called upon; but now there was peace, and with the frontiers secure, what need was there of soldiers in Rome? Of politics he knew nothing that would make him useful. He wrote a hasty note to Kira telling her that he was beginning the long journey home and delivered it to the Imperial posts; and then, his heart light, his step jaunty, he started out for Ostia.

Aurelian was not so pleased.

"We have lost an honest and dependable man", he said to Diocletian, "and just when I most needed such about me. Yes, I saw the expressions on the faces of some of the Senators, however much they tried to keep them smooth, but I will restore honest government and honest money to the Empire whatever the opposition and whatever the cost. I have not won all these wars to lose the peace to thieves and scoundrels."

Diocletian was frowning; he was as displeased as Aurelian, but his cautious nature prompted him to look for deeper reasons.

"Can we trust these Christians, Augustus, to be fully and entirely devoted to the State?"

Aurelian gave him a sharp look.

"Diocletian, I have often said that I prefer to woo men back into the Empire. I will add to that: I intend to unite, not divide them."

PART THREE
275 – 285 A.D.

CHAPTER TWENTY-SIX

"Why did God make dust?"

Giorgios was looking very earnestly at his father as they sat in the sunshine of an autumn morning in the peristyle of the villa. The homecoming from Rome had been joyful and Anastasius was spending all the time that his duties allowed with his son, now a sturdy, intensely curious boy. Anastasius had been relating the story of Aurelian's triumph in Rome for the tenth time, when this interruption had been prompted by the bustling of the house maids as they dusted the ornaments and furniture of the atrium.

Anastasius, stumped for an answer, grasped at the first one which occurred, "It might be to stop people being idle."

"Why?"

"Well", Anastasius paused to think, "because work is good for people."

"Uncle Andrew doesn't do any work", Giorgios said, with the utter simplicity of the curious child.

Anastasius half choked in suppressing a laugh. It was something he had thought to himself many times. However, it wasn't strictly true any more. A few days after his return, Andrew had received his longed-for commission as a Junior Tribune in the Xth. This meant that he would serve a year in the legion, chiefly on commissariat duties, after which he would either return home, transferred to the reserve, or be eligible for a post in provincial administration.

Anastasius had observed him with a smile as he had strutted about in his gilded armour, slipping around corners when he thought no one was watching to remove his helmet and admire the ostrich feather crest, or draw his sword and stab and slash at empty air.

"Uncle Andrew doesn't need to work because he's rich", Anastasius replied, rather lamely.

"Isn't work good for rich people, then?" Giorgios asked, clearly struggling with the problem.

"Well, yes . . ." his father answered cautiously, "but different people do different kinds of work. Uncle Andrew is away learning to be a soldier."

"But Uncle Andrew likes being a soldier", Giorgios protested. "He writes to Grandfather and says so."

"There's nothing wrong in liking what you're doing. It's still work."

"Do the maids like dusting every morning?" Giorgios was determined to wrestle with the problem until he was satisfied.

"I think so", his father replied, "they're always singing."

"Would they have to do it even if they weren't happy?"

"Well . . . yes, I suppose they would."

"Why?"

"Well, because they're servants. They have to do what your mother tells them. We all have to do as we're told by somebody."

"Does the Emperor have to do what he's told?"

"In a sense, yes".

"Then who tells the Emperor what to do?" Giorgios demanded.

For a moment Anastasius was stumped. He supposed that the easy answer would be "the Senate", but he knew that that was not true now, if it ever had been.

"Well, the Emperor should do what God tells us is right. If he does, he'll be a good Emperor; if he doesn't, then in the end God will punish him."

Giorgios pondered this and suddenly switched back to the maids, who had now finished dusting and were running off, chattering and giggling.

"If the maids weren't servants, they could all do the work they liked, the same as Uncle Andrew."

Anastasius laughed, "I suppose that's true, but it would be very difficult to make all slaves free."

"Why?"

"Because a lot of them wouldn't have anywhere to go; this is their home, and if they left they'd have nowhere to live and no one to protect them from wicked men."

Giorgios' forehead furrowed as he thought this over, and then he suddenly smiled.

"They could all get married, like Nanna Iris."

Anastasius laughed. "You'll be a philosopher, and maybe even an advisor to an Emperor."

The days passed pleasantly. Giorgios could now read Greek, with some stumbling, and could converse in Latin. He had grown out of Totti-Totti and had a bigger pony, the little Shetland being ridden by Lucius. Then one morning there was a great deal of bustle about the house; maids conversed in excited whispers, Grananna strode about administering rebukes and even light slaps to those who raised their voices. Auntie Claudia came hurrying into the atrium, clutching Lucius by the hand, a maid following her with Cyrennius. They and Giorgios were ordered out into the peristyle in charge of the maid, and told to "play and keep out of the way". Giorgios sensed the atmosphere of mixed anxiety and excitement and fell silent.

Sometime in mid-morning, Anastasius, pacing in the atrium, heard the awaited cry of a newborn child. Mansour, seated at a small table, began to write the hour and the day. Grananna came out of the lying-in room bearing a naked infant on a linen sheet.

She came to Anastasius, and placed the child in his arms.

"Praise God, you have a daughter, Domine. How is she to be named?"

Anastasius smiled; the matter had already been debated and decided with Kira. "Martha."

Grananna first looked amazed, then delighted, and then, as tears welled in her eyes, said, "But that's my name!"

"Yes, I know", Anastasius replied. "We thought it appropriate."

Giorgios was taken to see his new sister in the early afternoon. His mother lay in bed, Grananna fussing over her, and the baby lay in a cradle. He beamed in delight as she frowned and mewled. "I must have a sword now", he told his father.

"Why's that?" Anastasius asked, quizzically.

"To protect my baby sister from barbarians and dragons", Giorgios replied, as though the answer ought to have been obvious.

"Well", said his father, "Perhaps it's time for a wooden one."

Grananna seemed strangely content with life. She had held the daughter of her darling in her arms, and her name was perpetuated in the new generation. What more could one whose life had been one of service, need? She hummed, and then sang softly, an old Greek lullaby, her voice quavering on the high notes.

Gently, without any snapping or criticism, she took Giorgios by the hand and led him out. They were joined by Lucius and made their way to the stone bench by the peristyle pool.

"Tell us a story, Grananna", Giorgios said.

"What kind would you like?"

"One about brave men", Giorgios replied promptly, "but a new one, one we haven't heard before." Lucius echoed this request and Grananna thought for a while and then said, "Very well. I'll tell you the story of a man who was brave in a different way."

"Who was he?" demanded Lucius.

"You must listen to the story to find out", Grananna replied with unaccustomed patience.

"A long time ago, long before Jesus was born, a wicked king conquered Jerusalem and he said that all the people must worship his false gods and that the priests must hand over the Scriptures to be burnt. Any who refused would be cruelly put to death. Many people were afraid and did what the wicked king ordered. Many more, even though they didn't worship the false gods, pretended that they were not Jews and stopped worshipping God and keeping His Law, hoping the king would leave them alone. The king's governor who was even more wicked than his master, thought of a plan to trap these people. He ordered everyone to assemble and eat swine's flesh. Those who refused, he told them, would be stretched on a rack and beaten with clubs until all their bones were broken."

Grananna was interrupted by an indignant exclamation from Giorgios; but when she stopped, both boys pleaded, "Go on! Go on!"

"There was a very old man, named Eleazar. He was ninety years old and was a scribe in the Temple – that's someone who studies the Scriptures and explains them.

He refused to eat the swine's flesh. The soldiers forced his mouth open and put a piece of meat into it, but he spat it out and went up to the rack and stood by it, waiting. Some of the soldiers whispered to him, 'Send home for meat which you are permitted to eat, and pretend that it's pig meat, then they will let you go, and will even reward you.' Eleazar looked at them with scorn. 'You can kill me first,' he said. 'What would the young men of Israel say if they saw me do that? They would say, 'Here is Eleazar, a Scribe in the Temple, who is ninety years old, and has one foot in the grave already, but he loves life so much that for just a little longer he is ready to defile himself and defy God's Law. Why shouldn't we, who have all our lives before us, save ourselves by doing what Eleazar is doing?' It would be my fault that they were led astray, and though I should escape the anger of the king I would certainly not escape the anger of the Almighty.' 'Very well, then,' said the soldiers, 'you've made your choice', and they fastened him on the rack and stretched his arms and legs and beat him with clubs until he was dead."

"What happened then?" Lucius wanted to know.

"Why", said Grananna, "Many of those who had hidden their faith and even some of those who had worshipped the false gods, began to praise the Almighty who has made the whole world out of nothing, and to despise the idols and the demons who live in them."

Giorgios, except for his one interruption, had sat silent, drinking in every word. It was Lucius who asked the next question.

"What happened to the wicked king?"

"Ah!" said Grananna with a certain relish, "God punished him as he deserved. He fell from his horse and wounded himself so badly that his flesh rotted on his bones and he smelt so horribly that his slaves couldn't come near him to wash or feed him. Too late he repealed all the edicts he had made against God's People, for he died soon after."

Giorgios heaved a great sigh.

"I will always remember that story, Grananna."

The old woman smiled down at him and stroked his hair.

"I think you will", she said.

*   *   *

The next morning Grananna did not appear at her usual time.

Kira sent one of the maids to see what was delaying her. The girl came running back, incoherent, but at length Claudia was able to calm her and get her to say what was the matter.

"Grananna", she said, "It's Grananna. She's lyin' on her bed with her hands crossed over her chest, an' she's smilin', an', an' – she's dead!"

110

CHAPTER TWENTY-SEVEN

Giorgios mourned in silence, standing forlorn by the stone bench. When his father had left for the wars he had always returned, and trepidation had been turned to joy. Somehow he understood that this was different, Grananna would never return, that she, her stories and her honey cake had gone forever. It was not until the funeral that he began to understand this. A priest, Theodore, came from Lydda. He was dressed in black, he had a large black beard and black locks, and a long, lean face, reposed but unsmiling. They crowded into the atrium, the bier standing at one end, and Theodore began to chant the requiem, the floating melody rising and falling. All were standing, as the Liturgy required, and Giorgios' legs soon grew tired. He had a new nurse, Irene, another Greek girl with plain, sad features, who was fond of children. She sat Giorgios on the floor out of sight behind her, and there he went to sleep. When he awoke the Liturgy was nearing its end and the bier was carried away. It was then that Giorgios understood that he would never see Grananna again, or hear her voice, but he did not cry out loud.

"Why do people die?" he asked his mother after the funeral.

Kira was quiet now, and calm; somehow she too had taken one of those big steps that bring, not year by year, but in sudden leaps, a new maturity. She pondered the question, wondering how much to say.

"Well, they grow old and tired, and are glad to go to heaven."

"Then why do children die?" Giorgios asked.

"Well, sometimes they have accidents, or sometimes they get ill."

"Will you die, Mamma?" There was deep anxiety in the little boy's voice.

"Not for a long time yet, I hope, not until you and Martha are grown up and married; but we all die in the end and go to live in heaven. Grananna is happy and is surrounded by God's love."

A few days later Giorgios and Lucius were sitting on the stone bench, Cyrennius being at home with his mother. Both boys were silent and gloomy until Giorgios suddenly found his tongue and turned to Lucius.

"Grananna is in heaven now, with Jesus and the angels. It's very nice there, and she's very happy." He paused. "But I think I'd rather stay here."

Lucius looked up at him; Giorgios was already his model and his leader.

"An' I think I'd rather stay here with you too", he said.

Both boys laughed a little, then Giorgios cried, "Look, there's a butterfly. Let's catch it!"

*   *   *

A few days later Theodore returned.

"Abba Theodore has come to baptize Martha", Kira explained to Giorgios. "He will dip her in the water three times and say 'The servant of God is baptized in the

Name of the Father and of the Son and of the Holy Spirit,' and then she will be a Christian."

"Was I baptized?" Giorgios wanted to know.

"Of course", his mother replied.

"Well I don't remember being dipped in the water", Giorgios said stoutly.

"Of course not, you were only a baby like Martha."

The ceremony greatly intrigued Giorgios, whetting his curiosity. Abba Theodore arrived with two deacons and half a dozen acolytes. He tied up his robes around his knees and went down into the pool in the atrium. Martha was handed to him, wrapped only in a linen sheet. To Giorgios' great terror Abba Theodore plunged her three times into the water and held there, his hand over her mouth and nose, for what seemed an endless time, but was in reality only a few seconds, whilst he pronounced the words of baptism. He lifted her up and held her out to Anastasius and she began to howl, and went on howling whilst Kira dried her and wrapped her in a warm, linen towel. As Theodore climbed from the pool his deacons began to sing hymns and the acolytes to clash cymbals and blow horns. Then everyone began to drink wine and chatter and laugh and it seemed to Giorgios, though he could not have put it into words, that new life had filled up the vacuum left by the old.

*   *   *

Anastasius sat with his father-in-law under the colonnade of the peristyle. The autumn was growing late, but it was still mild enough to enjoy the late sunshine and the warm wine of Lebanon. Giorgios sat alone, playing with some pebbles a little distance away. Mansour came through the atrium. He stood politely until asked to sit.

"There is grave news, Domine", he said, addressing Dionysius, "There has been an uprising in Rome."

"An uprising! Who?" Anastasius exclaimed.

"The moneyers", Mansour replied. "Apparently, the Augustus Aurelian issued an edict. It ordered the moneyers to sell to the State all the trash they have been coining, for which they would be paid only the value of the alloy."

"Rough justice", interrupted Dionysius.

"Perhaps so, Domine, but they saw it as the withdrawal of their privilege to rob the people."

"Who led the uprising?" asked Anastasius.

"Felicissimus, controller of the mint, and of course one of the richest men in Rome. He secretly gathered an army outside the city: criminals, degenerates, run-away slaves, perverts, all the scum of Rome. They were to rush the Palatine and Capitoline hills and seize the city. They were thwarted by Aurelian's Gallic cavalry – his clemency has earned him their gratitude. The rebels took refuge on the Caelian Hill and fortified it."

"Have they been put down?" asked Anastasius.

"Yes! But at a great cost. One report says that the army lost 7000 men in storming it."

Anastasius knew that Mansour had his own sources of information, so he merely nodded.

"Aurelian", Mansour went on, "was enraged by these losses, and ordered that all those taken prisoner were to be executed on the spot." He paused.

"Yes?" Dionysius prompted.

"One of those taken prisoner was his nephew."

"His nephew!" Anastasius exclaimed.

"Yes, Domine, his sister's son, who foolishly believed that he would be the next Emperor, 'advised', of course, by Felicissimus in all financial matters."

There was a shocked silence on the part of the others. They were both weighing the dilemma Aurelian had faced.

"Did – did he have his nephew executed?" Dionysius asked.

"No!" replied Mansour, "He would not lay upon anyone but himself the responsibility of shedding the blood of a member of the Imperial family."

There was a long silence.

"You mean, Aurelian himself put his nephew to death?" Anastasius asked at last.

"Yes, Domine." Both men were stunned.

"He could not do otherwise", Dionysius said grimly, "He could not execute others and spare the greater traitor."

Dionysius knew as well as Anastasius and Mansour the strength of the Roman sense of family; it was unthinkable that a man would execute his sister's son.

"Everything he has achieved will be wiped out by this", Anastasius said bitterly, "the mob will howl 'murderer' after him in the streets."

"The hypocrites behind the rebellion have already organized protest marches and demonstrations", Mansour said, "but Aurelian may survive yet."

"How?" both demanded at once.

"He has appeared before the Senate again. He declared that he, as First Magistrate of the Roman People, and he alone, was responsible. That he had acted without hesitation to save the State, and without fear or favour. Then he announced that as an act of reparation for the slaying of his nephew, he would build a great new temple in the northern suburbs, dedicated to the Unconquered Sun."

"How did they take that?" asked Dionysius.

"They took it very well, Domine", Mansour replied. "The building guilds, the goldsmiths, the silversmiths, the sculptors, the marble polishers, and all the other guilds which would make a profit from it, were enthusiastic. The tax-farmers and moneyers found themselves in a minority. Then Aurelian, to great applause, pledged that the statues, ornaments and vessels of gold and silver, which he had taken from the Temple of Bel in Palmyra, would be donated to the new temple." The other two let out audible sighs of relief. "There is one other cause of worry, though it might be nothing."

"What is that, Mansour?" asked Dionysius.

"Why, he reminded the Senators that, as Tribune of the Plebs, his person is sacrosanct."

"That is correct", Dionysius said, "the Augusti have held the office of Tribune of the People from the beginning."

"Yes, but then he went on to claim that the Emperor is the manifestation of the Deity."

His two listeners looked grave. Anastasius remembered his dream of Aurelian in blood-spattered purple proclaiming himself a god. Yet it was the venality and greed of men which was driving him to make the claim.

"He said nothing of sacrifice?" asked Dionysius.

"Not yet."

Giorgios, sitting quietly in the colonnade, had listened with avid curiosity to the conversation of the adults. He understood little of it, but he understood that it was a serious matter. What little he did understand, he stored in his memory.

*   *   *

The Saturnalia came and went, and Giorgios' fifth birthday was approaching. For some time now Lucius had joined him in his lessons with Mansour, and it was with the latter that Anastasius was discussing the future.

"Giorgios is reading well, both Greek and Latin, and we have started arithmetic and music", Mansour was saying. "I leave it to the priest, Theodore, to teach him the Scriptures."

"He must also start training in athletics", Anastasius said. "No! Don't worry, Mansour, I'm not expecting you to run and jump! We must get a retired legionary from the Xth, a decurion will always be glad of a wage to top up his pension. If we find a suitable man he can start after Easter."

An instructor was duly found by Andrew. He was Marcus Laeta, a standard-bearer of the IVth cohort of the Xth Legion, a widower – for the ban on legionaries marrying was now honoured more in the breach than in the observance. He was indeed glad of the position, not only for the salary, but also for the opportunity it gave him of finding a new wife. His army nickname, "Square Marcus", suited him well, for he was short of stature, deep of chest and broad of shoulders. He had keen grey eyes under bushy eyebrows, a short thick neck, broken nose, furrowed forehead, jutting jaw and grizzled hair. He was no handsome hero, he well knew, but, he reasoned with himself, a plain, sensible girl with a life of servitude before her might well find him a good catch, and jump at the freedom he could offer her.

Marcus, when he arrived at the villa, was apportioned a room in the slaves' quarters, to which he immediately objected. He was then given quarters above the stables, which suited him well, since in his off-duty times he was able to "tut tut" and roll his eyes heavenwards as he watched the grooms at work. He would then tell them how the job should be done, regale them with stories of campaigns and battles in which, apparently, he had always distinguished himself, and complain about his two daughters who did not write to him. He supervised the boys' riding, swimming, running, jumping and, later, weapon training. He taught them how to throw the pilum and how to fence with wooden swords and toy shields. Giorgios and Lucius enjoyed their work, in spite of being rather frightened of him, for he had a fierce countenance and a gravelly voice. What he intended as a friendly smile, whenever Irene came to collect them from his charge, appeared to them, and to her, as a snarl of still greater ferocity!

* * *

It was golden October, the last of the wine harvest was coming in, the olive plantations had given a record yield of oil, and the corn harvest had been bountiful. Anastasius was sitting in the peristyle with Mansour. They had been going over accounts and various papers and were enjoying a jug of wine. Dionysius was with Andrew who, having completed his year with the Xth Legion had returned home and was impatiently – waiting a posting.

"Ha! Mansour", Anastasius said, "You remember our journey across Cappadocia?"

"Who could forget it, Domine?"

"Well what do you think of your gloomy prophesies now, eh? Here we are at peace, the Empire restored, the frontiers secure and the harvest one of the best ever; tolerance of our religions, the tax farmers compelled to be honest and bad money being replaced by good."

"I did say if no one could be found to save the Empire; and who then could have foreseen Aurelian?" Mansour defended himself.

"Nobody! Not even you Mansour, I'll grant you that. Nobody could even have dared to hope that such a man was waiting in the wings, much less that he would restore everything in five short years. He is one of the great Emperors, Mansour."

A porter hastened out of the atrium and crossed to where they were sitting.

"An Imperial messenger, Domine."

"Bring him in!" Anastasius ordered, and turned to Mansour, "Much as I would be honoured, I hope the Emperor isn't summoning me to join him. Of course it might be for Andrew, he'd be glad to go."

The messenger, looking hot and dusty, walked across to them, bowed and handed Anastasius a scroll. He glanced at the seal, "S.P.Q.R." – it was a dispatch, not from the Emperor, but from the Senate. He rose to his feet, as custom demanded, to read it standing. Breaking the seal with a strange feeling of trepidation, Anastasius unrolled the scroll and began to read.

Mansour saw his face contort in shock and deftly caught the scroll as it fell from his nerveless fingers.

"The Emperor" Anastasius said, his voice strangled, "has been assassinated."

CHAPTER TWENTY-EIGHT

The household was gathered in the atrium, even Giorgios, for no one was deemed too young to receive a Senatorial command. He stood between his father and grandfather, over-awed by the solemnity and silence. His grandfather motioned to Mansour to read:

"Greetings: From the Senate and the People of the Romans, to all Provincial Governors and Officers.

"Following the foul murder of the August Lucius Domitius Aurelianus, Restitutor Orbis, in a conspiracy led by the freedman Eros, this august assembly has elected as Censor, Imperator, Tribune of the People and Pontifex Maximus, the First Consul of Rome, Marcus Claudius Tacitus, with the titles, Imperator, Caesar, Pius, Felix, Augustus. All Governors are commanded to assemble their households, their civil staffs and military officers and administer to them the oath of loyalty to the City and to the Augustus Tacitus. This oath is to be sworn by the name each man gives to the Deity."

A tremor of relief went through the Assembly; the oath could be taken by all.

*　　　*　　　*

Marcus was watching his charges with approval. Almost two years had passed since the assassination of Aurelian and on a personal level they had been good years for Marcus. There were other children on the villa besides Giorgios, Martha, Lucius and Cyrennius. There were the children of freedmen, of the household slaves and of the field slaves. Giorgios, growing beyond confinement to the house and peristyle and accompanied by the faithful Lucius, ventured further afield. He gathered a dozen or so boys of his own age around him. They looked up to him as their leader, not only because he was the son of the Dominus, but because he was always the first to climb any tree, to raid any orchard, to get into scrapes, to invent new games and devise new adventures. He never dared his followers to do anything he had not done, but most of all, he was loyal to them not only in taking blame but in claiming "rights" for them.

"Why shouldn't my friends be taught by Marcus?" he had demanded when he wanted them to join in the foot-racing, jumping, swimming and other athletics. This pleased Marcus for it increased his responsibilities and, as Anastasius was a just man, increased his salary.

Marcus' progress however owed a great deal to the political situation. Tacitus had ruled for only six months. In spite of his age he had joined the army which Aurelian had mustered in Thrace and crossed with it into Asia Minor. There in the spring of A.D.276 he had defeated a barbarian force. Unhappily it was also there that he learned of the extortions and fraudulent activities of his relatives. Whilst preparing to return to Rome to investigate the mounting complaints against them, he was murdered, whether by his relatives or by their victims was never known.

The Senate, exercising the authority Aurelian had restored to it, had elected Florianus emperor. He immediately went to Asia Minor to continue Tacitus' campaign, and within a matter of weeks had brought the barbarians to the brink of defeat. Probus was aggrieved at having been passed over by the Senate, and with the Egyptian and Syrian legions supporting him, he proclaimed himself emperor. Florianus broke off his successful campaign and marched his army to Tarsus where he stood poised to invade Syria.

There he was murdered by supporters of Probus. Three Emperors had been murdered in a single year, and the Senate, reverting to its fits of cowardice, voted Probus the Tribunic dignity, which legitimized his assumption of power. Mansour's gloomy forebodings were being proven all too true. The Empire was returning to anarchy. Worse, envy, greed and venality were marking down for destruction any man with the ability to save it.

These events had happily passed by Lydda and the Vale of Sharon. Life there was secure and peaceful. There was no hunger and no indigence, until suddenly the peace was shattered.

Riding in from the desert beyond the Jordan, a nomad raiding party poured into the valley, intent on looting what they could and destroying what they could not. They left the villas alone and attacked the farms of the free tenants. Loaded with all they could carry, and driving off live stock, they made their escape unscathed.

"They will return", Dionysius warned his neighbours, "and when they do we must be ready for them."

So it was that Marcus' duties had been greatly increased and with them his *salarium*. He now had the responsibility for training sixty men in the use of the bow, the spear, the sling and the sword. He had acquired from somewhere an old and battered helmet with the red horse-hair crest of a centurion, which he wore with great pride. Anastasius smiled at this self-promotion, but asked himself, "Why not? A lot of less honest men have promoted themselves Emperor!" Very soon everyone was referring to "Centurion Marcus" and so, as he watched his pupils at play, he had every reason to feel pleased with life. He had a good post here, was likely to be needed for a long time to come, and his combined pension and earnings were sufficient to keep a wife. That, he told himself, was all he needed to complete his contentment, a plain, serious girl who would be grateful to him for marrying her. He discounted the possibility that anyone could actually fall in love with him!

"Good!" Marcus said aloud, as he watched Giorgios throw a taller boy in a wrestling bout. As Marcus attributed Giorgios' victory to his own training, he was much gratified; so much so that he broke into a grin, a natural one which lit up his weather-beaten face and grey eyes. He became aware that someone had come up behind him and turned quickly. It was Irene, come to collect Giorgios. She stopped still, surprised by the unaccustomed good nature on Marcus' face. She smiled too, a smile which lit up her plain sad face. They stood looking at each other for several moments, and then, Marcus, without thinking, loosened a tongue that had too long been tied.

"My! You *are* a pretty girl!" he said in a voice far less gravelly than usual; and suddenly so she was, for love turns sand into gold.

"I've come to collect the young master", she said, pretending to ignore the compliment.

"I'll walk back with you!" Marcus said hastily, surprising even himself.

"Cheek!" said that too-haughty maiden, and as Marcus' face fell she quickly corrected herself, "No! but I'd like that, I mean yes, really I would." They both became aware for the first time that Giorgios was at her side, looking up at her and listening intently to every word.

"Will you marry Centurion Marcus, Nanna Irene?" he asked innocently.

"Yes!" exclaimed that worthy centurion on behalf of them both.

"Well, then", said Giorgios, "You'll have to ask Mamma if she'll let you; but I think she will, she likes people getting married. When I grow up I'm going to marry a kind lady like Nanna Irene, but only if she can ride a horse."

CHAPTER TWENTY-NINE

The raiders did return, as Dionysius had warned. Their numbers had increased, and now forty or more came sweeping down the valley, intent on plunder. Marcus, however, had prepared well.

He had set up a chain of beacons on hill tops. At the first sighting of the raiders a signal fire blazed up. The nomads found themselves facing a stiff resistance, one they had not expected and had no liking for. They were driven off with heavy losses. Dionysius however, leading the counter-attack on horseback, was severely wounded. He was carried home where the villa surgeon cleaned the wound with wine and oil. He turned to Andrew and silently shook his head.

"Can nothing be done?" Andrew appealed in anguish.

The surgeon shook his head again, "It isn't only the wound. At his age the loss of blood and shock are too great."

Abba Theodore was, fortunately, at the villa. He confessed the old man and anointed him in the ritual for the dying. Dionysius rallied for a while and the family gathered around his bed, Giorgios and Martha round-eyed, if not with fear, then with trepidation. Dionysius managed a wan smile, "It seems", he said, "I am to die, and I die a Roman."

"Do you die in the Faith of Our Lord Jesus Christ?" Theodore asked.

"I do, as I have lived. No one of my family at any time has been a worshipper of idols and false gods. Before we were Christians we were Hebrews, the chosen of the true and only God. I die in the Faith of my fathers." Then Dionysius turned to Andrew. "My sword I leave to my only grandson, Giorgios. It was my father's and his father's before him. It is said that it is the sword with which the Blessed Peter cut off the ear of Malchus in the Garden of Gethsemane. See that he has it when he comes of age."

"I will, Father, I will", Andrew promised, choking on his sobs.

Dionysius gave three little breaths; they heard the death rattle in his throat, and suddenly the light went from his eyes and he seemed much smaller.

Giorgios' grief was silent. This was his grandfather whose presence and care had comforted him in those long months when his father had been away with the army, the grandfather who had taught him to ride Totti-Totti. He could not really grasp the idea that, like Grananna, he would never see him again, that something had ended. Who else might die? he wondered.

His mother was weeping aloud, not only tears but sobs; Martha and the maids joined in, and an ululation of mourning filled the house. Uncle Andrew and his father stood, eyes unmoving, faces rigid. Roman men might not give way to public expressions of grief, and Giorgios knew that he must do the same. Mansour stood silent, head bowed, face grave. Auntie Claudia entered the room to put her arms around his mother and to add her lamentations to the rest. Giorgios felt a lump form in his throat and a prickling in his eyes. It was at that moment that

Nanna Irene took him and Martha by the hand and led them gently away into the atrium.

The funeral of an Imperial Count could be no private affair. It must take place in Lydda in the presence of the Magistrates and the curia. There would be a funeral oration and the citizens would file past and only then could the family take the body for burial. It was a pity, the magistrates felt, that Christians did not hold funeral games in honour of the dead; they were always popular, but there would certainly be a donation, a distribution of corn and wine and oil to the townspeople. Dionysius had been a good governor. Men remembered how he had saved the city from Rome's anger after the Palmyran revolt and the large donation he had made to the empty treasury. It was expected that all the townspeople, citizen and servile, would file past the body and its military escort; but before all this there would be the requiem in the Christian church in Lydda, attended by the family and the other Christians on the estate. The day of the funeral would be a long day indeed.

At the requiem Giorgios listened, rapt to the floating melody of the chant, led by Abba Theodore. Halfway through his eighth year now, and Mansour's diligent pupil, he noted each word, trying to understand its import. Tentatively, he added his clear treble to the ancient lament of the dead.

> "Out of the depths I have cried unto Thee,
> Lord hear my plea, listen to my supplication,
> If Thou O Lord weigh my sins, how shall I endure it?
> But with Thee there is mercy and forgiveness.
> In keeping Thy Law I have waited for Thee
> My soul has trusted in Thy Word,
> My soul has hoped in Thee.
> From the morning watch, even until night
> Let Israel hope in the Lord.
> For with the Lord there is Mercy
> And with Him a plenteous redemption,
> And He shall redeem His People,
> Redeem them from all their iniquities."

The requiem came at last to its end, and Giorgios was startled as he emerged into the sunlight. More people than he had ever seen crowded the long street which led to the basilica.

Lamentation arose on all sides as the cortege passed. Standing on the steps of the basilica to receive the cortege were the magistrates and curia, principal citizens, and the decurions of the guilds. There was a long oration by the first magistrate and then the citizens began to file past. Giorgios grew tired and began to fret. Kira signed to Nanna Irene to lead him away unobtrusively. She took him to a shady corner of the square where they sat and ate grapes. Finally it was over and his grandfather was borne away to be laid in the family grave in the necropolis outside the city. Only now, with no witnesses but Nanna Irene, did he cry.

Giorgios, always a serious child, now became solemn. Somewhere below the level of consciousness was an ache, a loneliness; he missed his grandfather.

Shortly after the funeral, Kira called Giorgios to her side, "Mamma is going to have another little baby. Do you want another brother or a little sister?"

Giorgios' brow furrowed in thought.

"Well", he said at length, "I have a little sister already, so I think I would like a little brother."

Kira gave a little laugh which left Giorgios even more puzzled. He could not see anything faulty in his reasoning.

*   *   *

It was late autumn and preparations were being made for the Saturnalia. By "baptizing" the day as a kind of "official" birthday of Christ, Christians were able to celebrate the season, though in a more subdued and decorous way than their pagan neighbours. The more puritanical, followers of Tertullian, pointed out that sheep could not have been on the hills of Bethlehem at that time of the year, and in any case celebrating alongside the festivities of pagans, who were shortly to be struck down by the Right Hand of God's wrath, should not even be thought of by any right-minded Christian!

Giorgios wondered why his mother had been absent for the past couple of days whilst all this preparation and excitement was going on.

"She is confined to her room", Irene told him, "Your new baby is expected any day now." Then came the day of hushed excitement among the maids, of anxiety on father's and uncle's faces, of Auntie Claudia being officious about the household, of the physician and two middle-aged, serious-looking women arriving from Lydda; and then, at the end of it all, Giorgios and Martha being taken to their mother's room where she lay on a couch holding a tiny baby in her arms. She smiled at them and said, "This is your new little sister, Katherine. She has come just in time for Christmas."

CHAPTER THIRTY

Mansour read the coded message again. There was nothing he could put his finger on to disprove its authenticity, yet he felt uneasy. The message was to the point. The Samaritan brethren in Egypt were grateful. Much of their wealth was secreted in Persia thanks to Mansour. They desired to replenish the gold which had been spent in getting it there. As an earnest of what was to come they had sent a messenger with a bag of gold. He would meet Mansour at The Golden Ass, a wine shop in the back streets of Lydda. There was no single thing to justify a doubt and he could not leave the messenger adrift in the city. With some trepidation he fastened to his belt a Scythian blade. He put on a voluminous cloak with ample inside pockets and rode his mule to Lydda, wondering wryly if it was he who was "The Golden Ass". He arrived, on purpose, a little early, just before the autumn dusk fell, and entered the wine shop. It was empty. He chose a table in a corner and sat on a bench with his back to the wall. The innkeeper, a taciturn man with grey hair, came over and Mansour ordered a jug of wine and two cups.

A stranger entered, looked about him and made straight for Mansour's table. He was not, Mansour noted, an Egyptian, however the greeting with which he identified himself was correct, and Mansour replied in the same code. The man sat down and Mansour poured wine. Quickly the man slid onto the table a leather bag tied at the neck. Mansour drew it toward him; it was heavy, but it disappeared smoothly into the inner pocket of his cloak.

"You are an Egyptian?" Mansour asked pleasantly.

The man looked at him quickly, "No!" he replied, "but I serve those who dwell in the Land of Egypt."

"Well, that at least", Mansour thought, "was the truth", so perhaps he had been uneasy for nothing.

They drank the wine, and the man, speaking low, said, "It is best that I leave first."

Mansour intended to examine the contents of the bag before stepping into the street, so he readily agreed. The man stood up, bowed and went out.

Mansour poured himself a second cup of wine. The innkeeper was busying himself opening an amphora and was taking no notice of him. He slipped his hand into his pocket and expertly untied the knot that held the bag shut. He drew out a coin with finger and thumb, palmed it and brought it onto the table. It was gold, it was heavy and it was Persian. He took out a second coin and then a third, all were Persian. He leaned back against the wall to reflect. He had a bag of Persian gold on him, so what would happen next? He pictured the likely scenario. He would step out into the street, a city police patrol would happen to come along. They would arrest him on suspicion of something or other, march him away to be searched and discover the bag of Persian gold.

Well that was not a crime, gold circulated freely across the world, and Roman coins went as far as India, or even the mysterious Cathay. But what, they would ask, was a poor scribe doing with a heavy bag of gold? Would he be accused of theft?

That was hardly likely; someone would have to come forward to claim the gold and that would expose the identity of the conspirators. Then it came to him. He was not the target, Anastasius was! The poor scribe had a bag of gold, Persian gold, because he had received it for his master! Of course that was not a crime either; Rome was not at war with Persia and trade flowed freely between the two. But what had been exchanged for the gold, for what was it payment? It was a neat trap.

"Galerius!" Mansour breathed softly.

Carefully, Mansour slipped the three coins back into the bag. Skilfully, he drew the cords together but did not knot them. Slowly, and without as much as a chink, he lifted the bag from his pocket and lowered it to the floor, and with his heel he pushed it back under the bench against the wall. He would come back in the morning. With luck the bag might still be there, but if not, it was not his loss but the conspirators'. He would like to see Galerius' face when the police report mentioned no gold among the prisoner's possessions!

Mansour called for the bill – it amounted to a few denarii. The innkeeper insisted upon accompanying him to the door, bowing him out. Mansour noticed a large amphora of water standing inside the porch. It struck him as odd; then he stepped out into the street and looked down it for the expected police patrol.

What he saw made his blood freeze. Not ten yards from him was a man in the act of throwing off his cloak. He stood naked except for sandals and a sword belt, his body gleaming with oil, and a Scythian blade leapt into his hand. Mansour snatched a glance in the opposite direction; another man, naked and oiled, was crouching there, Scythian blade at the ready. "Sicarii!" The word exploded in Mansour's brain.

The Sicarii had begun, two centuries since, as a Jewish resistance group to Roman occupation. Over time they had degenerated into assassins, prepared to murder anyone, Jew, Christian, Samaritan or Pagan, provided the price was right.

Mansour leapt back into the porch, wrenching at the door handle. The door was bolted from the inside. Desperately, he reached for his own blade. He felt his hair grabbed and his head jerked back. He barely felt the razor-sharp blade slice across his throat. The assassin pulled him back, blood spurting, into the street and the other man drove his blade under Mansour's ribs into his heart. Quickly, the assassins washed blood from arms and body in the amphora of water, then tipped it over to wash sandals and feet. They pulled tunics and girdles from pouches inside their cloaks. Donning the cloaks, they walked quickly down the street and turned into another, where two horses awaited them. They met nobody on their ride to Joppa, but if they had there would have been no sign of their crime upon them. On the quay they walked calmly to a fishing vessel and climbed aboard. Back at The Golden Ass the innkeeper had already unhitched Mansour's mule and sent it trotting down the street. It was less than half an hour since Mansour had died.

The following morning the innkeeper swept and sanded the floor. He found the bag of gold beneath the bench and buried it, calculating how long he should wait before selling the inn and slipping away to Persia.

*   *   *

Claudia's shriek rent the air, terrifying Giorgios and the other children. The city police had found the body at dawn and their superiors had identified it immediately. The city had been alerted to find the murderers and the body brought to the villa, where it had been laid in the atrium. Claudia had by chance been visiting Kira and there was no time to prepare her for what she must see. Shrieking still she flung herself prostrate upon Mansour's body, her anguish filling the atrium. Kira knelt beside her, trying to raise her, but she clung stubbornly to the body. Ignoring all words of comfort she knelt, tearing her hair out with fearful force, raking her cheeks with her nails and ripping her garments. The others, even Kira, stood helpless before such grief. Then Claudia raised her clenched fists.

Words of some ancient tongue, long forgotten, came to her lips as she called upon heaven for justice and vengeance in fearful curses.

"Strike those who have done this thing", she shrieked. "Let their flesh melt from their bones. Let them be wax in the flames. Let them be accursed in waking, accursed in sleeping. Let them see their children wither. Let their children bring them down in sorrow to their graves."

At last, passion spent and grief exhausted, her face grey and haggard, she permitted Kira to lead her away.

Giorgios stood, hot-eyed, looking at the corpse. This was unreal, ungraspable. There lay the body of his tutor, the one who had opened to him the joy of learning; no harsh pedagogue ever ready with the rod to punish inattention or inability, but kind and gentle. Was there no end to death? Somehow God was involved in it, but he could not understand how. Why should God want his tutor, his grandfather, his old nurse to die? He remembered his serious infant words to Lucius, that heaven was a happy place, but that he wanted to stay here. Surely Mansour had wanted to stay here, had wanted to stay with Auntie Claudia and Lucius and Cyrennius? This thought brought the realization that his two friends must be suffering greater sorrow than he was. It was their Dadda who lay there, his throat gashed, a blood stain spread across his tunic. He turned to them. Lucius was weeping quietly, tears streaming down his face. Cyrennius was sobbing aloud, Martha and Katherine were crying with terror. He could no longer hold tears back and he too began to sob. His mother, distraught, realized for the first time that the children were present. Frantically she called maids to take them out into the peristyle.

Centurion Marcus arrived hurriedly, still buckling on his armour. He had been told what had happened and now he saw the boys standing bewildered and weeping.

"Right!" he shouted, command in his voice, "You boys get your swords and shields, we must practise to avenge Mansour."

124

It seemed unseemly to Giorgios. He placed his arms around Lucius and Cyrennius; the maids were hurrying Martha and Katherine away.

Marcus shouted again, "Enough of that. I want soldiers; fetch your weapons."

The boys blindly obeyed and, magically, the effort of fencing, of warding off blows with the wooden swords, eased their grief and dried their tears.

Anastasius, his attention caught by the sound of fencing, collected himself and turned urgently to Andrew.

"We know who's behind this, but it mightn't be the only thing he plans; the villa may come under attack. I can't take Marcus away from the boys; gather some of his trained men together and arm them. Send a messenger to Lydda to the cavalry commander there. We need protection."

Andrew, glad of action, hastened away.

Anastasius, left alone, looked down at the body of one who had been his friend more than his servant. He remembered vividly the winter journey and Kira's matchmaking; how the two women had cozened him, and how he had been glad that they had. He recalled their pleasure in the wonders of Antioch and the transparent happiness of Mansour and Claudia on their wedding day. He wrestled with his agony and cried aloud, "There will be justice! Mansour, my friend, there will be justice! Justice will be done." He could say no more. He knew that justice would be the hardest thing to obtain. There was no evidence, not the slightest, the police chief had informed him – of who had committed the crime, or even why. There was no sign that the body had been rifled; robbers would have taken the cloak, the few small coins, and the Scythian blade would have been a prize indeed. There were no witnesses, no one had seen any suspicious characters; the innkeeper had sworn that his wine shop had remained closed that evening and all night because he himself was ill and had only been aroused by the police.

Finally, there was the mystery of why Mansour had been in that place at that time and of why he had been armed. Only Claudia might know the reason and she could not be questioned, might never be able to be questioned. Anastasius clenched his fists till his nails bit into the palms of his hands. "But there will be justice", he repeated, and then, almost as an afterthought, "Have no fear for your sons, Mansour, I will adopt them as my own."

The funeral took place quickly, in accordance with Samaritan custom. The High Priest officiated and the body was buried in the city's necropolis. Claudia listened silently to the prayers; she was neither Christian nor Samaritan, nor scarcely Pagan in any religious sense. Silently she returned to the house which Mansour had had as freedman scribe to Anastasius. Only then did she turn to Anastasius and ask, "What is to become of me?"

Anastasius laid his hand upon hers.

"Put your mind at rest, you may remain here as long as you live. I will adopt Lucius and Cyrennius as sons. No! Don't be afraid, they will remain with you until they are old enough to choose their own ways."

Then at last Claudia began quietly to weep. At length she spoke.

"I do not understand your Christian God. He chastises the just and lets the wicked prosper; but if my sons are to be your sons, let them learn about him. Perhaps they will understand."

*   *   *

Galerius was in one of his rages. Probus had placed him in command of the garrison at Heliopolis. This had suited him well, for here, within a day's journey of Lydda, he could plan the murder of Mansour and the destruction of the Theognostas. As a bonus, Heliopolis harboured a "Temple", served exclusively by "priestesses" of exotic eastern beauty and skilled in the arts of sex. Galerius had become an enthusiastic neophyte of the cult and a regular "worshipper" at the shrine.

Now he was pacing about his cabinet in the garrison headquarters, talking to Licinius. One of his agents had procured a copy of the Lydda police report and he was reading it for the second time, searching in vain for the listing of the bag of Persian gold among the victim's possessions.

"There's no mention of the gold!" he said at last.

"Perhaps the police found it on the body and stole it", Licinius suggested.

"No!" exclaimed Galerius in exasperation, "No! They knew they'd be questioned."

"The courier might not have given it to Mansour", Licinius pointed out.

"The innkeeper observed the transfer, I made sure of that. No! Those serpents the Sicarii have stolen it. I paid them a high price to forego their booty from the murder. They've double-crossed me, taken the gold as well as the fee."

Galerius' face was purple. The gold found on Mansour would have been taken as proof of his accusation that Anastasius was spying for Persia.

"That gold would have had Anastasius' head", he barked.

Licinius shifted uncomfortably. Galerius was becoming more unpredictable and he was fearful that the rage would eventually be turned against himself: he had to choose every word with care.

"Well, at least you're rid of Mansour."

Galerius hurled the scroll across the room, "I'll not be made a fool of!" he shouted. "I'll not be laughed at in every souk across the East. What I'll do to the Sicarii will choke every tittle-tattler from Antioch to Persepolis. Where's Rufio? Send for Rufio!"

*   *   *

Rufio, grown older and ever more wicked in the service of Galerius, chose a starlit night to lead a score of the latter's Huns out of Heliopolis and along country track-ways, the horses' hoofs muffled. They came to a modest house, prosperous but not opulent in appearance. The figure of a man was silhouetted on the flat roof. Rufio made a gesture to the Hun next to him. An arrow sped silently on its flight and took the man in the throat.

He fell with barely a sound. Noiselessly the Huns surrounded the house, sliding like shadows to the windows and doors. They were as adept at this business as the Sicarii themselves. Each man drew from his cloak a jar of oil and smouldering tinder box.

At a sharp command from Rufio, blazing jars were flung through the windows. Fire leapt up, there were shouts of alarm as those within found both rear and front exits ablaze. They rushed for the windows only to be cut down by arrows. When no more scrambled out Rufio walked around the house counting the bodies: six, the full tally. The Huns hurled the dead and wounded into the inferno. The white heat shrivelled the flesh and melted it from their bones, like wax in the flame.

CHAPTER THIRTY-ONE

"Hup! hup! hup! Keep your shields up!" Marcus was shouting, as Giorgios, Lucius and Cyrennius advanced toward him in line. "I wan' to see nothin' but y'r eyes over them rims. Draw swords! Now, thrust, right side-step, one, two, thrust, left side-step, one, two. The Legions fight in line, the Legions fight by numbers." It was Marcus' endlessly repeated mantra. Dutifully, the boys thrust with their wooden swords, side-stepped to the left to ward off an imaginary spear, thrust and side-stepped to the right. "Shields hup", repeated Marcus, "keep 'em up t' y'r eyes."

Anastasius watched. It was a month since Mansour's murder and he had got no further in his search for justice. He was up against a blank wall. No one had seen anything or heard anything. He had to concur with the police chief's opinion that the deed was the work of professional assassins and he had his own opinion as to who was behind it.

He was joined by Kira. "Isn't this rather a waste of time? Giorgios is set on being a cavalryman, the same as you."

"He's learning to be a soldier from the bottom up", Anastasius replied; "there are too many cavalry commanders who don't know how infantry fight."

"Well, Claudia doesn't wish for either Lucius or Cyrennius to go into the army, she wants them to be scholars like their father."

Anastasius was taken aback, "But what way other than the army is there for them, now that they're Giorgios' foster brothers?"

"I only say what Claudia thinks."

"But she doesn't understand. For our people admission to the world's affairs is through the army; that's the only way. Once they've served a year as junior tribunes they can be scholars if they choose, but a man without military service cannot advance in public life."

"Well, there's plenty of time anyhow", Kira said rather lamely.

Anastasius frowned and fidgeted: the conversation had reminded him of a task not done and which he did not relish.

"I must find a tutor for them and for Martha", he said at length.

Kira looked at him sympathetically.

"You'll find it hard to replace Mansour won't you?"

"Yes! Very hard. Every time I think of it I put it off."

Kira laid her hand upon his arm, "Then leave it till after the Saturnalia. The boys won't mind missing lessons. Time will heal."

Anastasius looked at her gratefully. She struck while the iron was hot.

"Marcus has asked for Irene. Irene is willing and Giorgios no longer needs a Nanny, so I've said yes."

"Well, that's your province", Anastasius replied hastily. He always felt on unsure ground when it came to female politics.

"I know, but it's you who have to emancipate Irene so that Marcus may marry her, and to fix a dowry on her."

Anastasius felt a stab of grief. He had been about to say, "I'll tell Mansour to arrange it", and remembered, as he did every day, that Mansour was no longer there.

"I'll see to it, and I must also look for a new secretary."

Kira looked at him earnestly, "You'll see to it in time for the Saturnalia, won't you?"

"Yes, of course", he replied; then, "Irene is a Christian – I don't see Marcus at the Liturgy on Sundays."

"He's what Abba Theodore calls a 'three-times-a-year Christian'." Kira's expression fell between a grimace and a smile.

"There seem to be a lot of them about; I don't know how they'll stand it if there is another persecution." Anastasius was gloomy, but then he brightened, "One thing's certain, Irene's a serious girl and she'll soon put Marcus on the straight and narrow!"

"Will there be a new persecution?" Kira asked anxiously.

"Not as long as Probus is Emperor, but Galerius hates us, and if he becomes Emperor we'll be in great danger."

Kira felt fear, "Why is he such a wicked man?"

Anastasius gave a short laugh, "I suppose he doesn't think he is. In his own way he's dedicated to Rome, the Eternal City, and he doesn't want it to change, nor the old gods forgotten."

Kira leaned against him, taking his hand, "Then we're safe as long as Probus lives."

*   *   *

The new tutor, Philip, came after the Saturnalia. He was a Greek, naturally, and was astonished when he learned that part of his duties would be teaching Martha to read and write. Tutoring girls he evidently thought to be *infra dignitatem*. The Roman woman had always enjoyed more freedom than her Greek sister; an important reason for this was that both citizenship and social status passed through the mother, not the father. Whilst the Greek wife was confined to her home, the Roman matron, in control of her own income, might be at the bourse bidding for shares in the next harvest. Upon being widowed she was entitled to half of her late husband's property before any division among his heirs.

If the daughters of Patrician and Equestrian families were to manage income and estates well, it was necessary that they be literate and educated. It was also thought necessary that they speak both Latin and Greek correctly, so whilst Roman girls did not go to school as most boys did, upper-and middle-class girls were taught by tutors. Kira may have grown out of spinning and weaving with her maids as she played at being the classical Roman matron, but she still saw herself as Roman and was insistent that her daughters be educated as Romans and not as Greeks.

Philip was a tall, dark-haired young man, who took his duties seriously, but he was no Mansour. He also nursed the prejudice that an "instructor", as he referred to Marcus, was inferior to a "Tutor", as he styled himself, so Anastasius had to arbitrate between them.

"I'm a cavalryman", he protested to Kira, "I'd have to be an Egyptian juggler to keep those two both in the air at the same time!"

"Leave it to me", Kira replied in the no-nonsense voice maturity and experience had taught her. Anastasius gratefully left it to her, and the disputes mercifully ceased. The boys had their Latin and Greek, their geometry and music with Philip, and their physical and weapons training with Marcus. Martha learned to read and write, to speak well and to play the flute, whilst the infant Katherine spent the happy hours at play.

Mansour was missed and his absence was tangible. Claudia withdrew into mourning; Lucius and Cyrennius had a subdued air which Giorgios shared. Marcus, acquainted with the death of comrades, kept them busy; Anastasius fumed, frustrated in his quest for justice, but there was peace again. Probus had restored what Aurelian had achieved. He was appreciated but did not enjoy the popularity of Aurelian. With his long, mournful face and creased brow there was something sombre about him which distanced him from both army and people.

*   *   *

Easter came, followed by Giorgios' tenth birthday, and shortly afterwards a summons from Diocletian. Anastasius was not a man to shirk his duty, but he would very much have preferred to have been overlooked by Diocletian in his choice of subordinates for a new inspection of the Syrian legions. As it was, Anastasius kissed Kira and the children goodbye on a bright morning in late April and set off with his string of horses and mules to Caesarea to meet Diocletian. Kira comforted herself with the thought that he was not going to war, and that the inspection should take no more than a few weeks.

Caesarea was altogether a more imposing city than Lydda. It had been founded by Herod the Great and built on the Roman plan with forum and market in the centre. A broad highway led down to the quaysides, protected from the open sea by a great mole. On Herod's death, when his Empire had been divided between his four sons, Rome had taken over the city as headquarters of the Xth Legion and of a naval squadron. Barracks, arenas, parade grounds, stables, workshops, storehouses, granaries, baths, a hospital, and the houses of the Legate and the centurions, had doubled the size of the city. Anastasius came by way of the coast road and the quaysides. The sailors were mainly Greek or Syrian; Romans had no liking for the sea and naval service was looked upon as inferior to military service. He threaded his way through the forum and into the Legionary fortress, and made his way to the principia.

Diocletian's greeting was friendly but brief: "Dine with me tonight."

Diocletian, as usual, ate both sparingly and in silence, drinking watered wine. Only at the end of the meal did he call for undiluted wine from the slopes of Mount Lebanon. He looked at Anastasius as the wine was poured.

"You have something on your mind?"

Anastasius started, and then wondered how it was that this man could always startle him.

"Justice", he replied.

Diocletian arched an eyebrow, "Justice?"

"Yes", replied Anastasius, a little hotly, "Justice for my freed – my friend, Mansour. He was murdered in cold blood in Lydda."

Diocletian looked at him and spoke evenly, "Six men were struck down by archers and flung into a burning house, shortly after."

Anastasius caught his breath in surprise. They had heard in Lydda of this outrage in Heliopolis, but it had never occurred to him that it might be connected with Mansour's murder. As it was, he could only protest weakly, "I know nothing of that."

"Assuredly", Diocletian said with a faint smile, "for if you did you would not be alive now. The men were Sicarii, a secret society which never forgets and never forgives."

Anastasius was again taken by surprise, then he remembered what the police chief had said; that Mansour had been murdered by professional killers. Suddenly things became clearer.

"If they murdered Mansour, they were the instrument, not the author, and I know who – "

"Name no names to me!" Diocletian interrupted him sharply.

Anastasius fell silent, and Diocletian continued. "Your friend was murdered. Six men have died, some of them terribly. They were certainly the murderers. That is sufficient vengeance, let it be enough justice also."

Anastasius replied evenly, "I do not seek vengeance, least of all upon those who were merely the instrument. I seek justice, not for myself and Mansour alone, but for the Law of Rome. However high a man sits he must be subject to the Law."

"What do you know of Rome and the Empire?" Diocletian demanded. "You have buried yourself on your estates. If you had taken the advice given you in Rome and stayed there you might now be but a few steps away from the purple – there are few better suited. You will not pursue this matter further!" Anastasius was silent. "I am waiting for your reply", Diocletian said, an edge on his voice.

"As you command, Domine. I am a soldier."

Diocletian visibly relaxed. He had known that it would be useless to warn the man sitting opposite that if he pressed the matter his life would be in danger. That would not have deterred Anastasius, but he had judged rightly that a military order would be accepted and obeyed. He called for more wine.

"Now there are other matters that I must apprise you of: they concern our mission which is not simply an inspection. The Emperor takes the view that idle hands find mischief to do. It is his fixed intention to put the legions to work on civil projects, and our task is to prepare them for that."

Anastasius was too taken by surprise to reply. His only thought was that this was going to create trouble, and probably serious trouble.

The following morning, Anastasius went for a ride outside the city. He sorely missed what would have been Mansour's penetrating observations on the previous night's conversation.

The scents of spring were in the air, the orchards were in blossom, and in the distance were the brown Galilean hills. The shepherds would be taking their flocks up on to the high pastures now. Rounding a corner, Anastasius' thoughts were interrupted by the approach of a string of donkeys carrying wine amphorae. They were led by a man he instantly recognised. The man recognized him too, and a flicker of consternation crossed his face.

Anastasius reigned up, "You are the landlord of The Golden Ass!" It was a statement, not a question.

The man had recovered his composure, "I was, Domine", he replied with a sad shake of his head, "but since that wicked murder occurred, on my very doorstep as it were, trade has slumped. I've sold the place for less than it was worth and taken to trade."

Anastasius glanced at the wine amphorae, "You won't sell much wine hereabouts, they grow enough of their own."

"Not hereabouts, Domine, I'm going to Caesarea to join a caravan for Persia."

"Persia", echoed Anastasius. The man's story was plausible enough, but he did not forget that momentary consternation. "They've plenty of wine in Persia as well."

"But not like this, Domine; this is wine of Mount Lebanon: the perfume of the cedar trees enters it as it ferments. There is no wine in the world like our wine. When the Persians taste it, I'll need twenty donkey-loads for my next trip."

So, the man intended to return! Anastasius' suspicions were allayed, but remained.

"You heard absolutely nothing that night?" he asked bluntly.

"No, Domine, not a sound, I was ill. There's nothing worse than a coughing, sneezing landlord for driving away custom, so I left the place locked up and stayed in bed."

It was convincing but it was smooth. Anastasius gnawed his lip. He was handicapped by Diocletian's order, and he saw that he was unlikely to get anything out of the man. He came to a decision.

"Well I won't detain you longer. Good fortune to your venture", and he rode on.

Twenty yards up the road Anastasius turned in his saddle to check if the man had quickened his pace. He hadn't, nor had he when Anastasius turned again a few minutes later. The man himself was exerting great self-control to prevent any appearance of fear or panic. He knew that on no account must he break into a trot. The bag of Persian gold hidden under his cloak weighed heavy; the money he had got for the wine shop weighed almost as heavy. He would be glad when he was safely across the frontier, never to return to Roman jurisdiction.

That evening Diocletian held a dinner party. The guests included the Legate of the Xth (a large man who was anxious to remind Anastasius that the Xth was Julius Caesar's own legion), his Prefect, staff officers and the five junior Tribunes. Also present were the senior centurion of the legion, and the senior centurions of the other nine cohorts. Diocletian sat at the head of the table, saying little. The Legate was on his right and Anastasius was facing him across the table on Diocletian's left.

There was a general buzz of conversation to which Anastasius, turning over in his mind the bold policy Diocletian had outlined to him, was paying little attention, until suddenly the words of one of the centurions penetrated his thoughts and he became alert.

"My cousin's bought the wine shop in Lydda."

"The one where the murder took place?" another voice asked.

"Yes! The Golden Ass, and a right ass he was to pay a high price for it. The trade will decline once the novelty fizzles out."

"Is the trade good now?" the second speaker asked.

"Good? The place is packed every night – morbid curiosity; but like I said, that'll fizzle out."

Anastasius' head was in a whirl. The inn-keeper had lied!

He had lied about the state of trade and about the price he had got for the inn, but why? Because, confronted unexpectedly, he had to have an explanation for leaving Lydda. And why was he leaving Lydda? Because he was implicated in the murder!

Suddenly he became aware that the Legate, sitting opposite, was speaking to him. He made an effort to put aside his cogitations and listen.

"This latest scheme of the Emperor will cause trouble!"

Anastasius felt it prudent to say nothing. The Legate thought further explanation was necessary, "I mean this business of putting the legions to work."

Anastasius still remained silent. The Legate looked at him with an expression which clearly said, "How can you, an Imperial Count, appear so stupid?"

"You know what I'm talking about?"

"I'm afraid you'll have to explain more fully to me."

"Why! Now the frontiers are secure, and the barbarians thrashed, thanks to the legions, the Emperor intends to put us to work, repairing the roads, bridges and aqueducts, and the defences destroyed by the barbarians."

Anastasius did not want to get into an argument, but he had to say something.

"The legions have the engineers and surveyors", he pointed out, "and the skilled carpenters and stonemasons. They've always built roads and defences."

"Yes! As they advanced", snorted the Legate. "All the roads were military roads to start with, but it's a long time since the soldiers did the labouring on civil roads. That's work for slaves and prisoners. I can tell you my men won't like it. They are, after all, Caesar's legion, not mules and work-horses."

Anastasius made a non-committal murmur. He could see the soldiers' point of view, but a legion was expensive to maintain, and it wasn't any cheaper to keep it idle.

CHAPTER THIRTY-TWO

Anastasius had spent a restless night. Diocletian had ordered him not to pursue the matter of Mansour's murder any further, and he had acceded to that order. It was hardly his fault that he had run into the inn-keeper, nor that he had overheard the conversation the night before, but was he justified in going out to search for the man? Something else had suddenly occurred to him. Mansour was on foot when he was murdered; but where else would he have dismounted, save at an inn? If he had dismounted, he would have hitched his mule in the yard behind the inn. Who else would have known it was there and unhitched it and sent it on its way, except the inn-keeper? This was the weak link in the man's claim to have spent the evening in bed and heard nothing. There was an order from a superior officer but there was also the Law, the Law of Rome, without which civilized life was impossible. It was not vengeance that Anastasius sought, but the vindication of the Law. Anastasius now had no doubt that Diocletian intended to be Emperor – but what had Diocletian meant when he had said that he himself might be but a few steps from the purple? He did not want that, but it was disturbing to think that Diocletian was including him in plans of which he wanted no part. Perhaps it was his annoyance that influenced his decision.

Anastasius rode out through a city just awakening to the bustle of the day. He made for the Agora, the open space outside the city proper, where caravans were mustered. Already the air was filled with the braying of donkeys, the harsh coughing of camels and the shouts and curses of the drovers. Anastasius had no great hopes of spotting his quarry, so he was surprised when he saw the inn-keeper suddenly appear around the corner of a wagon not twenty yards ahead of him. The man saw him too, and dodged back before taking to his heels in the direction of the gates. Anastasius, handicapped by being on horse-back, struggled through the crowds, riding down the lines of camels, seeking a gap, often only to find that he had to ride back again up the other side to find a gap in the next train. By the time he got to the gates of the agora his quarry was long gone. There was only one road that he could travel, winding between vineyards and orchards and out to the desert beyond. Anastasius rode furiously. Turning a corner in the road he saw the donkeys not half a mile ahead, beyond a plantation of olive trees. He was gaining ground rapidly when three cavalrymen rode out of the olive plantation.

"Dacians!" Anastasius noted. The three were riding toward him and he moved to the left of the road. The troopers passed him without a glance and, deeply annoyed, he reined up his horse. "Halt!" he shouted, turning in the saddle. "Do troopers in your ala not salute superior officers?"

The men turned almost lazily. "Certainly", said one, and Anastasius recognized him. It was Rufio. Before he could think further, Rufio had hurled his pilum. Anastasius jerked sideways by reflex action, but the missile struck him in the shoulder and flung him to the ground.

Winded and bleeding, he struggled to rise. One of the troopers rode up and, looking down at him, sneered, "A gift from Galerius", and hurled the pilum down, piercing Anastasius' heart.

The Dacians recovered their weapons and, turning, galloped after the inn-keeper. He wondered what they could want. He had played his part, delaying his departure in the belief that Anastasius would be unable to resist searching for him. He had made sure that Anastasius had seen him leaving ahead of the caravan and had been lured into the countryside. He had been paid in advance and so the matter was finished as far as he was concerned. Nevertheless, he grew uneasy: it was now he who was alone and unprotected by the presence of witnesses. The three cavalrymen overtook him, brought his donkeys to a halt and surrounded him.

"You are in a great hurry, inn-keeper", Rufio said, a grim smile on his face.

"Take the wine, take the wine", the inn-keeper squawked, his voice high with fear, "take it all."

"It isn't the wine we've come for", Rufio replied. "You have something belonging to Count Galerius."

"I?" the man squeaked. "I? I know nothing of Count Galerius, how should an inn-keeper know anything of such as he?"

"Don't insult us with lies", Rufio barked. "Did you think the Count wouldn't hear of your selling your inn when custom was better than ever, and making for Persia? The Count has eyes and ears everywhere. He knows you stole his gold."

The man collapsed with fear, "I swear I didn't know it was his", he wailed. He put his hand into his cloak and brought out the bag. "Take it! Take it back to the Count." Rufio took it from him. "Now let me go", the wretch begged.

Rufio shook his head, "So that you can go telling lies about the Noble Count? No, it's too late for that, but, as a concession, we'll kill you mercifully."

The man shrieked in terror and fell babbling to the ground. Rufio gave him a well-aimed kick in the head which tumbled him over.

"Have some wine, coward", he said; and, going over to a donkey, wrestled a large amphora from its harness. He raised it on high and brought it crashing down on the inn-keeper's head. Rufio stooped down and drew from the man's cloak two more bags. He weighed the larger in his hand.

"The price of the inn", he said to the others. "The Count claims that as compensation for the inconvenience he has been put to."

He weighed the other, smaller, bag in his left hand.

"The fee for this business. Galerius says we can keep that; half for me and a quarter each for you."

"It's a pity to leave the donkeys and the wine", one of the troopers said.

Rufio eyed him sharply.

"Don't get greedy. Try to sell the donkeys and we'd be marked men, not the kind of people Count Galerius likes having around. Leave them here till the caravan catches up. There are plenty of rascals who'll share them out and take them over the frontier to disappear in Persia. Drag him into the trees and run your gladius through his throat, just to make sure." The two troopers hastened to obey. Claudia's cry for justice had again been heard.

*   *   *

Kira received the body in the Atrium, standing, her face carved from marble, her hands resting on the shoulders of Giorgios and Martha, who stood on either side of her. Andrew, her brother, stood behind her, and Claudia, withered, her face aged and her hair greying, stood to one side. Four centurions of the Xth escorted the bier, carried by legionaries. There was a message of regret and condolence from Diocletian. Kira stepped forward; now indeed she stood like the mother of the Gracchi, erect and calm. She laid her hand upon her husband's head, noticing how the fair hair curled around the temples, and spoke slowly and deliberately.

"This was a good man, who harmed no one. He had no ambition to stand in another's way in the glory and power of this world, nor did he ever compete for it, doing only his duty. Yet the murderers feared that he obstructed their plots and took evil steps against him and his household. I am required to forgive them, but I leave them to the judgement of God."

She stood back and Abba Theodore began the opening psalm of the liturgy:

"Judge me, O God, and distinguish my cause
From the Nation that is not holy.
Deliver me from the unjust and deceitful man.
For Thou, O God, art my strength."

The chant rose and fell, passing over Giorgios' grief without assuaging it. As the deacons fell silent Abba Theodore turned to the household congregated in the atrium and began the opening reading of the liturgy.

"The Lord became my protector and he brought me forth into a large place. The Lord is my firmament and my refuge and my deliverer."

Numbly, Giorgios stood as the prayers rolled on and was hardly aware that he had become the centre of attention when Abba Theodore commanded him to kneel. Laying hands upon the boy's head, he said, "Receive the Holy Spirit", and then, anointing his forehead with oil, "In the Name of the Father and of the Son and of the Holy Spirit." Giorgios realized that, in that moment, childhood had passed. Later in the liturgy, Abba Theodore admitted him to Communion for the first time, and then the body of his father was taken for burial in the city necropolis.

The funeral procession was met by the city magistrates and curia. They led it through streets crowded with citizens. There were some shouts of "Justice! Find the murderers!" But for the most part the mourners were silent, subdued. Where was safety for any man if a just governor could be struck down on the road in broad daylight and no enquiry made, no measures taken?

Giorgios listened silently to the orations of the magistrates as they enumerated his father's virtues and expressed the anger of the citizens; and then it was all over and they returned to a house that had suddenly become empty.

*   *   *

Kira faced the future numbly. It was agreed, almost without discussion, that she and her children should continue to live in her father's villa, now the property of Andrew. They had never lived on Anastasius' own Lyddan estate which lay near to Andrew's, and half of which was now Kira's own property; nor had they used the Governor's residence, except for state business.

Once a week Anastasius had gone there to hear the suits concerning debts, unfair trading, the moving of boundary markers, the depredations of cattle and sheep and the seemingly endless disputes of neighbours and rivals. He had always returned home with a throbbing head and ragged temper, furious at dishonest litigants and bribed witnesses. Now a new governor would be appointed. Who would he be? What manner of man? What of his family? It was a relief to her when she heard that the new governor was a Christian and that his name was Justus.

CHAPTER THIRTY-THREE

In due course Kira and her children received an invitation to visit the new Governor. She led Giorgios and Martha, followed by a maid with Katherine, along the familiar path to Mansour's cottage. They did not go all the way to the cottage, however, but turned at the little wicket gate which opened onto a gentle slope of goat-cropped pasture dotted with Rose of Sharon shrubs.

The crest of the slope was marked by a hedge of the same shrub with a gap in the centre. Oddly, Giorgios in his many explorations of the estate had never ventured up this slope. He knew that beyond lay the Governor's residence, used only by his father for official business, and, in some mysterious way, that it was forbidden territory to children. Now, with his mother and sisters, he started up the incline, heading toward the gap, his mother merely remarking, "This is a shorter way than the road."

Reaching the gap in the hedge, Giorgios gave a cry of delight. Across a stretch of level ground, dotted with olive, peach and orange trees, all in blossom, was a low, single-storeyed building, gleaming white in the sun, and covered with vines and wisteria. They walked across and came to the door of the atrium where a major-domo received them courteously and led them in. The new governor and his wife were waiting to greet them. Giorgios had expected a young man but, to his surprise, Justus appeared middle-aged. He had very little hair and what he had was greying. In spite of the heat, as a mark of esteem for his guests, he had donned the toga, the all enveloping, hot and uncomfortable garment woven from lamb's wool. His features were undoubtedly Roman, the hooked nose being prominent, but lacked Roman severity. Instead Justus was smiling and bowing to them as he presented his wife, Julia. She also had dressed in the formal attire of a Roman matron. She was small, middle-aged, a little plump, with a round, pleasant face.

"I hope, Domina", Justus said, addressing Kira, "that we have not caused you to leave your home. We would rather have lived anywhere else than that, but protocol requires us to take up residence here."

Kira looked at him and decided that he was sincere. His wife was nodding her agreement.

"Do not be troubled on that account, Domine", Kira replied. "We never lived here, preferring to live in my father's villa after the death of my mother."

"I'm so glad!" exclaimed Julia. "We simply couldn't have been happy here if we had added to your sorrows."

It was at this point that a little girl of perhaps nine or ten, with light flaxen hair unbound, peeped around from behind her mother's ample skirts. She looked shyly at Giorgios, her grey eyes turning to blue as she saw Martha and Katherine. Julia drew the child in front of her.

"This is our Justina", she said. "She did so want to meet your children, especially when she learned that there were two girls."

Justina hid her face in her mother's gown.

"What a beautiful child", Kira exclaimed involuntarily. The faces of both parents glowed.

"Let the maids take the children to play in the gardens while we talk." Julia said, stroking the girl's hair.

"Giorgios, I am sure, would rather explore by himself", Justus intervened, and turned to Giorgios. "Consider the house and gardens as your own", and he began to lead Kira toward the door of another room.

Giorgios, for his part, had the sudden and pleasant sensation of realizing that the little Justina was pretty. It had never struck him before that his sisters, or indeed any of the girls on the estate, were delightful to the eye, but this one certainly was. However, he definitely did not wish to spend the afternoon playing girls' games, and once out of the atrium, determinedly made his way in the opposite direction to the one the attendant maids took!

Justus led Kira over to a table where cakes, fruit and wine were laid. A slave offered her food and poured wine before, to Kira's surprise, being dismissed by Justus. He turned to Kira.

"I have heard much of your late husband's virtues and qualities." This was Kira's second surprise. "Oh yes, your husband's fame had gone beyond Lydda. He was known far away as a just man, all of whose ambitions were for the safety of Rome. He was known as a brave commander who did not glory in battle, who preferred peace to war. It was whispered that Diocletian intended to raise him high, whether he wished it or not, knowing that his sense of duty would make him accept."

It was difficult for Kira to suppress a sob. All this she had known, somehow, when so many years ago the young tribune had appeared in a shaft of sunlight in the atrium of her father's house.

Justus was speaking again, "As you may know, Diocletian's wife, Prisca, is sympathetic to us and is much attracted to the Faith."

"I didn't know", Kira said. Almost every sentence of this man brought a new surprise.

"Well, it is the case", said Justus, "and being a Christian would have been no deterrent to your husband's rise. Indeed, given Prisca's influence on Diocletian, it might even have been an advantage."

Kira was silent. Anastasius, she knew, would not have wanted this, but would she have wanted it? In her heart she knew that the answer was "Yes!"

"You have seen", Justus went on, "that I have no son."

Kira nodded, and Julia joined in, "We married late, you see, and consider ourselves blessed that we have Justina, but - " she moved her hands helplessly, "a man needs a son."

"I believe in first impressions", Justus went on, "and I am impressed by your son. He will be everything his father was, and more."

Kira's mind was in a whirl; she remembered the soothsayer and Anastasius' own prophecy at Giorgios' birth. Might it be that her ambitions for Anastasius, long put aside, would be fulfilled in his son?

"However", went on Justus, "if he is to progress in the army, and in the councils of the Empire, he will need a man of influence behind him. He will need education: education in all branches of knowledge, like Plato's 'philosopher king', and", he paused, his voice becoming grave, "he will need protection, protection against those who have chosen to see your house as a stumbling block to their schemes and conspiracies."

A cold hand laid itself upon Kira's heart. She could not suppress a gasp of terror, and she looked wildly about her. Julia laid her hand upon her arm.

"We have no son", she said, and Justus took up her lead:

"I will be as a father to Giorgios. I will guide and guard him in his career." Kira said nothing, and Justus went on, "Think upon this, Domina, but now let us turn to other things. Let us have the food taken outside and we will join the children in a picnic."

Everything had been astonishing, but Kira grasped at the one thing that had not been mentioned.

"Giorgios has two foster brothers!" she all but whispered.

Justus smiled a gentle smile, which showed him well pleased with what she had said.

"They will not be neglected", he assured her.

CHAPTER THIRTY-FOUR

Justus, amiable though he might be, was a determined man. He dealt with the litigious Lyddans who brought their quarrels to the weekly court by warning that anyone giving false evidence would lose ten times the amount he hoped to gain by his falsehoods and that litigants wasting his time with trivial matters would be driven from the court by the rods of the lictors. There was an immediate fall in the number of actions. It soon became apparent that Justus also loved learning. Perhaps, thought Kira, he had married late in life because he had been so busy with his studies. He had brought with him quite a remarkable library of scrolls, all classified and neatly shelved. He did not forget his promises to provide for the education of Giorgios, Lucius and Cyrennius; on the contrary, Kira began to feel that he was over-zealous in implementing them.

Part-time tutors began to appear at the villa, much to the annoyance of Philip, who felt himself slighted. Justus dealt with him by flattery and firmness. He mollified Philip by assuring him that the employment of part-time tutors added to his importance rather than diminished it, at the same time making it plain that if Philip would not co-operate the door was open for his departure. The boys' secondary education began with the history of Greece, Herodotus' account of the Persian war, and Thucydides' account of the Peloponnesian, wars.

Giorgios and his friends were still young enough to re-enact, in play, such stirring events as Leonidas holding the Pass at Thermopylae. The words of Simonides, carved on the memorial stone, particularly struck Giorgios to the heart: "Go, Stranger, tell Sparta that here we lie, obedient to her laws."

After Greek came Roman history, with tutors to guide the boys through Tacitus and Livy, and Caesar's Gallic Wars. Yet another tutor came to introduce them to Josephus' History of Israel. A young student, Eusebius, from the seminary at Lydda, was brought in to teach them the history of the Church. Kira became alarmed, "Don't you think that all this is too much for the boys?" she asked anxiously.

Justus was reassuring, "Not while they enjoy it."

"They must not be overtaxed", Kira said firmly.

After two years the peaceful life of Lydda was interrupted by the assassination of Probus. The Emperor had never been popular. There was open rejoicing in the legions at the news of his murder. The general populace was indifferent to or critical of his achievements. He had completed the walls of Rome, but in the popular mind they were "The Aurelian walls." His rural resettlement schemes had failed because those whom he tried to benefit, the urban proletariat living in wretched slums, were the most resentful. They preferred idleness and their doles of corn, oil and wine, and, in return for their votes, the begrudged bribes of wealthy Patricians. Those who were enthused by Probus' policy of "Back to the Land", were thwarted by the Roman fiscal system. No sooner had they gathered in their first harvests than the tax-farmers descended upon them. By the time of Probus' murder, disillusioned, they were returning to the cities where idle penury could be relieved by the games and the slaughter of beasts and criminals.

*   *   *

In the spring of A.D. 282, Probus, satisfied that he had won the argument with the legions, had set out on a campaign against Persia. In his absence the commander of the praetorian guard, Marcus Aurelius Carus, had rebelled. The news of this rebellion led to a mutiny in which Probus was murdered after taking refuge in a watchtower. By the September of that year, Carus, with the support of the army, was in control of the Empire. To everyone's surprise, Carus conferred upon his eldest son, Marcus Aurelius Carinus, the title of "Augustus", entrusting him with the government and defence of the Western Empire, while he himself, with his second son, Numerian, to whom he gave the title of "Caesar", established his capital at Nicomedia and took charge of affairs in the East.

"What do we know of Carus?" Andrew asked.

"A mediocre man", Justus replied unhesitatingly, "and at fifty-eight hardly likely to last long."

"What then?" asked Andrew.

"That's what I am afraid of", Justus replied. "The hand behind this usurpation is Carinus."

"And what of him?" asked Andrew.

"A man of evil life", Justus answered promptly; "he'll turn the Palatinate into a brothel. There are no excesses to which he won't go, and no perversions either. It will be the evil Caligula, Nero, Caracalla and Commodus all over again."

"Carus has another son", Andrew pointed out.

"Numerian?" Justus asked with a laugh, "You can count him out, he's a harmless fellow, a poet, and not a bad poet at that, but no soldier and no statesman."

Giorgios listened intently to the adult conversation.

"Why should a murderer become Emperor?" he asked. "Why doesn't the Senate refuse to vote him the powers which make him Emperor?"

Justus gave another short laugh, "The Senate refuse! With ten thousand Praetorian Guards in the city, all promised a generous donation by Carus? The Senate does what it's told."

"And if the new Emperor doesn't do what he promised the army?"

"The worse for him", Andrew put in, a sour note in his voice.

Andrew, feeling embittered at not having been confirmed in his father's office of Count, was becoming cynical about public affairs. He would be loyal, he declared, to whichever Emperor had troops in Lydda, and meanwhile he would mind his own business. His business at the moment was to find a wife, and he was successful in winning the heiress of an estate on the northern slopes of Mount Lebanon. His choice was approved by all his relatives, for the bride was his fourth cousin, and the marriage would keep the estate in the Gamayal clan.

"I thought your name was 'Theognosta' ", Justus had said.

"That's our family name", Andrew explained, "Our tribal name is Gamayal."

Andrew brought his new bride, Susannah, to the Villa, and Kira began to feel uncomfortable. She considered the idea of moving to Anastasius' estate, but arrived at no firm decision.

Certainly the villa was large enough for both families, but she was no longer mistress of the house.

Such tensions passed over Giorgios unnoticed. These were the last days of childhood, and of the imagination which can turn a stick into a sword, a bench into a horse, a plank into a bridge and a crowd of boys into a cohort. He, Lucius and Cyrennius, re-enacted Livy's account of the Horatii defending the Tiber bridge, the estate boys swarming up to drive them across it before the make-believe carpenters and masons could bring the make-believe bridge crashing down into the make-believe Tiber. There was rough and tumble and whacks with wooden swords, laughter and the rueful inspection of bruises and scratches, and then suddenly the days of childhood were gone.

At thirteen the old magic ceased and there was a distance between him and the estate boys. Giorgios began to notice that his companions shifted uneasily when he joined them. They were learning also, but pruning and ploughing, sowing and reaping; not Greek and Latin. The gulf was widening.

"They're letting me win", he complained to Lucius.

"You're the Dominus", Lucius said simply, and Giorgios realized that Lucius and Cyrennius thought that too. This divide he was determined to bridge, but he knew that he could not bridge the gulf between himself and the rest. So Giorgios, bereaved of his father and of Mansour, was now bereaved of comradeship, suffering the pangs of desolation, the past locked against him, the present miserable and the future unknowable.

It was at this point that Justus decided that the three boys ought to have at least an acquaintance with Hebrew. He arranged with the head of the Beth din at Lydda for one of the senior students, who would receive a generous stipend, to come twice a week to teach them. A young man by the name of Raphael ben-Ezra was appointed. He was tall and lean, with side locks on his cheeks and his head veiled. Taken to the schoolroom he stepped back from the door in consternation.

"I regret, Domine", he said to Justus, "I cannot serve you here."

He pointed, his hand taking in the walls decorated with paintings of pastoral scenes. Justus was taken by surprise.

"But they are not graven images", he said, "only paintings. Many Christians who will not tolerate graven images will accept paintings."

"And some Jews too", Raphael replied. "But it is well written, 'Do not approach too near the Law. Do not touch the Law'."

Justus looked at the young man keenly. The principal of the college had spoken highly of him, and in his book a man who stood by his convictions was a man to trust.

At length he said, "There is another room at the Residence, next to my library; there are some faded paintings on the wall which I can have white-washed over. Return here a week today and the room will be ready for you."

"What an odd fellow", Lucius said.

"He was willing to forego his stipend for his faith", Giorgios replied, "and he probably needs the money; he is a poor man."

"How do you know that?" demanded Cyrennius.

"His sandals were tied with string, and his tunic was frayed at the hem and the cuffs", Giorgios answered.

The room Justus referred to had been built onto the residence at some time in the past. It was lime-washed and had a low pitched roof of yellow and orange tiles. Inside it was admirably suited as a school room. The height of the walls from floor to roof beams was equal to the width, and the width was one third of the length. Three round arched windows admitted clear northern light, so perhaps it had been a painter's studio. Now, pristine white, the room was quiet, still and timeless. Raphael clapped his hands in rapture when he saw it.

"A place for Solomon to consider his judgments", he exclaimed. "Here I can teach."

The opening of this new schoolroom was to have important consequences for Giorgios. He had seldom been to the Residence after his first visit, and although his sisters frequently went there to play with Justina, he had caught no more than a rare glimpse of her. Now, taking the shortcut up the grassy slope beside Claudia's cottage, he would sometimes see her at a window, passing silently down a passage or tripping through the orchard with a nanny in tow. He did not take a great deal of notice for he was absorbed in the difficulties of mastering the Hebrew syllabary. Lucius and Cyrennius found it even more difficult and he could sense the growing distance between them and himself. He began to feel more and more desolate, and took to coming up to the residence at other times, simply to sit in the room which, peaceful and silent, seemed to enshrine a moment of eternity. Here he found solace in prayer, formal prayer at first, but slowly developing into meditation. Afterwards he would collect scrolls from Justus' library to read, while Lucius and Cyrennius went about their own affairs.

CHAPTER THIRTY-FIVE

The death of Carus, barely a year after his seizure of power, came literally as a thunderclap. He was on the Tigris frontier, having defeated the Persians and taken Ctesiphon, when his tent was struck by a bolt of lightning; but it was whispered that he was not in it at the time.

"The hand of God", Andrew remarked sourly.

"You think so?" asked Justus. "More likely the hand of our friend Diocletian, Commander of the Imperial Bodyguard."

"In that case, why not the hand of Aper, commander of the Praetorians?" Andrew countered.

"Perhaps so, time will tell."

"Aper's daughter is married to Numerian", Andrew pointed out. "If Numerian succeeds as Emperor, which Carus clearly intended when he gave him the rank of Caesar, his wife will easily persuade him to name her father as Praetorian Prefect. Aper will have the real power and leave Numerian to write his poetry."

"Which would not suit Diocletian", Justus pointed out. "He hasn't waited so long and worked so patiently to be thwarted by the succession of a son. But as I said, time will tell."

There now unfolded one of the most bizarre episodes in the history of the Empire. Numerian contracted an eye infection which left him partially blind. Having concluded peace with Persia, he ordered a withdrawal, spending the winter of 283 in Syria. In the spring he recommenced the journey to Nicomedia.

Incapacitated and travelling in a closed wagon, he was murdered at some place on the journey. The crime was kept secret, Aper appearing each morning at the entrance of the Imperial tent to reassure the army that the Emperor was "improving". Diocletian said nothing until they reached Nicomedia. Then he struck, swiftly and effectively. Aper was seized and hauled before a full military assembly. Indignantly, Diocletian revealed the truth and accused Aper of the murder of Numerian, together with a long list of other crimes. Outmanoeuvred, Aper's defence was drowned by the shouting of well-placed cohorts acclaiming Diocletian as Emperor and saviour of the honour of the army.

Diocletian humbly accepted the ovation and then, in a second rage of indignation against Aper, drew his sword and cut him down. A roar of approval came from the well-placed cohorts, which spread through the entire assembly. The Empire had a new master.

In Lydda, Justus read aloud an account of these events.

"Well, I doubt if we'll ever know the truth", he concluded, "Diocletian's rage may have been genuine. If it was, he didn't murder Carus and Numerian. If it was play-acting, then he did, and Aper too."

"What of Carinus?" Andrew asked. "Will he march east to avenge his brother and father? Will there be another civil war?"

Justus remained calm.

"Emperors come and emperors go", he declared, "but the power and beauty of good literature remains forever. It is now time that Giorgios and his foster brothers were introduced to it."

* * *

Carinus did indeed turn the Palatine into a brothel, filling it with harlots and pimps. His pleasures were not so much indulgence in sex as the exercise of power. He took a perverted delight in humiliating Senators and Patricians by seducing their wives. If seduction failed he took even greater delight in forcing the woman's submission with threats against her husband's life and property, threats he was known to have carried out. He took the opportunity of power to avenge slights, real or imagined, murdering old school fellows against whom he had harboured a grudge. Growing reckless he began to test just how much humiliation the Romans would endure, appointing a brothel-keeper as city prefect, and replacing the prefect of the city guard with a notorious procurer named Matronianus. He contemptuously dismissed the lack of opposition to these outrages as cowardice and turned his attention to the wives of his army commanders. In the spring of 285, he marched east to meet Diocletian near the modern Belgrade. Carinus had the larger army, and the battle was going in his favour when one of the wronged officers took the opportunity to stab him in the back. Diocletian's long wait for power was over.

* * *

It was summer and Giorgios, now fourteen, was making his way up the grassy slope to the Residence when a girl appeared in the gap in the hedge. It was Justina; he recognized her immediately.

She was tall and lithe and her flaxen hair was lifting in the breeze. She was about thirteen, an age at which Roman girls might marry. She saw him coming up the hill and waved and smiled; a tinkling silver laughter floated down to him. A nanny came hastening up, clucking disapproval and shooing Justina away.

There were a hundred myths and folktales in Giorgios' reading to tell him why his feet seemed to have wings as they sped across the grass, why his heart sang, why happiness thrilled through him, why he repeated her name, "Justina", for the joy of hearing it. He had fallen in love as Perseus had after rescuing Andromeda, and what dragons would he, Giorgios, not slay for Justina! But this was more than a story, it was a reward. All the sorrows which had fallen on him were wiped away. Justina was his promised one: this was what God had prepared for him, to love Justina always and forever; and loving her would be his supreme happiness. Of course, Justina would fall in love with him once he had had the chance to prove his worth to her. When and how was scarcely important, for it would happen, and meanwhile it did not matter because even the thought of her was sufficient happiness. He scarcely needed to see Justina; the love he kept secret in his heart made her always present. But actually seeing her, at the end of a passage, running across a lawn, that was happiness indeed. His visits to the library increased in frequency. There was pain in loving, but it was a sweet pain.

*   *   *

"This Diocletian seems to be a man in a hurry", Justus said to Andrew as they sat in the sun drinking wine. Justus had become a frequent visitor at the villa, and Andrew, feeling more and more that official life had passed him by, was glad to welcome him. The household slaves whispered among themselves that Justus came to escape a garrulous wife as much as for Andrew's company, but in fact both enjoyed a conversation between equals.

"You have news?" Andrew asked eagerly. Public life still had a fascination for him.

"An edict! arrived by Imperial courier today." He produced the scroll. "The Senate have voted Diocletian the pro-Consular and Tribunic powers, appointed him Pontifex Maximus, and elected him Consul."

"To be expected", Andrew remarked, disappointed that there was nothing more exciting.

"But wait", said Justus, enjoying the moment, "Diocletian has granted his old companion-in-arms, Maximian, the title of Caesar, with full authority in the West."

"Obviously taking a leaf out of Carus' book", Andrew mused.

"And equally", said Justus, "it is the shape of things to come."

The year turned, Giorgios' sixteenth birthday came and went. His opportunities of seeing Justina increased, for his sisters often came to the residence to visit her, and Giorgios would join them as they walked through the orchard or sat in the peristyle chattering together, a nanny hovering in the background. These meetings were to a certain extent disconcerting for Giorgios.

Justina had been an object of admiration, adoration even, but an object nevertheless, all her perfections existing in Giorgios' mind. He had not expected her to have opinions, and certainly not opinions which differed from his own. Now he found a girl who, while always cheerful, was not giddy, and who required that he should justify his opinions and tastes to her.

"Why do you read so many books?" she demanded.

Giorgios was taken aback; he could give no reason except, "I like learning things", which seemed a weak and obvious reply.

"So do I", said Justina, "but I like learning things from *people*, about plants and trees and birds, or music."

The realization grew that she was a person, not just a dream.

"Why do you want to be a soldier? My father wasn't and he's still a governor."

"He must have had a year as a Tribune with a legion", Giorgios countered.

"Well perhaps he did", Justina retorted, with a toss of her flaxen hair, "but that was years ago, and he never talks about it."

"My father was a soldier", Giorgios countered, "so I want to be one too."

"But soldiers kill people", Justina exclaimed. "Why do you want to kill people?"

Giorgios was completely nonplussed, "I don't", he said, "I don't want to kill anyone."

"Well you'll *have* to if you're a soldier. Anyhow, we're going for our music lesson."

She skipped away, followed by Martha and Katherine. She always seemed to skip or dance when she walked, her adorable feet as light as thistledown. Giorgios watched her out of sight, devastated. He had no one to tell him that maidenly pride required a girl to put on a show before others, of being at least a little scornful of the one she secretly admired.

To win her, it seemed, he must abandon his ambition to be a soldier of Rome; but Justina had struck far deeper than day dreams, far deeper than ambition. A soldier must kill people. Could that be right? Would God forgive?

Giorgios' doubts troubled him for several weeks. He went to the library and took out the scripture scrolls, searching through them thoroughly without finding a solution. His father had been a soldier and there had been no better person, no juster man. If, like Lucius and Cyrennius, he turned his back on military service, would that win him Justina? Cogitating in this manner he went one morning to Raphael's lecture room, there it would be silent, and there, if one were quiet and calm, a voice would speak to one.

To Giorgios' surprise there was a noise of hammering in the room, and entering it he saw Raphael busy with hammer and other tools, mending a stool. Giorgios remembered that at the last lesson Lucius had been tilting the stool onto its back legs, and the pegs holding the legs had splintered. Apparently Raphael had come early to mend it.

"You should have told the carpenter to do that", Giorgios said.

Raphael looked up with a smile, "I am a carpenter", he said, and returned to his task.

"But you're a student", exclaimed Giorgios, "How can you be a carpenter?"

Raphael paused in his work, "Because my father was a carpenter, and taught me. As the Rabbi Gamaliel has written, 'What are we to think of the man who does not teach his son a trade? He might just as well teach him to be a thief and a robber'."

Giorgios thought that over. "My father was a soldier, and I've been taught that trade, and always wanted to be one."

"And a scholar?" Raphael queried with a laugh.

"Yes, that too."

Raphael finished re-pegging the stool and looked long at Giorgios.

"But antiquities and speculations are not what have troubled you these past weeks?"

Giorgios shifted on his feet uncomfortably.

"Sit down", Raphael said, "and let us talk."

Giorgios sat down and hesitantly began to speak.

"The Scriptures – your Scriptures – our Scriptures say, 'Thou shalt not kill'. Cain had a mark placed upon him, David was punished for plotting the death of Uriah, but then we are told that Saul slew his thousands and David his tens of thousands, and that the angels came down to blast the Assyrians when they attacked Israel."

Raphael remained silent for a few moments.

"Men of all nations honour the soldier, do you agree?" Giorgios nodded. "But no one honours the brigand. Why do you think that is?"

Giorgios thought for a while.

"I suppose because brigands kill to steal."

"That is partly right, but the chief reason we do not honour the brigand is this: he is prepared to kill. He is willing to murder. He is ready at all times to slay other men. What is the difference between that and the soldier?"

Giorgios frowned, "I'm not sure", he said at length.

"Ah! But there is a great difference. We honour the soldier, *not* because he is prepared to slay, but because he is prepared to *be* slain. That is the pledge which the soldier makes to his people. He pledges that when the moment of peril comes he will stand in the gates and hold them or die. In return his people give him honour and privileges."

Giorgios let out a long sigh.

"I see", he said, "so I *can* be a soldier?"

"That's not for me to say", Raphael replied, "Only you can answer that before the Lord; but you should speak to your Abba Theodore. He is a wise man. He and I have many disputations together."

Giorgios took Raphael's advice, and after the morning lesson he sought out Abba Theodore. Satisfied with Raphael's explanation though he was, he had a further problem which he related to the priest.

"Our Saviour's words in the Gospel are 'Love your enemies, do good to those who hate you, pray for those who ill use and persecute you.' How can a Christian be a soldier?"

"A very difficult question", Abba Theodore replied. "Have you read these words in the Latin as well as in the Greek text?"

"No", Giorgios admitted, "but I can't see that that would make any difference; and besides, Our Saviour did not speak Latin."

"Indeed not, the words were spoken in Aramaic and were translated into Greek, and later, Latin. You know that Latin has two different words for 'enemy'."

" 'Inimicus' and 'hostis'! " Giorgios exclaimed, a door beginning to open in his mind.

Abba Theodore went on, "'Inimicus', someone who dislikes you, perhaps for no reason, or whom you dislike. 'Hostis', the public enemy, the criminal or one who plots to overthrow the state or an invader. We are commanded to put aside, to drive out from our hearts, hatred, personal spite, revenge, animosity, anger, malice: we must neither do ill nor wish ill to those inimical to us, indeed we must try to do and wish them good and we must forgive them: that is what loving means." Abba Theodore paused and smiled, "We are not commanded to like the 'inimicus'. Liking and loving are quite different things."

"But what of the 'hostis'? What of the public enemy?" Giorgios asked.

"This is a different matter. The question of hatred does not come into it. We do not hate the 'hostis', we oppose him, we prevent his aims, and if he is punished it is by the state, impersonally."

"And what of the soldier?" asked Giorgios, eager now to have his last doubts settled.

"The soldier does not hate those opposite him in battle. He may often respect them as good soldiers. They are the enemies of his nation and must be defeated, but they are public enemies, not his personal enemies."

"I see! I see!" Giorgios cried. "Excuse me, I have someone to tell!" and he rushed off.

He arrived at the Residence breathless. Justina and his sisters were playing a rather leisurely game of "catch" with a ball.

"Justina!" Giorgios cried, "I want to speak to you!"

Justina tossed her hair, "Well, speak", she said.

"No, over here", Giorgios said determinedly. "Come and sit down beside me."

Rather surprised at herself, Justina did as he said.

"I can be a soldier", Giorgios babbled, "and a Christian, and soldiers don't hate the enemy, and they are prepared to die to save others, and that's the greatest love, and I am going to be a soldier, and, and, and, I'm going to marry you and no one else ever, but just for now it must be a secret."

CHAPTER THIRTY-SIX

Katherine, being the youngest of the family, enjoyed the role of "tell-tale".

"Mamma", she said, interrupting Kira's perusal of the family accounts, "Giorgios is in love with Justina."

"Is he?" Kira replied absently. "How d'you know?"

Katherine screwed her face up and prepared to dispense some cruel mimicry.

"Because whenever he's with us, it's 'Justina, yes', and 'You are right, Justina', and 'Let me reach that fig for you, Justina' and he said he's going to marry her, and I know 'cos I was there."

At this Kira became alert.

"When was this?"

"Yesterday. Giorgios said he was going to be a soldier and that he would marry no one else but Justina, ever."

"Where was her Nanny when all this was going on?"

"Domina Julia had called her away. She often calls her away when Giorgios comes out of lessons. Martha noticed it and says that it's very odd."

"Yes it is, but – perhaps not so odd. You mustn't go about saying anything about this, Katherine. Justina's father will decide whom she marries."

"Won't Domina Julia decide as well?" Katherine asked.

A stab of memory sent a flicker of sadness across Kira's face, but then she smiled, wanly.

"I suppose Domina Julia will tell him what to decide, and then he'll decide it."

"I like Justina", Katherine volunteered. "She has grey eyes, but when she's glad they turn blue, and when she's mad at anybody they turn green. They always turn blue when Giorgios comes."

Kira considered what Katherine had said. This might develop into an awkward situation. Justus had been more than generous in his patronage of Giorgios and, for Giorgios' sake, of Lucius and Cyrennius, but that might not include marriage to his only daughter. Katherine was now pursuing another train of thought.

"If Giorgios marries Justina, she'll really be our sister, won't she? Martha and I would like that."

"Katherine", Kira said sharply, "I've told you, you must not go about saying things like that."

At the first opportunity, Kira sought out her brother and related what Katherine had said. To her surprise Andrew was not disturbed in the least by this development.

"Good for Giorgios!" was his response.

"But it's improper", Kira's voice rose slightly, "it's improper for him to speak to Justina before speaking to her father. Justus might not wish it. We might not wish it."

"I don't see what objection Justus can have." Andrew said with a shrug. "Our family are Patricians, the same as his. We're better in fact, when you consider our pedigree. And why we should object is beyond me. Justus has plenty of influence in the right quarters, villas in Sicily and Gaul, hoards of gold, and the lot will come to Justina. Giorgios couldn't do better."

Kira had listened to this with growing agitation, "What's happened to you, Andrew? You talk and think of nothing but money and how to grasp more and more of it. How about Giorgios' happiness, and Justina's? He's a scholar and will soon be a soldier with prospects of high command. Justina's a beautiful child, I know, but that's all, a child, light-hearted and light-headed and no wife for a man of affairs."

Andrew tilted his head indignantly.

"I remember well a child, and a pampered child at that, who grew up after she was married and now runs her own affairs, and seemingly everybody else's."

Kira regretted her outburst; Andrew had hit back shrewdly; she was, after all, a guest in his house.

"I know, Andrew, you may be right, and perhaps a girl like Justina would make Giorgios a little less serious about everything, but why are you so engrossed with money?" Andrew looked away.

"I played my part during Zenobia's revolt. I fought well against the desert raiders when our father was killed. I served my year with the legions with credit, but time and again I'm passed over, ignored, just because I'm a Christian."

"Other Christians aren't discriminated against, Andrew", Kira said gently. "The Imperial officials look for men who are generous, who make donations or endow public parks and gardens or baths – " her voice trailed off, and she was afraid that she had said too much.

Andrew flared again, "Well, if Rome doesn't want my services, I'll keep my gold. When you've got gold you're safe."

He strode from the room, leaving Kira's problem unresolved.

*   *   *

Unknown to Kira, a similar conference was being held in the Residency. Julia dismissed the slaves and poured Justus some wine. He continued to peruse the scroll he was holding, the book of the Psalms.

"Do you still think highly of young Giorgios?" his wife asked.

Justus sighed and put aside the scroll.

"Yes! He confirms my first opinion."

"I thought so too. He's a splendid young man."

"His father might have had the purple, Diocletian told me."

"So might Giorgios", Julia replied. "Of course, if he were married to Justina he really would be our son and you would be Caesar's father."

Justus sat bolt upright, "Married to my Justina! Why she's only a child!"

"She's nearly fourteen", Julia replied. "I don't mean married now; when Giorgios has served as Tribune there will be time enough."

"Why!" said Justus, "I wouldn't even think of her marrying till she's eighteen at least."

"You have to let her fly the nest, you know", Julia said, "and Giorgios is such a splendid young man, and of our class."

"Well, perhaps so", Justus ruminated, "but I'm not greatly taken with military marriages: there are long separations, and always the danger of being a young widow. No, I wouldn't want that for little Justina."

"Well, whoever she marries he must be a Patrician, and if he's a Patrician he must have been a soldier at some time, and Giorgios is likely to rise high enough after a few year's service to live on his estates between commissions."

Justus was not convinced.

"You overlook one thing; his people might not agree."

"I don't see why not", exclaimed Julia, bridling. "I'm sure our Justina's good enough for anyone, and whoever she marries will be a very lucky man."

Justus sighed again. His wife could worry a subject better than most dogs could worry a bone. He began patiently to explain.

"It's not just a question of Roman status and class: both our families are Patrician, agreed; but they are Syrian nobility, they are Shaikhs. They don't say it openly, but they consider themselves superior."

Julia let out a squawk of indignation.

"We are Romans!"

"And, as they see it, they were living in cities and writing books like this", he gestured to the Psalms, "when Rome was a collection of wooden huts on a muddy hilltop."

"But we're all Christians! Surely that's the important thing?"

"Maybe so, but so are all the cousins Giorgios might marry. The fact is that they regard themselves as the first Christians and they marry among their own Gamayal kindred to keep the land in the tribe. Andrew has recently married his fourth cousin for that very reason."

He picked up his scroll and began searching for his place, but Julia had not finished.

"Justina is in love with Giorgios!"

Justus dropped the scroll, "How do you know that? Has she told you?"

"She doesn't need to tell me. I'm her mother."

"A childish fancy; it will pass."

Justus sat frowning. Justina was the child of his heart. He was well aware that as an heiress there would be many suitors; but generally he refused to think about it, and each time he did he pushed back the age at which she might marry. He thought of balding senators in Rome, rich provincials with pot bellies and heavy jowls, hard-bitten, battle-scarred legates, and then of Giorgios, young, upright, serious, gentle, with the looks and stature of a Greek hero – to which of these would he willingly give his darling? There was no contest.

"Very well", he said, "We'll say nothing more of this till she's fifteen, and then we'll see how matters stand with his family. She need only be betrothed; it might be a year before she marries."

CHAPTER THIRTY-SEVEN

Giorgios paid a visit to Claudia; though he was sixteen he still addressed her as "Aunt" as a matter of courtesy. After his talks with Raphael and Abba Theodore he was full of high resolve to rise above vengeance and to put away hatred. Claudia was sitting, as she so often sat, in the garden, staring vacantly.

As Giorgios crossed the orchard a shaft of sunlight fell upon him, and Claudia, looking up, gave a start and a sharp cry of "Oh!"

"What's the matter, Aunt?" He hurried over. She stared at him intensely.

"I thought it was your father."

"My father's dead, Aunt Claudia, you remember?"

"Yes, murdered; and Mansour my husband, murdered. All murdered. But why was he there outside that tavern? Why?" She twisted her hands together and then suddenly stopped, and a light dawned in her eyes. "I remember now – seeing you appear like that – there was a letter."

"A letter?"

"Yes! Mansour had a letter. He said that it was important, nothing to do with the estate, and that he would soon be back."

Giorgios' curiosity was aroused, "What happened to the letter?"

"I suppose he put it in his private chest; I've never looked. It's all come back to me now."

"Let's see if it's still there!"

Giorgios felt excited – a mystery might be solved. They went into the cottage and into Mansour's cabinet. It was as he had left it: an iron-bound chest stood on the desk, locked.

"I'll have to break the lock, Aunt Claudia, is that alright?"

"Let us find the truth", she answered.

Breaking the lock took some effort, but at last the lid was thrown back. Resting on top of a pile of papers was a scroll, the last thing Mansour had put there. Giorgios opened it and began to read.

"It's in code, there must be a cipher." He looked helplessly around the room.

"In here!" Claudia said, "I remember now."

She placed her hand under the desk; there was a click, and she drew out a sheet of papyrus. Giorgios sat down and began to decipher. Eventually he looked up.

"The letter is from the Samaritan merchants of Egypt, or so it pretends. It asks Uncle Mansour to meet a man at The Golden Ass who will give him a purse of gold to repay the expenses of the Samaritans here in assisting Samaritans from Egypt to pass into Persia. It promises more to follow. It was a trap, it's easy to see that now."

Tears had begun to well up in Claudia's eyes.

Giorgios hastened on. "When my father was murdered, the innkeeper of The Golden Ass was found murdered too. We didn't think there was any connection, but now it's obvious that he was murdered to silence him."

Claudia was only half listening; she had heard all that she needed to know and her tears were flowing unchecked.

"All this time", she sobbed, choking on the words, "All these years of doubt, of not knowing why he was there, not remembering what he had said – all the torment."

Giorgios stood awkwardly: he did not know what to do; it was unthinkable that he should put a comforting arm around Aunt Claudia. He could only listen helplessly. Besides, his own mind was now in turmoil. Were those who had murdered Mansour and his father 'inimici' or 'hostes'? How soon his high resolutions were being put to the test, and how hard the test! If inimicus, could he forgive? If hostis, need he forgive? Yet he must forgive. He made a supreme effort of will and thrust the turmoil aside: if inimicus, God would judge, if hostis, the state would one day judge them. He turned to Claudia. Her sobs had ceased, but her tears still flowed.

"Uncle Mansour died nobly", he said to her, "he died for his brethren. He laid down his life for his friends."

She looked at him, her eyes no longer vacant.

"Yes!" she said, "I had lost everything, every memory, but now I have everything back, now I have Mansour back."

Giorgios did not understand, but he knew that her thoughts were too intimate to be shared with him.

"Come and see mother soon, and talk to her", he said, and made to leave the cottage.

"No wait!" There was a new note in Claudia's voice. "I told your father I did not understand your Christ. Now I do. Take me to Abba Theodore so that I may become a Christian."

Giorgios, who, like any adolescent, might have been thrown into confusion by this request from an older woman, found a new assurance, and confidently bowed his acquiescence; hearing plainly the words he had so often read, "Blessed are the peacemakers".

*   *   *

Imperceptibly, lectures and lessons had moved from the Villa to the "New Room" in the Residency. Eusebius introduced the Christian Theologians, Origen and Tertullian. Philip intended that Philosophy would follow: Plato and Aristotle, Plotinus and the neo-Platonists. The culmination would be training in Rhetoric, the absolute essential in the Roman world for any man hoping for a career in law or politics. Raphael was delighted that he was entrusted with the study of Philo Judaeus, for he was being "raised", as Philip put it, from being a language instructor, to the dignity of pedagogue. Philip made a point of referring to the part-time tutors as his "assistants", and was becoming an irritation. Justus, though often tempted, did not dismiss him, for Justus was well named. Not only did he recognize that Philip's organizing and curriculum qualities outweighed his vanities, but, expecting loyalty from subordinates, he too was loyal to them.

"The good governor and the good general", Justus would tell Giorgios, "do not blame subordinates when things go wrong."

The move to the Residency gave Giorgios more opportunities to be with Justina. His sisters were always there, and Lucius and Cyrennius too, and the Nanny hovered anxiously at a distance, missing nothing, but he could walk and talk with Justina.

Bereaved and lonely, cut off from old friends as he had been, his heart found a lovelier home than it had ever known. To Justina he confided his most secret thoughts and hopes. She shared them, became part of them, and by a subtle reciprocation they were reshaped to fit hers. When their eyes met and held, her gaze would be one of admiration, and his of adoration. She was the image by which he lived. When indeed Giorgios' conversation became too serious, too heavy, she would skip away through the orchard, laughing as he chased her; until he, laughing with her, caught her adorable hand. Between them, after the first infatuation, there had grown that special pure but passionate friendship of boy and girl which concentrates all its beams into a single shaft of fire, and lights in the heart another sun.

Kira called Giorgios aside.

"Another year and you will be joining the army", she said.

Giorgios nodded, wondering what might be coming next.

"It would be best if you were betrothed to a serious girl before you go. I have been talking to Andrew about it, and he thinks a betrothal with one of your cousins should be arranged."

Giorgios replied promptly.

"I will marry no one but Justina. If I cannot marry her, I will never marry."

"You can't say that; no one knows the future, and her father might object."

Giorgios' reply was simple but forceful.

"Then I will not marry."

His mother made up her mind.

"I will go tomorrow, with Claudia to support me, and speak to Domina Julia. We will see what can be arranged."

Julia, who was a little plumper and as cheerful as ever, received her guests. She took Kira by surprise by coming straight to the point.

"How fortunate, Domina, you are to have a son as fine as Giorgios, of such good character, and clever and handsome too. If we had been blessed with a son he is just the one we would have wished."

"And how fortunate you are, Domina", Kira replied, choosing her words carefully, "in such a daughter as Justina, so beautiful and yet a serious girl. My own daughters love her as a sister."

Julia beamed, she was not one to cast around for subtleties.

"I have often thought, indeed I have often said it to Justus, that if Giorgios and Justina were to marry, we should have the son we have wished for, and your daughters the new sister they desire." Kira was surprised at this directness and decided to be equally direct.

"That is the very matter I have come to see you about. Giorgios says he will marry

156

only Justina, and if he cannot marry her he will never marry. Perhaps Justina only sees him as the brother she does not have, and he will be disappointed. Has she spoken to you?"

"She does not need to speak to me of her feelings; I am her mother and a mother knows these things. She wishes to marry Giorgios."

Kira felt a wave of relief.

"Then we can arrange matters?"

Julia nodded. "You and your brother must see Justus to settle the matter of the dowry, of what will be settled on Justina should she become a widow, and all the rest of that business. Can you come tomorrow?"

"Yes!" Kira said eagerly. "Do you think the Dominus will agree?"

"Of course! And now let us have some refreshments."

Giorgios was on tenterhooks. A betrothal was neither a simple nor an easy matter. It seemed to him that those negotiating the settlement regarded financial and property questions as more important than the affections of the two most concerned. He heartily wished that Uncle Andrew was not his legal guardian and had no part in the business. He imagined him driving so hard a bargain, demanding more and more, that eventually Justus would reject the suit in disgust.

There were several meetings over a period of weeks, with notaries and scribes arriving and departing, their pens ever busy, and during all this time Giorgios scarcely saw Justina, who seemed to be kept indoors. At length, early one morning, a slave arrived with a peremptory message that the Governor wished to see him at the Residency, right away. Giorgios' heart sank; such a message, and such a manner of delivering it, could only mean that Justus had refused to allow the betrothal, and would probably order him never to speak to Justina again. He set off in trepidation, walking along the path to Claudia's cottage until he came to the wicket gate and the short cut to the Residency. He hesitated; but then, with a silent prayer, opened the gate.

Before him was the gentle slope of goat-cropped pasture, dotted with Rose of Sharon shrubs in bloom and wet with the morning dew. Several nanny goats and their kids were grazing the new grass. He looked up the slope to the hedge which marked its crest. A girl was standing there among the golden blooms. She waved and laughed and began to run down the hill, her flaxen hair lifting in the breeze, her feet scattering the dew drops. The hem of her silken frock, damp and clinging with the dew, rode up above her ankles. As she drew near she reached out her hands and began to speak. He read as much as heard her words, "Giorgios! Giorgios! Father agrees!"

He caught her hands in his as she reached him. She looked up at him; her eyes were blue and shining; and, bending, for the first time he kissed her lips.

CHAPTER THIRTY-EIGHT

The formal betrothal of Giorgios and Justina took place before the magistrates in the basilica at Lydda. She was gowned in white silk, the skirt pleated, Roman fashion, the result of several hours of skilled ironing. Her hair was gathered up to cascade from the crown in ringlets; her toes peeped through gilded sandals, though perhaps in deference to the memory of Old Nanna her toenails were not painted scarlet. Giorgios wore the toga, Roman symbol of manhood, with a gilded capulet.

A second ceremony took place in the atrium of the Residence. Abba Theodore blessed the couple, sprinkling them with water, reminding them of their duties to one another, and, impromptu, chanted from the Song of Solomon,

> "Arise my beloved, my fair one,
> Come, thou whom my soul desireth,
> for lo! the winter is past,
> the rains are over and gone
> and it is spring in our land.
> It is the time of singing,
> and of the cry of the turtle dove;
> the fig tree and the vine are in blossom,
> their fragrance fills the air.
> Arise my beloved and come,
> for the spring has returned to our land."

This was the happy year. For these two, it seemed that never had two others known such happiness, and never had two others loved so much; and mirroring their happiness the little world of the Vale of Sharon blossomed for a bountiful harvest.

In April, Diocletian further surprised the Empire by raising Maximian from Caesar to Augustus. They would rule jointly, Maximian in Rome and the West, Diocletian in Nicomedia and the East. More astonishing was the declaration that he and Maximian would abdicate in the year 306, exactly twenty years from the day. It was taken for granted that the Senate would take back all its lost powers and elect new Emperors for a fixed term, restoring the Republic in fact as well as in name.

The hope that Diocletian's constitution would put an end to assassinations and civil wars was short-lived. In November of the same year, Carausius, Count of the Saxon Shore and Admiral of the Northern Fleet, proclaimed himself Emperor of Britannia.

Further, he claimed that the province of Belgica was, geographically, ethnically and linguistically, part of his new Empire, and seized control of the great port of Gesoriacum and with it the entire Northern Fleet. Without a fleet Maximian could do nothing; He and Diocletian duly recognized Carausius' fait accompli. The latter celebrated by minting a new silver coin depicting the three Emperors, and inscribed "Carausius and his brothers".

"What do you know of this Carausius?" Giorgios asked Justus. They were, as usual, sitting in the peristyle.

"He's no barrack-room Emperor. He's a good general and commands great loyalty, especially from his sailors. Most of them are Saxons, recruited from beyond the Rhine and from the Frisian Islands. As Count of the Saxon Shore he followed a policy of settling the veterans on farms among the Burgundians and other Germans whom Probus planted in Britannia. That way he has a reserve of experienced sailors to call on."

"Is that why that coast of Britannia is called 'The Saxon Shore'?", Andrew asked, suddenly curious.

"Yes, you'll hear more Frisian or, as they call it, Englesc, spoken there than Latin, or even British Latin."

"Is Carausius a Roman?" Giorgios asked.

"Yes and no. He's a Roman in his own eyes, more Roman than the Romans in fact. He calls himself 'Marcus Aurelius Mausaeus Carausius', but his father was a Saxon pirate and his mother Irish, taken in a slave raid. It's said she was a princess, but I know nothing more. He is in many ways an elusive person, but not one to be underestimated, especially as he holds the mastery of the seas."

"He chose his time well", Giorgios remarked, frowning with thought. "Even if Maximian does gather a fleet together, he'll have to wait for the winter storms to pass before he tries crossing the Channel."

"What of the legions in Britain", Andrew asked, "will they accept Carausius?"

Justus frowned, "The XX Valeria Victrix and the II Augusta have been there for two hundred and fifty years, even the VI Victrix has been there for nearly two hundred; the troopers are almost entirely British-born, and Carausius is clever enough to present himself as both British and Roman at the same time. I think the legions will trim with the wind, but if Maximian does succeed in landing a Roman army, they'll trim back again. The man I really fear is the one Carausius has appointed as his Praetorian Prefect, Allectus."

"What of him?" asked Giorgios.

"A nasty, treacherous, crop-headed German. It's suspected that he allowed Saxon pirates to raid the coastal towns and then intercepted them as they made for home."

"What good would that do him?" Giorgios asked.

"Why, that's obvious. He claimed everything on the ships he took as prize of war, and that included everything the pirates had robbed."

Giorgios found it difficult to express his disgust, "Can anyone be so vile?"

"Well Allectus can. There was a commission of enquiry on its way from Rome, when Carausius rebelled. My opinion is that he was prodded into it by Allectus. I also think that Carausius would be wise to watch his back."

*   *   *

At Trier, in faraway Gaul, the newly-created Emperor, Marcus Aurelius Valerius Maximianus, pored over the maps of the coasts of Gaul and Britannia. He turned to his chief-of-staff, Flavius Valerius Constantius Chlorus, stabbing the mouth of the Seine with his forefinger.

"We will muster a fleet here, embark a legion, and be in Britain before Carausius can establish himself."

Constantius drew a sharp breath.

"We have no ships, Carausius has the whole fleet."

Maximian dismissed the objection with a wave of his hand, "I will bring the Rhine flotilla up to the coast and down the channel."

"But they are freshwater sailors", Constantius protested, "useless at sea; besides Carausius controls the mouth of the Rhine, they would never get past, and if they did his war galleys would annihilate them in the channel."

Maximian clucked with impatience, "Merchant ships, fishing boats, anything, we'll commandeer them."

"It's a sixty-mile voyage in uncertain weather, and Carausius controls the seas."

"Why are you always obstructive?"

"Landing an army on a hostile coast is something nobody has done since Claudius. We have no experience of it. We must take time to prepare."

"Time! I have no time. If I, the new Augustus, do not retake Britannia, I will be a laughing stock."

"If you fail, and in a make-shift fleet you *will* fail, you will be an even bigger laughing stock."

Maximian was a stubborn man, but he was not a fool; he knew that the opinion of one of Rome's greatest generals was to be listened to, even if it was then rejected.

"Very well then, what would you do?"

"Bring the transports from Portus Julius into the Channel and begin building war galleys here", Constantius pointed to the map, "at the naval yards at Forum Julii. Fortunately, Carausius didn't seize that, and that may be his first mistake."

"That would take months", Maximian exploded; "the transports could not venture beyond the Pillars of Hercules till the spring storms are passed, and how many galleys could we build in that time? Precious few!"

"We would not be idle", Constantius said patiently. "We must first retake Belgica, Gesoriacum and the smaller ports, and bring the transports into them; that will cut the crossing down to twenty miles."

Maximian snorted, "It would need three legions to do all that. It would need months to capture Gesoriacum."

"Meanwhile", Constantius countered, "we could be recruiting Saxon seamen to man the ships."

Maximian stared at Constantius, "Saxons! Saxons! What would I want a bunch of savages for?"

"They understand the tides, they know the coasts; Mediterranean sailors don't."

"Tides! Tides!" Maximian exclaimed, "everyone talks of tides as though we knew nothing of them, ever since Julius Caesar had to tuck up his kilt and run for his ships before the tide lifted them off the beach. That was three hundred years ago. Our sailors have learned a little since then."

Constantius kept his patience, "At least recruit a Saxon pilot for each vessel, and an oars' master too; they're not the savages you think, they've learned something from Rome this past hundred years."

Maximian puffed and harrumphed but eventually made up his mind.

"I'll send for the troop transports, as you suggest, and build as many war galleys as we can in the time; but I will embark from here", he stabbed the map again. "I will not spend time and money retaking Belgica and reducing Gesoriacum, and I will not have Saxons."

Constantius listened in dismay. There was one hope; the legions might be needed elsewhere on the Rhine, and that would give time to muster a proper fleet. In the event it was three years before Maximian could put his plan into operation.

*   *   *

The Saturnalia came and it was the happiest in Giorgios' life, for he was with his beloved, sharing the feast with her.

They attended the midnight liturgy together, standing side by side in the midst of their family: Justus and Julia, Kira, Andrew and Susannah, Claudia, Martha, Katherine, Lucius and Cyrennius.

Abba Theodore began the chant and the response was taken up by the deacons and acolytes:

"The Lord has said to me: thou art my Son, this day have I begotten thee."

"This is that night, that holy night,
The hope and expectation of the ages,
Filled with the splendour of true Light."

And so it seemed indeed to Giorgios and Justina as the mystery and wonder of the night enveloped them and drew them together, heart to heart and soul to soul. Afterwards, as wine and honey-cake, raisins and apples were carried around by the household slaves, they danced and sang together; Justina floated above the floor like thistledown, so light, so fragile. The following day she joined Kira, Andrew and Giorgios in waiting upon the slaves, pouring their wine and serving their food with a cheerful grace and humility which brought tears of joy to the eyes of the old grey-haired retainers and their wives.

Kira watched and remembered previous Saturnalias and Anastasius. Giorgios was more like his father every day, and could she herself have chosen a better bride for him? She thought not. And Julia, looking fondly at her daughter, could not imagine a better husband for her, nor a better foster son for Justus.

There was an added delight for Giorgios: Justus presented him with a pure white Arab filly, a yearling. He stroked her neck and nose, spellbound by her beauty.

"What will you call her?" Justina asked, skipping with glee.

"Assjadah", Giorgios answered without hesitation.

"What is that in Latin?"

"Daughter of the Morning."

The year turned and the spring came; and at seventeen, duty called. Giorgios left a tearful Justina to care for Assjadah and embarked upon the long voyage to Nicomedia and the army; and the lament of the turtle dove was heard again in the land.

PART FOUR
A.D. 289 – A.D. 303

CHAPTER THIRTY-NINE

Giorgios' gaze switched from Centurion Dacius to the boy standing beside him. "Boy" seemed hardly the right word, for the youth was almost as tall and as broad shouldered as himself. He was square-jawed with a short thick neck and large pale blue eyes. Nevertheless, he could not have been more than sixteen years old. He stood now with clenched fists – large and bony – at his sides, rigidly to attention. Giorgios looked back at the balding centurion with his weather-beaten face and scarred cheeks, but said nothing. The cavalry school at Nicomedia was housed in the barracks of the Imperial Guard. Discipline was in the hands of the officers of the Guard, hence Centurion Dacius.

There were cadets who scoffed at the belief that Centurion Dacius had the gift of omnipresence, only to be stricken in the midst of their blasphemies by the manifestation of the Centurion amongst them, when they were in the very act of some depredation.

Giorgios had only once made that mistake. Now he waited for Dacius to speak.

"I want you to look after this wolf-cub, show him the ropes, keep him out of trouble, that's why I'm putting him under your command." Giorgios bit off the words "Why me?" and Dacius, exhibiting another of his attributes, that of omniscience, went on, "You're the one least likely to get into trouble yourself", and with this enigmatic remark he left Giorgios' cubiculum.

Giorgios had completed his year as a cadet and had returned home. He had hoped that he and Justina might marry, but Justus remained adamant that she should not marry until she was eighteen; nevertheless, there had been a blissful month of leave before he had received orders to return to Nicomedia. He had hoped for a posting to an active service unit, perhaps to Gaul for the expected invasion of Britannia – for that far-off province was beginning to fascinate him. At Nicomedia he learned that he was to remain on the training staff for a year with the rank of decurion, in charge of ten cadets. That year was half run without his collecting any black marks, but now a raw recruit had been placed in his squad and somehow he had to bring him up to the same standard as the rest, and quickly.

Giorgios turned to the truculent boy. "Centurion Dacius didn't mention your name."

The boy looked at him, his eyes opaque.

"Perhaps he left it for me to decide."

"Well, we must call you something."

He wondered why the boy was so prickly and guarded.

"Constantine", he said, and then, after a momentary pause, "Yes, and before you ask, I am the son of Constantius Chlorus, and my mother is Helena, his lawful wife."

The bitterness was unmistakable. Only months before, Constantius Chlorus had publicly repudiated his wife, Helena, in the Temple of Jupiter in order to marry Theodora, step-daughter of the Emperor Maximian. The marriage was mutually beneficial. It made certain Constantius' succession to the purple and he as nephew to the legendary Claudius Gothicus gave a legitimacy to the upstart Maximian. Giorgios sympathised with the angry boy who stood before him. He knew, as everyone knew, that Theodora, not content with Constantius' public humiliation of his wife, had spread the story that Helena had never been married to him, that she was merely a concubina.

Giorgios spoke lightly to the lad, "Lots of people use influence to get into the army under age, but that just shows how keen they are to serve."

"I didn't ask my" – he paused as though dragging out the next word – "father for any favours, he offered this one and I took it; but now I'm in, I don't want any more."

"You won't get any", Giorgios assured him, "not here anyway."

At that moment the trumpets sounded for evening meal.

Giorgios led Constantine out of the barrack block and skirted the parade ground as they made for the mess. Several large horse troughs stood around the perimeter, and lounging against one of these were four senior cadets. Giorgios knew them well; Maximin Daia, a thickset, thick-headed bully with blubbery lips, and his three henchmen. They were the last people in the world Giorgios expected, or wanted, to meet at this moment, but to turn back was impossible. He continued on his way, Constantine beside him.

As they approached, Daia, smirking at his minions, sauntered forward, blocking the way.

"What have we here?" he asked, "A nursemaid with a truant schoolboy?"

Before Giorgios could intervene, Constantine had stepped forward, "My name is Gaius Flavius Valerius Constantinus, son of Julius Constantius Chlorus. I am not a schoolboy, truant or otherwise. I am a soldier of the Roman Army, the same as you."

"My! My!" Daia drawled, "What an insolent fellow; I don't hear no 'Domine', or even 'Sir'. We know who you are. We've heard all about you and how regulations were waived for you, just because you're Constantius' bastard."

Constantine's right fist drew back until it was level with his ear, then it shot forward to smash into Daia's face. The bully went down flat on his back, blood pouring from nose and mouth. Constantine half turned to the right, where one of the minions was making a grab at him. His left fist drove into the man's solar plexus and he doubled up fighting for breath. The other two stepped back. Daia had scrambled to his feet, murder in his eyes as he drew his sword.

164

Giorgios' right foot swung up and kicked the weapon out of his hand. Daia stumbled back against the horse trough and Giorgios, shouting "Cool off, you idiot", tipped him into it with a quick, wrestler's throw.

A crowd had gathered, seemingly from nowhere, cheering on the combatants, at which moment Centurion Dacius appeared. He took in the scene at a glance.

"Grudge fights to be settled in the gym", he barked. "Get along there."

Daia had struggled out of the trough, dripping water and wringing his hand, "I can't" he said, "they've broken my fingers."

"Well, get along to the surgeon", Dacius roared. "Anywhere but on my parade ground."

He turned to look for the henchmen, but they had melted away, so he turned to Giorgios.

"I had expected better of you", he said and strode off.

Giorgios' exasperation turned to dismay as he saw Constantine climb onto the rim of the horse trough from where he began to address the delighted audience of cadets.

"My name is Constantine", he bellowed.

"Get down you fool", hissed Giorgios.

"And I am the son of Constantius Chlorus."

There were some ironic cheers from the crowd.

"If you resent my being accepted here under age, I'm sorry, I didn't ask for the privilege; but I took it when it came and I'm not ashamed of that. Who would not want to be a soldier of Rome?"

The ironic cheers turned to shouts of approval.

"Get down *now*!" Giorgios hissed again, but Constantine ignored him.

"My mother, the Domina Helena of Naissus, was my father's lawful wife; if any of you want to call me 'bastard' come over here and do it now!"

Another cheer went up; someone shouted, "Hail Constantine, victor of Maximin Daia!" Daia, being a bully, was unpopular, but now, publicly defeated in a fair fight, he was no longer feared, and a forest of hands shot up in salute as the cry was taken up. Constantine stood calm and erect until the shouting ceased.

"One more thing: it's been spread abroad that my mother was the daughter of an inn-keeper. Well, so she was, if owning a chain of mansiones on a Cursus Publicus is being an inn-keeper."

It was just the right note. The crowd laughed aloud, there were more shouts of "Constantine! Constantine!"

Desperate, Giorgios reached up and grabbed Constantine by his belt, "If you don't shut up and get down I'll tip you into that trough."

When they entered the mess the hubbub of voices ceased and all eyes turned to look at Constantine. Whether it was because he was the grand nephew of Claudius Gothicus and the son of one of the greatest commanders in the army, or because he was the boy who had thrashed Daia and his gang, or whether it was simply because of the way the youth held himself and walked tall, Giorgios could not tell. He only wished that he had not drawn the short straw for mentoring this stormy petrel. Constantine paid no attention to the eyes following him. He walked over to the bar, collected his jug of watered wine, bowl of lentil and mutton hash and hunk of black bread and waited for Giorgios to lead the way to a table. They sat down and gradually everyone took up their interrupted talk. Giorgios noted that Constantine ate delicately, but not fastidiously, breaking his bread neatly before pouring a little olive oil onto it. He made no comment upon the food, except for one brief grimace when he tasted the wine; however, he drank without further sign of distaste.

"I suppose you realize", Giorgios said as they finished eating, "that you've bloodied the nose of the nephew of the Count Galerius, who's fast becoming Diocletian's right-hand man, and knocked the stuffing out of Maxentius, son of the Augustus Maximian. You've made powerful enemies already; luckily, they're nearing the end of their term here and'll be gone in a few weeks."

Constantine pondered this for a few moments.

"Well", he said at length, "I suppose I'll have to execute them when I'm Emperor, anyway." Giorgios was too astonished to speak and Constantine went on, "My father spoke highly of your father. He remembered how he saved the day at Palmyra after the left flank collapsed under Galerius, and the march up the Rhône with Aurelian when your father defused a near mutiny."

Giorgios was gratified by this praise of his father. "My father is dead, you know", he said, his voice softening.

Constantine turned his pale eyes on him.

"Yes", he said, "murdered; but *your* father is still alive to you."

Giorgios felt a pang of pity. This youngster who sat opposite him was destined to rise high; those in the mess had sensed his charisma when he walked in, but if he carried in his heart, unhealed, this wound, this betrayal of boyhood trust, this bitterness at desertion, then woe to Rome.

"We'd better get back and I'll show you how to lay out your kit", he said, anxious to escape further introspection.

Diocletian's long-meditated army reforms had started to take shape. The army was to be raised from 300,000 to 500,000 men. The auxiliaries were to provide the garrison troops for the frontiers, and the legions the field army. The big innovation, however, which would absorb most of the increase in manpower, was cavalry brigades, highly mobile and stationed in key positions. This strategy probably originated with Galerius, who increasingly had Diocletian's ear. The army was to be given a separate command structure, no longer subordinate to provincial governors. On each section of the frontiers the army would be commanded by a "Duke" who would be directly responsible to the "Master of Cavalry" and the "Master of Infantry." These two "Marshals of the Empire" would be at the Emperor's side at all times. It was to train the officers of the planned brigades that the cavalry school had been established at Nicomedia.

*   *   *

The cadets' cubicles were small by any standard. There was a narrow window in the wall opposite the door and beneath that a table and stool. A straw mattress against one wall took up most of the floor space and there was a row of hooks on the wall opposite. Constantine's kit lay in a heap on the mattress.

"You'll share the services of a slave with two other cadets", Giorgios explained. "Your man is Crispus, comes from Britannia, but speaks good Latin. He'll take your mattress down to the hypocaust furnace once a week, burn the straw and refill it with clean straw. Army issue is two cotton loincloths and two cotton tunics; you change every day and Crispus launders the dirty ones. When laundered they are to be folded neatly and placed on the bottom edge of the mattress." Giorgios laid them out, and went on, "You have two outer woollen tunics: the shorter, lighter one for barracks wear, that is to be hung on the first hook; and the other, for field service, on the second hook."

"What happens if they're hung on different hooks?"

"Your whole turma gets extra drill, six times around the parade ground at double pace and in full kit. You won't be very popular if you drop your comrades in it like that; but more important, the layout of kit, like the design of barracks, is exactly the same in every part of the Empire. You have to be able to put your hand on any piece of equipment in the dark. The enemy doesn't always have the good manners to wait for daylight before attacking." Constantine merely nodded and Giorgios showed him the rest of the lay-out. "Keeping your equipment cleaned and maintained is your responsibility; there aren't any slaves to do it for you on campaign."

Constantine lifted a sandal from the mattress and inspected it; the leather was supple with oil and the soles were about an inch thick, studded with round-topped nails.

"Why don't we wear boots?"

"Because if your feet get wet, in boots they stay wet, and if they sweat they stay sweaty; and at the end of the day your feet will be sore and the skin split."

Constantine nodded, satisfied, and picked up another lighter sandal with no studs, "And I suppose these are for wearing in barracks?"

"Correct. Now, let me go through it with you."

Constantine rattled off the instructions, word for word.

"You've a good memory", Giorgios said approvingly, "but make sure that you do it; don't be tempted to try to beat the system, because you can't, nobody can. Oh, and one more thing: if you want good service from Crispus, be generous, give him a tip once a week, just a few denarii."

"What does a slave want money for?" Constantine asked. "He has his food, clothes and shelter."

Giorgios paused; could this boy, young as he was, really be so insensitive? His reply was abrupt, "He can squander it in the wine shop, in which case for a few hours he's as free as any other man with money in his pouch; or he can, as Crispus does, hoard it until he has enough to buy his freedom."

Constantine did not miss the note in his mentor's voice. He reddened, "I hadn't thought of that", he said, humbly.

Giorgios immediately warmed to him. The boy was biddable and knew when he was wrong. He was just about to leave to put his own cubicle in order when he noticed a small scroll still lying on the mattress. He picked it up.

"Virgil?" he queried, *The Eclogues?*"

"Why yes", Constantine replied, "I often read them."

Giorgios unrolled the scroll until he came to the Fourth Eclogue, so strangely out of context with the others. He scanned the Latin hexameters, reading aloud while, by long habit, silently rendering snatches into Greek,

"The great cycle of the ages begins anew....
the son of the Most High will descend...
Justice will reign again...
Pollio, it will be in your Consulship...
for a time there will still be wars...
but in the end Justice will rule supreme.
The earth will yield its bounty...
The time is now at hand...
Oh may I live so long as to see his coming."

"I didn't know Christians read Virgil, or any other pagan author", Constantine said as Giorgios finished.

"Why yes! We call him 'The Isaiah of the Gentiles'."

"Who was Isaiah?"

"A prophet of Israel, who foretold the coming of a Messiah."

Constantine's lip curled slightly: the scene in the Temple of Jupiter, his father repudiating his mother, flashed through his mind.

"And you really believe the Son of High Jove will be born among men and restore justice?" he asked, a note of mockery in his voice.

"Why yes", Giorgios replied, as he turned to leave the cubicle. "He already has been."

CHAPTER FORTY

Giorgios, returning to his cubiculum, wrote to Justina, using one of the army "postcards": two thin pieces of timber, hinged and coated on the inside with wax. The writing could be smoothed out with a warm knife and the "postcard" re-used for the reply. He and Justina had several of these passing between them so that only a week at most was spent in eagerly awaiting the next letter. He then sat down to ponder the quandary Constantine had put him in. It was a serious offence to strike a brother cadet, and the penalty was expulsion. Constantine had crowned his first day by laying out two brother cadets, and those with powerful connections at that. He himself was not in a good position, although his defence, that of disarming Daia in the only way possible, might be accepted. Hopefully Constantine's defence – his mother's honour – might also be accepted, for the Roman Mother stood high in army iconography. It seemed that his training in rhetoric might come in useful sooner than expected.

With these disturbing thoughts he lay down to try to sleep.

*   *   *

Giorgios collected Constantine for breakfast and, as they ate, outlined the situation to him.

"What should I have done?" Constantine demanded.

"You should have challenged him to a fight in the gym, with a referee and witnesses. I'll do my best to argue that, as a new man of only one day in the service, you didn't know the rules."

With that they made a morose journey back to prepare for parade.

First parade was on foot. The cadets were drawn up in their turmae, facing a line of centurions and lictors. It was at this parade that disciplinary matters were dealt with by a Tribune of the Imperial Guard. Standing on a dais, the Tribune addressed the parade, Giorgios waiting tensely for the axe to fall. Four cadets, the Tribune announced, had, against regulations, gone into the city in uniform. There they had not only got drunk in a wine shop, causing a disturbance, but had then proceeded to a brothel where one of them, supported on the shoulders of the rest, had chalked over the entrance the words, "Vestal Virgins".

The city magistrates were even now complaining to the Legate, the curials were waiting to complain to the Legate, the flamens from the temple of Vesta were waiting to complain to the Legate, even the brothel-keeper had come to complain. The defaulters' names, the Tribune went on, were known. It would be better for them if they fell out now, rather than have him denounce them. He paused and waited. Four cadets marched out to the front.

"Six strokes", the tribune announced. The cadets bent their backs and four lictors marched up to administer six strokes across the shoulders. The swish of the rods and

169

the thwack of the impacts were plainly audible, but as the cadets were wearing their cloaks and scale armour the pain was minimal, though the humiliation was great. The Tribune would report to the Legate that punishment had been inflicted and the Legate would assure the complaining citizens that the culprits had received condign retribution. The army, Giorgios reflected, looked after its own, and he hoped desperately that the same attitude would extend to Constantine's offence.

The Tribune had not finished. Two cadets had left the barracks after curfew. They had been seen returning in the early hours by a slave who had duly reported them. Would the defaulters now step forward? No one stirred. Very well then, the Tribune thundered, they would be discovered, even if he had to spend a lifetime interviewing every man in the army, and then it would be the worse for them. Still no one moved. Tensely, Giorgios waited for the Tribune to order those who had taken part in yesterday's brawl to step forward. To his surprise the Tribune ordered the parade to dismiss. Centurion Dacius might not yet have reported the incident, but it was inconceivable that Daia had not done what bullies always do, gone whining to authority when they had a taste of their own medicine.

Giorgios' anxiety would have been abated if he could have witnessed the night's events in Galerius' quarters. The two cadets who had absented themselves were none other than Daia and Maxentius. They had gone to the Palatium to enlist Galerius' aid in vengeance. Daia's version of the incident was that an unprovoked attack had left him with a broken nose, split lips, loose teeth, bruised hand, and soaking wet. Galerius listened frowning, but without speaking.

"Who spoke first?" demanded Licinius, as usual in attendance upon Galerius. Taken aback, Daia mumbled something about having jovially called Constantine a 'bastard'. Everyone knew that Helena was Chlorus' concubine; how could a Patrician have married an inn-keeper's daughter anyway? Constantine would have to get used to such friendly twitting.

"It would seem", said Licinius drily, "that Constantine has a defence and also a counter-complaint, since you drew a sword on a brother cadet."

Daia bridled, "That was self-defence. He struck me without warning, and I'm going to get him kicked out if it's the last thing I do."

A stinging slap on the side of the head sent him staggering.

"It will be!" snarled Galerius. "You know nothing, you fool. Why do you think I persuaded Diocletian to let the brat come here under age? He's a hostage, you fool. Bastard or not, he's Chlorus' son, and while I have him here I have a grip on Chlorus. You get him kicked out and he returns to his father at Trier, out of our reach and the certain successor to his father. The one who would rule the Empire would then be that mother of his and her Christian friends."

Daia was looking at his uncle, stupefied. To save face he switched his attack to Giorgios. Galerius listened, but Licinius interrupted, "He disarmed you, that's all. You should be grateful: he saved you from a murder charge."

Daia glared at Licinius; Galerius snarled, "I thought I'd got rid of the Theognostas; now here's the cub causing trouble."

Daia brightened, "I could kill him for you", he exclaimed, "a training accident."

He caught the flat of Galerius' hand across his head for a second time.

"Are you an utter and complete idiot? A leader does not murder his opponents, a leader picks subordinates who are eager to outdo each other in anticipating his wishes, and who have enough sense not to inform him that they've done it, something he neither needs nor wants to know. Now this is what you will do: you will apologise to Constantine, say it was just a feeble army joke and that you meant no offence." Daia opened his mouth to protest, but Galerius cut him short, "Do what I say if you wish to remain my heir." He turned to Maxentius, "And you, if you don't want Constantius Chlorus to succeed your father in the West, do as I say. Now both of you get out."

While every day which passed made it less likely that Daia would complain, Giorgios' anxiety remained high. He could not understand why Centurion Dacius had not reported the incident, but then perhaps Dacius considered it was up to Daia to complain.

It came as a surprise, a few days later, when Daia and Maxentius approached Constantine and himself in the mess.

"Look here", the former said to Constantine, "I meant no offence the other day. Soldiers often call each other 'bastards', it's just a habit really, nothing to be taken badly. Can't we forget it?"

Constantine looked at him without change of expression.

"I already have", he said, and walked away.

Giorgios, though he disliked both men, made an effort to be conciliatory.

"Thank you for not making a complaint", he said to Daia; and then, turning to Maxentius, said, "I should think you know a great deal about Carausius; when will we fight him?"

"A slight, meritless fellow", Maxentius drawled, flattered at being looked upon as an authority, "just another barbarian. His mother was an Irish slave – of course, he claims she was a princess, but among these barbarians every wretched village has its king and its princes to herd the pigs, and its princesses to milk the cows. My father'll soon put him down now he's got a new fleet together; shouldn't be surprised if a legion isn't already embarked, but I rather hope they'll wait till I've finished here."

"Thank you", said Giorgios, "I'm sure you'd do well in any campaign there."

Gratified by this further flattery, Maxentius and Daia strolled away.

Several days later the news of the British disaster reached Nicomedia and the cavalry school. The invasion army had embarked on the troop transports at the mouth of the Seine and had started the sixty-mile crossing, protected by an inadequate number of war galleys. Carausius' fleet had swept out of inlets and estuaries: fast long-ships which rode lightly on the waves, propelled only by oars, and manned, not by chained slaves, but by the fighting men themselves. They circled and darted about the transports, dashing in to shear off the oars from one side leaving the heavy vessels floundering in circles before being caught by wind and tide and swept away down the Channel to run aground wherever they could. The Roman losses of sailors and soldiers had been high, of transports total. Maximian, commanding the fleet from the rear, watched in despair as his armada was destroyed. He turned to Constantius and said weakly, "But they had no sails!"

"But they had Saxon oar-masters and pilots, and they had control of their ships against wind or tide."

It was noted in the mess that Maxentius absented himself from public life for several days after the arrival of the news of the debacle.

CHAPTER FORTY-ONE

Training at the cavalry school was rigorous. Immediately after the morning parade the cadets fell in under their decurions for the daily route march in full kit. "Full kit" included a forty-pound pack, but those under Giorgios' command knew better than to empty their water skins to lessen the weight. He always checked. They moved off in a long column, two abreast, at the legionary pace of one hundred and twenty a minute. The Roman mile was a thousand yards, and as each squad completed the first mile they changed to "double pace". This alternated with the marching pace for five miles. As the column swung into the parade ground, Giorgios noted that Constantine had kept up well.

From the parade ground it was straight to the baths for swimming and then a hurried midday meal of "iron rations" – bread, raisins, olives and water. The afternoon was spent on horseback, tilting at targets, forming columns, dividing columns, wheeling, charging to the front, and fencing on horseback, until at last the trumpets sounded and the weary cadets led their mounts to the stables to be groomed and fed until the trumpets sounded the summons to the mess. After the evening meal there would be a lecture on Military Law, Civil Law or Military History, and then a couple of hours leisure before the trumpets sounded curfew. All of this Constantine took in his stride.

"The cub is half horse", Giorgios said to himself, "and as strong as a horse too." What was equally surprising was the amount of good will Constantine generated among the other cadets. They remembered how he had thrashed Daia.

Winter closed down, and it threatened to be a hard one. Before the Saturnalia there was snow on the mountains, and sometimes on the coastal plain. Roman agents beyond the Danube reported movement among the barbarians. The nomads of the steppes, finding pasture failing early, began to raid the agrarian folk further south; they in turn thought of the store-houses across the Danube.

Galerius sat in his cabinet studying reports and maps. He was a good strategist and had been a good cavalryman. His mistakes were partly due to the distractions of debauchery, but more to his conviction that he was looked down on as a Dacian. Periodically he would have an uncontrollable urge to prove himself, to show them that he was as good a Roman as they. These moods, unfounded as they now were, resulted in wild strategic mistakes. They were also at the root of his obsessive plotting. Now he spoke to Licinius.

"The reports are bad. The movements south are growing in strength. If the Danube freezes, and that is likely, there'll be eruptions all along the frontier."

Licinius' old admiration for the man was briefly rekindled.

"You must seek an audience with the Emperor!"

"I will", Galerius replied, "and I'll do it now!"

The Roman soldier did not have leave or weekend passes. He spent his off-duty hours in the camp, or, at the most and if he had civilian clothes, in a neighbouring

173

city. Tribunes, however, were able to return home when a campaign was finished; in effect, a transfer to the Reserve. Giorgios spent the Saturnalia in the cavalry school, waiting with the other officers upon the legionaries and cadets. It brought back fond memories of watching Justina waiting upon the household slaves the previous year. After the dinner there was a good deal of drinking, wrestling and horseplay before curfew was sounded and he was able to throw himself on his straw mattress and nurse his aching head.

The following day, although not an official feast day, was relaxed. There were no parades and no drills and the cadets were able to wander off to the theatres, wine shops and arenas of Nicomedia.

"Would you like to come with me? I'm visiting my mother", Constantine asked.

Giorgios was surprised, "Your mother? Why, where is she?"

"She's living at Drepanum, an hour's ride with the ferry."

"I thought you came from Naissus."

"Mother has a house there", Constantine replied, "but she's taken a house in Drepanum."

"You never said", Giorgios sounded reproachful.

"D'you think that would have been wise?" Constantine asked, "Just imagine what Daia would have made of it – 'Mumsy moves house to be near her ugly son', and that sort of thing."

Giorgios laughed, "I see what you mean, but I'll gladly come with you, I could do with the ride."

"Actually, she moved to Drepanum because my uncle lives there. After my father deserted us she felt it better to be near her brother."

"I can see that", Giorgios replied, anxious to soothe Constantine's feelings.

"Well, at least we'll have some decent food and wine and some civilized company", Constantine replied.

Giorgios found himself introduced to a tall, slender woman. Her red-gold hair was greying, but that she had once been extraordinarily beautiful there could be no doubt. With her Grecian features and grey eyes she was still handsome in spite of an aura of sadness.

"Constantine often mentions you in his letters", she said. "It seems you're quite a hero of his."

Giorgios blushed slightly, "I'm sure, Domina, that he would have made his own way very well if I hadn't been there", he replied.

"Don't underestimate yourself. But tell me, you come from Lydda, in the land of your prophet?" There was a sudden eagerness in her voice.

"Yes!" he replied, "We're not far from Jerusalem."

"I've heard a story", Helena went on, "that when Adam died he was buried with a pip in his mouth, a pip from an apple which grew in Paradise."

"I haven't heard that one before." Giorgios was mildly amused.

"The story goes on", Helena continued, "that a great tree grew from his grave, living through all the ages of man, and from it was cut the living wood of the cross on which your prophet was crucified. Is this story true?"

Giorgios laughed, "I can say with certainty that it isn't."

"Oh!" Helena was clearly disappointed, "but I thought that all your scriptures were true?"

Giorgios pondered this, "All in our scripture is true, but this story, and many others like it, are not in the Scriptures. They are inventions of a later date, at the best pious fantasies."

"Oh! Is that all?" Helena appeared quite crestfallen.

"Some may have a basis in truth", Giorgios went on, "for instance among my own people there is a story that our clan, the Gamayal, are descended from the great rabbi Gamaliel. Perhaps we are, or perhaps it's only wishful thinking based on a similarity of names. What we do hold as certain is that the Apostle Peter took refuge among us, because the Scriptures say that he 'visited the saints at Lydda and Sharon'."

Helena shook her head sadly, "I see what you mean. It's very intellectual, but I prefer the story of a real apple and a real tree. One day I'll go to Judea and visit these places."

"I hope you will, and should you come you'll be more than welcome at my mother's house."

Slaves carrying platters of honey cakes, raisins, almonds and cups of wine interrupted the conversation. Giorgios savoured the sweet, unwatered wine and the cakes and looked about him at the other guests. It was obvious that there was great affection between Helena and her son and that she had considerable influence over him. What was intriguing was the way that Constantine's eyes would light up whenever his glance fell on a certain girl of about fourteen. Her name was Minervina and she appeared to be a protégé of Helena. Giorgios was delighted to discover that his young friend was in love, and, remembering his own hesitations, was sympathetically amused by the realization that the bold, brash, forward Constantine had not yet gathered sufficient courage to declare himself, but worshipped in silence and from afar.

CHAPTER FORTY-TWO

The following morning all was bustle and excitement. Galerius was moving four alae of cavalry to the Danube frontier and had decided that the cadets would go with them to gain experience of commissariat problems. The cadets, five hundred or more, were divided into sixteen turmae to make a fifth ala. Giorgios, to his surprise, found himself commanding a turma with Constantine as his-second-in-command. It was Constantine who gave voice to a dark suspicion, "Perhaps he hopes we'll be killed!" The rest of the day was taken up with issuing equipment, particularly woollen trousers.

"It's going to be cold", Constantine remarked; "Double tunics to be worn, you notice?"

The next day the long dragon of men and horses, war machines, supply wagons, and pack mules moved off. They were ferried across the Bosphorus to Byzantium and lodged there ready for a start at first light the following morning. Constantine was absorbed in memorizing everything he saw, particularly the marshalling of the column in the morning and at its halts for food and drink. He judged rightly that efficient marshalling was the skill a general must have. A week's march brought them to the Danube and they saw the first ice forming. Galerius issued his orders. The cadets would patrol the banks in both directions, at Turma strength. They were not to engage any force crossing the river, but were to return with exact information of its strength and equipment. The regular troops would do any fighting. The next morning the river was frozen hard.

"Who are we expecting to fight?" Giorgios asked one of the regular turma commanders.

"The Sarmatians", the man replied briefly.

"Who are they?"

"Horsemen from the steppes, they've been moving further south for a century. They've beaten the Goths, so don't expect them to be a pushover."

The first Sarmatian sortie came a few days later. They were spotted by patrolling cadets, crossing the river about a hundred strong and in a long line to spread the vibration on the ice.

Galerius was waiting for them and few escaped.

"They'll try further up the river", Galerius told his turmae commanders. Once again Galerius was right and was waiting for the invaders. Now he strengthened his patrols, interspersing the cadets with turmae of regular troops. Several more forays were driven back.

"They're estimating our strength", Galerius told Licinius, "and by now they know it. We can expect the main attack soon."

"What do you intend to do?" Licinius asked, "attack first?"

"No!" replied Galerius, "I intend to light some large fires and keep them burning. Detail men to fell trees."

Giorgios' turma was riding through leafless forest overlooking the frozen river when the sound of battle came to them. They moved cautiously out of the trees. A clear space on the river bank came into view. A troop of Gallic light cavalry, perhaps twenty in all, was desperately fighting off twice their number of Sarmatians. There was no time to ride back to report: the Gallic cavalry would be overwhelmed long before reinforcements could reach them. Giorgios came to a decision.

"Column will divide. The right wing will charge to the right.

Decurion Constantine in command. The left wing will follow me.

Trumpeters, sound the charge and keep sounding it as loud as you can."

The two wings of cavalry swept down in curving columns, threatening to surround the Sarmatians. The latter had no desire to fight superior odds, and turned to make for the river.

Giorgios called his turma to a halt and watched them cross over. A tall, lanky Gaul rode up to them.

"Thank you!" he said in Gallic Latin. "You saved our lives, they had us pinned down. My name is Crocus of Noviomagus."

Giorgios studied the man closely, "We are honoured, Prince Crocus."

"Ha!" laughed the Gaul, "You have a quick mind, but I do not use the title here. At home, where my father is a king among the Gauls, it is different."

"I am Giorgios Theognosta of Lydda, and this is Constantine, son of Constantius Chlorus."

The Gaul's eyes widened, "Constantius Chlorus! Why, as soon as this damn river thaws we're on our way to serve under him. He will need light cavalry for the reconquest of Britannia and we are the best in the Empire."

The main Sarmatian attack came a few days later. The invaders had even brought up wagons to cart away their expected loot. To succeed, they had to destroy the Roman army facing them. The Sarmatians came across in a great wave, five or six deep but spread wide. As soon as they reached halfway, Galerius gave his orders. The sappers raked red-hot stones from the fires along the river bank and loaded them onto the catapults. Clouds of steam rose from the ice as the stones struck it, the ice clanging like a bell. The catapults were re-wound at top speed and twenty more stones struck the ice, breaking its surface. Cracks began to appear and the Sarmatians panicked. Horses slithered as they were jerked around. Some riders whipped their steeds to a gallop to reach the Roman bank before the ice split.

Galerius gave a second order, and a line of bowmen sent a barrage of arrows into the mass. There was an ominous cracking sound and horses and men were tipped into the freezing water. Galerius watched with satisfaction.

"Tomorrow", he said, "we build a bridge."

The Sarmatians fought fiercely to prevent the building of the bridge, but Galerius had secured a foothold on the opposite bank by sending the Gallic light cavalry across further up stream during the night. The "bridge" in fact was more a timber causeway resting on the refrozen ice, and as the Roman army poured across it, the Sarmatian chiefs came to ask for quarter.

"What mercy would you have shown to the people you came to rob?" Galerius demanded. They stood silent. "You think farmers are there for you idle vagabonds to rob and kill", Galerius thundered, "and now you ask for mercy?" The chiefs were cowed. "Very well then, mercy you shall have, but you chiefs must bring your sons and daughters here to me, as hostages. You must bring to me every piece of gold or silver your people have. You must remove yourselves from Roman land to the other side of those mountains." He pointed to the distant Carpathians.

"But there we will starve", one old chief protested.

"That is your affair. The alternative is that my troops slaughter all your menfolk, burn your tents and wagons and take your women and children into slavery. You yourselves will be hanged as criminal enemies of Rome. If you break these terms, Rome's vengeance will be terrible, every one of your people will be crucified."

The chiefs began an agitated debate and then bowed down in submission. Later that day Galerius conferred with his staff officers.

"We stay here and patrol the river until the ice melts."

To Licinius he said, "Send a wagon of barley after the Sarmatians."

"But I thought they were to starve", Licinius protested.

"Never leave an enemy without an option", Galerius replied.

Licinius looked at him with something of his old respect. Away from the palatium and its abundant whores, the manliness of battle had cleansed him.

CHAPTER FORTY-THREE

It was early spring when the cadets returned to Nicomedia, only a few days before the completion of their year's training.

Galerius decided that their active service qualified them: all had passed with proven merit. A delighted Constantine hastened to find Giorgios to tell him that he had been given a place in the Imperial Guard with the rank of decurion. Giorgios had other things on his mind. He had been to the legionary post office to collect letters from Justina and home, and to his dismay found that all mail had been forwarded to the Danube frontier only a week before. He fretted and fumed at this delay in hearing from Justina and was about to write to her when he was summoned to appear before Galerius.

"You disobeyed orders." Galerius greeted him with a scowl.

Giorgios, surprised by this, said nothing.

"You led a turma of cadets into battle against my orders."

Light dawned on Giorgios.

"Domine, we went to the rescue of Roman forces."

Galerius scowled the more; he knew that he had no case against Giorgios.

"So the Prince Crocus has informed the Emperor, in a no doubt exaggerated report: but for that, you would be court-martialled." Giorgios suppressed a sigh of relief. "However", went on Galerius maliciously, "I have no room for instructors who give a bad example to cadets by disobeying orders. You are relieved of your commission here. Go home until you are wanted elsewhere."

Choking with indignation, Giorgios saluted, about-turned and marched out to pack his few belongings. Galerius smiled in satisfaction. He had got rid of a Christian and, as a bonus, of a Theognosta. Giorgios would vegetate in Lydda with his uncle.

Giorgios' fury at his unjust treatment abated a little when he heard that there was a merchantman sailing from Nicomedia for Sidon and Joppa at first light the next morning. It would be a rough voyage in winter, but faster and surer than riding overland. He bade a hasty farewell to Constantine, giving him a brief account of events. The latter was as furious as himself.

"I'll write to my father; he'll see Diocletian is informed", he said between gritted teeth.

Giorgios knew how much it would go against the grain for Constantine to approach his father, and thanked him profusely. He led out his horse, wondering if this was the end of his military career, and rode down to the port.

He had no intention of missing the sailing by staying in the college overnight.

*   *   *

It was a bright morning in early April when Giorgios finally rode from Joppa to his family villa. His heart was high; in a few weeks he would be twenty and in a few months Justina would be eighteen and they would be married. One of the field slaves saw him coming and ran to the villa. Giorgios rode through the gates, dismounted, and strode joyfully into the atrium. His mother, his sisters, Uncle Andrew, Lucius, Cyrennius and Claudia were there to meet him.

"Mother!" he hastened over to her, "I'll stay but a few minutes, before I go to Justina."

He stopped. There were no smiles, only grave countenances. His mother laid her hand upon his arm.

"Oh Giorgios, didn't you get our letters?"

"Letters! Why no, the fool of a postal clerk sent our mail chasing after us to the Danube and we passed it on our way back."

Tears had sprung to his mother's eyes. "Why, what's the matter?"

"Oh Giorgios, oh Giorgios", she said again. "It was the winter fever – it was worse this year – many died." Giorgios was listening, but not comprehending, "Justus died, Justina . . ."

"No!" said Giorgios quietly, his mouth drying, "No! No – I will not hear it – it is not true – I will not listen."

"Giorgios", his mother said again, "the physicians did everything – she was so fragile, so delicate – she could not fight it."

Giorgios howled like a beast in pain. He hurled himself against a pillar, striking his head against it before Lucius and Cyrennius could drag him away. He flung them off and threw himself onto the floor. Andrew motioned and a slave hastened over with a flask. Giorgios tasted a sweet, sticky liquid trickling down his throat and slowly subsided into unconsciousness.

*   *   *

Giorgios came to his senses in his own room, his mother sitting beside him. Memory returned and with it black despair.

He refused to eat and drove from the door whoever came. After two days Kira sent for Abba Theodore. It took him an hour to gain admittance and he remained in the room for another three.

He emerged grey with fatigue.

"He is reconciled to the ways of God, now let him rest."

Giorgios emerged the next morning, pale and shrunken.

"I will go", he told them, "to my estates in Cappadocia, to see if the emancipation of the field slaves ordered by my father has been carried out." No one tried to dissuade him. "First I'll visit Julia; she has lost a husband and a child. Then I'll see her grave before I leave."

"Won't you go to the stables and see Assjadah?" Katherine asked.

Giorgios smiled sadly, "Of course, I'd forgotten. Justina looked after her for me."

He went, with his mother and Claudia, to the familiar wicket gate and the slope of goat-cropped pasture topped by the hedge of Rose of Sharon. No glad girl ran down the slope this time, and he made his way to the house. Julia met him at the door. She was an uncomplicated woman whose happiness had been her husband and her child, and now, seeing Giorgios, she burst into tears, throwing her arms about him. He found that he was the comforter and before they left she had ceased to weep and even smiled wanly.

As they left, Claudia spoke *sotto voce* to Kira, "He is indeed a comforter of the afflicted, a son of consolation."

Lucius and Cyrennius accompanied Giorgios to the grave in the necropolis of Lydda. It was marked by a flat marble slab on which was carved her name and the symbol of the fish.

Giorgios stood in silence for a long time and then said, "I will bring a shrub of the Rose of Sharon from her house and plant it at the head. Will you help me dig it out and carry it?"

The two nodded dumbly.

"Tomorrow", he told the family, "I'll travel to Antioch on the vessel which brought me here. I'll ride Assjadah." He had another visitor in the evening. Raphael ben-Ezra came to tell him that he had completed his studies.

"I've been invited by the Hebrew congregation in Sidon to be their rabbi", he said. He placed his hand on Giorgios' arm. "I know of your great sorrow. One day God's providence will become clear to you."

"I cannot think so", Giorgios replied. "God has stripped my soul bare, even the army casts me aside. You remember how we talked of the soldier's duty? Even that is denied me."

Raphael nodded, "But you will marry some day, when time has healed."

Giorgios shook his head, "No! I'll never marry. She will live in my heart forever."

Raphael took his leave, but as he went he prayed silently with simple piety, "Lord, if this is the way you treat your friends, who shall wonder that you have so many enemies?"

CHAPTER FORTY-FOUR

Giorgios was furious. The factors, far from emancipating the field slaves, had re-enslaved those whom his father had already freed after judging their ability to support themselves and their families. The factors had also re-absorbed the small-holdings into the estate. He dismissed them, driving them in righteous anger from the villa with blows. He sent for surveyors, notaries and scribes. With them Giorgios pored over plans, parcelling out the arable land.

"Perhaps ownership in common would be the easiest way", one of the notaries suggested.

"No" replied Giorgios, "That's the worst kind of ownership, it means responsibility without empowerment."

They returned to the plans, went out to inspect the land, drew lines, and the notaries began to make up grants and title deeds. A stream of men answering his summons arrived at the villa door, still with hands and faces smudged with toil. One by one they received from his hands the deeds of their smallholdings.

"The gods favour you", they would say, calling down blessings upon him, and Giorgios would reply, "There is but one God." They would look at him, uncomprehending.

Only one God? No Apollo to drive the sun chariot? No Diana to ride the night? No spirits of tree and stream to leave offerings for? No smoke of sacrifice to rise in the calm of the evening? What kind of empty world was this? But the young Dominus must know best, so they would say, "May that god follow you with blessings and let him be our god also", and then, in spite of his protests, they would crouch down to kiss the floor before him.

At length the task was complete and he rode around the estate watching the men begin the autumn ploughing with a new zest.

He took to riding further afield each day, especially along the coasts of the Euxine. He found the sound of the waves soothing; there was nothing else in his heart. One morning, unable to sleep, he had ridden out at daybreak and, giving Assjadah her head, had gone much further than usual. He was over a bluff when he saw smoke rising on the other side. He urged Assjadah forward and, gaining the top, looked down on a dreadful scene.

There was a small fishing village, perhaps a dozen huts, all ablaze. Screaming women and girls were being ferried out to a long, sleek vessel which was riding out a couple of hundred yards from the shore. Even as he galloped down the hill, the last of the boats with its terrified captives was reaching the pirate vessel and the prisoners were being dragged aboard with blows and kicks.

Helpless rage seized Giorgios. If he'd had a turma of cavalry, and if he'd been half an hour earlier, not one of the pirates would have left the beach alive, but there are no "ifs" in life. If he hadn't been determined to join the army, Justus might have agreed to Justina marrying before she was eighteen. If he'd been there he might have saved her. There were no "ifs", only mistakes.

He rode down the hill to the beach and moved among the bodies. It struck him as odd, but there were no pirates among the dead. The slain villagers were mostly old or middle-aged men, so the young had been taken as slaves. Something else was missing: there were no weapons on the beach, not a spear, not an axe. One or two of the dead grasped cudgels, a few, wooden staffs, but that was all.

There was a noise from some bushes. He rode over and dismounted. A boy of about ten years of age crouched by a grey-haired man. Giorgios dismounted and knelt beside him. The boy shrank back with fear. One glance at the man's wound told Giorgios that it was mortal. He reached for his waterskin. The man shook his head, "Not yet", he croaked in Greek. "Not yet. You are Roman?"

"Yes", replied Giorgios.

"Save my grandson." Giorgios nodded. The man gripped his arm, "He is no slave. He was born free."

"He will remain so", Giorgios replied.

"You swear?" Giorgios looked at the old man, and he felt a sudden impulse. "He will be my foster brother."

The man looked at him, searching his face, and, satisfied, said, "Now water." Giorgios held the water skin to the man's lips. He gulped, drank, shuddered and died. Giorgios continued to kneel beside the man – stunned, in spite of his military experience, by the suddenness of death.

He was brought out of shock by the howl of anguish from the boy whose face had crumpled in grief. He could think of nothing to say, but "Come!" The boy clung to the corpse. Giorgios placed his hand on his shoulder but the boy shrank away.

"Do you speak Greek?" The boy nodded. "What is your name?"

The boy looked at him, large-eyed.

"Pasicrates."

"Come, Pasicrates. We must leave here."

The boy stood up and looked at his grandfather. "Bury him."

"We will bury them all, but we must get help. Where is the nearest village?"

The boy pointed to a track which wound inland.

Giorgios mounted and, reaching down, swung the boy up onto the horse; he weighed almost nothing.

"Why did the men not fight?" Giorgios asked. The boy was silent.

"Why did they have no spears, no axes?"

"The soldiers. They came and took them away."

"Which soldiers? Why?" Giorgios was convinced that the boy had not understood him.

"The Edict said so."

"Edict? What Edict?"

"I don't know. Everyone talked about the Edict."

They rode on in silence until they came to the village; about a dozen cabins grouped among pasture and orchards. A little apart was a more substantial dwelling.

Giorgios presumed that it was the house of the landlord and rode up to it. A slave stepped out. "What d'you want", he asked in distinctly uncivil tones.

"Tell your master that Giorgios of Lydda wishes to speak to him."

They were invited in. Giorgios handed Assjadah to a groom and took Pasicrates with him. A grey-haired, coarse-featured man greeted them in Greek.

"I am Xenophon. What d'you want?"

"There has been a pirate raid. There are many dead. I want to hire some men from you to bury them; I'll pay, of course."

The man cocked his head and looked at him through one eye.

"And who are you to hire men to bury the dead?"

Giorgios was taken aback by the hostility in the man's tone. He decided that if he stated his rank the man would realize that he could commandeer labour without paying anything.

"I am a decurion in the Roman Army", he stated firmly, "and I require a burial party."

To his astonishment the man spat on the floor.

"Then you're responsible for the slaughter. Have they sent one man and an urchin to protect the entire coast?"

Giorgios was baffled; he had not the faintest idea what the man was talking about.

"I? Responsible?"

"You. Your lot. You confiscated our weapons last week."

"Confiscated your weapons? How? Why?"

"The Edict, you fool!"

"Edict? What Edict? What is going on?"

The man glared, "The Disarmament Edict! Issued by Diocletian, and the confiscation orders signed by that pig, Galerius."

Giorgios' head was swimming, he had immured himself on the estate for months, what had been happening?

"I know nothing of this! What Disarmament Edict? I've been out of active service for six months." The man looked at him, eyes hard with suspicion, and he spoke slowly and with deliberation.

"The Emperor has issued an edict forbidding arms to any below the rank of Eques. You're telling me you know nothing of it?"

Giorgios was dumbfounded, "Nothing", he said, "I've been out of touch with things, I told you so. But it's madness, how can men defend themselves without weapons?"

The man spat again, "The army or the police will protect everyone in future, or so the edict says. No one is permitted to protect themselves, their family or their community, not even against criminals."

Giorgios was slowly grasping the situation, "But why? Why should the Emperor disarm everyone?"

"You wouldn't ask that if you saw the latest tax demands", Xenophon replied bitterly. "After the last increase the tax-gatherers come with an armed escort. If the people had weapons they'd cut their throats; the Empire would explode in riot and revolution. Now only criminals have weapons, and criminals don't pay taxes."

Giorgios was silent. Pasicrates was gazing round-eyed with terror at the fierce face of Xenophon. At length Giorgios spoke.

"I don't understand all this, but I still need to bury the dead; will you hire me some labourers?"

Xenophon cocked his head again.

"Who's the boy?"

"The only survivor. I promised his dying grandfather I'd take care of him."

"Leave him here, I'm short of field hands, he'll soon learn the work."

Giorgios looked back at the man, "He is not a slave, and as I told you, I promised a dying man."

"Ha! And what happens when you're recalled to the army? Who'll look after him then? If you land him on your wife she'll think he's your bastard."

Giorgios fought down a desire to hit the man, "My mother will care for him."

Xenophon again closed one eye and weighed Giorgios up with the other.

"So, not married, eh? I've a daughter, sixteen, a plain, plump, motherly girl, too plain to get a husband, she'd look after the brat if she were your concubina. That would solve your problems. You can have her for the bride price."

"You'd sell your daughter?" Giorgios was almost spluttering.

The man glared back at him, "I'm not a pander!" he shouted, terrifying Pasicrates even more, "I want to see her settled in life. I want to see her protected by a strong man. Those pirates, they've raided before, and once they know about the edict they'll raid inland, and how can I protect my family and my people if we have no weapons?"

Giorgios was shocked, shocked that so misguided and misjudged an Imperial Edict should put a man in such a quandary.

"I'm sorry", he said, "I'm sure your daughter's a very good-natured girl and would be a mother to this boy and to her own children, but my religion doesn't permit me to have a concubina."

The man spat again, "Ha! A Christian! Well take my word for it, Galerius is going to get you lot, you'll soon be glad of a good pagan girl's skirts to hide behind."

Giorgios felt that they had wandered far enough from the subject.

"Will you hire me labourers or not?" he demanded.

The man, he had concluded, was plainly eccentric, asking first for the boy as a slave and then offering to sell his own daughter, but such people usually had money at the back of their minds. "I'll pay."

"How many men?"

"About twenty."

"In gold?"

Giorgios fished around in his pouch, fumbling through the silver denarii until his thumb and finger fixed upon a gold *as*. He held it up and Xenophon positively salivated as he reached for it.

Giorgios snatched it away.

"When the job's done", he said, "and I'll stay to watch it finished. and if you're thinking of any funny business", he touched the hilt of his sword, "Remember I'm the only man here with a blade and that I'm trained to use it."

Giorgios felt decidedly uneasy as they rode back to the villa. Had he made a rash promise? The child should remain with his people. Did he have any right to take him away to what was a far distant land?

"Have you a mother and father? he asked.

"Dead", came the reply in a choking monosyllable.

"Uncles? Cousins?"

"No. All dead."

"Would you like to live with me, my mother, sisters and brothers?"

The boy looked up at him uncomprehending, his eyes wide with fear. Giorgios did not press him further and there was silence until they rode through the gates of the villa.

Pasicrates stared about him in wonder and turned to Giorgios.

"Are you the Emperor?"

For the first time in six months Giorgios laughed, "Why no! What makes you think so?"

"This is such a great palace."

"Only a small one compared to the Emperor's, and his is covered in marble and gold."

Pasicrates said no more, and Giorgios handed him over to two maids to bathe and dress him in clean clothes. The boy pulled away in terror from the hot bath, struggling to break away, but cried with delight at the tepidarium and, flinging off his tattered tunic, leapt in, swimming strongly.

The maids returned with the boy, wrapped in a blanket.

"He refuses, Domine, to change into clean clothes and to let go of his old."

"They're all he has left of his life. He must keep them."

"But Domine, they stink of fish."

Giorgios drew the boy to him.

"Pasicrates, these kind women will wash your clothes and dry them, and they will mend and patch them and you will have them back in a bundle to keep forever. Do you understand?" Pasicrates nodded. "Now I want you to put on the clean clothes these good women have found for you, and then we shall have supper."

Pasicrates played with the food, without appetite, bewildered, choking on each mouthful. Giorgios was worried, but then he remembered Grananna with her stock of honey-cake and raisins. "Bring some honey-cake, raisins, apples", he ordered.

Slowly Pasicrates began to relax and, gaining confidence, reached for more. At last the platter was empty and Giorgios asked, "Do you want anything else."

"Can I have a fish please?"

Giorgios laughed for the second time in six months.

"As many as you can eat", he said.

CHAPTER FORTY-FIVE

Autumn was now advanced and Giorgios was puzzling over the problem of the return journey. With the Disarmament Edict being more and more rigorously enforced, soon the only ones carrying spears or sword would be pirates, brigands and common criminals.

The solution seemed to be to join a caravan. Pasicrates could not ride, so he would have to get a light carriage. They would both ride in it, which had the advantage of sparing Assjadah his weight for the entire journey.

"What will you do with the house?" the senior notary asked, a few days before the caravan's departure. "You can hardly sell it without an estate."

"The household slaves will be emancipated, and I will give the house along with the orchard, vineyard and paddock, in gift to Nicholas, the bishop here, on condition that he employs the freedmen and women and provides dowries for the maids if they should marry. Draw up the deed."

After several days the caravan reached a large mansio off the road but approached by a by-road which followed a rushing torrent. Giorgios was surprised at the size of the place, its stables, store-houses and accommodation. Conversation at the evening meal was dominated by a veteran centurion who appeared to be a permanent guest. He announced that his name was Rufio, centurion of the IX Hispana, a legion unjustly traduced, as he himself was unjustly traduced. Once he had been master here, under the patronage of his good friend the Count Galerius, whom he had served well. As a reward for faithful service Galerius had pensioned him off here in his old home. The wine bill, Giorgios thought, must be considerable. The patron was plainly bored by an oft-told tale and the Patrona bristled whenever Rufio mentioned that his bills were being paid by his generous patron, Galerius. Rufio however, amidst all this talk, did give one piece of useful information. The Count Galerius had built a new road from the mansio. It would take them to Antioch in time for the last sailings before winter. Giorgios had found Rufio's talk of the IXth Legion fascinating. The legion had disappeared from military history more completely than the XVII, XVIII, and XIX, lost in Germania by Varrus.

After the evening meal Giorgios saw a sleepy Pasicrates to bed and went in search of Rufio to satisfy his curiosity about the IX. The patrona informed him tartly that the old reprobate would be sitting in what had been the cabinet before he'd taken it over as his personal domain; and would, no doubt, be guzzling the best wine in the house as though he still owned the place.

Giorgios soon found the room. It was long and lit by a row of windows from which a hill top with several crosses could be seen. Rufio was sitting in a chair at the far end, a jug of wine and a cup on a low table before him. As Giorgios entered, the last of the evening light was slanting through the windows.

Rufio looked at him, rheumy eyes narrowing, then suddenly he started up, pointing with a shaking hand at Giorgios.

"Anastasius!" he rasped. His face, contorted with superstitious terror, turned purple. "Leave me! You're dead! I saw you dead, I killed you outside Caesarea."

Giorgios started back, horror and fury struggling for mastery. Suddenly Rufio clutched his chest, croaking with pain, and collapsed back into the chair. Giorgios hastened to him. The man was mumbling something unintelligible, then he was seized by a final spasm and fell forward, dead. Giorgios hastened in search of the Patron.

"No doubt about it, a stroke, and a big one to take him off that quick", the Patron opined. They were joined by the Patrona.

"Rufio is dead", the Patron told her. She spoke abruptly.

"About time, we've dined and wined him long enough."

"The last of the IXth Hispana", the Patron remarked, a touch of awe in his voice.

"Good riddance. I'm sick of hearing of it, night after night", and crossing over to the corpse with a business-like stride she wrenched a gold ring from a finger, unclasped a gold brooch from the tunic, and tugged a purse from the belt. She tipped out the contents of the purse onto the table, a heap of silver denarii.

"This will pay something toward what his 'good friend the Count Galerius', was always 'just about to pay'."

"What about the funeral?" her husband asked.

"What funeral?" demanded the wife. "We're not expected to pay for that are we? Drag him out onto the hillside and leave him for the jackals."

Giorgios had listened to all this with growing agitation. Here before him was the corpse of the man who had murdered his father, and had probably had a hand in the murder of Mansour too; and here was the Patrona consigning, with bitter words, the body to the jackals.

"He ought to be buried", he said at length.

The Patrona turned on him, "Well you bury him", she snapped.

Giorgios' brain was all confusion. *Inimicus* or *hostis*, which one was the dead man? He could not be hostis, the public enemy, for he had served Rome, had put his life on the line for her in many battles, had obeyed his superior officer, blindly perhaps, wrongly certainly, but obedience was a soldier's way of life. So then the man was inimicus, his personal enemy. The man who had terrorized his family was now a corpse, defenceless against malice, spite, vengeance, against being kicked and mutilated and flung out upon the hillside for the jackals. "Love your inimicus. Do good to those who hate you." The struggle was intense.

"Well?" snapped the patrona, interrupting his thoughts, "What are you going to do about it?"

Giorgios looked at her, and then at the Patron.

"I will need to borrow a spade", he said.

188

CHAPTER FORTY-SIX

There was an unexpected surprise awaiting Giorgios, a letter from Constantine. The latter now had the command of a turma of the Imperial Guard, a rank equivalent to the legionary centurion. He also sent the joyful news that he was betrothed to Minervina – his mother had arranged it. He had written to his father about the injustice done to Giorgios. Whether as a result of this or not, a few weeks later an Imperial dispatch arrived at the villa; Andrew was to succeed his father as Count of Lydda. It was signed by Diocletian. Andrew examined the *codicillus* of installation which accompanied the dispatch with unconcealed delight. This specified his title, the area under his authority, and a list of his personal staff, Giorgios being named as prefect. The cover bore Andrew's insignia as Count of Lydda, a picturesque map of his county beneath a golden Rose of Sharon.

"Well, this is one in the eye for Galerius", Andrew exclaimed.

Kira laid her hand upon her brother's arm, "Oh Andrew, I'm so pleased for you."

A Roman soldier's life did not consist entirely of fighting. It is probable that the greater part of his long service was spent peacefully. Giorgios was glad to throw himself into the work of praetorian prefect to his uncle, often taking his place in the weekly court. He was an imposing figure as he sat in the judgement seat wearing the toga with its purple stripes. At something over six-foot in height he stood like Saul among his brethren. With his fine Grecian features and red-gold hair curling about his ears, and the nape of his neck beneath the bronze capulet, he looked like a hero from the frescoes. His method of dispensing justice was different from that of Justus and certainly different to that of his ever more testy and impatient uncle.

"Why" he would ask an appellant whose complaint was clearly bogus, "have you lost more by being away from your business, than you can ever gain in compensation?" The man would bluff and bluster about it being the "principle of the thing."

"But you know in your heart that you are in the wrong", Giorgios would reply.

The man would feel the fathomless blue eyes searching him and would start to shuffle, "Perhaps I was mistaken."

"You know you were. Go away and attend to your business honestly, for if there is one thing certain, it is that it has need of your attention. But be warned, do not come back with more foolish accusations."

The man would suddenly realize that he had been granted mercy rather than justice, and would hasten away. Others waiting in the crowded court with similar ill-founded accusations would sidle out.

Pasicrates presented a problem, at least for Kira, though Giorgios saw no problem at all; and Martha and Katherine saw only a little brother to fuss over. Anastasius had legally adopted Lucius and Cyrennius, but Kira was firm that this could not be the case with Pasicrates.

"A bachelor cannot adopt a son", she told Giorgios, "it would create a most difficult situation, especially when you marry."

"But I shall never marry", Giorgios would object.

"That's for the future to decide. Even if you wanted to marry you could not, no woman could accept that an adopted son would take precedence over her own children and inherit before them."

Giorgios had to admit the force of this argument while still protesting that it did not apply to him, since he would be faithful to the memory of Justina, forever.

"A woman, a widow, can't legally adopt a son", Kira pointed out, "but there is nothing to stop her fostering a child. I will foster Pasicrates, and he will grow up as one of the family. You must make provision for him in your will, since he will have no rights of inheritance."

Giorgios was happy with this. He was keeping his promise to a dying man and, legally at least, not taking the child from his own people.

Philip, although his school tasks were now completed, had become a fixture at the villa. He would wander up to Justus' library to spend the day in reading and study, and wander back to the villa for the evening meal. He was, after all, a poor scholar and philosopher, and the rich had a duty to support poor scholars and philosophers. In an abundant land and amidst an hospitable people no one questioned this assumption. He was quite happy to take up the task of teaching Pasicrates to read and write, Greek first and then Latin. The boy was not quick to learn, but he obediently plodded through his lessons. Giorgios taught him to ride, presenting him with a pony of his own when he had mastered the art.

As for Pasicrates himself, he lived in a world of wonder to which he could only slowly adapt. During this long period he would suffer spasms of homesickness. At these times he would scarcely eat and spend nights in disturbed sleep. This troubled Giorgios. Teaching the child, seeing him solve problems, learn new skills, enlarge his vocabulary, express new thoughts, brought the teacher's rewards to him. The child filled a place in his heart without invading the empty space left by Justina. He hit upon the idea of taking Pasicrates to Joppa and the sea. Joyfully, Pasicrates would run across the beach, search the shore line, dive into the waves and return hungry, refreshed and reassured.

"When did your mother and father die?" Giorgios felt it safe to ask him one day.

"Before the pirates came."

"How long before? A long time?"

Pasicrates screwed up his face in concentrated thought and at last said "I do not know."

Perplexed, Giorgios asked, "How did they die, if not the pirates?"

Pasicrates answered that promptly, "The winter fever, many died."

So that was it! The child's parents had died at the same time as Justina, and of the same cause. He looked out across the sea, wine-dark, stretching forever. Where did the sickness come from? How did it pass from one person to another? Justina and her father had eaten well, slept warm, bathed daily, always had clean clothing, yet they died the same as the boy's parents who had lived frugally. Why did some recover and others not? The physicians' medicines seemed to make no difference. After the same medicine some died and some lived. Could it be, as the Alexandrian physicians maintained against the Athenians, that sickness struck those whose minds were troubled, and they died because they had no will to live? The tormenting thought came to him of Justina pining during his long absence, being stricken because of him. But then, what of Justus?

Giorgios turned abruptly to Pasicrates, "We will ride home now"; and, seeing that he wished to be silent, the boy said nothing. As they rode toward the villa, Giorgios recollected that he was a rich man and came to a decision.

"I will build a hospital", he thought, "A place where there is great quiet and tranquillity, and the sound of water. It has soothed me and it soothes Pasicrates."

*   *   *

Lucius had found his vocation: he would practise law. That made it imperative that he should serve a year with the legions as a junior tribune; no man who had not done so could get his foot on the first rung of the legal ladder. After that his rise depended either upon his ability to win cases, or his means to bribe magistrates. Presented with this argument, Claudia withdrew her opposition to her sons entering the army.

"After all", she said to Kira, "he wouldn't be Mansour's son if he didn't want to be a lawyer!"

Giorgios and Pasicrates arrived home to be met by the glad news that Andrew's efforts to get Lucius an appointment as a junior tribune in the Xth Legion had been successful, and he was to leave for Caesarea the next morning.

"And what do you want to be, Cyrennius?" Giorgios asked. Cyrennius looked at him diffidently. "Come on! You must have some idea by now?"

"A Physician", Cyrennius said at length.

"A Physician? That indeed you shall be!"

*   *   *

The valley was formed by a fold of the Galilean hills. The slopes were green and dotted with clumps of cedar and wild olive. A torrent, fed by the winter rains and melting snows of the mountains, cascaded down the centre of the valley. Giorgios and Cyrennius sat their horses at the top, and looked down.

"About there", Giorgios said, pointing to where the valley widened out, briefly, to form a basin. "It will be a long, low building, with plenty of windows overlooking the river. The only sound will be cascading water, all else will be silent and tranquil."

"How long will it take?" asked Cyrennius. "There's no road here for carting the timber and stone, only a track."

"One reason why I chose it", Giorgios replied. "But it will be finished by the time you've finished at Alexandria. You have three or four years of hard work ahead of you."

191

Cyrennius' eyes glowed at the prospect. The medical school at the University of Alexandria was famous throughout the Empire and beyond. It drew its tutors from as far afield as India, whose artists led the field in anatomical drawing. Cyrennius was to go there to study medicine and, qualified, return to supervise the hospital Giorgios intended to build.

"What is the name of the valley?" Cyrennius asked, curious.

"El Kudr", Giorgios replied.

A hundred years later a convent, dedicated to Agios Giorgios, was added to the hospice, and for more than fifteen hundred years Christians, Muslims and Jews were to bring the mentally ill there for healing.

CHAPTER FORTY-SEVEN

It was the year A.D. 292 and Giorgios was twenty-two years old. Imperceptibly, the centre of gravity in the villa had shifted to the younger generation. Lucius, having completed his year as a junior tribune was home again. Cyrennius had left for Alexandria, Abba Theodore reminding him that he would be following in the footsteps of Luke, Paul's "Dear and beloved physician", and author of a gospel and the "Acts". Giorgios was in the cabinet working on the Imperial dispatches with Lucius when Kira came into the room in a state of great agitation.

"Is it true?" she asked, "Has Diocletian raised Galerius to the purple with the rank of Caesar?"

Giorgios tried to calm his mother.

"Yes, but it means that Galerius will move to the Danube frontier, permanently, out of our way."

"When?" asked Kira, "When is it to happen?"

Giorgios picked up the scroll of the Imperial Edict.

"On the 1st March next year to be exact. On that day Diocletian in Nicomedia will formally adopt Galerius as his son and raise him to the rank of Caesar, and shortly afterwards Galerius will marry Diocletian's daughter, Valeria."

Kira wrung her hands, "He will murder us."

Giorgios placed his hands upon her shoulders.

"I think not. On the same day and at the same hour, Maximian in Rome will adopt his son-in-law, Julius Constantius Chlorus, and raise him to the rank of Caesar. When the time comes for Diocletian and Maximian to abdicate, as they intend, the two Filii Augusti will succeed them. I think we're very much small fry now in Galerius' calculations."

Kira left, still far from reassured, Andrew passing her as he came in.

"Your mother seems agitated."

"She has heard of Galerius' elevation."

Andrew pursed his lips.

"We must certainly keep our heads down and not look for trouble. What are the details?"

Giorgios picked up another scroll.

"The Empire is to be divided into four. In the East, Galerius will govern Greece and everything between the Adriatic and the Danube. In the West, Constantius will govern Britannia, Gaul and Hispania."

Andrew grunted, "Too much government". He went moodily over to the maps, tracing borders with his finger-tip. "Who is to pay for it?"

"There's more", Lucius said, "The Provinces are to be reorganized."

Andrew became alert and turned to him abruptly, "Amalgamated?"

"Not quite. Some provinces will be divided, but in reality all the old provinces will be nothing more than provincettes with a civilian governor, grouped together in twelve dioceses, each governed by a Vicar, responsible to one of four Praetorian prefects."

Andrew looked decidedly sour at this news, no doubt because he had begun to entertain thoughts of getting the governorship of Lebanon in addition to his military office of count.

"What do you think of it?" he asked Giorgios.

"The same as you, Uncle", Giorgios answered promptly, "Too much government, two new tiers in fact. The governors will not be responsible directly to the Emperor, but to the vicars, and they in turn to the Prefects, and they to one of the four Augusti."

Andrew was silent while he chewed this over.

"Diocletian's genius was organization. He was outstanding when it came to commissariat, but the trouble with that type of man is that he begins to think that every problem can be solved by more organization, and paper organization at that! Diocletian thinks he has decentralized government with this new hierarchy; in fact, he's centralized it more. Soon no one will take an initiative or make a decision; they'll kick every problem upstairs."

"His army scheme's worked well", Lucius pointed out.

"Ah!" said Giorgios, "But there he really did simplify things by taking military authority off the governors and making the dukes and counts directly responsible to the two Imperial Marshals."

Andrew was still gloomy.

"We've had a tax hike to pay for the new field army, but it will be small compared with what will be needed for two more palaces and all the hangers-on and parasites that go with them. There's going to be trouble!"

*   *   *

Trouble did come, later that year, though it seemed to have nothing to do with taxation. The new Persian king, Bahram III, was not pro-Roman, but he preferred peace to war and negotiation to fighting. Skilful diplomacy might have brought a permanent settlement to the long-standing problem of the eastern frontier.

Diocletian, increasingly under the influence of Galerius, ignored the peace overtures from Persepolis and this in turn encouraged the Persian "war party." Bahram was overthrown by Narses, the Persian Commander-in-chief.

The news from the West, that Constantius Chlorus had, after long and careful preparation, moved against Carausius, had retaken Gesoriacum and all the Gallic coast and had started preparations to invade Britannia, did much to take minds off the Persian situation. The news that Carausius, by now looked upon as Rome's major enemy, had been assassinated by Allectus, his Praetorian Prefect, increased optimism. Carausius, with his undoubted leadership qualities and his mastery of sea warfare, was one thing; Allectus was a shabby little adventurer who would soon alienate both the Roman cities and the native kings. In these circumstances the first intelligence reports that Narses was massing troops on the border of Rome's client kingdom Armenia came as a shock.

Diocletian was galvanized into action by the news, and the action he enjoyed most – mobilizing and commissioning an army. The Persian move also gave him the opportunity to test his new field army. Reserve officers were summoned to Nicomedia.

Giorgios and Lucius took a ship to Antioch, hoping for another to Nicomedia, whilst Andrew, the Imperial Commission in his hand, mobilized a force of numeri for the defence of Lydda and Galilee. Pasicrates, now eleven, begged to accompany Giorgios and Lucius.

"I can read and write now, I could be your scribe", he urged.

Giorgios laughed, "Well, perhaps one day you will be, but for now you can stay at home and protect your mother and sisters. Perhaps Uncle Andrew will let you ride with the numeri if there's no danger of fighting."

Upon arrival at Nicomedia there were three welcome surprises. First they were greeted by Constantine wearing the gilded armour and red plumes of a Tribune of the Imperial Guard.

"I command my own ala now", he told them proudly, "and not just because I'm the son of Constantius. Diocletian himself assured me that I had earned it."

The second surprise was that promotion awaited Giorgios; he too was promoted to Tribune and given command of an ala of light cavalry. He felt, in his own mind, that he could not have merited this. Was Diocletian compensating him for his father's services, for his father's murder even? Had Constantine anything to do with it, using his father's influence?

The third surprise went some way to explaining the first two. Galerius was not in Nicomedia, he had moved to his new capital at Thessalonica from which he governed Illyricum, his quarter of the Empire.

"So you see", Constantine assured Giorgios, "with Galerius no longer around to whisper against you, Diocletian has recognized your merit, which was plain to everyone at the cavalry school and on the Danube."

Diocletian moved his army along the coast of the Euxine toward Armenia. He made a lot of noise about it and Narses got the message. Rome would fight for Armenia if it had to. Narses withdrew from the Armenian frontier, but Diocletian was wary. He would take the field army back to Nicomedia, but the auxiliaries would stay in the East, reinforcing the legions on the Tigris-Euphrates frontier. Giorgios and Constantine were among the commanders ordered to Syria, but Lucius was returning to Lydda, on the reserve.

CHAPTER FORTY-EIGHT

The desert was hot, dusty, and boring. It was not in fact "true" desert, but a semi-arid region, with human habitation wherever wells might be sunk. The little clusters of houses were surrounded by date palms and fig and olive trees, while goats, the desert makers, survived on scrub and tough grass. To the east were the Roman frontier forts and the fertile crescent; to the west, the fertile coastal plain and the cities.

The ala pitched their tents and established their horse lines to the great dismay of a nearby hamlet. The headman came, fearfully, to protest.

"Will you drink our wells dry? There is no grazing for so many horses."

Giorgios listened sympathetically. This was something far-away government did not consider, or if it did, dismissed it out of hand.

"As for the grazing, you have no need to fear; our horses are fed on oats brought in from Antioch. As for the water, I will do all I can to have our supplies brought in, and we will only use your water in a dire necessity."

The headman went away reassured.

Giorgios rode over to the hamlet the following morning. It consisted of a circle of houses, the doorways and windows facing inward, the outer walls blank. The houses were like inverted plant pots, wider at the bottom and sloping upward to a flat roof, the wattle and daub covered over with a layer of clay and lime-washed. The whole so practical and economic, Giorgios thought to himself. Entering the headman's house he was surprised to find how cool it was. The only furniture was a long low table, evidently a matter of pride to the headman, and rugs and cushions. Cooking and eating were outdoors for most of the year.

The generosity of his hosts posed a problem for Giorgios. Figs, olives, barley bread and goats' cheese, together with a thin poor wine were spread out; he ate and drank out of courtesy, conscious that these people could ill afford such hospitality. The slaves at home lived better than these free cultivators, and he wondered if his freeing of his own slaves in Cappadocia might doom them to a similar frugality; had it been a kindness after all? Total poverty, the degrading poverty of indigence, was rare in the Empire, but frugality such as this was common. The alternative was to drift into the cities and join a rootless proletariat, dependent upon the state doles of corn and wine. Many, too many, Giorgios knew, were doing just that. A vision rose before him of palaces of dressed stone, tessellated marble floors, colonnades and shaded gardens, pools and fountains, hot baths and heated rooms. Surely if the rich had a little less, the frugal might have a little more?

"My men are well disciplined", he reassured the headman, "there will be no thieving. They will pay for what they want."

"Of what use is money to us?" the headman asked, spreading his hands.

Giorgios was nonplussed. Rather lamely, he said, "They will pay in kind. If they want fruit or cheese they must pay for it from their corn or wine ration. I will so order it."

There were ten such hamlets in Giorgios' sector of the front. Constantine held the sector to the north of him with an ala of light cavalry, whilst to the south a tribune whom he had never met also commanded an ala. Their business was to watch the frontier, to meet and repel any Persian attack which broke through the static defence of the legions. Giorgios accordingly kept his patrols eastward away from the local population. In this he made a mistake.

The raiders came with the full moon, striking the hamlet farthest from the camp. A gully gave them a concealed approach to within a few hundred yards before they charged across open space with battle yells which sent the villagers fleeing. The raiders took their time emptying the storehouse of barley and rounding up the goats and chickens, which they slaughtered, carrying off the carcasses. There was hardly anything else worth looting.

Giorgios went to the stricken hamlet immediately the news reached him. He found the people in despair.

"We will starve", the headman told him. "We have nothing left."

"You will not starve", Giorgios assured him. "I will buy two goats from each village for you and I will get barley from Antioch."

Giorgios' pledge was not so easy to fulfil as to make. The other hamlets would not sell goats for money, but eventually agreed to barter them for barley. Neither the civil governor nor the military dux between whom the new administration divided authority would accept responsibility for replenishing the barley store.

"Their weapons were taken from them with the promise of military protection", Giorgios told the dux angrily. "The state has not protected them, so it must compensate them."

"What were you doing?" the dux demanded of him. "Why didn't your patrols intercept these raiders?"

"I accept that. I will buy the barley myself."

"It will cost you dear", the dux replied with a smirk; "Our intelligence reports show that Persia is paying the nomads to raid across the frontier. You would do better to change your tactics."

Giorgios reddened. It was a rebuke and one that he had earned.

*   *   *

The maps were spread out on a table and the turmae commanders gathered around Giorgios.

"We have ten settlements to protect. It is safe to assume that the nomads will not raid the same place twice, nor will they raid the two hamlets on either side of us. That leaves seven. We will station a turma in each, as hidden as possible among the trees. No tents, the troops will bivouac in their cloaks with their horses beside them." Giorgios spread his hand across the map. "I think we can reduce the odds a little. This village was attacked because a gully gave cover up to the last half mile. There are four other hamlets similarly situated", he jabbed his finger at each of them, "but this one", he pointed again, "is on a track which leads straight back to the Euphrates. That is the one which will be raided next, and at the next full moon."

The turmae commanders nodded eagerly in agreement.

"I will take two troopers from each turma to form a new turma, which I will command, and I will be there", he pointed again at the map, "to take responsibility for my tactics."

What was to puzzle Giorgios over the next few days was the press of volunteers to join his new turma.

"You're taking all the best men", his commanders said to him, but without any hint of complaint or grumbling.

When Giorgios led the wagon of barley and the little flock of goats into the stricken hamlet, cries of gratitude filled the air. The headman greeted him in the centre of the village.

"Hope of the hopeless!" he cried theatrically, "Aid of the helpless! Succour of those in distress", and prostrated himself.

"Get up! Get up!" Giorgios cried, "Roman citizens do not grovel. Listen to me! All of you! The Imperial Edict denies you weapons, and we must obey the law; but there is no law against digging a ditch around your village and filling the bottom with sharp stones so that horses cannot get a footing, and there is no law against building a beacon fire and keeping watch throughout the night." He dismounted and went across to the headman. "Take me to your house and I will tell you what you must do."

*   *   *

The raiders emerged from the gulley and fanned out across the level ground. They began their war yell as they whipped their horses to the gallop. The first of them had reached the ditch around the hamlet and pulled up, milling about in confusion, when the trumpets sounded and a flying wedge of Roman cavalry emerged from the trees. Everything happened quickly after that. There was a crash of horses, a flashing of swords, clouds of dust obscuring everything and, after five minutes of blind turmoil, the raiders were galloping away.

Giorgios reined in Assjadah and, as the dust settled, looked about him. None of his men was down, but neither were any of the raiders.

"Always the same, Sir, in a cavalry skirmish."

He turned, a battle-scarred trooper was grinning lopsidedly at him. Giorgios checked the impulse to rebuke the man for insolence; "You been in many?"

"Why 'undreds, Sir. Most of the cuts and bruises are on arms and thighs. I was keepin' close to you, watchin' y'r back, like. You gave more swipes wi' the flat of th' sword than wi' th' edge. Most do in a skirmish, it all 'appens so quick like."

Giorgios liked the man, even though he could see at a glance that he was a rascal.

"What is your name, trooper?"

The man answered without a blink, "Scipio, Sir."

Giorgios laughed, "Not Scipio Africanus by any chance?"

"Why no, Sir, not even a great, great, great-nephew four times removed, otherwise I'd be at least a centurion."

"It wouldn't stop you being a rogue; but rogue or not, you are now standard-bearer of my turma."

CHAPTER FORTY-NINE

"Pharmacos" – the healer – his men had named him, because he had himself tended the wounded, pouring wine into their cuts and gashes. It had caused great amusement, at least to those who had no wounds, to hear tough men who had no more than winced at the slash itself, yell aloud as the cleansing wine stung them. After the wine he poured oil into the wounds and sent the men to the care of the ala surgeon.

The raiders came again several times. Giorgios did not always anticipate them, but where he did not, the signal fire would blaze up and the turma he had stationed in the hamlet would hold the field until reinforcements arrived.

"My best cavalry commander", the Dux wrote to the Magister Equium "and young Constantine learns from him."

The Nomads were losing their taste for raiding, and attacks came less frequently until, after a year, they ceased. The ala remained on service for a further six months before it was withdrawn. Giorgios, transferred to the reserve, returned to Lydda. To Scipio he gave a golden *as*.

"On condition that you spend it on wine", he joked.

In court, Giorgios found his Uncle Andrew as testy as ever; and at home, still complaining bitterly of tax increases. Lucius had become a pupil to a quaestor in Lydda. Katherine was awaiting Giorgios' consent to her betrothal to a distant cousin. Cyrennius had left for Alexandria, and Martha was disinclined to marry.

"Be careful what you agree to in dowries", Uncle Andrew advised. "If you're wise you'll check everything with me first. Just because they're cousins doesn't mean that they are either friends or honest."

Abba Theodore had been promoted to be a bishop in Jerusalem. Pasicrates, now thirteen, black-haired, dark-eyed and olive-skinned, still seemed small and slight for his age.

"Does he lose his appetite still?" Giorgios asked his mother. "He seems so thin."

"He eats well", Kira assured him. "Perhaps he's just naturally small in stature. Philip says he's of the Ancient People, the Shore Folk, who were here before us, before the Helenes even; they were small."

"How does Philip know that?" Giorgios demanded.

"I don't know, but he seems very sure. All these philosophers do."

"Well, whatever! Pasicrates and I will go riding tomorrow, and maybe down to the sea."

Pasicrates had been overjoyed at Giorgios' return. He had adapted to his new life and knew that he had Giorgios to thank for it. Giorgios was both father and big brother, and Pasicrates was eager for the promised ride, eager for the stories of skirmishes and fights, eager to hear of Giorgios' victories and the enemy's routs. The weeks slipped by into months and the Saturnalia came again with its poignant memories for Giorgios and its sorrow for what might have been, and the year turned to spring, and it was then that Narses struck.

The Persian army swept, without resistance, into Armenia. Tiridates, the Roman client king, barely escaped to seek refuge in Nicomedia. Narses' declared policy was to make the Mediterranean coast, as it had once been, the frontier of the Persian Empire; but fortunately for Rome, he was not able to move immediately against Antioch. Diocletian entrusted Galerius with meeting the Persian attack when it came. Giorgios expected his recall to Antioch every day, but when his commission came it was not a recall to the Persian frontier, but a transfer to the West to serve under Constantius Chlorus.

"It's easy to see", Constantine wrote to him, "who is behind this. Galerius wants to split a partnership which might outshine his nephew Daia who, incidentally, grows more brutal every day."

He added a footnote: "My mother decided that I ought to be married before going off on the Persian campaign, so here I am, a happily married man." Giorgios was astonished by this casual mention of what he would have thought the most important news; but, he reflected, Constantine was a very private person.

Constantine was not entirely right. His father had requested that he be posted to Gaul. Galerius had no intention of letting a potential hostage slip through his fingers. Seeing the opportunity of breaking a growing partnership which might pose a danger to his ambitions, Galerius had replied that Constantine was unenthusiastic about joining his father, and that instead he would send Giorgios Theognosta. Constantius, reading the letter, gathered from it, as he was intended to, that his son had refused to serve under him, and so accepted Giorgios in his place.

The voyage from Joppa to Arles took three weeks, and was not one that Giorgios wished to subject Assjadah to, so he left her behind in the devoted care of Pasicrates. From Arles he began the long journey to Trier where he fell in with Prince Crocus and his Gallic cavalry on their way to Gesoriacum.

*   *   *

Standing in the hall of the basilica with the other Tribunes, Giorgios waited expectantly for the appearance of the man who was a living legend, the heir of Claudius Gothicus. He was not disappointed. Constantius' entrance, heralded by trumpets and preceded by his staff and the legates of three legions, was dramatic. He was tall with the classic Roman nose. A cloak of purple silk draped his gilded armour. He wore a golden diadem, studded with pearls. A forest of hands shot up with the cry, "Hail Constantius! Hail Caesar!"

Constantius began to speak. His voice was strong, his diction perfect, his Latin precise. The time had come, he told them, for the liberation of Britannia from a tyrant, and its reconciliation with Rome. Intelligence reports, he went on, indicated that both the Britanni and the Britons would welcome them. The British legions would not fight for Allectus, so this was to be no civil war, but a war of liberation against the mercenary rabble Allectus had imported. These barbarians were terrorizing the population. They were looting, murdering and raping. The months of waiting, he assured them, were now over. They had nothing to do but prepare themselves and their commands for the coming battle and pray to their gods for a quiet sea. He finished, and every man present felt enthused, impatient to be boarding the transports; and again there was a great shout of acclamation as a hundred hands were held high.

Giorgios sought out Crocus, "What did Caesar mean when he spoke of the 'Britanni', and the 'Britons'? Are there two nations in Britannia?"

"There's no hard and fast dividing line", Crocus told him. "The Britanni are the citizens of the Roman towns and villas, Roman colonists, retired legionaries, mainly Saxons and Franks. There are also the Burgundians and Vandals that Probus planted, and of course the native Britons, Romanized and Latin-speaking. Rome's interest is their interest. The 'Britons' are chiefly in the North and West, the 'People of the soil', who have kept their own territories and their own tongue and their own ways. Rome recognizes their kings, gives them Roman titles, and protects them from the Barbarians beyond the seas or beyond the great wall, to whom in fact they're related by blood and tongue."

Giorgios was turning this information over in his mind when he received a summons to the presence of Caesar. Constantius was studying maps and charts with his Praetorian Prefect, Asclepodotus. He looked up as Giorgios entered.

"You know my son?"

"Yes, Augustus."

"Why did he refuse to join me here?" Giorgios started.

"He did not, Augustus. He did not know you had requested it."

Constantius studied Giorgios' face for so long that he began to feel uncomfortable.

"I see. Well, no matter, now you are here. I have good reports of you." Giorgios did not know if he was expected to say anything, so he remained silent. "It seems", Constantius went on, "that you are something of a persuader rather than an enforcer. A diplomat in fact. I have you to thank for saving my son from being expelled from the cavalry school."

Giorgios reddened, "There was no complaint made, Augustus. I didn't do anything."

"Ah, but you did. You buttered up Maxentius and Daia, and that's what I need now, a peace-maker. Come here and look at these maps."

Giorgios crossed over and Constantius moved his finger across South-East Britannia.

"When we land here and defeat Allectus, as we will, his rule will fail throughout the country before Roman government can be re-established. There's likely to be chaos and bloodshed. The Picts, sensing this, will swarm over the wall. The Scotti and the Atta Cotti", he pointed to Ireland, "will pillage the west coast."

Giorgios nodded. He wondered what was coming and what he was expected to do about it. "I want you to sail tomorrow with a turma of cavalry from Prince Crocus' command, and a horse transport, down here." His finger traced a route down the Fretum Gallicum and around Cornwall into the Bristol Channel. "Carausius was a good strategist. He built a fortified port here – the Britons call it Caerdydd – to defend the South-West from the Atta Cotti, and manned it with a new kind of soldier – marines, trained to fight on both land and sea. I want you to go there and obtain not the surrender, but the reconciliation of that garrison. Assure them that if they loyally continue their duties, Rome will forgive."

Giorgios had not the faintest idea as to how he could do that, but any excuse would be lame, and to refuse impossible.

Constantius was searching his face again, a slight smile on his own. His finger moved over the map. "This is Segontium, an outpost of the XXth. There ought to be a cohort there. Assure them there will be no inquisition if they renew their loyalty to Rome." His finger moved on to Deva, "The headquarters of the XXth, I need them back on our side." The finger went on till it came to Porta Sisuntorium. "This is the second of Carausius' fortified ports, for defence against the Scotti. We must have the garrison back to their duties. From there you will cross the mountains – there is a good road – and meet me at Eboracum. If I'm not there, it means I'm dead, so get back across the hills and sail for Gaul. Any questions?"

"Will a turma of cavalry be sufficient, Augustus?"

"A legion would not be sufficient if you were going to fight your way to Eboracum; but I'm not sending you to fight, I'm sending you to persuade. Do not get involved in any fighting; if you meet with hostility, get out quick and go on to your next port of call. Anything else?"

"No, Augustus."

"Good! You have not asked how you, a tribune, may treat with legates."

"It had not occurred to me, Augustus."

"No! It wouldn't have done. Well I'm instating you as a count of the Empire, as your father was. Your credentials will be ready for you and your men and horses will be embarked tomorrow. You will sail on the afternoon tide. Now get some sleep."

Giorgios, assuming that the interview was ended, saluted, about-turned and began to march away. Constantius called him back.

"When you meet my son again, tell him that there are orders no one may disobey. Orders given by the Emperor for the sake of the Empire. Tell him I loved his mother, and still do."

For a brief moment Caesar's eyes pleaded, and then he turned away.

CHAPTER FIFTY

Giorgios was intrigued by the Saxon pilot and rowing-master. They were gigantic men with red beards and yellow hair, braided into ropes on either side of the head. They spoke dog Latin to the captain of the vessel and to him, but conversed together in a guttural, barbarous tongue. The rowing-master, beating the stroke, would break out into a rhythmic chant which Giorgios took to be some kind of poem. Both wore trousers, bound with cross gartering, and (Giorgios could not repress a shudder of Roman distaste) sheepskin jerkins. He concluded that they were not frequent bathers. The oarsmen were not slaves or criminals but trained sailors who could handle both oars and sail.

The vessel sped down the Channel, accompanied by its horse transport, hugging the Gallic coast. Watching the crew about their work, Giorgios wondered why naval service was considered inferior to army service; perhaps the stigma of galley slavery overshadowed it. They crossed to the British coast before the Channel merged with the dread Oceanus, where a ship, caught in its currents, would be carried remorselessly to the edge of the world and plunged into everlasting night, or so the pilot said.

The earth, Giorgios explained to him, was round – all the philosophers were agreed. The man looked at him pityingly, scornfully pointing to the sea, flat and level to the horizon.

Rounding Land's End, they kept close to the shore until the pilot judged the tides right to make a run for the opposite coast. Again, they sailed close in to the land, keeping watch for Carausius' naval station, for the map was vague as to its location. Giorgios was studying the coast as they sailed past.

"How green it is", he said to the pilot, "one of the most pleasant lands I've seen."

The pilot snorted, "It's a fat land, full of cattle and horses and rivers full of salmon, and fields of grain and grapes."

The conversation was interrupted by a shout from the shore. A man had appeared from the sand hills, waving a flag. The pilot called for him to come across and he launched a small oval boat of wickerwork and skins which he paddled with great skill. He came aboard, asking to see the commander. Giorgios was intrigued. The man was small and wiry and he seemed unable to keep still. He had black hair and black, gleaming eyes. His arms and legs were disproportionately long and he seemed to grovel on the deck. He spoke Latin with an odd sing-song accent which made him appear even more obsequious. Giorgios, however detached he tried to be, regarded him with distaste.

"I am Annwyn, a Roman scout."

"A spy", Giorgios corrected briefly.

"I prefer 'scout', noble Count."

"And what have you to tell me, scout?"

The man glanced around him furtively, "For your ears only, Noble Count."

Impatiently, Giorgios led the way to the rear of the vessel; he doubted if the man knew anything of importance.

"Now, what have you to tell me?"

"You have not heard? You do not know? The news has passed you by?"

"Let us say that I do not know", Giorgios replied, "and that the news has indeed passed me by. What information have you?"

The man scratched his head and rolled his eyes.

"My anxieties! My debts! It is difficult to collect my thoughts."

Giorgios took a purse of denarii from his cloak and passed it to the man who weighed it in his hand.

"Your news?"

"Allectus is dead. Slain by the mighty Caesar who has won a great victory."

Giorgios looked at him unbelievingly.

"You swear this?"

"Yes, Noble Count, it is the truth, these are the facts."

"What are the details?"

The man cringed, his hand went back to his head to scratch again.

"My wife and children starve. It is a long time since Rome paid me my salary."

Giorgios took another purse from his cloak.

"The great Caesar sent Asclepodotus across the sea with half the fleet, straight for the coast. Allectus left Londinium to meet him. then the Caesar took the other half of his fleet and landed near Londinium. He marched after Allectus who was caught in the trap; his barbarians are fleeing in all directions, burning and looting as they go."

Giorgios noted that the man knew the name of Constantius' Praetorian Prefect, but then, conmen knew things like that.

"How do you know all this?"

The man gave him a sidelong glance, "I know that you are now a noble count."

"Granted! But you are sharp enough to have noted my insignia."

The man spread his hands, "I am a scout, a spy. It's my business to know. Let us say the birds tell us."

"The magpies, you mean! Will you sail with us or trust your boat to the waves?"

The man laughed, "Scouts are heard and not seen; I will leave you here."

On an impulse, Giorgios took another purse from his cloak and handed it to the man. Annwyn looked at it and then looked at Giorgios; a long, appraising look. He spoke without any trace of obsequiousness.

"Such a man as you does not know what it is to receive without begging, to be given without wheedling. I will tell you this; you are but a few miles from the fortress, 'Caerdydd' in our tongue. Gerontius, Legate of the II Augusta, is already there; he has marched a cohort from Isca Silurum, which we call 'Caerleon,' to take possession in the name of Rome. With him is Ambrosius Aurelius, a wealthy Roman noble. He owns many villas in Western Britannia, and in Italy, Gaul and Armorica. He is the most powerful magnate in the West. Do not be haughty with these two as if you came to judge them. Let them know that you come to accept them as allies against the rebels. There are also three kings of the Britons in Aurelius' villa; treat them with respect."

Giorgios could not but be impressed by the transformation of the man.

"Thank you, Annwyn", he said. "Permit me to see you to your boat."

*   *   *

The sail had been lowered. They approached the quay under the steady sweep of oars. Giorgios had dressed carefully, his armour polished and his count's insignia on his cloak. He would be accompanied by five attendants: the captain of the galley, the turma decurion, the standard-bearer and two troopers; a sufficient number for dignity but not so many as to be threatening. He studied the reception party as he disembarked, recalling Annwyn's advice. There was Gerontius, Legate of the II Augusta, of British extraction, surrounded by his staff officers.

Beside him was another man, his expression aloof. His features, delicate and refined, indicated generations of good breeding. Spanish by blood, Giorgios decided. He was sumptuously dressed in white samite, a heavy gold chain hung about his neck, gold rings adorned his fingers. A massive gold clasp held his white silk cloak which was embroidered in gold thread from knee to shoulder with a sinuous dragon. There were at least a dozen slaves in attendance upon him. Who could this man be who so boldly displayed the emblem of Emperors? It must be the Aurelius of whom Annwyn had spoken, and he must either be, or claim to be, of the Aurelian *gens*.

Giorgios strode across the quay and saluted, first the Legate and then Aurelius, handing his credentials to the former.

"I come in the name of Julius Flavius Valerius Constantius Caesar, to welcome you back into the comity of Rome."

The legate gave a tight smile.

"There is to be no inquisition?"

"There is to be no inquisition. The Caesar requires only that you maintain the Roman Order and defend the province against the Atta Cotti."

The Legate gave another tight smile. "As you see", his hand swept the empty quay, "our naval squadron is already on patrol. But you say 'Province'; is there to be no division of Britannia into several provinces as has happened throughout the Empire?"

Giorgios knew he must tread carefully. Constantius intended to constitute Britannia as a new diocese of five civil provinces; Britannia Prima, Britannia Secunda, Britannia Flavia, Britannia Maxima and Valentia, with a vicar resident in Londinium. There would be a Dux commanding the northern defences and a Count, the southern. Giorgios did not think that the legions would welcome that!

"The noble legate", he said, measuring his words, "will forgive me, but I have no remit in the matter of a political settlement. My commission is concerned purely with a military settlement."

The legate appeared to dismiss the matter from his mind.

"Your troops must be weary of the sea, and your sailors no doubt want to stretch their legs. Your horses must also long for green pastures. The noble Aurelius", he turned and bowed toward the magnate who up to now had remained silent, "offers them rest and entertainment, and he asks you to honour him as a guest in his villa."

Giorgios bowed to the magnate, but carefully addressed the legate; protocol required that he should not speak to the Patrician until the Patrician had spoken to him.

"Such hospitality will indeed be welcome, it has been a long voyage."

*   *   *

To cross the threshold of the Aurelian villa was, in this far-flung province of the Empire, to step back into the World of Rome. Three other guests were presented to Giorgios, with all the ceremony that Roman protocol demanded: Riothimus, king of the Dobunni; Ceretic, king of the Demetae; and Creoda, king of the Silures. Their goodwill was essential to Rome, and Giorgios saluted them with due deference to their rank. Always fascinated by human variety, Giorgios silently noted that they were tall, had auburn hair and high colour. They spoke good Latin, wore Roman attire and conformed to Roman etiquette. Their slaves however seemed to Giorgios to be outlandishly attired. They were wearing white linen smocks and trousers of woven, multi-coloured squares and rectangles. Most of them were of the same black-haired, swarthy type as Annwyn and prattled away together in a tongue utterly strange to Giorgios.

Creoda was speaking to him, to his surprise, in Greek.

"You are here to assure yourself of our acceptance of the new Caesar?"

Aurelius had made no mention of his mission when the kings had been presented to him, so Giorgios welcomed the opportunity to broach the subject. He weighed the situation carefully. Creoda was addressing him in Greek either to emphasise that he and his fellow princes were cultivated men, or to limit the audience of what he had to say; probably both motives were present. Giorgios replied in Greek.

"I bring greetings from Julius Flavius Valerius Constantius Caesar, and his welcome to you on your return to the comity of Rome after your enforced", he stressed the word, "separation."

"Be assured of our acceptance of the authority of Caesar Constantius", Creoda replied, "which we do as allies of Rome."

So, they were allies, not subjects, Giorgios noted, and he wondered if he would ever master the subtleties of this diplomatic game.

"The Caesar Constantius asks only that you uphold the Roman Law and maintain the defence of the West against the depredations of the Atta Cotti."

Riothimus pounced, "Then we are to understand that the Disarmament Edict will not apply in our territories?"

Giorgios groaned inwardly. Here was that idiotic Edict again. These three princes could, he knew from his briefing, muster ten thousand spears, enough to repel even the most determined Irish invasion; but now the Disarmament Edict ordered them to depend on the regular army for defence and protection.

"My understanding", Giorgios replied, "is that the decree does not include numeri mustered when necessary by the magistrates."

Riothimus merely smiled, "Every one of our freemen has his ash spear and his oaken shield on the wall of his cabin, ready for the hosting. Without weapons there can be no hosting."

The logic of this was undeniable.

"I will urge this upon Caesar Constantius as strongly as I can", Giorgios promised; but the princes had not finished with him yet.

"We have heard that the II Augusta is to be withdrawn from the West to defend the Saxon Shore."

The implication was clear. If the princes' numeri were disarmed and the II Augusta was withdrawn they would be defenceless. Why then be allies of Rome?

"I will stress to Caesar Constantius the folly of any such move", Giorgios assured them.

Riothimus struck again, "And the XXth?" he asked. "The XXth guards our northern flank against the Scotti."

Giorgios was learning the diplomatic game, "I cannot say anything of that", he replied, "until I have visited Deva and Segontium, and know the situation."

The call to the dining room led to a general drift in that direction. Riothimus placed his hand on Giorgios' arm.

"King Coel Hen of Rheged spoke highly of your father, although he met him but once in Gaul; but then Coel had the second sight. You have your father's qualities and you listened well to Annwyn."

Giorgios glanced at the man in surprise, but Riothimus' face was impassive.

The banquet was lavish by the standards to which Giorgios was accustomed. At Lydda the rule had been, except at the Augustales and the Saturnalia, plain food and watered wine. This had prepared him well for army life. Here a slave stood behind every guest to serve his food and pour his wine or *methglyn*, a potent variety of mead.

Now that news of Allectus' defeat was running ahead of him, Giorgios' mission was of increasing importance. He was determined to sail on tomorrow's tide, and so ate and drank sparingly.

"You sail tomorrow, Count?" Aurelius asked him.

"Yes, Domine", Giorgios replied.

"You must change your Saxon pilot for a British one who knows the sea between here and Deva. If you are agreeable I will send one of my own men with you, and a rowing-master."

"I would be very grateful for that."

"I will also give you letters of introduction to Lucius Artorius Castus, Legate of the VI Victrix at Eboracum. He is my brother-in-law, as is the legate Gerontius.

Unfortunately, Clemens Maximus, Legate of the XXth, is not at Deva. Though his family came over here with the IXth, they kept one foot in Hispania. He was at one of his estates there when Carausius rebelled, and he was unable to return; but Caius Maximus, his Praetorian Prefect has been loyal and has managed things well."

"They are related?" queried Giorgios.

"Cousins", Aurelius replied, "as they are also, some degrees removed, of myself."

CHAPTER FIFTY-ONE

The new pilot was one of the "Red" Britons, and the rowing master one of the "Black" Britons. The pilot was loquacious, the rowing master taciturn, merely giving his name – "Mervyn."

"My name is 'Geraint', the pilot told Giorgios, "that is the Brythonic form of 'Gerontius'."

"Are you related to the Legate?" Giorgios asked, curious.

"My eighth cousin."

"Do you all keep such a close tally?"

"Why yes. Is that not the sensible thing to do? The Brethon Law provides that if a man dies without children or nephews, his land is divided between his kin up to the ninth degree. It is the same in Hibernia where the Brethon Law was framed, and in Caledonia. It is well to know your relatives."

The boat was skimming the waves across a great bay; a headland lay behind, and rising dimly in the distance was another. The far shore was a panorama of mountains, mist and sunbeams.

"I wonder", said Giorgios, "that any of you have enough land to stand on if that is the case."

Geraint laughed, "Men are always dying, and land comes back to you when a cousin dies childless; or when you wed, a wife brings land with her."

Giorgios mulled this over, "I understand that the Britanni follow the German custom of the oldest son inheriting. Whilst you scatter your land they consolidate theirs and grow wealthier."

Geraint shrugged, "There will be no trouble between us while the legions keep the peace."

Giorgios laughed, "That's true, and the legions are here forever."

Geraint nodded, "But if the barbarians should sweep the land, we are the stronger, for every man has land to fight for. Who among the Britanni will fight for a brother's inheritance from which he is excluded?"

It became evident to Giorgios that the Britons looked upon the Britanni with a mild contempt – they had grown 'soft,' living in their cities and their heated villas; besides which, they were not poets.

"I heard their minstrelsy once; it was like listening to a frogs' chorus, not enough vowels in their words you see. Now our bards" – he stopped speaking abruptly and pointed to a high double peak with a deep saddle, which had appeared on the skyline: "'Cader Idris', the seat of kings."

Giorgios caught his breath at the sight. Golden sunlight bathed the summit and golden mists swirled about the upper slopes.

Giorgios was intrigued by the pilot's attitude toward the Old Romans. It seemed to be one of respectful familiarity, if there could be such a thing, indicated by their contraction of the Latin names into Brythonic forms. Ambrosius Aurelius became

"Lord Emrys", Caius Maximus, "Lord Kie", Clemens Maximus, "Lord Macsen", and Lucius Artorius Castus, "Lord Arthur".

"Do you address your eighth cousin as 'Geraint'?" Giorgios asked.

"Not to his face", Geraint replied. "But now we are rounding the headland, we must keep clear of the islands; the currents there are bad, very bad.

*   *   *

They came to the harbour of Segontium under oars, and Giorgios noted two war galleys beached on the mud banks of the estuary. The fort itself was on a low hill with a great cave in its rocky face, half a mile from the port. They were met by Caius Maximus and a small escort of legionaries. Giorgios went through the formalities. They accepted the authority of the Caesar Constantius, and were reconciled to Rome. Caius was anxious to justify his collaboration with the usurpers during the nine years of Britannia's secession from the Empire.

"Our duty is to guard the frontiers. We accepted the authority of the nearest Augustus – what use to plunge the province into civil war by defying him?"

Giorgios had to admit to himself that this was the practical attitude; but he pointed to the two war galleys stranded by the tide.

"The Caesar Constantius, being now on his march to Eboracum, is the Augustus nearest to you, and he desires that your galleys be at sea on patrol against Atta Cotti raiders."

They remained overnight, long enough to watch the two war galleys floated off the mud banks. Caius gave them a pilot to take them through the narrow straits between the mainland and a large, low-lying island devoted to the growing of corn. Geraint and the new man quarrelled fiercely, or so it seemed to Giorgios, in their native tongue, and he let out a sigh of relief when they were through the straits.

A while afterwards they came to a wide, sand-filled estuary.

"Deva", Geraint cried, pointing down the estuary, and immediately began another argument with the local pilot over who should give orders to the helmsman.

The galley drew into the quay at Deva. This time the magistrates and curia of the city, as well as the officers of the XX Valeria Victrix, greeted them. The formalities were gone through. Of course the city had never approved of Carausius' rebellion, but what could they do with all his Frankish and Saxon cut-throats at his back? Giorgios had his hands full. There were the soldiers and sailors to be billeted and then a banquet to attend. The horse transport had caught up with them, and Giorgios determined to remain in Deva the next day to give the horses exercise. Geraint assured him that he could pilot the ship to Porta Sisuntorium, and Mervyn broke one of his long silences to say that he was willing to remain.

They left Deva on the morning tide which carried them out to the open sea and the journey north, keeping the coast of golden sand in view. A birch forest stretched inland to a range of mountains.

"The Romans call those 'The Pennines' after their "Apennines", Geraint told him.

Giorgios broached a subject which had been intriguing him.

"Are there two Peoples among the Britons, a fair and a dark? You speak the same language, but are very different."

"They are the Old People", Geraint replied. "The Ancient Folk; they live in the hollow hills."

Giorgios wondered what to make of this, "Caves?"

"Not caves", Geraint replied, but offered no further explanation. "It does not do to offend them. They have the evil eye and can put bad luck on a man."

Giorgios laughed, "Surely you don't believe that?"

Geraint looked at him, "Well, put it this way: I take care not to quarrel with them."

Giorgios sensed that Geraint was uncomfortable and changed the subject, "What a beautiful land, so green, even the mountains."

Mervyn left his station, since the wind was carrying them at a speed which outmatched the oars, and came across to them. His gaze was penetrating as he looked at Giorgios, murmuring something in a forgotten tongue, then he spoke in Latin.

"You will return once more, and after that, not in the flesh."

Giorgios felt his scalp prickling and the hairs on his neck rising. Mervyn looked at him again, this time his eyes dancing with an ancient merriment.

"You see", he said, "The Ancient Ones can bless as well as curse"; and then, as the wind dropped, he strode back to his pulpit to beat out a fast stroke on his drum.

At Porta Sisuntorium there was more recent news. Constantius had established his headquarters at Eboracum, the garrison here had already made its submission to him and Giorgios and his turma of cavalry were to proceed to Eboracum with all speed after a day's rest from the voyage. They were to have an escort of light cavalry and Giorgios, to his great pleasure, found it was commanded by Crocus, who boasted, "Constantius couldn't do without us! We had the routing of Allectus; his barbarians fled the field at the sight of us."

"What happened to them?"

"Those who fled straight to their boats we let go. Those who stopped to loot or rape on the way, we rode down." He passed his hand across his throat. "Some, the better trained of them, surrendered and are now being formed into an auxiliary ala."

Giorgios nodded; it was the Roman way.

The horse transport having arrived they set off for the mountains a day later. The road climbed through the great birch forest to emerge on wild moorland clothed in heather. The air was clear and sharp and felt like wine. They camped that night on the other side of the summit and continued their journey downhill the next morning. The green sunlight of the birch forest enclosed them again and then, as evening was approaching, they emerged from it into a landscape of fields green with corn and barley and, in the far distance, the gatetowers of Eboracum.

"I will return to it once more", Giorgios repeated to himself, "and after that, not in the flesh." What could that mean?

*   *   *

Constantius listened in silence to Giorgios' report. He merely nodded when Giorgios stressed the fears of the Britons over the disarmament edict and the withdrawal of the II Augusta from the West. Lucius Artorius Castus, Legate of the VIth Victrix was also present; "Lord Arthur", Giorgios said to himself as he studied the man. Undoubtedly Spanish, he concluded. To his surprise, the Legate supported him.

"The Britons ought to keep their weapons and the II Augusta is in the right place to guard the Western Approaches."

Constantius nodded, "The story of the II being withdrawn is merely a foolish rumour, such as are always going around armies. As for the weapons, it is I who will interpret the Edict, and when I do I will bear in mind what you have said. Meanwhile, you have done exceedingly well. With the navy at sea and the garrisons on the alert, certain of whose authority they are under, we are ready for raids by the Atta Cotti and the Scotti." Giorgios could not help but feel a glow of satisfaction. Constantius continued, "I am sorry to say this is not the end of your labours. Orders have been received for you to return to the East, to Antioch. Prince Crocus will accompany you. I haven't the transport to send so many by sea, so you will have to go from here to Rutupiae, take ship to Gesoriacum and travel through Gaul for a ship to Antioch. I want you to be ready to start in two days' time."

"Yes, Domine", Giorgios replied, rather relieved not to be confined to the ship again.

Suddenly Constantius stood up and crossed to a table spread with maps.

"You have seen something of the Britons, and of Britannia; what do you think of this?"

He pointed to a map on which lines had been drawn dividing the province into five parts. Giorgios studied it.

"I think that the division of the province will divide it into three nations, Domine."

Constantius frowned, "You question the wisdom of the Emperor?"

"I had not considered the matter before now, Domine, but it seems to me that what may be appropriate in one part of the Empire may well be inappropriate in another."

Constantius continued to frown: "I see, but the matter is settled. Now that Britannia is back in the Empire it must be organized as the rest is; that is the Emperor's decision."

Giorgios recalled what his Uncle Andrew had said about Diocletian's obsession with organization. "I'm probably wrong, Domine."

"Yes! Yes!" Constantius said. "Well, you will be wanting to rest now".

And thus dismissed, Giorgios left, remembering the British king's question: "Will men fight for their brother's inheritance from which they are excluded?"

CHAPTER FIFTY-TWO

Galerius, in Antioch, heard the news of Constantius' successful campaign in Britannia with envy. Who – when he succeeded Diocletian, and Constantius succeeded Maximian – would be the senior Augustus? Obviously, he pointed out to Licinius, he who had the most laurels.

"A victory on the Persian frontier would more than even things up", he said.

Licinius saw, or thought he saw, what was in Galerius' mind, a strike north to recover Armenia.

"We have been ordered to hold Antioch, Domine. If we move the army north to recover Armenia, the Persians could take the city and cut the Empire in two."

"Not Armenia, Licinius, I'm not interested in recovering a province. I mean a strike southward at the heart of the Persian Empire. With their best troops in Armenia we can take Persepolis; we can do what Alexander did, conquer Persia. I will be Emperor of Persia first, and then of Rome."

"It means defying Diocletian."

Galerius dismissed Licinius' caution, "When Persia is conquered, he will be grateful. If we move quickly we cannot fail. Bring me the maps."

The army moved out from Antioch to cross the Euphrates north of Dura Europos, following a fateful route. Three centuries before, the Roman Triumvir, Crassus, had conceived of exactly this plan to give him ascendancy over his fellow Triumvirs, Pompey and Caesar. He had marched his legion into the desert and, at a place called Carrhae, the Roman Army had suffered one of its worst defeats at the hands of the Persian heavy cavalry and their Parthian bowmen. In July 297 A.D. the same fate overtook Galerius, though unlike Crassus he escaped with his life.

Giorgios and Crocus knew nothing of this until they reached Antioch. Hearing of Galerius' folly, Diocletian had dispatched two alae under the command of Constantine to provide a cavalry shield for the legions. They had crossed the Euphrates too late; Galerius was already in full and disorderly retreat, the Persian cavalry cutting off groups of infantry and slaughtering them.

Constantine had placed his cavalry between the Persians and the retreating Romans, and slowly restored order, gathering the scattered centuries into cohorts and, eventually, the cohorts into a column of legionary strength.

Concerned for Constantine's safety, Giorgios asked their informant if he had reached Antioch safely.

"Oh yes", was the reply, "but that young Constantine's a bit of a showman. He halted his column two miles outside of the city, rather than enter it at dusk, and in order to give his troops a good night's rest. Then next morning they marched in, standards held high, drums beating, trumpets blaring. It was like a triumph – but then, what do you think happened?"

"Tell us!" Crocus demanded.

"As Constantine entered the city, Galerius, in silver armour and wearing a purple cloak, with his Praetorian Prefect, Licinius, and his staff officers, rode out to lead the march, just as if it was his personal triumph." Giorgios' face flamed with anger; Crocus gave an exasperated snarl. "But it did him no good. The crowds gathered along the route began to shout, 'Hail Constantine, Hail Constantine.' Galerius turned purple with rage, but there was nothing he could do about it."

"Serves the bastard right", Crocus chortled.

Giorgios remained silent. There was nothing to be said in Galerius' defence, but at the same time he could not bring himself to gloat at another's shaming.

"But that's not the end of it. As the procession turned into the Via Caesarea, a golden chariot drawn by six white horses came in the opposite direction. Everyone fell silent. It was the Emperor himself, clothed in purple and wearing a kind of diadem of sun rays. He wheeled the chariot broadside to block off the road, and Galerius was forced to halt. Galerius dismounted and went over to the Emperor and made the obeisance."

"An obeisance!" exclaimed Giorgios, his voice rising in anger, "The Emperor is first citizen of the Republic, not a Persian potentate."

The other looked at him keenly, "That is the custom now, Count. It would be unwise to raise your voice against it."

"Since when?" demanded Giorgios. "A custom is something we inherit; when did grovelling become a custom for Roman citizens?"

The man shifted, looked around, embarrassed, "It's what is expected, what's required, in the presence of the Divine Emperor."

Crocus, sensing a scene was developing, cut in hastily, "What happened next?"

"The Augustus spoke to Galerius, very quietly, and then Galerius stood up and placed his hand on the rim of the chariot, and in that way walked the entire length of the Via Caesarea. Only at the end, before the palatium, did the Emperor permit his son-in-law to remount his chariot."

Crocus was chortling with glee, "He's finished now, surely, there's nothing for it but to fall on his sword."

Giorgios was silent; he was remembering Galerius' own words, 'Never leave an enemy without an option.'

"But there is more good news. Constantine has been made commander of the Imperial Guard. The Emperor knows that it was he who saved what could be saved of the army."

Giorgios' face brightened; his friend's advancement was something he could be glad to hear about.

*   *   *

Bitter anger consumed Galerius as he cast around for some justification of his action and exoneration of his failure.

"It was the Christians", he fumed to Licinius; Licinius said nothing. "There are many Christians in Armenia. Perhaps they prefer Persian rule to Roman rule."

"They hardly caused us to attack the wrong front, Domine", Licinius said mildly. Galerius' scowl made him regret not keeping silent.

"They used their black arts and magic to confuse me. Constantine's mother, that concubina, Helena, is almost a Christian. She wants a triumph for her son in vengeance for his father's desertion."

Licinius recognized the symptoms. In his obsession with plots and conspiracies, Galerius would assemble facts, rumours, assertions and occurrences, no matter how utterly disconnected and random, and build from them a tottering tower of "evidence" against his enemies, real or imagined.

Galerius strode about the room searching his brain for further justification, "Even if they had no malice toward me, they still bring ill luck on the Empire by their refusal to sacrifice to the immortal gods. It was ill luck the Persians had moved their army from Armenia to Carrhae, and it was the Christians who caused that ill luck."

Licinius thought to himself that it might have been the fact that Galerius, impatient of immediate success, had doubled his strength with ill-trained numeri, who had run away at the first charge of the mailed Persian cavalry.

*   *   *

Giorgios, Crocus and their cavalcade made their way through the narrow streets which connected the port of Seleucia with Antioch. Constantine was waiting to welcome them at the palatium.

"Congratulations!" Giorgios exclaimed, "No one has worked harder than you or deserved it more."

Constantine was delighted at Giorgios' praise.

"And you too. An Imperial Count no less, and so you should be."

"I don't think it will carry much weight in the East. I'm more of a 'temporary gentleman,' a count of the Western Empire, and was not even made such by the Emperor Maximian, but by your father."

Constantine's face clouded at the mention of his father, and Giorgios remembered what Constantius had asked him to say when he next met Constantine, and so repeated the message, ending, "Perhaps if you knew all, and understood all, you could forgive?"

Constantine's countenance remained dark.

"My mother does so, and urges me to do so too. Perhaps you are right. Perhaps he has suffered as much as we; but", his voice hardened again, "he has suffered in a great deal more comfort and with the consolation of his whore."

Giorgios was startled by this recklessness.

"Not so loud. Perhaps she was as unwilling as he, but being the Emperor's step-daughter she had no choice but to obey."

"Perhaps so", Constantine grudgingly conceded.

Giorgios urged, "Be reconciled to your father, Constantine, I know that it grieves him to have lost you, and I know that he is proud of you."

"Well, perhaps I'll try. Meanwhile", his face brightened, "I've asked the Emperor to appoint you Millenary Tribunus Militum of an ala of the Imperial Guard, and he has agreed."

Giorgios was lost for words to express his gratitude. An ala of the Imperial Guard was of double strength, that is to say it was a thousand men, and the rank of Tribunus Militum was a high one.

"Don't thank me too much", Constantine said, "before you hear the rest of it. As soon as the army is marshalled, and us with it, we are off to war against Persia under the command of Galerius!"

Strangely, Diocletian had not stripped Galerius of the purple, nor had Galerius thrown himself upon his sword.

"Galerius! I would have thought that he was finished", Giorgios exclaimed.

Constantine shrugged, "Having diminished him in public, Diocletian raised him in private, but perhaps not so high. He ordered Galerius to muster a new army, even though that will mean taking troops from the Danube frontier and from Egypt, and to recover Armenia before the year is out."

Giorgios had hoped to return for a short time to Lydda, not an impossible distance from Antioch by sea.

"When do we start?" he asked.

"In a week's time", Constantine replied, "Long enough for you to get to know your officers, if not all your men."

CHAPTER FIFTY-THREE

"I said the new taxes would cause trouble", Andrew exclaimed as he read the dispatch, "and now here it is. Egypt has rebelled, and it started with a tax riot."

The Egyptian rebellion undoubtedly had its roots in the defeat at Carrhae – that a Roman army could be defeated was a lesson gladly learned. The spark came when tax-farmers demanded from a widow stall-holder in Alexandria an amount which she did not have. She became hysterical. The tax farmers tipped over her stall and began to beat and kick her. An angry crowd gathered. A large, well-built man picked up a large, well-made amphora and brought it crashing down on the head of one of the enforcers. The crowd seized other makeshift weapons and attacked the tax-farmers.

If the tax-farmers had escaped, the thing might have blown over. Unfortunately for them they did not – the crowd lynched them and the Rubicon was crossed. The mob swarmed out of Alexandria's slums intent on looting, and it was quickly apparent that nobody in the city was in command or would admit to being so. The civil governor referred the matter to the Vicarius of Oriens, the new diocese which included Egypt, and awaited instructions. The military Count referred the matter to the Prefect and also waited instructions.

In these circumstances a tribune, Lucius Domitius Domitianus, took control of the situation, turned out the troops and dispersed the mobs. Much to his surprise, he found his troops and the city curia hailing him as Emperor. He allowed vanity to outstrip common sense and accepted the title, fortifying the city and demanding the submission of Roman garrisons along the Nile valley. He lived only five months to enjoy his Imperium before being murdered and succeeded by an equally obscure tribune named Aurelius Achilleus. The date was December A.D. 297, and Diocletian was forced to postpone the Armenian campaign and deal with Egypt himself.

Giorgios and Constantine, ordered to Caesarea, waited for the Emperor, who was sailing down the coast with the infantry. At Caesarea they would be joined by the Xth Legion.

As they were encamped overnight at Lydda, Giorgios took the opportunity to call home for a few hours. Katherine was now married and had gone to her husband's house. Martha had declared her intention of being a nun, living in seclusion in her family home. Lucius had been recalled to the Xth and was about to set off the following morning for Caesarea. Pasicrates, now a youth of sixteen, begged to accompany Giorgios.

"I can read and write both Latin and Greek now", he protested, "I can be your scribe and write reports."

Giorgios looked doubtful; Lucius sided with Pasicrates.

"There'll be no danger, this will be a one-battle war; once the army arrives at Alexandria, the city will surrender."

Giorgios reluctantly agreed and the three set off with their train of horses; Kira, Martha and Claudia watched them go.

*   *   *

The army marched along the coast road following the fleet.

Pasicrates wrote enthusiastically, recording every incident of the march to Alexandria. The fleet was there before them, blockading the two harbours. From the top of a low rocky outcrop Giorgios and Pasicrates surveyed the city. They looked in wonder at the Diabathra, the mile-long breakwater which curved out into the sea, with its palace and temple of Isis. From the Diabathra the eye was carried to the crescent of the esplanade, lined with palaces and public buildings, the quays crowded with ships.

Ships also filled the docks and repair pens quarried out of the island of Antirrhodus. From the esplanade, colonnade opened upon colonnade; the university colleges, the museums, the library and the observatory. The Caesareum, rivalling the Parthenon at Athens, rose white and gleaming. Plainly visible were the two obelisks before the soaring Gateway of the Sun, and towering over all, the high white mass of the Pharos. Here before them was the greatest city of the Empire, perhaps of the world.

The city's surrender was demanded, pardon being promised. It was refused, and the siege began. A ditch was dug around the city and a stockade erected. Mining proved impossible, for tunnels were quickly flooded by ground water, so the siege engines were brought to bear. After eight weeks Diocletian judged the breaches sufficient for an assault.

The night before the attack Diocletian held a council of war with his commanders. Giorgios was disconcerted to find a scarlet-robed flamen present, a priest from the temple of Apollo. The Law of Rome was plain, Diocletian said: a rebellious city was offered pardon; if pardon were refused, surrender on harsher terms could still be offered until the moment the first battering ram touched the walls. After that the city would be levelled, the survivors crucified, and the women and children sent to the slave market. This would be, must be, the fate of Alexandria if the city did not surrender the following morning. There could be no exceptions. Yet everyone present knew that Alexandria was an exception, that it was the jewel in the crown of the Empire.

Giorgios spoke; he had come to know Diocletian during his bodyguard duties.

"Augustus, the walls have not yet been touched by a battering ram. What if they are not? What if we bring down the gates with catapults and enter the city that way?"

There was a murmur of agreement; everyone present was seeking a way out, except the flamen. With a look of pure malice at Giorgios he flung his arms wide, crying in a high-pitched voice.

"There is the cunning of the Christians, enemies of Rome, enemies of the immortal gods. The auguries have been read. They prophesy that unless the blood of that accursed city touches the knees of Augustus' horse, a great disaster will befall Rome."

Constantine joined Giorgios in his protest.

"Augustus, there are many people in the city who have had nothing to do with the rebellion."

"Then why didn't they rise against the rebels?" Diocletian demanded. "It is every citizen's duty to resist subversion of the Roman Order."

"They had no weapons, Domine", Giorgios pointed out, "because of the Disarmament Edict."

Diocletian harrumphed.

"If we storm the gates the resistance will collapse", Constantine pressed home the argument.

Giorgios felt his blood run cold; Cyrennius was in Alexandria, studying medicine. There were thousands like him, students of mathematics, astronomy, geography, engineering, literature, philosophy, theology: Alexandria was civilization! The flamen was speaking again, his voice rising to a screech.

"Disaster will follow defiance of the law of Rome; the Emperor's life itself will be in jeopardy. The auguries have been taken, the fates have spoken."

Diocletian, like most soldiers, was a superstitious man.

"I cannot defy the gods. The city has until the first battering ram touches the walls."

Sick at heart, Giorgios pondered what he must do.

Diocletian decided to attack the gates at the same time as the tortoises advanced against the walls. He wanted a wide entrance for his troops. The gates gave way as the first ram touched the walls and the attackers surged forward. Diocletian, on horseback, followed, with Giorgios and Constantine riding on either side, Giorgios still hoping to stop the carnage. They passed under the gateway. Across the cobbles lay the body of a woman; blood had pumped from her slashed throat and lay in a pool, already congealing. Diocletian's horse shied from the body; its front hoofs slipping in the blood, it pitched forward onto its knees. Diocletian would certainly have been severely injured, if not killed, had he been thrown over the horse's head.

Constantine and Giorgios seized his arms and pulled him back. Diocletian regained control of his mount and brought it upright.

Giorgios glanced down and saw the salvation of Alexandria.

"The auguries have been fulfilled. The blood of Alexandria has touched the knees of the Emperor's horse", he cried aloud.

Constantine, seizing the situation at a glance, joined in.

"Augustus, stop the slaughter, lest the gods be offended."

Diocletian hesitated; he was shaken by his near fall and superstition again got the better of him.

"Enough!" he shouted, "Enough have been slain to fulfil the auguries. Death to any soldier who kills another after hearing my command."

Constantine turned to the trumpeter, "Sound the recall", he ordered.

Giorgios turned to one of his decurions, "Ride ahead, cry the Emperor's order to everyone."

*   *   *

Diocletian took up residence in the palace of Cleopatra. He still ate and drank sparsely and retired early, but he made a special point of entertaining Giorgios and Constantine.

"You undoubtedly saved my life twice today, first by saving me from being thrown, and again when you saved me from the wrath of Apollo."

Constantine smirked behind his hand at Giorgios' discomfiture.

When they left the dining room he turned to Giorgios, "How do you square proclaiming the auguries with being a Christian?"

The little furrow appeared between Giorgios' eyebrows, the sign of serious thought.

"I didn't proclaim the auguries, because the auguries are falsehood. I mocked the auguries by so easily twisting them."

Constantine laughed, "You're worse than the philosophers. Let's go and have a drink of unwatered wine."

*   *   *

Giorgios was sitting in his billet with Lucius. Pasicrates was busy at a desk writing out his account of what had happened, liberally exaggerating Giorgios' courage and presence of mind, when four men in dalmatics were ushered in. Giorgios rose to greet them. They stood before him in a semi-circle and bowed.

The one who was obviously the leader spoke.

"I am Alexander, Patriarch of Egypt and Ethiopia. These are my deacons. We have come to salute you as saviour of the city and to thank you for our lives and those of all the people of Alexandria. Your name will live forever in our Church, inscribed in our liturgy, blessed in Egypt, Ethiopia and Nubia."

Giorgios was taken aback.

"Will my lords take wine?"

"A little", the Patriarch replied, "that we may do you no discourtesy."

The Patriarch had hardly left when another group was ushered in. Giorgios looked at them with even greater surprise for, judging by their curled hair and philosophers' cloaks, they came from the University. They were well-fed men for philosophers, he thought, and all wore a superior expression which irritated him; nevertheless, he greeted them politely.

They bowed, "We have come to thank you for saving the city; the wisdom of centuries would have been lost if it had been put to the torch."

"And you yourselves would have been among the dead, rather than in Plato's cave contemplating the shadows of the ideal forms."

221

They started; Giorgios could have laughed at the expressions on their faces.

"You have read Plato?" one asked.

"And your master, Plotinus", Giorgios replied. "But though I treasure wisdom, it was men who concerned me most, the meanest as well as the loftiest."

There was a slight spasm of distaste on the face of the spokesman, "The generations of men are but leaves which fall; wisdom is eternal."

Giorgios smiled, "Nevertheless, I think you are relieved that it is not yet autumn."

The other went on hastily, "Your name will be inscribed in our college as one to whom future generations of scholars must be grateful."

Giorgios was genuinely pleased with the tribute and thanked them sincerely.

"Snobs!" exclaimed Lucius when they had gone.

The next visitors were members of the city curia. They assured him that his name would be carved upon the basilica and that his fame would live forever. Giorgios thanked them, but when they had left he said to Lucius, "I do wish people wouldn't do this; I hadn't an idea what to do till the horse stumbled."

Sometime later Raphael ben-Ezra arrived. Giorgios was glad and surprised, "I thought you were safe in Sidon", he said.

"Alas!" replied Raphael, "I wish that I were. But for you I would now no doubt be lying with my throat cut. The whole city knows what you did and is resounding with your praise."

"I know! They're all going to remember me forever, even the philosophers. But you haven't told us what you are doing here."

Raphael grimaced, "Recognizing the brilliance of my intellect, our elders decided to send me to teach at the Hebrew College here, so here I am, still alive after eight weeks of siege, and glad to be coming to thank you for it."

Giorgios laughed and clapped him on the shoulder, "If I'd known you were cooped up here as well as Cyrennius, I'd have thought twice as fast. What do you intend to do now?"

"Why! Stay in Alexandria. In spite of all its perils there's no place like it on earth for a scholar; it would take a lifetime to read a tenth of the scrolls in the library. The important thing is to keep out of arguments in public; they always turn into a fracas, and a really good one, into a riot. I'll settle down here and marry, and teach my sons philosophy."

Giorgios was delighted for his friend. "Well in that case I can say with certainty that there'll be a Raphael ben-Ezra, your grandson, teaching philosophy here in a hundred years' time. Let's have a cup of wine to that."

"You haven't seen my brother, Cyrennius, by any chance?" Lucius asked.

"Why yes! As it happens, I saw him yesterday with a gang of medical students, busily searching out anyone with the smallest cut they could pour oil and wine into. The wounded were fleeing from them in all directions."

This did nothing to allay Lucius' anxiety, and, smiling, Raphael said, "Don't worry. I saw him in the atrium as I came up. He was deep in debate with another student, so I didn't interrupt him. I've no doubt he will be here soon."

At that moment Cyrennius himself walked into the room. He glanced around, crossed to the table, carefully swirling his student's cloak, and poured himself a cup of wine.

"Well, you all took your time getting here", he said. "Eight weeks is a jolly long time to go without a decent drink. By the way, what was all that hoo-ha down by the gate this morning?

CHAPTER FIFTY-FOUR

The army remained encamped around Alexandria for several weeks. Aurelius Achilleus and his staff officers were beheaded; the Magistrates and Curia, after impassioned pleading of their inability to prevent the military rebellion, got off with fines which left them poor men. They were also barred from public office for life. Diocletian appointed new magistrates and curials from the pro-Roman party, who at his mere suggestion immediately voted him a donation exceeding the expenses of the campaign, to be met by the city treasury.

Always fascinated by foreign climes and people, and treasuring their differences rather than the similarities, Giorgios, having a day free of duty, decided to explore with Pasicrates the canals of the Nile Delta. They set out on horseback at dawn. Warned that there were deserters who had taken to robbery, Giorgios took his sword, shield and two javelins, while Pasicrates carried two more.

Every square foot of land, Giorgios noted, was cultivated. There were clusters of hovels built with mud bricks and thatched with papyrus, evidently the homes of the many peasants they saw tending the crops. After two or three hours' riding, Giorgios realized that they were lost.

"If it grows dark", Pasicrates said, "we'll be able to see the Pharos."

"Of course", Giorgios exclaimed, "I hadn't thought of that; but we've hours of daylight to find our way anyhow."

He did not want to tell Pasicrates that, Pharos or not, it would be impossible to strike a straight line across the network of canals and ditches.

They came, not to a canal, but to a sluggish channel of the Delta with an earth road running alongside it.

"Ah! A road", Giorgios exclaimed, "I think we'll be home for supper, Pasicrates."

They followed the track which presently left the river, to skirt a thick plantation of papyrus which grew above their heads. Suddenly they heard a shriek of pure terror.

Giorgios urged Assjadah through the papyrus, drawing one of his javelins, to find himself in a riverside clearing, which was evidently used for building papyrus boats and rafts. A single tree stood there with a girl of perhaps fourteen bound to it. She had fainted, her head fallen forward, her raven-black hair covering her face.

Giorgios scanned the clearing and saw the reason for the girl's terror. A huge crocodile was emerging from the river and clambering up the bank. With a yell, Giorgios charged at it.

The long jaws gaped, exhaling a wave of foul breath. Assjadah shied away, but Giorgios managed to thrust the javelin down the reptile's throat. The jaws snapped shut and bit the shaft cleanly in two.

Distracted from its prey, the reptile was wildly thrashing about, trying to disgorge the javelin. Giorgios turned Assjadah and galloped back. Black blood was seeping from the creature's mouth, and Giorgios hurled his second javelin. It bounced harmlessly off the beast's thick scales. Pasicrates had now burst through the papyrus, and taking in the situation, rode alongside Giorgios, handing him a javelin. The beast had decided who its enemy was and rushed at Assjadah. At a touch of Giorgios' knee she skipped nimbly aside, and this time the javelin went straight and true into the reptile's eye. It stopped short, rolling over as it tried to dislodge the weapon, its tail lashing violently from side to side.

"Quick", Giorgios shouted, and Pasicrates handed him the remaining javelin. Giorgios slipped from Assjadah's back.

Holding the javelin with both hands, he ran at the crocodile and plunged the weapon into the soft skin under its shoulder. Black blood spurted from the wound and another wave of foul breath enveloped him. The creature's lashing tail struck Giorgios on the thigh, sending him sprawling. Grasping desperately for a handhold, Giorgios found the javelin he had cast in vain.

Scrambling to his feet, he ran in again and thrust it through the beast's throat. There was a tremendous spasm and then the stillness of death.

Anxiously, Giorgios scanned the river for signs of any more reptiles. There was none, and calling to Pasicrates to collect Assjadah, he hastened to the girl and hacked off her bonds. She was still in a faint, or else helpless with terror, and collapsed into his arms. He laid her down and chafed her hands until she opened large gazelle eyes.

"Do not be afraid", he said in Greek. She looked at him dumbly. "What is your name?" he asked. She shook her head.

"Your name", he repeated gently, "What is your name?"

She tried to speak through dried lips, but no sound came.

"Wine", Giorgios called to Pasicrates, who ran up with the wineskin.

"Drink", Giorgios poured the wine into her mouth, "Don't be afraid, we will not harm you."

"The dragon", the girl said, in Greek, pointing at the beast.

"It's dead", Giorgios assured her, and she seemed to understand.

"But what is your name?"

"Cleosolinda."

"Where do you come from, Cleosolinda? Where do you live?"

"Sylene", she said, pointing toward the bank of papyrus.

"There's a path through the reeds", Pasicrates said, "perhaps it leads back to the road we were on."

"Good", Giorgios said, and picking up the girl, sat her on Assjadah to ride in front of him.

CHAPTER FIFTY-FIVE

Sylene could not be called a "city", but neither was it a village. It was built on one of the rare rises in the land which lifted it above the swamps, and surrounded by an inadequate wall of sun-baked brick. The four main streets of the town centred upon a forum, and on one side of this was a substantial building, not the basilica of a self-governing city, but the palatium of a petty lord. Opposite it was a Christian church. Many of the houses had workshops attached to them, and in one quarter there was a market square. Giorgios drew up at the gates of the big house and waited. The door was opened by a slave and an elderly man came out, neatly dressed in blue linen. As soon as she saw him, Cleosolinda let out a little cry of joy and, slipping from Assjadah, ran to him, calling "Papa! Papa!"

The man stood astonished, and then weeping cried "Sabra, my little Sabra", and caught her in his arms. As if this were a signal, people began to emerge from their houses and crowd into the forum.

Giorgios sat Assjadah; his thigh was aching and his temper was short. From the hubbub of voices around him he divined that the townsmen spoke Greek, so he shouted.

"Silence! I require an explanation of what has happened here: who has attempted to murder this maid?"

A man with a round face and villainous squint pushed himself forward.

"I am Amon, priest of Isis." He turned to the crowd. "Sacrilege!" he shrieked, "Sacrilege! This man has robbed the gods, now their vengeance will be terrible. The dragon will descend upon you, breathing fire; it will devour you all. What must we do with this blasphemer? Who is he to rob the gods?"

An angry murmur rose from the crowd. Giorgios drew his sword and moved toward the man, holding the blade to his chest.

"The dragon, as you call it, is dead, slain by me. As to who I am, that will soon be evident to all criminals. I am Giorgios of Lydda, Millenary Tribunus Militum to the Augustus Diocletian."

A murmur ran through the crowd and the agitator lost his confident expression. Cleosolinda's father called out, "Giorgios of Lydda! Merciful deliverer of Alexandria", and the crowd began to edge away from Amon.

Giorgios addressed him, "You will remain silent while I hear what has been done, and by whose instigation."

Another man, wearing a dalmatic, came hastening to join them.

Bit by bit the story was pieced together. The town's economy, boatbuilding, paper-making and basket-weaving, was based on papyrus. The "dragon", as the townsfolk believed it to be, had made its lair in the swamps several days before. Two men working in the papyrus beds had been taken by it, and now nobody dared to go there. The flamen, Amon, had announced that the dragon was sent by the gods as a punishment for deserting their worship. The dragon would remain until a maiden, chosen by lot, had been sacrificed to it. The lot had fallen on the lord's daughter, Cleosolinda.

Giorgios turned to the man in the dalmatic, "You are the priest of this town?"

"Yes, but when I stood against this man I was taken by force to my house and locked in. Only now have I been released."

Giorgios turned to the girl's father, "Why didn't you arm the citizens and slay the beast or drive it away with fire?"

The man looked up at Giorgios shamefacedly.

"We have no weapons. They were taken from us under the Disarmament Edict." Giorgios permitted himself one of the milder of soldiers' expletives; that idiotic edict again. He turned to the crowd.

"Listen to me, you foolish people. What you call a 'dragon' is only a beast of flesh and blood and bone, the same as the jackals you drive away with rods or the rats you set your dogs upon. It is not immortal, it is not magic, and it does not breathe fire, only foul breath. These crocodiles live on the banks of the Nile. This one has found its way here and, not being driven away by fire brands, made its lair here. Now it is slain and you have nothing to fear. You who have had the Gospel preached to you know very well that there are no gods and goddesses, for there is but One God who rules over the whole world. Why have you listened to this charlatan? Why have you ill-used your priest? Why have you returned to the evils you were saved from?"

The crowd stood silent and Giorgios continued, "Go to your priest and confess, and tomorrow attend the holy liturgy and receive the body of the Lord." He turned to the flamen. "You have plotted a most wicked deed. Leave this town before tomorrow's sunset."

The man began to utter curses and Giorgios crossed himself. "Do not curse me" – his voice was calm – "for I am protected against all your malice. I have shown you mercy not justice; for if I were to take you to face justice, the magistrates would surely hang you. Now go!"

The man began to edge himself away, to the jeers of the crowd.

"Silence", thundered Giorgios, "What right has any of you who did his bidding to mock him now?" He turned to the priest, "And you, Abba, go to the church to hear those who come to you."

The crowd began to disperse, and Giorgios dismounted, grimacing with the pain in his thigh. He turned to the girl's father, "Can you give us a guide back to the city?"

The old man looked up at the sun, "It is too late to travel now, Domine. I will be honoured if you will sleep under my roof tonight. My name is Philemon, a widower with but this daughter, my little lamb, to comfort me. I am lord of this town and the surrounding land."

Giorgios accepted gratefully. He felt in need of a hot bath, of salves for his bruised thigh, and of clothes washed clean of the crocodile's blood.

Throughout the evening meal Cleosolinda looked at Giorgios with awe; but when she turned her gaze on Pasicrates, her large innocent eyes glowed in her golden brown face with a light Giorgios knew well. Pasicrates for his part gazed at her with equal admiration whenever her eyes were not upon him. Giorgios smiled. He felt a tenderness himself toward the girl, a tenderness which lifted his heart. After the meal when the girl had left the table and a slave had poured wine, Giorgios said, "You call your daughter Sabra, but she told me her name was Cleosolinda?"

"Sabra was our pet name for her when she was a child, but I must talk to you of another matter concerning her." He waited for Giorgios' assent, which was given with a nod of the head. "When my child was dragged from me and carried to the river, and I myself held prisoner in my own house, I made a vow, that if she were saved, he who saved her would have her hand in marriage, and half of all my estates. You saved her, and to you I redeem my vow."

Giorgios listened, not daring to look at Pasicrates; but he spoke gently to the old man, "I also have made a vow, and that is not to marry. Your daughter is the most beautiful maid, save one, whom I have ever seen, and if I had not loved elsewhere I would be honoured to take her as my wife" – Philemon seemed about to interrupt – "No, I beg you do not pursue the question, it is not possible." Giorgios glanced quickly at Pasicrates, "I think, however, that you may see more of my brother when he has come of age."

The matter closed, Giorgios retired to bed and, as he slipped into sleep, the thought of Cleosolinda was like a little bird singing in his empty heart; and as he breathed a prayer of thanksgiving for her beauty and innocence, he knew that the memory of her would always ease his pain.

*   *   *

The following morning, early, he was called to the door.

The flamen stood there.

"Can I be forgiven by your God?" he asked.

Giorgios studied him.

"So that you may remain here?"

The man looked abject, "No! My mule is packed, I take only my tools, I cannot stay here for shame."

"Where will you go?"

"Further down the river, away from the Delta, wherever papyrus grows."

"What is it you desire now?"

"To know your God and be cleansed."

"As to the first, my God, as you call Him, is the God of every man; and as for the second, you must go to the priest to learn of Him and be baptized – but you must learn first. Go to the priest here and he will give you a letter to take to whatever city you settle in."

*   *   *

The church was crowded for the morning liturgy and, on leaving it, Giorgios and Pasicrates noticed a small group standing outside, the flamen among them.

"Who are they?" he asked another of the congregation. The man studied them with surprise, "Most of the pagans in Sylene. I wonder what they want?"

"To be baptized, I think", Giorgios replied; and, going over to the group, called the flamen aside.

"Have you money for your travels", he asked.

The man shook his head, "I've had no work since the dragon made its lair here."

Giorgios took a purse from his cloak. The man took a step back, "Let it be a loan between us", Giorgios said, and pressed the purse into the man's hand.

"You have shown me mercy twice", the flamen said.

"Then, you also show mercy", Giorgios replied, and went to collect Assjadah and their guide to Alexandria.

Once safely back in the city, Pasicrates took out a new scroll, unrolled it and began to write:

"There was a city named Sylene in Egypt which prospered by the river until a great dragon, breathing fire and pestilence, made its lair in the swamps, devouring all who came there. The foolish citizens of Sylene, instead of doing battle with the dragon, offered it a goat each day so that it would not devour them, but when they had no more goats they cast lots, and the lot fell on the King's daughter, who is the most beautiful maiden in the entire world. In spite of the entreaties of her father she was led, dressed as a bride, to the river. Just as the most horrid and monstrous dragon appeared from the swamps, the Tribune Giorgios, greatest warrior of Rome, rode by on his snow-white mare, Assjadah, which in Greek is 'Daughter of the Morning.' Making the Sign of the Cross, the Tribune Giorgios, whose courage is greater than that of any other man, charged the monster, piercing it through the throat with his spear" – At this point he heard the trumpets sounding for the evening meal, so he sprinkled sand on what he had written, rolled up the scroll and put it away, to be completed another day.

CHAPTER FIFTY-SIX

Constantine had received a letter from his mother informing him that he was a father; Minervina had borne him a son and named him Crispus. Giorgios was over-joyed for his friend, who whilst obviously delighted, took it calmly. Nevertheless, they both drank quite a deal of wine in the mess.

Alexandria had returned to normal, and the spring gales had spent themselves. Diocletian ordered the army back to Antioch for the campaign to recover Armenia. Giorgios and Constantine were waiting to embark when another letter for Constantine arrived – it was from his mother. Constantine read it silently and passed it to Giorgios. It was brief and plainly agitated.

Minervina had died a few days after giving birth. Giorgios looked at his friend, stricken, but Constantine was wooden-faced. There seemed to be nothing he could say, so he merely gripped Constantine's arm. Only then did Constantine turn to look at him.

"I keep trying to remember her face."

Giorgios swallowed a lump in his throat, "You never will, if you try; but the memory will come unbidden."

Together they ascended the gangplank.

*   *   *

Galerius knew that this was his last chance; he would not get another command if he failed. His preparations therefore were meticulous; he even overcame his prejudices sufficiently to appoint Constantine and Giorgios as his cavalry commanders. The army he led from Antioch was well equipped and highly disciplined. The presence of King Tiridates ensured a general uprising of the Armenians, for Persian rule had been oppressive.

"I see that all the Armenians have spears and shields to take down from the wall", Giorgios remarked drily to Constantine.

The Roman and Persian armies met on the frontier and Galerius' victory was complete. He drove through Armenia in a series of skirmishes, decided by the torrential cavalry charges with which Giorgios and Constantine rolled up the Persian wings.

Having liberated Armenia, Galerius turned south into the fertile crescent, driving Narses before him until the Persians had only the desert at their backs.

"One stroke will finish it now", he told Licinius, "a surprise night attack by light cavalry. We'll seize Narses in his camp."

"It will be fatal for the cavalry if the surprise fails", Licinius pointed out.

"That's why I'm putting Constantine and the Theognosta whelp in command", replied Galerius with a smirk. "Either way, I win."

The attack, however, was a complete surprise; within minutes of riding down the Persian pickets, the Roman cavalry was in the heart of the camp. Narses fled, leaving behind his wives, children and sisters, and also his treasury. Giorgios entered the pavilion where the terrified women were clinging to each other. He bowed to the Queen.

"Have no fear, Madam", he said, "You are under the protection of Constantine, son of a Roman Caesar and a man of honour, and of myself. I am placing around you a guard of decurions for whose behaviour I hold myself responsible."

The Queen looked at him gratefully.

"I thank you on behalf of myself, my children and my sisters. We are your prisoners, but no longer afraid."

Galerius had learned from his experience of the desert and declined to follow Narses. Instead he sat in his camp and waited for Narses to negotiate. The treaty which followed was highly favourable to Rome. The territory along the upper Tigris, which Narses was obliged to cede, carried the frontier almost to the point reached by Alexander, and gave Rome control of the headwaters of both rivers. In return, Narses' family was restored to him. Giorgios escorted them to the Persian squadron sent to receive them.

After the formal ceremonies were concluded, the Persian Queen spoke, "I owe my safety and my honour and that of my children and sisters to this noble soldier who has been our protector from all assault and insult, who has treated us with deference and honour. Let his name be known in Persia for evermore as 'Jirgis Baqiya' and let the oppression of the Christians in Persia cease. As a pledge of this I offer him this ring, which, it is said, once adorned the hand of Alexander."

She took from her finger a great ruby which Giorgios, bowing, accepted.

*   *   *

Galerius had every reason to be pleased. His victory had enlarged the Empire for the first time since Trajan had conquered Dacia two centuries before; and it was he, a Dacian, who had done it! This put Constantius' achievement in Britannia into the shade. He had merely recovered a lost province; Galerius had conquered a new one! Who could doubt now that when Diocletian and Maximian abdicated, he would be senior Augustus!

"And, knowing Galerius", Constantine remarked to Giorgios, "who can doubt that his ambition will be to be sole Augustus?"

"You must get to the West and join your father in Britain", Giorgios urged him, "because from now on, you're disposable!"

The heavy taxation imposed by Diocletian had also led to rebellions in the Western Empire. A confederation of five Berber tribes, known to the Romans as the "Quinquegentiani", had broken through the Imperial frontier in Africa. Several African cities, acting on the dictum, "Better the barbarian than the tax-farmer", had rebelled, joining the invaders. Maximinian had despatched his son, Aurelius Maxentius, to Africa. He had defeated the Berbers and then set about levelling the rebellious cities in an orgy of brutality. Nevertheless, his African campaign counted as a victory for which Maximian took the credit, as he did for the victories of Constantius Chlorus in Britain and on the Rhine frontier.

Galerius, however, was content that these victories paled before his own. He made a triumphal entry into Antioch, continued on a triumphal march to Nicomedia, and from there to his new capital of Thessalonica. He had not forgotten his earlier humiliation, nor his conviction that the Christians, and not himself, had been to blame. Settled in Thessalonica, he began to plot his revenge.

CHAPTER FIFTY-SEVEN

With victories in Egypt, on the Persian frontier, on the Rhine Frontier, in Africa and Britannia, a Roman Triumph was mandatory.

In comparison to that of Aurelian, however, the Triumph of A.D. 299 was Spartan. Rome itself was no longer the home of the Emperors, for Maximian had moved his capital to Mediolanum to be nearer the Rhine-Danube watershed, the favourite route of barbarian invaders. In Diocletian's reorganization of the Empire, Italy had become a diocese of eleven provinces, not even exempt from taxation as Rome had been.

Diocletian and Maximian in the robes of Triumphators led the procession in a gilded chariot drawn by six white horses. The lictors marched on either side in the old way, bearing the fasces of axe and rods, but the relegation of the Praetorian Guard to the rear of the procession left no one in any doubt that the days when they made and unmade Emperors were past, and many saw it as their humiliation. The procession wound its slow way to the temple of Capitoline Jupiter which Diocletian and Maximian entered alone for the sacrifice, emerging blood-spattered, to announce a distribution of corn, wine and oil to the cheering mob of plebeians.

From the temple Diocletian made his way to the Senate house. There the Senators elected him to his eighth Consulship and confirmed him in the Pro-Consular and Tribunic powers; but it was plain to all that Diocletian was Lord and Master of the Empire with or without the consent of the Senate. He emphasized the fact in a way that was all his own. The Senate voted him a new title, "Alexandrius", to commemorate his victory. He thanked them courteously, but said that with their consent, he would grant the new title to the Empress, who would be known as Prisca Alexandra. The Senators, dumbfounded, nodded their assent. With the Emperor disposing of triumphal titles, the gift of the Senate, they finally understood who was Master.

From the Senate, Diocletian and Maximian processed to the banquet which would bring the Triumph to a conclusion. Diocletian as usual ate sparingly, drank watered wine and spoke little. Aurelius Maxentius took the opportunity to circulate among the disgruntled Tribunes of the Praetorians and the smarting Senators, to assure them that if he and not Constantius Caesar, were to succeed his father as Emperor in the West, he would restore Rome as the capital of the Empire. The City's glory would be assured, and the Praetorians would regain their rightful privileges. The rewards, he hinted, to those who assisted him to the purple would be matched only by his displeasure at those who opposed him. Maximian Daia, becoming bored, selected several of the decorative girls who stood around the banqueting chamber and disappeared. Aurelius Maxentius, becoming drunk, as was usual, collected several more of the girls and took them away for a playful slapping around, from which they emerged bruised and tearful but refusing to speak. Constantine advised Giorgios, *sotto voce*, to drink little but appear to drink much, since it was on occasions such as these that careers were made or broken. Diocletian sat and noted everything, storing it away in his phenomenal memory. Constantine himself, though yet unaware of it, had caught the eye of Maximian's daughter, Fausta.

He was even more unaware that Fausta had decided that this commanding grand-nephew of Claudius Gothicus would go far with the right woman behind him, and that married to him she would be Empress of Rome. He was equally unaware at that time that what the Lady Fausta wanted, the Lady Fausta got.

*   *   *

The following morning Giorgios was summoned to the presence of the Emperor. He was surprised at how quickly the palatium had been adapted to the new order. The great audience hall to which Roman citizens had had easy access, had been divided into a series of ante-chambers. Giorgios was passed through these by a succession of ever more gorgeously attired flunkeys. Finally, he entered the Presence. Diocletian was not sitting on the throne, and had discarded the sun-ray coronet and purple silk, to sit at a desk.

Giorgios gave the military salute, bowed, and stood to attention. An angry chamberlain barked, "Prostrate yourself before the Emperor." Giorgios remained at attention.

Diocletian studied him shrewdly, and turned to the chamberlain, "This is an informal occasion. You will leave." The chamberlain scuttled through a doorway which had a muslin curtain instead of a door. Diocletian continued to study Giorgios who remained rigidly at attention. This, he realized, was a battle of wills, and if he so much as twitched he would lose it.

Diocletian continued his scrutiny for what seemed an eternity and then suddenly gave a short laugh, "You are like your father, but more stubborn."

Giorgios did not move; Diocletian had spoken, but had not given him leave to stand at ease. The scrutiny went on, then Diocletian shrugged, "At ease, Tribune." Giorgios relaxed.

Diocletian stood up and walked around the desk. "Why do you refuse to perform the prostration?"

"I am a Roman citizen, Augustus, as you are. I respect and obey you as First Citizen, Marshal of the army, and Tribune of the People, vested with the Pro-Consular powers."

Diocletian shook his head, "That notion of yours, that the several offices of the Republic are vested in the person of one man, is a legal fiction. It always was, even before Octavius Augustus. Do you imagine Sulla or Marius were elected by the Senate? No! They made themselves autocrators."

Diocletian's argument was unanswerable, but it did not affect Giorgios' conviction that the Republic must be upheld, even as a legal fiction, in the hope of better times. He stood silent.

Diocletian had not finished, "The Senate has for long been a city curia, nothing more. A town council cannot rule an Empire, that can only be done by one whose

234

authority is granted from on high." Giorgios still remained silent; one did not argue with Emperors, especially one who had heaven on his side. "Your father, if he had stayed with me in Rome, as Aurelian urged him to, would now be Caesar and my successor. He refused and returned to Lydda to vegetate."

Giorgios felt keenly that this was a rebuke to his father's memory and was stung to reply, "My father would never have divorced my mother for the sake of the purple, Augustus."

Diocletian looked at him sharply.

"Are you criticising Constantius Chlorus or me?"

"I meant no criticism of anyone, Augustus, I only say what is true."

"I see that you are as bold as your father. But suppose that I was to instruct Constantius to name you Caesar and Filius Augustus, when he succeeds Maximian, what then?"

Giorgios was stunned.

"But everyone expects Constantius to name Constantine"

"I have already decreed that sons shall not succeed their fathers, but that during his lifetime the Emperor must adopt a man of proven ability as his heir; but apart from that, what then?"

Diocletian's eyes never left Giorgios' face, and he felt that the Emperor was reading every thought he had ever had; but he did not hesitate.

"No!"

"Why not? You have no wife to divorce and Constantius has a daughter for you to marry."

"Constantine is my friend."

"Ah!" Diocletian's expression changed and Giorgios realized that he had passed some kind of test; though what, he could not imagine. Diocletian called for wine and said nothing until the slave who brought it had left.

The Emperor returned to his desk and sat down.

"I have made a great mistake! When I abdicate, as I am pledged to do, and Galerius becomes Emperor of the East, he will name his nephew, Maximinus Daia, Caesar and Filius Augustus – I did not think of banning nephews!"

Giorgios gave a start; Diocletian looked at him, "You don't approve?"

"I think Maximinus Daia unsuitable, Augustus."

"So do I", Diocletian replied drily, "but there is worse. Maximian is pledged to abdicate on the same day that I do. He has been a good general, and a good colleague, but I had not considered the fact that blood is thicker than water. Aurelius Maxentius plots to seize Italy and Africa and proclaim himself Augustus; his father will do nothing to prevent it. Galerius is in on the conspiracy, Aurelius Maxentius having agreed to marry Galerius' daughter, my own grand-daughter. On that basis he will claim the Western Empire and go to war with Constantius for Gaul, Hispania and Britannia."

Giorgios was aghast. Not only would a drunkard and sadist rule the Empire, but everything Diocletian had achieved would be destroyed. While one faction fought another the barbarians would pour across the frontiers.

Diocletian was watching him carefully.

"You say that you are Constantine's friend?"

"Yes, Augustus."

"And you have proven it by rejecting the offer I made you. Now you can prove it again." Diocletian drew a scroll from his robe. "This has been written by my own hand so that only I know its contents. You see that there are no doors in this room for eavesdroppers to lurk behind", Giorgios nodded, "and outside each window is a decurion of the Imperial Guard, his ears blocked with wax? Since it is necessary for you to know the importance of the contents of this scroll, you may read it now – silently."

Giorgios unrolled the scroll. He scanned the customary opening greetings and read the text, his expression growing more serious with each word. He read it through a second time and then handed it back to the Emperor without a word. Diocletian rolled it, melted wax, sealed it with the Imperial seal and only then did he speak.

"Now only you and I know the contents. No one else is to do so, not even Constantine, much less that mother of his. If anyone else were to learn of its contents your life would not be worth a fig."

"What am I to do, Augustus?"

"You are to sail to Arles, tomorrow, and from there go to Trier. If Constantius is not there you are to follow him, even to the great wall in Britannia, but the scroll must be placed only in his hands, no one else's." He handed the scroll to Giorgios, "Guard it with your life".

"I will, Augustus."

Diocletian called for more wine, and continued speaking while the slave poured, "Yes, as I was saying, the Empress and my daughter, Valeria Galeria, desire to go shopping in Rome; they have heard of a perfumier who has over five hundred different fragrances in his stock. No doubt they will spend money like autumn leaves. They will require an escort. The Empress has particularly asked for you. Go to the Empress' suite and present yourself." The slave departed.

"Is this so, Augustus?" Giorgios asked almost in a whisper.

"Of course", replied Diocletian. "Go and enjoy yourself being dragged around the forum; make an afternoon of it – but remember tomorrow!"

*   *   *

The Empress Prisca Alexandra and her daughter were perfunctory in selecting and purchasing perfume. Once they had finished, Prisca turned to Giorgios, "Tribune, kindly order the bearers to take us across the river to the Vatican hill."

Giorgios was startled, "There is no chariot-racing in the circus today, Augusta."

"I am aware of that, Tribune, but it is not chariot-racing that we have come for."

Giorgios' surprise changed to puzzlement. Transpontine Rome was distinctly unfashionable; what could the Empress want there?

The slope of the Vatican Hill was steep and the bearers were breathing hard when they at length put the litters down at the entrance to a narrow alleyway between two rows of tombs, some as large as modest houses. The Empress and her daughter dismounted and, beckoning Giorgios to follow, they entered the passageway. It sloped upward to a short flight of steps. Mounting these, Giorgios followed them through a doorway and found himself in a courtyard flagged with green and white tiles. His military eye noticed that it was large enough to hold a small assembly of people. Turning to look at the doorway by which he had just entered, he saw that it was set in a red plastered wall. Knitted into that wall, to the left of the door and at a little above eye level, was a horizontal marble slab, supported at its projecting front end by two columns. In the floor beneath it was a simple, unadorned tomb. "This is the tomb of the Apostle Peter", Prisca said, "and we chose you as our escort, as we chose the bearers, because we know you are a Christian."

Giorgios gazed from the tomb to the Empress; at the tomb with wonder, at the Empress with amazement. His faith had grown in the hard ground of reason; "Hold fast the form of sound words, which thou hast heard from me in faith" – Paul's admonition to Timothy was the text which had shaped his thought. Now, standing before the tomb of Peter, he experienced *emotion* – joy and wonder at this revelation of God's providence. Here was the tomb of Peter, the Rock upon which Christ had built his Church, the Apostle who had visited Giorgios' own ancestors at Lydda. Three centuries had elapsed, but Peter was still here, still venerated, still heard; and the Empress of Rome, humble before his tomb, was a Christian.

Giorgios had escorted the Empress and her daughter in obedience to a command. He had appreciated that it was an honour, a high honour, but he had not been overwhelmed by it; he had kept his place, conscious more of the imperative of duty than of the honour. Now he looked at Prisca in a new light. She was the Empress; her daughter, the wife of a Caesar; and he, their servant; but they were all Christians, reborn in the waters of Baptism. For a moment, God's Providence illumined history. Something of the timelessness of the Church was revealed to him, a sudden insight in which the centuries past and the centuries to come became one, a single thing, and he cried aloud in Latin, "Portae inferi non praevalebunt!" – the gates of hell shall not prevail.

To Prisca it seemed that Giorgios' face was lit by more than the light of the sunbeams which slanted into that shaded space. Breathlessly she whispered, "We must pray", and the two women crossed themselves three times and held out their hands, palms up, in the Eastern fashion. Giorgios also prayed, the words flowing from his heart, without an awareness of the passing time.

He was startled when the Empress touched his arm. "There is one more thing we must do before we leave."

They left the courtyard and descended a few steps to a door in the opposite wall. Prisca tapped on it, and it was opened by a priest. For a few moments he gazed at the Empress in astonishment; but, collecting himself, he bowed them in. Giorgios found himself in a sparsely furnished ante room or cabinet. A trestle table covered in scrolls and writing materials, at which two scribes were working, occupied one side. Opposite the door, seated on a chair, was a man Giorgios immediately took to be the new Patriarch, Marcellinus.

The Patriarch's delight at receiving the Empress was unconcealed; he stood up to greet her and led her to the rear of the room in earnest conversation. After a few minutes Prisca beckoned Giorgios to join her.

"This is Tribune Giorgios Theognosta; he is from Lydda."

Marcellinus looked at him keenly. "Visited by the Blessed Peter himself," he said with a smile.

Giorgios, for once, found himself deprived of clear thought. Here was the successor of Peter at whose tomb he had just prayed. Twenty nine Patriarchs led back in an unbroken line to the Prince of the Apostles, and others would follow to the end of time. Giorgios was in such a turmoil that he heard himself stupidly replying, "I have returned the visit."

Marcellinus smiled broadly, but then became serious. "I give you my blessing, the blessing of Peter, for a great thing is expected of you"; and, following the Latin custom, Giorgios went down on one knee. When he arose he was aware that another had entered the room, silently, almost like a shadow, and was regarding him closely.

"I am Marcellus, Deacon to the Pope," he said, introducing himself. Giorgios' instinct told him that here was a man who was an efficient administrator, one for whom no detail would pass unnoted or unprovided for; a true Roman, with the lively, intelligent features of the race which had conquered the world. Something told him that the Church of Rome, and hence of the world, was in safe hands.

After the audience, Marcellus called Giorgios aside. "My friend", he said, "let me give you some advice. I do not know how important it is, what you are carrying, but I do know that you are carrying it, because you keep touching it, surreptitiously as you imagine – any enemy agent would know the same. Satisfy yourself that your message is securely fixed to your body and then forget that it is there. On no account feel to see if it is still there."

Giorgios looked at Marcellus in astonishment; the cleric, it seemed, was also a courier of the less official sort.

When finally, the audience over, they emerged into the dazzling sunlight of the Roman evening, Giorgios said as firmly as courtesy permitted, "We must hasten back, Augusta; not even the longest shopping trip can have taken as long as this."

"Of course; but it's all downhill, and you must use the journey to forget everything you have seen and heard today, except of course the purchase of the perfume!"

"My lips, Augusta, are sealed", and Giorgios touched anxiously the scroll hidden in his tunic, before snatching his hand away and ostentatiously scratching his ear.

CHAPTER FIFTY-EIGHT

Giorgios sailed in a merchantman which was returning light to Arles. The ship skimmed the waves, promising a speedy voyage.

There was a number of passengers on board, one of whom had a private cubicle from which he did not emerge. The sea remained calm until they had passed north of Corsica, and they were within a day's sailing of Arles when one of the Mediterranean's sudden storms blew up. A great wave hit the ship broadside on, and carried the helmsman with it. The oarsmen lost their stroke and the vessel wallowed before the next wave rushed upon it, swamping the decks. For a few moments there was panic, men cried aloud in terror, rowers cursed the oarsman in front of him, passengers clung to anything near them. It seemed to both crew and terrified travellers that the next wave would sink the vessel.

Giorgios ran to the helm and seized the swinging tiller. By main force he swung the rudder and the ship came around. The oarsmen picked up their stroke, the sailors trimmed the sails, and the ship ran before the storm. To the passengers, huddled together, Giorgios, standing braced and tall at the tiller, appeared more than human.

As suddenly as it had blown up, the storm abated and they were running on choppy seas. Giorgios was scanning the waves for a sign of the lost helmsman, when a passenger called, "You saved our lives", and another hailed him, "Protector from tempests". A third cried "Son of Neptune". Yet another called, "The sea obeys him." More voices joined in acclamations.

Giorgios, horrified at these plaudits, shouted back, "There is no such being as Neptune! There is but One God, who is the Lord of all; thank Him for your lives;" but as this did nothing to still the shouts, embarrassed and confused he hastened to go below deck. In his hurry he collided with the mysterious passenger.

He was astonished when he recognized the deacon, Marcellus. The latter beamed as at an unexpected pleasure. "We have met before? Yes! You were with the Empress. If you wish to escape your admirers come into my cabin."

Giorgios, wet through, excused himself, "I must dry and change."

His chief concern, however, was for the scroll in its waterproof wrapping, hidden in a pocket of his tunic.

"Very well, but call in afterwards. I am on my way to Arles, do you go further?"

Giorgios now had his wits about him; "I will see how I like Arles", he replied.

Marcellus gave him a flash of approval, as if to say "You learn quickly." Instead he said, "If I do not see you again before we disembark, I must thank you for saving my life, and something else of great importance to the Church. Your saving of us who were in peril on the sea will not go unrecorded, or unremembered."

The two parted, Giorgios to examine the wrapping of the scroll while he dried himself, and the deacon to his cabin.

*　　*　　*

Constantius, Giorgios was informed, was in Lugdunum. There was nothing for it but to make all speed up the Rhône valley, changing horses frequently to spare Assjadah. Arriving at Lugdunum he was informed that Constantius had returned to Trier.

The city was famous for its jewellers and silk-dyers and Giorgios took the opportunity to have the Queen of Persia's ruby set in the pommel of his grandfather's sword. Was it, he wondered as he admired the setting, really the sword of the Apostle Peter, or was that just a family legend? And again, was it really the ruby of Alexander?

At Trier, Giorgios found that he had missed Constantius once again, and the following day he set off for Gesoriacum. From the cliffs of that port he looked out over the narrow seas to the white cliffs of Britannia, and the white sails of Constantius' transports half-way there! Next day he secured a passage on a ship bound for Londinium. This time he intended to arrive first and be waiting. The Imperial warrant which had carried him thus far would gain him immediate audience with the Caesar.

Giorgios had bypassed Londinium on his previous visit to Britannia, being in haste to reach the coast and a ship for Gaul. Now he saw it for the first time. This was no provincial town but a thriving city, capital of a diocese of the Empire.

Carausius had boasted that he would make Londinium the principal port of the Northern seas, and as they tied up at the quayside among vessels not only from Gaul and Hispania, but from savage lands of the far North, Giorgios had to admit that Carausius had fulfilled his boast. Constantius had arrived only a few hours before, Giorgios learned, and hiring a guide, he set off for the Basilica. The guide, holding Assjadah's bridle, led him down the Via Decumana, the principal thoroughfare of the city. It was lined with elegant villas and meticulously attended gardens.

Silk-gowned matrons thronged the shopping streets; slaves bore litters from which richly dressed women peered at the passing scene; sailors from every part of the Empire headed for the numerous taverns; the scent of cooking food wafted from the restaurants. Everywhere there were the symbols of prosperity, a prosperity ensured by Constantius' wise government.

At the Basilica, Giorgios paid off the guide and presented his warrant. He was admitted immediately and ushered into the presence of the Caesar, no ceremony delaying him and no flunkies barring the way. Constantius was at his map table when Giorgios entered, and he looked up with pleasure, speaking in his precise Latin, "I have had a letter from Constantine, a friendly letter; I think that was your doing, and I thank you."

Giorgios saluted and handed the scroll to Constantius, who broke the seal and read it.

"Are you aware of the contents?" he asked.

"The Augustus required me to read it, so that I might understand the importance of delivering it to nobody but yourself."

"You have spoken of this to nobody?"

"Nobody."

"Good! It must remain an absolute secret. It would not go unnoticed if you returned to Rome immediately. Aurelius Maxentius' agents would not take long to work out that such a journey could only have been made for a special purpose, and it would not be difficult for them to guess what."

Giorgios nodded in agreement.

"I do not think that I was followed, Augustus."

"No you wouldn't – that is the business of Arcani, not to be seen but to see. As it happens I need a good cavalry commander. There is trouble with the Picts who have now realized that they can outflank the wall by sailing around it in their skin boats. I will write to Diocletian requesting your transfer to my staff, if you are willing."

On his first visit Giorgios had felt a strange attraction for Britannia, almost as if the land called to him; and now he had the same feeling, not to mention the desire to be far away from painful memories. He did not hesitate:

"As you wish, Augustus."

CHAPTER FIFTY-NINE

Eboracum, wasted some time before by a Pictish raid, had been restored by Constantius. Its walls rose from the river bank stronger than ever. It was garrisoned by cavalry alae able to hunt down and destroy even the largest bands of raiders.

Giorgios renewed his acquaintance with Lucius Artorius Castus, who surprised him with the greeting, "Count Giorgios, hero of Alexandria". News travelled fast throughout the Empire, not only by the Imperial posts but through the semi-secret network of the Centurions.

Eboracum retained something of the austerity of a legionary camp, with smithies and weaving sheds busy all day. Exploring the city, Giorgios was distressed by the number of harlots who hung about the barracks. Solicited, he took to giving the women a handful of denarii, saying "Go home, do not sin at least tonight." Most would snigger behind his back as he strode on. Others, a few, wept and found the throne of grace.

Giorgios was delighted to find that Prince Crocus was in the city, but they had little time to renew their acquaintance, for Constantius was a man who moved quickly; and soon the long dragon of a Roman army on the march was making its way northward. Two cohorts of the VIth and two alae of Gallic cavalry with all their baggage train and strings of remounts stretched for miles along the road. Roman intelligence was good, Constantius had seen to that; and he knew that a force of several hundred Picts was at sea in large coracles, intending to land well south of the wall and plunder the villages of the now disarmed Britons.

They came across the raiders beached on the estuary shore, and Constantius drew his troops up in the classic Roman manner, the infantry in the centre with the cavalry on the wings. The Picts, however, had not come to fight, but to pillage, and at the sight of the defenders they took to their coracles and made out to sea.

"Always the same", Crocus confided to Giorgios. "If we could but bring them to battle and show no mercy we might settle this border problem; but brigands as they are, they refuse to fight."

"If we still had the armed numeri", Giorgios replied, "defending their homes and their land, we might not have the problem."

The autumn was spent repelling such forays, with the occasional skirmish when Pictish bands were caught away from the shore. The cost of defending the coasts, Giorgios reasoned, must be bleeding the economy dry.

Winter came and Giorgios awoke one morning to find the world transformed into a wonderland of white. This was different from seeing snow on distant mountains. It took him back to his boyhood and the rare occasions when the snow had spread from the Galilean hills to fall on the plain. Going out into the streets of Eboracum he was delighted with the mock battles the children were playing, he laughed aloud when a well-aimed snowball hit his hood and the icy crystals cascaded down his face. His heart longed to join in, but the dignified stride of Lucius Artorius

Castus bearing down on him persuaded him otherwise. Instead, he headed for the Christian church where he attended the Liturgy each Sunday. On entering it he was again transported to faerie land. The church was garlanded with holly and ivy and ablaze with candles. The keeping of the Saturnalia as Christ's birthday was evidently more popular in the Western Church than in the Eastern Church.

After the dismissal, *Ite missa est*, he was carried away by greetings and invitations and astonished at the grumblings of Britannia veterans. The snow did clog the roads, it was cold, exhilaratingly cold – but it was wonderful!

"Wait till you've been here ten winters", a gnarled Centurion said to him.

"I wish that I could stay in Britannia for ever", he replied, and then remembered Mervyn's strange words: "You will return once more, and after that not in the flesh."

*   *   *

Constantius looked up from his maps as Giorgios entered the room.

"Does he ever read anything else?" he asked himself as he came to attention and saluted.

"Not enough men, never enough men", Constantius was saying, as much to himself as to Giorgios. "I need you and your cavalry down in Britannia Prima with the II Augusta. The scout ships report that Scotti are moving south, and concentrating as they move. My feeling is that they're going to join the Atta Cotti for a big raid, maybe an invasion. It won't be on the north-west coast, they know they're watched there from Porta Sisuntorium, and any landing place is within marching distance of the XXth or the VIth." He stabbed with his finger, "There! With all the loot of Aquae Sulis as the prize."

"I understood that the Scotti and Atta Cotti were enemies", Giorgios ventured.

Constantius gave a short laugh, "If you're going to make your career in Britannia, there's one thing you had better learn from the start: treachery and back-stabbing aren't crimes in Hibernia, they're a way of life. How soon can you leave for Isca Silurum?"

"Tomorrow, Augustus."

They entered Isca Silurum to the cheers of the legionaries. Rumours of the impending raid had spread through the ranks, as they always do, and tension was mounting. Giorgios renewed his acquaintance with Gerontius.

"The reports of the sea scouts are that the Scotti vessels are now in Atha Cliath, joining up with Atta Cotti bands", he told Giorgios.

"I intend to move three cohorts to Aquae Sulis tomorrow; your men can rest and follow on the next day."

CHAPTER SIXTY

Gerontius was proven right. Within a week a large force had slipped past the Roman patrols by hugging the Devon coast, and landed within striking distance of Aquae Sulis. Gerontius marched out to meet them and blocked their way where the ground rose toward the Mendips. He drew up two cohorts in his centre, with the third in reserve, and divided Giorgios' ala between the two flanks. Sitting Assjadah on the high ground, Giorgios had a full view of the field. The slope of heather and uncurling bracken ran down to dark beech woods; through them, he knew, the enemy was moving and would suddenly burst out. Below him, and somewhat to the rear, were the legionaries, splendid in scarlet and silver, drawn up, century by century. Across the slope were the other half of his ala. The battle tactics were to be a simple pincer movement. Higher up, Gerontius, his staff officers, his trumpeters and his flagmen sat their horses beneath the purple dragon banner.

There was a sound of war horns, of bodies crashing through underbrush, and suddenly, out into the open emerged the mass of the Atta Cotti. Giorgios studied them and understood why they were spoken of with dread, accused of ritual torture and even of cannibalism. They were naked, except for a leather clout, and filthy, smeared with dirt and dried blood; their hair and beards long and matted. They were armed with oval shields and fearsome spears. They had stopped to drink, gulping from their horns. At the sight of the Romans drawn up before them they began screaming obscenities and curses, breaking into a wild dance to work themselves into a battle frenzy.

"Berserkers", Giorgios exclaimed aloud with the professional soldier's disgust for those who killed out of blood lust. At the sound of a war horn, the Atta Cotti charged, moving at a ground-devouring pace.

Behind them the Scotti emerged from the forest. They came in ranks and files, not unlike the Roman formation. They had no body armour, but all had an iron cap and a large round shield, limed so that it shone in the sunlight. Their spears were long with a hooked barb. That barb, caught in a joint of Roman armour, could drag a man out of the ranks for slaughter. Finally came the war chariots, about twenty in all, light wickerwork carriages on scythed wheels. They were drawn by a team of two horses driven by a charioteer. Each carried a war-chief attired in white linen and a scarlet cloak, wearing a gilded helmet and carrying a shield rimmed and decorated with red and blue enamel.

The Atta Cotti were still screaming obscenities as they charged up the slope toward the centre. At the sound of a trumpet, the front rank of legionaries flung a barrage of pila into the seething mass. Men went down in heaps, but it did not stop the charge; nothing, Giorgios knew, could stop berserkers – they saw nothing, heard nothing, felt nothing, through the red mist which blinded them. They flung themselves upon the first rank, bearing it back by sheer weight of numbers. There was the sound of trumpets and four ranks of legionaries retreated step by step to put distance between themselves and the attackers. As the Atta Cotti broke through the remaining two ranks in bunches, the pila went to work again, cutting them down. There was another blast on the trumpets and the legionaries began to advance, regaining the ground they had yielded, gathering up the knots of survivors from the first two ranks, and suddenly the berserkers were streaming away, their blind rage spent and their strength exhausted.

The war-horns sounded. To beating drums and skirling pipes the ranks of Scotti began to advance, first at a double pace, and then, lengthening their stride, at a run. Giorgios watched with begrudged admiration. These were warriors, and he wondered what part the chariots would play.

The Scotti were met by another barrage of pila, the last that the front lines had. The barrage cut gaps in their ranks but did not break up the charge. There was a clash of shield upon shield, rolling like thunder all down the line and the cries of men whom the Scotti's hooked spears had found. At that moment the signal flags gave Giorgios his orders. Calling to his trumpeter to sound the charge, he drew his sword and swept down upon the rear of the enemy infantry.

To the deep bass braying of the war horns, the chariots swept forward to meet the cavalry charge. Giorgios sensed fear sweeping through his ranks at the sight of the whirling scythes; the horses had seen them too, and began to scream. The manoeuvre would certainly have succeeded if the Scotti had brought more chariots, but they had not expected their attack to be anticipated. Giorgios shouted an order to his trumpeter and at a signal the ala split up into knots of horsemen, leaving space to avoid the chariots.

Giorgios, with half a dozen troopers, tried to circle round the leading chariot and avoid the scythes. The charioteer turned the vehicle in its own length and rode straight at him. Assjadah leapt aside. For a moment Giorgios looked the war-chief straight in the eye, grey eyes that shone hard and bright with the joy of battle. To his amazement he saw that the man was laughing, and then the warrior hurled a spear at him.

The shield took the full impact of the missile, but he felt the point pierce his shoulder armour. The heavy shaft dragged the shield down and almost pulled him from the saddle. He flung his sword arm around Assjadah's neck and lay along it awaiting the stroke which would finish him. He ventured a glance upward; the war-chief was lying athwart the chariot, knocked unconscious, his charioteer dead, a spear through his heart; and he himself safely surrounded by his own troopers.

Broken chariots littered the field and horses lying and screaming in pain were everywhere; the scythes had done their dreadful work. The seething mass of the main battle seemed far away, though in fact it was only a few hundred yards. The Scotti were forcing the legionaries back inexorably. Giorgios stuffed a piece of linen under his armour to staunch the blood. Distant trumpets sounded and a movement on the slope told him that Gerontius was throwing in his reserve cohort. He called for his own trumpeter to sound the recall. Knots of cavalrymen began to gather, sorting themselves out into three long lines. Looking up the hill, Giorgios saw the draconarius waver and then go down.

The Scotti were pushing the reserve cohort back. He signalled his orders. The three lines of cavalry coalesced into three wedges, one to attack the Scotti in the centre and the others to roll up their flanks. This would be the final throw; if it failed and Gerontius were overwhelmed, the land would lie helpless before the raiders. He ordered the charge and slipped slowly from his saddle.

*   *   *

The battle had been long and bloody. A large body of the enemy had fought their way out and escaped to the shore, the Romans too exhausted to pursue them. The fugitives had taken to the sea in their coracles. Giorgios knew little of this as the surgeons stitched the wound in his shoulder, gave him wine and honey to drink and told him to sleep.

There were a few prisoners, among them a war chief. He was brought before Gerontius. Giorgios, on his feet again, studied him. He was tall, over six foot, and broad, with vivid red hair and a yellow beard. A large brooch of fantastically wrought gold held his cloak. He stood before them, defiantly, his hands manacled. Giorgios recognized him as the man who had flung the spear at him. Gerontius looked at the man and asked one question, in Latin.

"Why?"

"For freedom, Lord Geraint", the man replied, in passable Latin.

"But Rome does not threaten you, we have not attacked you."

"Ah! But ye would have done had ye dared."

"If we had needed anything of yours, we would have dared", Gerontius replied sharply. He knew it was pointless to chop logic with the Scotti; no one, not even a Greek, could get the better of them in that.

The man laughed out loud, "Ye haven't, so ye haven't dared."

Gerontius turned to one of his aids, "Kill him!"

Giorgios was shocked into protest, "Domine! It would be a shameful thing to kill a bound prisoner."

Gerontius looked at him, "Well, what do you suggest? Are you going to fight him single-handed?"

Giorgios searched for an idea. He liked the man; surrounded by enemies as he was, he had not flinched, and if the tables had been turned he would probably have given Gerontius the option of single combat.

"This man is a king in Hibernia. Send him and the other prisoners back in one of their coracles with a message for his fellow kings. If they attack again, Rome will follow them to their lairs and destroy them."

The chieftain looked at Giorgios with a strange light in his eye. Raising his head high, he said, enigmatically, "Thank you, Lord of Courtesy. You send me and I will go. I will go where the Fenians are at feast and greet them in your name."

They watched the coracle put out into the deep water, the chief sitting in the midst of the oarsmen.

"Who are the Fenians?" Giorgios asked.

"Legendary heroes", Gerontius replied briefly.

"And what did he mean, that he will go where the Fenians are at feast?"

Gerontius, shifted uneasily, "You will see. These are a strange people. They are merry in their battles but are full of sorrows. They mourn for things that never were. They sing of a land that never was and of a time that has never been, an Otherworld of deathless heroes and magical women."

The vessel was now a good half mile from shore. The watchers saw a flash of steel as the chief, standing up, slashed through the wickerwork and hide of the coracle. Aghast, Giorgios saw the waves engulf the frail craft as it sank with all its crew sitting in their places.

"You don't understand, do you?" Gerontius said to him. "The shame of returning, not only defeated, but by Rome's favour, was too much for him. He would rather have been slain here, by the sword. Meanwhile you, Count, are being credited with saving the day. They are relating your deeds already in Aquae Sulis and in Isca Silurum."

CHAPTER SIXTY-ONE

It was high summer and the Pax Romana lay upon the land.

Giorgios had not been idle, having been appointed to train the numeri of Riothimus and Creoda. Constantius had interpreted the Disarmament Edict as not applying to tribal levies, and the two kings had put this down to Giorgios' efforts on their behalf. He also came to know the aloof Aurelius better, and found him an intelligent and sensitive man, and a fellow Christian. Indeed, Christianity seemed well established in the South-West, though some of its practices, such as kneeling at prayer and at communion, seemed strange to Giorgios. He asked Aurelius about it.

"The freeborn have the right to kneel and to bear arms before their lord, that is the Western custom", Aurelius told him, "Only the bondsman stands humbly in his lord's presence. Because by baptism all are freeborn of the Kingdom, everyone baptized has the right to kneel in church, for he is kneeling before the Lord."

Giorgios recalled his surprise when, at Riothimus' court, he had seen warriors go down on one knee before the king. It was odd; what to him had seemed a servile act, was for them a cherished right!

It came as an unwelcome surprise when Gerontius summoned him to his cabinet. Aurelius was there.

"I regret, Count, that we have to part with you." Gerontius passed him a scroll with the Imperial seal on it. It was an order for his return to the East and a warrant for his travel.

"I'm travelling to Ynys Afallon", Aurelius intervened, "It's on your way; perhaps you would like to accompany me that far?"

"Ynys Afallon?" there was a query in Giorgios' voice. He had heard of it, but was not certain of its significance.

" 'Isle of Apples' in Latin; the first Christian church was built there, it is said, by Joseph of Arimathea. Whether that's true I don't know, but there is no other church which claims to be older, and it was certainly there in my grandfather's time, for as a child he told me of it and of the legend."

Giorgios smiled, "There's a legend in my family that Joseph was among our ancestors; perhaps I'll see his tomb?"

Aurelius shook his head, "There's no tomb, only a great peace."

The Tor at Ynys Afallon, though only four hundred feet at its summit, was impressive as it rose from the surrounding fens. Beneath its steep face was the church. It was a long, low building, half-timbered, with a row of narrow windows down each side and the wattle walls limed white, within and without. It was empty except for a stone altar at the far end. For Giorgios it recalled the schoolroom at Lydda; it had the same atmosphere of tranquil light, the same silence. They walked down to the front and Ambrosius knelt. Giorgios found himself thinking that that was the most comfortable position in this place, and so he too sank to his knees.

"You will return once more and after that not in the flesh." The words came back vividly and with them an inspiration. He stood up and Aurelius rose also.

Giorgios touched the hilt of his sword, "This was my grandfather's sword. There is another legend in our family, that it was the sword with which the Apostle Peter cut off the ear of Malchus." He drew the blade; the sun slanting through the windows caught it and it flashed fire. "The ruby in the hilt was the gift of the Queen of Persia, who believed it to have been Alexander's." He held up the hilt to Aurelius who peered into the depths of the ruby where mysterious light played.

"Just now", Giorgios continued, "I was told, almost, that when I come to die, whenever that may be, I must send the sword here, as an offering, to lie beneath the altar stone."

Aurelius smiled, "And I am to be the one who places it here for you?"

"Yes! If you will do that."

Aurelius touched the hilt, "I will do it for Britannia, for in a day of great need this sword will be the Sword of Britain."

They walked out into the sunlight and Aurelius said, "There is one more thing for you to see." He led the way to the foot of the Tor and stopped before a large thorn bush, which was in leaf but not in blossom.

"This is the holy thorn. The legend is that Joseph cut a staff from the bush from which Our Saviour's crown of thorns was woven. On reaching this place he struck it into the ground, and there it blossomed. It blossoms each year, but only in the depths of winter, and before the leaves open. Do you think this could be true?"

Giorgios considered the question.

"It's certainly possible; buds can lie dormant in a cut branch for a long time. If the branch is firmed in well-watered ground, such as this, it can strike root and the buds will sprout; that is how many shrubs are propagated."

"But did Joseph of Arimathea bring it here?"

Giorgios frowned, "Our family legend is that he was related to Joseph and Mary and a merchant in metals, especially tin, which he imported from Britannia. If his trading brought him here and he built the church, he might well have carried a staff cut in Judea. There is a rare thorn in the Vale of Sharon which blossoms in the winter."

Aurelius seemed disappointed, "So, the blossoming is not miraculous?"

Giorgios smiled and shook his head, "No! Just marvellous, as is all of God's creation."

Aurelius smiled ruefully, "Well, at all events, let us cut sprigs and wear them in our cloaks."

"Let's! and I will carry mine back to its native land", Giorgios agreed with pleasure.

CHAPTER SIXTY-TWO

Arriving at Nicomedia, Giorgios reported to the cavalry barracks and then went in search of Constantine.

"I'm betrothed", his friend announced.

"Betrothed! But who to?"

"Nothing romantic, it's more a political match: Maximian's daughter, Fausta."

Privately, Giorgios thought that he could never agree to such a marriage, but he said nothing. Constantine however was quick to notice his friend's change of countenance.

"You don't approve?"

"But that will make Aurelius Maxentius your brother-in-law!"

"That is a disadvantage, but I really have no choice. It's Diocletian's command."

"Do you love her?"

"I've hardly met her. She was at Rome, of course, for the Triumph, and she's a pretty little thing. The marriage won't be for a while yet anyway."

Giorgios realized that he must tread carefully if he were not to give any hint of what his mission in Britannia had been.

It was clear to him, however, why Diocletian had ordered the marriage. Constantine, as son of an Emperor and son-in-law of the Emperor Emeritus, would out-rank both Galerius and Aurelius Maxentius. He decided to appear naive.

"I can't see that it'll change anything; Diocletian's already decreed that sons can't succeed fathers, so that excludes both you and Aurelius."

"Yes, but the decree doesn't prevent a son becoming his father's Praetorian Prefect! That's what I intend to be, and when I am, I'll appoint you Magister Militum."

Giorgios caught his breath; a Marshal of the Empire! That was a legitimate ambition for any soldier, and one which would be a justification of his father.

"I'll hold you to that, Constantine. Meanwhile, shall we take a stroll down to the mess?"

As they walked through the shaded colonnades, Giorgios broached another subject that was puzzling him: "Does Galerius spend much of his time here?"

"Most of it! With all quiet on the Danube, he takes the opportunity to keep his grip on Diocletian."

Giorgios was surprised.

"I wouldn't have thought that anyone could influence the Emperor."

"A lot has changed in the time you've been away – nearly two years isn't it?"

"About that. But how can Galerius have become influential after all that's happened – at Carrhae I mean."

"Ha! Don't forget that he's married to Diocletian's darling daughter, his only child. She has Daddy round her little finger, and Diocletian himself is in ill-health. No! I'm afraid Galerius' influence increases every day; no one can get past him and the flunkeys he's surrounded the Emperor with." They had reached the mess and

Constantine ordered wine. "The trouble is that Galerius' influence is all for the bad. He reinforces Diocletian's organization mania."

"My uncle's always going on about that."

"Well, if he is, he has good reason; Galerius' is urging Diocletian to issue an Edict fixing maximum prices for practically everything, and a maximum wage for every trade."

"Is that a bad thing? Won't it stop prices rising all the time?"

Constantine gave his friend an odd look.

"You're a good soldier, Giorgios, but you think too straight to be a politician. If the maximum price doesn't cover the costs of production, men will stop producing, or else they'll sell under the counter. If the maximum wage doesn't allow a man to live, he'll stop working and join the unemployed in the cities."

Constantine was so vehement that Giorgios could only confess his ignorance in such matters.

"What can be done?" he asked helplessly.

"Only wait for better times", Constantine replied with a shrug.

"Galerius' bubble may burst, especially if the new currency doesn't do what he claims it will."

"New currency?" Giorgios realized that he had been very much out of touch with things when he was in far Britannia, especially as that province and Gaul had prospered under the benevolent rule of Constantius.

"Yes", Constantine was eager to talk, "A new edict lays down a minimum silver content for the denarius, and it's considerably higher than it was. Galerius' idea is that this will restrict the number of coins the mints can issue, and that will increase the value of each coin; in other words, he thinks that good money will drive out bad. What he doesn't seem to understand is that the cost of the increased silver content must be recovered from somewhere, ultimately from prices. That's why prices are rising, and that's why he now wants edicts setting maximum prices and wages in the hope of putting the lid on."

It struck Giorgios that his apt pupil had now become his mentor.

"Thank God I'm a soldier and not a politician", he said, and the conversation drifted off into talk of old friends and the grumbles of soldiers.

Giorgios had been kicking his heels around the barracks for a week; there seemed to be no position for him, and he was beginning to suspect the hand of Galerius, when he received a summons to appear before the Caesar. He had learned much in that week. There were traditionally four grades in the higher civil service. Now the grades had been transformed into a rigid caste system, distinguished not only by attire, but by the required manner of address. In descending order the administrators were *illustris, spectabilis, clarissimus* and *perfectissimus*. Sitting above and beyond this hierarchy was the Emperor, barely approachable by anyone below the rank of perfectissimus. Those who were admitted to the Imperial presence were required to prostrate themselves before the throne and kiss the hem of the purple robe. The earthly representative of God had become God-on-Earth. Giorgios considered himself fortunate that Diocletian had not sent for him, perhaps did not even know that he had returned, for perform the prostration, he would not.

Galerius, although Caesar and in the purple, did not surround himself with the protocol with which he had cocooned the Emperor. He was accessible to all, their trustworthy voice – as he repeatedly assured everyone – in the Emperor's ear. Now he sat in a chair at the head of the audience chamber, Licinius standing behind him, watching Giorgios intently as he walked the length of the room. Giorgios, with absolute correctness, halted, saluted and stood to attention.

He noted the change in Galerius. His cheeks had become purple-blotched jowls, his forehead creased, his hair receding and his body run to fat. Galerius, for his part, glared balefully at Giorgios.

"So! The hero has deigned to return, his fame as a dragon-slayer going before him."

Giorgios was startled, but kept his face expressionless. As he had been asked no question, he remained silent.

"Oh yes! We have received many reports of you, doubtless greatly exaggerated as is usual in your case. We have heard of your slaying of the fire-breathing dragon. We have heard how the winds and the waves obey you. We have heard how you drove the Painted People, almost single-handed, back into the sea; of how you repulsed the Scotti, with a little help from the Caesar Constantius; of how you became the commander of the armies of British kings; of how you searched for the tomb of your ancestor, Joseph of Arimathea, uncle of your Prophet; and of how your search, though fruitless, was nevertheless rewarded with the miraculous blossoming of a thorn bush, providentially transported from Lydda three centuries ago for just that purpose." Galerius was forced to pause to take breath. "We have even heard of how, in a secret place, you cure lunatics and hysterics – though not, apparently, those who believe these fantasies. We used to boast that we had eyes and ears everywhere, but in your case they are unnecessary, for your fame has gone abroad throughout the world."

Giorgios listened to this tirade uncomprehendingly. He had given a cursory account of events in his letters home, but surely such brief mentions could not be the basis of these accusations?

"You have nothing to say to all this?" Galerius barked.

Giorgios shook himself into some presence of mind, "I cannot understand, Augustus, where these reports could have come from."

Galerius gave a short laugh, "Where? Yes indeed, where? Where else but from yourself, to gain fame among the accursed followers of your superstition and to incite them against the State – you and your scribe, another Mansour in the making."

Light dawned on Giorgios: "Pasicrates!" Philosophers might dispute whether the pen was mightier than the sword, but there could be no doubt that in Pasicrates' hands it was more dangerous. The boy was a natural storyteller and his admiration for Giorgios was without bounds; he had obviously read Giorgios' letters home and his fertile imagination had transformed each item of news into an epic.

"I take full responsibility, Augustus. My scribe, who is but a youth, has no blame in this matter."

Galerius was triumphant. He had an admission of responsibility and that was what he wanted; he was not really interested in the scribe.

Licinius bent down and whispered in his ear, "There is no law against storytelling, Augustus. You know how these things are: bring this man to court and there will be a thousand fools to testify that they have seen fiery dragons and another thousand to swear to shrubs blossoming in the midst of winter; the stories about him will grow a thousand times more preposterous. Best to dismiss him, send him back to his estates to be a nine-day wonder."

Galerius scowled. He knew that Licinius was right, but somehow these Theognostas, father, and now son, always slipped his net. He did not consider that this might be because the conspiracies he attributed to them were all in his own mind. At last he spoke.

"I have no place for vainglorious boasters, Tribune, nor has the army. You are dismissed. Return to your estates, you will never serve in the army again."

Giorgios swallowed his anger. The only crumb of comfort was that Galerius had not thought to ask the one question he dreaded. He saluted, turned, and was about to march away when Galerius stopped him.

"What was your mission to Britannia, Tribune? Why did the Emperor send you to Constantius Chlorus?"

Giorgios turned slowly, "My mission, as you call it, was a kind of exile, Augustus. The Emperor felt that he had best send me into obscurity in Britannia in the service of Caesar Constantius."

Galerius stared hard at him, but Giorgios' face showed nothing. He had not lied, merely evaded a question which his interrogator had no authority to ask. Galerius gnawed his lip; he could not decide if he had been outwitted or not. On impulse he made up his mind.

"Go! And do not return to Nicomedia unless you come to die."

*   *   *

At the time when Giorgios was packing his belongings, seeking a ship for Joppa, and pacifying an infuriated Constantine, a chamberlain was sweeping through the audience hall of the palatium casting supervisory glances to right and left, pausing to rebuke a slave engaged in polishing the floor or in dusting the statues of gods and heroes which lined the hall. If the man's expression was not abject enough to gratify him, he would prolong the pause sufficiently to strike the man with his cane or aim a kick at him. This great hall was the chamberlain's domain: here he was master and the very worst of slave-masters, for he was a slave himself.

The chamberlain came to the top of the hall where the chairs of the Caesar and his notables stood upon a dais. Immediately to the right of the dais on a high pedestal, was the bronze statue of the Capitoline Wolf. Near to it, against a column, was a marble pedestal about four feet high, and upon this stood a bust of the Emperor. Before the bust was a silver lamp and a silver bowl of incense. Sacrifice to the Genius of the Emperor and worship of his divinity was made by sprinkling a pinch of incense on the lamp. The chamberlain paused and strode over to the pedestal to inspect it for the slightest mote of dust. As he put his weight on the marble paving slab on which the pedestal stood, it rocked and the flame in the lamp wavered.

The chamberlain loved matters of great consequence, so much indeed that he was apt to transform even the most ordinary happening into a drama. Imperiously he beckoned one of the cleaners, "Hasten to the carpenters' workshop and inform the first carpenter you see to come here immediately", he said, giving the slave a blow across the head to impress upon him the urgency of his mission, "and be quick about it."

There was only one carpenter at the workshop waiting for work. Receiving the message, he picked up his tool bag, summoned his apprentice, and hastened to the hall. However he was waylaid en route by another of the palace's chamberlains who insisted that he attend to some minor work. It was an hour before he arrived, breathless, to where the chamberlain was waiting in growing fury, having convinced himself that the carpenter's delay was an act of insolence.

"Idle pig, come immediately when I summon you", he barked, and struck the carpenter across the face. "See to this loose paving." The carpenter, his face burning with anger and shame, bent to inspect the slab, whereupon the chamberlain gave him a well-aimed kick before resuming his strut down the hall. The carpenter removed the lamp and the bowl and, with his apprentice, lifted off the bust of the Emperor. With the assistance of several of the slaves he man-handled the pedestal out of the way.

Except in the fields of civil and military engineering, the Romans were often jerry-builders. Their marble colonnades, marble interiors and marble baths were, more often than not, constructed of concrete, veneered with thin marble slabs. When the carpenter raised the loose paving slab, he saw immediately what was wrong. The joists on which the slabs rested lay flat on the beaten earth beneath. Dry rot had infected them.

The carpenter was normally a conscientious worker. He knew that at least sixteen square yards of the floor should be taken up and all the timber, whether infected or not, removed and burnt; and that the earth beneath should be excavated and the cavity purified by fire. He was, however, smarting with anger and humiliation. He removed only three slabs, one from either side of the unsteady one. He cut out the diseased joists and replaced them with pieces of new timber secured to the old by long nails.

He replaced the paving slabs, stamped on them to check that they were steady, and had the slaves manhandle the pedestal into place. The bust and the lamp and bowl now replaced, he packed his tools, called his apprentice, and returned to the workshop, gratified that he had avenged the blow and the kick. The fungus spores scattered on the beaten earth began their work again with consequences as yet unforeseen.

CHAPTER SIXTY THREE

Changes there had been, Giorgios found, on his return to Lydda, but not in the pattern of life of a Christian household which moved with the seasons, as it had always done. Moderation and contentment were part of the atmosphere of a pious home and loving family. Cyrennius had completed his studies at Alexandria and had opened the hospice at El Kudr. Lucius was a deputy in the Quaestor's office at Caesarea and Pasicrates was pleading to be allowed to go to Alexandria to study the world's literature.

Giorgios took the opportunity to administer a mild rebuke.

"I know that you love writing, but you must not exaggerate, Pasicrates, it could cause a great deal of trouble."

"But the pagan authors write of monsters, gorgons and centaurs; even here at Lydda they tell of how Perseus slew the sea-dragon and rescued Andromeda. Their stories thrill people, and I want mine to do so too. Why should the pagans have the best stories?"

"I have no doubt that the Pagan myths are exciting, but you must understand, Pasicrates, that I have no desire to become a myth, least of all one confused with Perseus, if there ever was such a person at Lydda or anywhere else. When Christian authors exaggerate and invent wonders and marvels, they discredit the Gospel. They even cause unseemly mirth in church when they creep into the sermon."

"Perhaps", said Pasicrates slyly, "a little study at Alexandria would teach me to understand the difference."

Giorgios smiled, he could guess at the difference which was attracting Pasicrates.

"I'm quite certain that it would, if directed by the right mentor. Well, you may go for a year; but do not be cast into utter despair if the maid is already married – and see that you study at least four days out of seven."

Pasicrates let out a whoop of joy, and all but overwhelmed Giorgios with his thanks.

*   *   *

Uncle Andrew had not done well out of the re-organization of the provinces. A new civil governor had been appointed for Galilee. This man had moved into the residency and Julia, loathe to leave Lydda, had come to live with Kira and Martha, bringing Justus' library with her. Claudia had also moved into Kira's villa, leaving the cottage which had been home to her and Mansour. With Giorgios' long absence the villa was almost entirely a female establishment. With three of the four women middle-aged there was much invidious comparison between the hardships of their youth and the good fortune and ingratitude of the new generation. Andrew sourly dubbed them "The Sisters of Perpetual Indignation".

With the legate of the Xth having been appointed Dux of the armies in Syria, Galilee and Judea, Andrew was left with little more than the title of "Count", a matter which grieved him greatly. Susannah had presented him, after several years of marriage, with two sons: Andrew, now twelve and Anastasius, ten; two cousins whom Giorgios had not had the chance of getting to know, until now.

Philip the tutor still made himself at home in one villa or the other. No sooner had Pasicrates passed through his hands, than young Andrew and Anastasius were ready to be his pupils. If he thought about the matter at all on his daily triangulations between the school room, the dining room and the library, he probably concluded that philosophers and poor scholars deserved such good fortune. Marcus, faithful old centurion, had died some years before and Giorgios was surprised to learn that no provision had been made to teach Andrew and Anastasius horsemanship or any military skills. He gladly undertook their education in this all-important field, and found them both apt and willing pupils.

Giorgios found that he was enjoying rural life. Remembering his own childhood, he gathered the children of the estate for lessons and games. Always, it seemed to Kira, her son was surrounded by children, teaching them to ride, to wrestle, to fence with wooden swords and to play ball games. He was, in fact, one of them at heart; a big brother and exemplar to the troupe which followed at his heels. She broached the subject of marriage several times, but he was adamant that no one would or could displace Justina. He would be faithful to her memory forever.

In spite of his mother's anxieties, Giorgios was content. He would, he decided, rather be a country squire, shaikh of his clan and a river to his people, than even Magister Militum of the Roman Empire. He put Constantine's forebodings of Galerius' economic policies out of his mind. "The eyes of the fool are on the ends of the earth", he told himself, and from now on his concern would be for his own people. As it happened, things were going well. No one was hungry, no one was ill-clad or ill-shod and no one was without a roof over his head. He was also gratified that most of the pagan slaves on the estate, and even some neighbouring Samaritans, were seeking baptism. He would have been astonished to know that many put this down to his example and influence.

This contented life was interrupted by two Imperial Edicts promulgated jointly in A.D. 301. The first set maximum prices for every conceivable commodity, without variation for climate, terrain or season. The prices were to be carved in stone in every market place. The second edict set maximum wages for every type of employment, from dock porter to schoolmaster.

"How is it proposed to enforce this? What are the penalties?" Giorgios asked his uncle.

"Death!" replied Andrew, "Death for charging more, death for paying more, and death for paying or accepting a higher wage!"

"But that's preposterous!"

"Edicts as preposterous as these can only be enforced by disproportionate penalties", Andrew replied.

The ill effects foreseen by Constantine were immediate. Others were long-term. Goods disappeared from the markets to be sold "under the counter". The maximum wage was circumvented by "gifts" of corn, wine or oil. The enforcement of the Edicts required an army of snoopers, *agents provocateurs*, who descended on the markets to entrap traders by offering higher prices.

These parasites, when exposed, were lucky to escape with their lives, and to protect them troops had to be withdrawn from the frontiers. As the snoopers were required to make a certain number of reports each week, they began to spy and report upon each other. A miasma of fear and suspicion spread across the Empire.

Longer-term trends were well illustrated by Andrew's reaction to the new gold coin, the Solidus. It was the one thing he approved of, and he set about acquiring and hoarding as many as he could. With many doing the same, the gold coin disappeared from circulation almost as quickly as it was issued.

This was one factor, though a major one, in the inflation of the denarius, forcing it back to its old value.

*   *   *

"Necessity", is the plea for every infringement of human liberty. It is the argument of tyrants, and the creed of slaves.

Galerius fully understood the appeal to "necessity". It had worked when the Empire was under siege, but with the frontiers restored, a new "necessity", a new enemy, had to be found – the defeat of inflation. If the first edicts were manifestly not working, Galerius reasoned, it was because they were not comprehensive enough and must be strengthened by further edicts.

To maintain the army and enlarged civil service, the Empire was turned into a taxation machine. Every holding of land was valued and a tax levied upon it which the smaller landowner and the peasant found it impossible to pay. If the landowner abandoned his land, the state seized it. Eventually the greater part of the land was to pass into state-ownership, as were industry and transport. Men left the land for the cities, and so a further series of edicts not only bound peasants to their farm, and labourers to their villa, but also bound their children to the land in perpetuity. Attempted escape from this new form of slavery was punishable by fearful penalties.

The city worker was not neglected. With the maximum wages insufficient to keep a man and his family, many gave up work, swelling the unemployed, maintained by the daily dole of corn and wine. New edicts obliged all to belong to the guild of their craft, binding them and their children to it. Whatever their employment, factory worker, shoemaker, baker, scribe – all were tied to their bench or desk. It became difficult to persuade honest men to accept election as curials and magistrates of their city – once an honour eagerly sought. A bleary-eyed clarissimus had hit upon the idea of making the curials responsible for the total property tax of their city and obliged to make up any shortfall. The honest citizen now avoided taking an office which was likely to ruin him. He was replaced on the curia by the dishonest, who justified the peculation of the city funds and the exaction of excess tax, as an insurance against failure to collect the full amount of the tax. It was not that the Imperial officials were wilfully perverse, on the contrary, the Empire was being strangled by good intentions. The bars which were intended to hold it together were the bars of its prison.

All this did not happen at once, but after as little as two years the trends were discernible.

"What can we do?" asked Giorgios.

"Nothing!" his uncle replied. "The cart is sunk too deep in the mire for it to be dragged clear."

Giorgios shook his head, "There will be one oppression too many, and then someone must do something."

CHAPTER SIXTY-FOUR

Galerius was well aware that his measures had gone wrong.

It was not entirely his fault: the Romans did not have a credit system and had never mastered the mysteries of monetary circulation and value. What was his fault was his failure to apply the first rule of battle: never reinforce failure. On the contrary, pride, vanity and the "Dacian" chip on his shoulder, made him stubbornly determined to reinforce his policy. As the unintended results became apparent, he sought for someone to blame.

"The traders", he fumed to Licinius, "if they had observed the maximum prices; the workers, if they had accepted the maximum wage, the new denarius would have bought more and everything would have worked out."

Licinius frowned, "Perhaps they were hungry, Domine."

Galerius scowled at him, Licinius was becoming too free-spoken these days.

"After the terrible sixty years the Empire has gone through, everyone has to make sacrifices", he retorted.

The Emperor was another problem. Diocletian had recovered his health and strength and his lassitude had left him. Now he was asking questions and wanting answers. Galerius' future was not so bright as it had been when he had drafted the Prices and Wages Edicts for Diocletian to sign. A culprit must be found.

As it happened, a culprit was found, and that without any effort on Galerius' part. In Nicomedia a group of wild men, their hair and beards long and unkempt, dressed in sheepskins, wandered into the city, which they insisted upon calling "Sodom and Gomorrah", threatening it with destruction by fire from heaven. When they were arrested, a number of scrolls were found in their possession and were brought to the attention of Galerius.

Galerius savoured his moment. At last he had the evidence which had so long eluded him.

"Who is this Tertullian?" he demanded of Licinius.

"A Christian author and controversialist, Quintus Septimius Florens Tertullianus; he died about eighty years ago."

"Ha, and here is his treason, plainly written for all to read. He threatens the Eternal City, urges the Christians to destroy civilization, and stirs up another Spartacus to lead a slave revolt. He even calls the sacred games a 'hideous offence against humanity'. Listen to this: 'He who shudders at the body of a man who died naturally, goes to the amphitheatre to gawp at the bodies of men broken and bleeding, torn in pieces, covered in their own blood. Even he who goes on the pretext of seeing murderers brought to justice, will call for a reluctant gladiator to be driven with lash and rod to do murder.' What do you think of that?"

Licinius shrugged, "I think I might read exactly the same sentiments in Seneca."

Galerius was about to ask who Seneca was, but thought better of it.

"The games are sacrifices to the immortal gods! This Tertullian denies the gods their due!" Licinius shifted uneasily, he was loathe to get into a dispute with Galerius; but something told him that another catastrophe was being hatched.

"As I said, Domine, you will find many who say the same thing about the games."

Galerius snatched up another of the scrolls, "See here! He says that slavery is immoral and inhuman: is that not inciting the slaves to revolt?"

Licinius took the scroll from him. "He also says that since slavery cannot immediately or easily be abolished, the master has duties to his slaves as they have to him; that he must treat them well and be as a father to them. Many of the Stoics say the same thing."

"That's exactly what I'm saying. The Christians are insinuating their ideas even among those who should know better." Galerius was reading another scroll and he smiled in triumph. "You won't find any excuses for this one, just listen to it. 'We are but of yesterday, and we have filled every place belonging to you: cities, islands, fortresses, towns, assemblies, the palace, the Senate, the law-courts; the only thing we have left to you are your temples.' Isn't that treason?"

"It's more like vain boasting, and it's greatly exaggerated, but it's true to a certain extent: some of the ablest and best-educated men in the Empire are Christians."

"You're singing a new tune, Licinius; this is not the way you used to think."

"I've learned, Domine, that's all. There's no evidence that the Christians plot against the Empire; some of them even say that the Empire is the work of Divine Providence. If you want to confiscate their funds, that's a different matter, but you'll need stronger evidence than the opinions of an eccentric to justify your actions; that horse just won't run."

Galerius was not going to let go of an opportunity; for one thing he had an audience with the Emperor in an hour's time, and his instincts told him that he would have to have a good case if he were to be successful in shifting any blame. He picked up another scroll and, ignoring Licinius, settled down to read.

"See here", he said, after a while, "this Tertullian of yours calls Rome 'The Great Harlot' and 'The Whore of Babylon'. He writes that the Christian God will destroy it. He says every act which serves Rome maintains idolatry and immorality. He tells Christians that they must refuse all civic duties. He says that the only true Christians are those who leave the civilized world to live in the desert. Doesn't that make it plain that it's the Christians who have ruined the economy?"

Licinius arched his eyebrow. He was wary of Galerius but no longer afraid of him.

"There's something about Tertullian that you don't know."

"What's that?"

"All his later writings are repudiated by the Christian bishops who expelled him from their Church."

"Well, they would, wouldn't they? He's exposed their secrets."

"It's not as simple as that. Tertullian's early books, in which he defended the doctrines of the Christians, were highly praised. The praise went to his head; he became more and more severe in castigating Christians who were not as ascetic as himself. Finally, he taught that the bishops might not absolve sinners more than once in a lifetime. There was a great row about it and the Bishop of Rome expelled him. It was after that that he began to rave against the Empire."

"What happened to him?" Galerius was suddenly interested.

"He took his own advice and went into the desert and nothing more was heard of him."

Galerius gathered up the scrolls.

"Well, I can assure you a great deal will be heard of him from now on. The Emperor will be convinced this time."

It was perhaps fortuitous that a fire broke out in Galerius' wing of the palatium a few nights later, and that scrawled on the wall was the Christian symbol of the fish.

CHAPTER SIXTY-FIVE

The Saturnalia at Lydda had been a happy one. Giorgios was delighted that the snow on the Galilean hills had spread down to the coast. He organized the boys on the estate into two armies and a grand battle was fought with snowballs, followed by a feast and the distribution of gifts. Pasicrates joined in the fun. He was happy because Philemon had agreed that he should marry Cleosolinda, when she was twenty-one. The holiday atmosphere lasted through January and preparations were in hand for the spring lambing and sowing when, in the first days of February, A.D.303, the Edicts against the Christians fell like a bolt from the blue.

Both Giorgios and Andrew were summoned to Lydda to hear the Edict read in the basilica. The protonotarius of the curia rose, holding a heavy scroll. The Emperor's greetings and the list of his titles and victories took quite some time before the substance of the document was reached. The impiety of the sect of Christians, the Edict declared, had become intolerable. It was notorious that their activities had caused upheavals in all parts of the Empire, that they had treacherously supported rebellion and false Emperors, that Christian traders had thwarted the Edicts on maximum prices and maximum wages, that they had hoarded gold and smuggled it to fellow Christians in the Persian Empire.

An angry murmur spread through the crowd. Further, the protonotarius droned on, felonious Christians had attempted to murder the Noble Caesar Galerius by setting fire to his rooms in the palatium. There was an angry shout at this, loudest from those who had frequently expressed the hope that someone would assassinate Galerius. The accusations were not yet finished.

The Divine Emperor, ever careful of the Roman Peace and the safety and security of all, had graciously called a council of the most eminent men in the Empire to examine the activities of this nefarious sect and to determine what their ultimate aims might be. The Council, presided over by the Noble Caesar Galerius, had concluded that the Christians intended to set up a state within the state, that they plotted to overthrow the gods and institutions of Rome, that they refused to worship the Genius of the Emperor, so bringing ill luck on the armies of Rome.

Further, they elected magistrates of their own who made laws at variance with the laws of Rome, and they unlawfully collected treasure to be used for the spreading of their blasphemous cult. So insolent had they become that they even planned to set up their own armed force in despite of the Disarmament Edict which had brought public safety and peace to the Empire.

By this time the entire audience was seething with indignation. The protonotarius paused for dramatic effect and then continued. The patience of the Divine Emperor was exhausted, he could no longer allow his natural clemency to sway his better judgement. This nefarious sect was to be suppressed. In every province of the Empire severe measures were to be taken against them. There was a general murmur of approval.

The first Edict was directed against Church property. All scrolls of scripture, of the liturgy, and of works defending the doctrines of the Christians, were to be surrendered to the magistrates and publicly burned. All property belonging to the sect was to be seized and sold and the money delivered to the Imperial Treasury under the control of the Noble Caesar Galerius. All temples of the sect were to be levelled to the ground.

Andrew and Giorgios hastened back to the villa and the first thing that Andrew did was to gather up his gold and hide it under a paving slab in the hypocaust.

"There'll be worse to come", he told the family. Giorgios' immediate concern was the scrolls. "Somehow", he told Lucius, "they must be saved".

Pasicrates had a suggestion, "I learned in Sylene that, far down the Nile, beyond the frontiers of the Empire, there is another Empire called 'Ethiopia', where there are many Christians; even, it is said, their Emperor is a Christian. Perhaps we could take the scrolls there for safe-keeping?" Lucius was doubtful if such a journey could be made, but Giorgios took up the suggestion.

"Our scrolls could be taken to Sylene and hidden there; it's a little-known place and there is papyrus-making in every house. They may be safe there whilst we arrange transport down the Nile."

"Who will take them?" Pasicrates asked, rather too eagerly.

Giorgios smiled, "Why, who else but he who thought of it?"

*　　　*　　　*

A second anti-Christian Edict followed, this time directed not against property, but persons. All in public office, whether Imperial, Municipal or Military, who refused to sacrifice to the Genius of the Emperor, were to be instantly dismissed. All Christians were deprived of Roman citizenship and could not seek restitution in the courts, defend themselves against an accusation or appeal from a judicial verdict. No Christian slave could be emancipated. A third Edict ordered the arrest of bishops and presbyters who were to be imprisoned and tortured until they publicly sacrificed to the gods. It imposed the death penalty for attendance at secret worship.

"You understand what this means?" Andrew asked, and then went on to answer the question himself. "It means that every suit at law against us will be accepted without question and any thief who steals from us, or even murders us, will be free from punishment. We are very likely to lose all our estates."

Giorgios sensed belligerence in his uncle's voice and stance.

"What does it profit a man if he gain the whole world, yet suffers the loss of his soul?" he asked.

Andrew, looking sour, walked away, but then turned and threw over his shoulder, "We're not talking about the whole world, but a pinch of incense and a scrap of paper." The "scrap of paper" was a "Certificate of Sacrifice".

Giorgios, on his next visit to Lydda, found a long line of people stretched halfway across the forum from the entrance of the basilica.

"Why, most of those are Christians", he exclaimed, recognizing a number of them.

"All are", replied Lucius, who had lost his position in the legal service.

"But what are they doing?"

"They're sprinkling a pinch of incense to the Genius of our Divine and Beloved Emperor, and getting a certificate to prove that they've done so."

Giorgios was aghast, "But that's apostasy, and by so many."

"They tell themselves that it isn't. They sprinkle the incense whilst denying its meaning under their breath."

The little furrow creased Giorgios' forehead, "And they really think that the heart can be the same after such an act?"

"I suppose so, but there's quite a trade in forged certificates, so which do you think is worse?"

There was no hesitation in Giorgios' reply, "Those who buy forged certificates, they may deceive the Emperor, but they can't deceive God."

"I can't see that one is worse than the other in that respect", Lucius replied, "but in practical terms, if the forgeries outnumber the genuine, the whole thing becomes a farce, so perhaps they're helping to defeat the Edicts."

Giorgios shook his head sadly.

"Forged or genuine, the scandal to others is the same. But I'd like to see one of these certificates; there might still be law in Rome."

His wish was granted sooner, and in a way which caused him more pain and consternation, than he expected. Andrew emerged from the basilica clutching a certificate. Lucius studied it eagerly; it read: "I have sacrificed to the gods in your presence and according to the terms of the Edict and I ask that you add your signature as witness", (signed) Andrew, Count of Lydda, and beneath, "I witnessed Andrew, Count of Lydda, sacrificing, and I append my signature."

"No loopholes in that", Lucius concluded grimly.

There was a long and painful silence between the three as they stood at the foot of the steps of the stoa. Andrew became visibly more truculent.

"Think what you like", he eventually exploded, "I'm not going to lose our family estates for a pinch of incense, and you'll both be grateful to me one day when all of this business is over."

"It can never be over if we don't stand firm", Giorgios said.

Andrew looked defiant, "Well, you obviously haven't heard. The Empress Prisca Alexandra and her daughter, Galeria Valeria, have been exposed as secret Christians, and have been obliged to offer public sacrifice to the gods. What's good enough for an Empress is good enough for me", and with that he strode angrily away.

Before Giorgios and Lucius could follow him they were stopped short by the appearance on the basilica steps of a wild figure, unshaven and unbarbered for many years. He was barefoot and clad in a sheepskin. He raised a staff aloft and began to harangue those entering the basilica.

"Beware, apostates! There shall be no return to salvation for you".

"A Tertullianite", Giorgios hissed to Lucius; "we could do without trouble-makers just now."

The man was working himself up into a fine fury, "The hand of God is already stretched out over the Great Harlot, the Whore of Babylon, drunk upon the blood of the saints. Fire and brimstone will descend upon her, and when her very name is wiped out, do not think that we will forget you, apostates. Do not, in your vanity and foolishness, imagine that you will be received back." A decurion and two troopers came hastening up.

"Here come the sons of Satan, the doomed and the damned whom you have – " He was cut short by a blow to the stomach from the decurion's spear butt. As he doubled up, the troopers seized him and dragged him away.

"Is there anything we can do?"

Giorgios turned to Lucius, "No! You know the Edict. He can be tried and condemned without hearing or defence. Let's hope the magistrates will be lenient, give him a scourging and throw him out of the city."

They heard later that the fanatic had been found guilty of threatening Rome, of defying the Divine Emperor and obstructing Roman citizens performing their duty, and had been condemned to be burnt alive.

CHAPTER SIXTY-SIX

Once he had returned to the villa, Giorgios went to the chapel and prayed, standing with arms outstretched before him, palms uppermost in the manner of the Eastern Church. He prayed earnestly for his uncle and for all those who had committed the greatest of all sins – apostasy, the flinging of salvation back into God's face. He remained in the silent room for several hours, consumed with zeal for souls. He emerged when he knew what he must do.

He first sought out his mother and told her of his decision.

"But why you?" she asked. "Why must it be you?"

"Because I'm here, Mother; there's no one else. Don't worry, Diocletian will listen to me."

Kira stood calmly, she could think of nothing to say; and when she did speak, she knew immediately how trite it sounded.

"Well, do be careful."

Giorgios bowed and left to summon Lucius, Cyrennius and Pasicrates to the library, and without any preliminaries told them of his intentions.

"I will go to Nicomedia and plead with Diocletian for justice and an end to this persecution."

"They will kill you", Lucius said.

"Please don't go", there was panic in Pasicrates' voice.

"You will not even get as far as the Emperor", Cyrennius said. "Just let us all stay here and keep our heads down."

Giorgios shook his head, "I am hoping that Constantine will get me into the Emperor's presence. Galerius will never have enough loot to satisfy his greed. I know, but can say no more, that once Diocletian and Maximian have abdicated and he is Emperor of the East, he intends to seize the West. There is never enough gold to meet the cost of that, and meanwhile souls are being lost. As for me, I ask of you, brothers and friends, only one thing; if they kill me, recover my body and bring it back to Lydda, and bury me beside Justina."

Pasicrates jumped up from the bench where he was sitting, his fists clenched.

"If you go, I go!" he exclaimed.

"And I", said Lucius.

"And I", cried Cyrennius, standing up in his urgency. "Otherwise how can we bring your body back to Lydda?"

Giorgios smiled, their support meant a great deal to him.

"You always were a clever one, Cyrennius, but we'll discuss who goes later. I want to deal with the practicalities. You're the lawyer, Lucius."

Lucius flapped his hands helplessly, "I was, I've been dismissed from the courts."

"But not from your learning. Let's get down to business. My own inheritance from my father's estate was the villa in Cappadocia. I emancipated the slaves years ago, and divided the land, as my father had wished. Can they touch that, Lucius?"

Lucius frowned.

"No! I would say not, it's only Christians who are slaves at the time of the Edict who cannot be emancipated."

Giorgios nodded, "Good! A half share of this villa is my mother's widow's portion, can they touch that?"

Lucius stood up and paced the room, "At present, no! The Edict seizes church property and money on the legal point that the church, not being a registered corporation, cannot own property or common funds. It also provides for the seizure of the property and money of bishops and presbyters who refuse to sacrifice, but it makes no mention of women or their property."

Giorgios crossed to the window.

"The other half falls in equal shares to the three of us. Can they take that?"

"If the Edict is extended to all Christians, yes!"

Cyrennius gave a brief laugh.

"In that case, why not give mother our shares as a gift?"

Giorgios pondered this.

"I'd need Abba Theodore's judgement on that, if he can be found."

"Nothing simpler", Cyrennius said, crossing to a table and helping himself to a cup of wine. "Your mother has him hidden away in our old cottage, pretending to be a head gardener. Anyone else want wine?"

Theodore was sent for and listened to the case.

"You are entitled to avoid the seizure of your property. That is a different matter from dishonestly evading just laws."

"What's the difference between 'avoidance' and 'evasion'?" Cyrennius asked, pouring wine for Theodore and another cup for himself.

"Not always clear, but clear enough. If I wish to travel from here to Antioch and I hide aboard a ship and pay no fare, that is evasion and theft. However, I am under no moral obligation to increase the ship owner's income by sailing first to Alexandria and from there to Antioch. I am morally entitled to avoid the extra fare by travelling straight to Antioch."

Cyrennius came and sat down, "How does that apply to paying taxes?" he asked.

"Plain enough. If I work hard and earn a thousand denarii of which I am lawfully required to pay a hundred in tax, I am under no moral obligation to work twice as hard to earn two thousand denarii, so that I might pay two hundred in tax."

Giorgios slapped his hand on the table. He did not want this to become an exercise in logic-chopping.

"Well, may we protect our property by gifting it to my mother?"

"Yes!" replied Theodore.

A slave knocked at the door to announce that the evening meal was ready. Rather testily, Giorgios dismissed him with the message that the meal should be delayed. He crossed to the window again and looked out. The first buds were bursting upon the trees and the first blossom opening. Blue smoke stood up from the cottages and the shadows of the cedar plantations were creeping across the pasture and the vineyards.

All his memories were here and the place had never seemed so dear. It would be hard, very hard, to leave it.

He turned, "Is it too late now to emancipate the slaves on the estate?"

Lucius nodded, "The Edict expressly forbids the emancipation of Christian slaves, forever."

"You could emancipate the pagan slaves", Pasicrates piped up.

Giorgios looked at him and smiled.

"That would only cause jealousy and envy, but I will provide for them in a different way. My personal treasure is considerable. Quite apart from my inheritance from my father I was not a squanderbug in the army, and a Tribune's pay is high. My Treasury is to be divided into halves. Half will be kept hidden, and I have no scruples about that, as a fund for the emancipation of the slaves if things should improve. If they don't improve, the fund will be used to emancipate all infants born on the estate, which means that those of Christian parents will be emancipated before they are baptized."

Cyrennius gave a hoot of laughter at this announcement,

"I bet Galerius never thought of that!"

"The other half of my treasury will be divided into ten shares. One share for my sister Katherine, who is married, two shares for my sister Martha, two shares each for Lucius and Cyrennius and three shares for Pasicrates, who has no other inheritance. I want you, Lucius, to get the paperwork done as soon as possible."

"Are we coming with you?" Pasicrates demanded.

"Yes, I've thought about that. I'll be glad of your support, but once in Nicomedia you must remain in a mansio and not interfere in anything I do. One last thing, Lucius".

Giorgios crossed to the wall and took down his sword. He unsheathed it and the blade blazed with reflected light. There seemed to be fire deep in the heart of the great ruby in the hilt.

"In Britannia, praying in the first church built there, I was inspired to pledge this sword as an offering. I will not carry any weapons in Nicomedia, but if I lose my life there, I ask you, Lucius, to take this sword to Britannia. Go to Ambrosius Aurelius, he is a great lord, known to all. He will receive the sword from you and place it under the altar stone of that church."

He handed the blade to Lucius who took it with tears streaming down his face. Kissing the cross of the handle, he said, "I swear it."

As they left the library for the dining room, Theodore detained Giorgios.

"Are you certain that this is the Will of God?"

"Abba", Giorgios replied earnestly, "in prayer today all my life came before me and I understood, as I was once told that I should, God's purpose in all that He has permitted, in all that I have done or that has happened to me. The question I have so often asked, 'Why did Justina die?' was at last answered. If I had married her I would not, could not, have accepted this cup, a cup that I heard a voice, as plain as I hear yours, tell me was of supreme importance in God's plan. Why or how was not revealed to me, but I know that all my life has been a preparation for this. I have drunk the wine of Cana, now I must drink the vinegar of Calvary, but with the promise of new wine in the heavenly Kingdom."

Abba Theodore listened silently with the growing sense that he was in the presence of holiness. He raised his hand in blessing and, having blessed, said, "It seems it is necessary that one man should die, that the People might not perish."

CHAPTER SIXTY-SEVEN

Giorgios' plan received its first setback when, arriving by sea at Nicomedia, he learned that Constantine was not in the city. Galerius had taken the opportunity of Diocletian's ill health and seclusion to dispatch him on a tour of inspection of the Danube frontier. While Constantine's mother, Helena, was living in Drepanum, Galerius was confident that Constantine would not slip away to join his father at Trier. Without Constantine's help, Giorgios could not get past Galerius, and this called for a change of plan.

"You three", he told the others, "are to remain here in the mansio. I will take lodgings with a widow who took in visiting parents of troopers."

"Why can't we all stay with you?" Pasicrates asked.

"Because if I'm not immediately arrested when I appear before Galerius, I may have to go to the Palatium daily, until I get an audience with Diocletian, and I'll certainly be followed. I don't want any of you arrested as well."

"I could come with you and return here tomorrow", Pasicrates protested. "You'll need someone to carry your helmet and armour."

Giorgios pursed his lips.

"I'll leave my armour here until tomorrow; nevertheless, you may come with me."

The two set off on foot for the outskirts of the city.

Giorgios had left Assjadah in the care of Martha, with instructions that she be exercised every day, but otherwise left to enjoy her remaining time in retirement. He arrived at the widow's hovel to find her lamenting that her 'little red cow' was grievously ill.

"Where is the cow?" Giorgios asked.

"What does a fine gentleman like you know of cows?" the woman demanded.

"I'm a countryman, mother; I grew up among those who tend cows and horses."

Grumbling her doubts, the woman led Giorgios to a stall at the rear of the house. The cow was lying down, coughing and labouring for breath. Giorgios crossed to the manger and dug around among the hay. He came up with a handful of "spear grass", with large, coarse seed-heads and broad, sharp-edged leaves. He shook his head; some rogue fodder merchant had mixed it with good hay.

"Have you any oil, a lot of oil?" he asked.

"How would a poor woman such as I have a lot of oil?"

Giorgios took out his purse and gave the woman a handful of silver.

"Go to the nearest merchant, or better still your neighbours, and buy a large jar of oil."

The woman left and Giorgios knelt beside the cow, stroking its flanks. He instructed Pasicrates to fill the widow's iron cooking pot with water and find some rope to tie the cow's forefeet and hind legs. It did not resist, and he took its head in his hands, mooing to it.

The old woman returned. Ordering Pasicrates to hold the cow's head firmly, Giorgios smothered his arm with oil, and thrust his hand down the cow's throat. Choking, the animal thrashed wildly, but Giorgios' hand closed on the spear grass that had stuck in its gullet. He pulled it out, threw it aside, and poured oil down the animal's throat. It promptly vomited and lay panting. Giorgios, enduring the stench, washed his arm with the rest of the oil and unloosed the animal's legs. The widow meanwhile was keeping up a constant wail that they had killed her little cow. She stopped in mid-note as the animal struggled to its feet, and dipped its muzzle into the pot of water, and drank, whereupon she fell upon her knees calling down blessings upon them. Giorgios begged her to stop, and when she did so he informed her, to her great delight, that he intended to lodge with her, paying a week's rent in advance.

He viewed his tunic, soiled by the cow's vomit, with distaste. Nothing, he thought, would induce him to wear it, and he was about to ask the widow if she had a sheet or blanket he could wrap around himself, when she hastened into the living quarters and emerged with a well-worn, but to Giorgios' satisfaction, well-laundered, linen tunic. It had been her husband's, she told him, and being poor she had never thrown anything away.

The following morning, Giorgios and Pasicrates made their way back to the mansio, where the first thing he did was to bathe. Then he donned the decorated bronze breastplate, plumed helmet and scarlet cloak of a Tribune, hired a horse, and set out for the Palatium. Pasicrates opened a scroll and settled down to write.

"The noble Giorgios, though unafraid, was nevertheless prudent and took humble lodgings in the obscure home of a poor widow. Here he cured her cow which was on the point of death." He read this over and, crossing out the last line, wrote instead, "and by God's grace raised her cow back to life and I, Pasicrates, his scribe, was a witness to this marvel." That, he felt, made the episode far more exciting; and in any case, the cow would surely have expired, and Giorgios would surely have restored it to life?

Meanwhile, Giorgios had dismounted at the Palatium and, striding past the startled sentries, whom long years of iron discipline had automatically brought up to the salute, entered the audience chamber. He strode down the marbled floor until he came before the dais upon which Galerius, flanked by his nephew, Maximinus Daia, and the Protonotarius, was sitting for the morning audience. Licinius was, as usual, standing behind Galerius.

Giorgios came to a halt, saluted, and stood to attention. Galerius, his face purpling with anger, stared at him for several moments before croaking, "So, you have returned to Nicomedia to die?"

"And without your bully-boy Constantine to back you up", Daia drawled. "That was very foolish of you."

Giorgios ignored him and addressed Galerius, "No, Augustus, I have not returned to die, but to claim my father's title, offices and salary."

Galerius was choking with fury and Maximinus Daia replied for him, "Why? Have you a certificate of sacrifice?"

271

Giorgios looked at him coldly, "Which Magistrate of the Roman People is asking me?"

Daia scowled angrily, "You are addressing the Second Consul, and it is he who is questioning you."

"If we are to debate legal niceties, only the Senate of Rome may appoint the Consuls."

Daia sneered, "The Senate does what the Augustus Maximian tells it to do, and he obliges his son, my friend, Aurelius Maxentius. I have authority to question you, and I have power to silence your impudence. I haven't forgotten the horse trough!"

Giorgios bowed his head slightly, "In that case, Noble Consul, I have not got a Certificate of Sacrifice."

"Neither, it seems, have you read the Edict. Those without a certificate may not exercise public office, therefore your claim to be appointed to your father's offices and titles is void."

Galerius now found his voice, "You have the remedy. There is the image of the Augustus", he pointed to the bust of Diocletian on its marble pedestal, "There is the lamp, perpetually burning, and there is the incense. Sacrifice to the Genius of the Emperor and we will consider your claim."

Giorgios looked calmly at Galerius, "No, Augustus, I will not sacrifice."

Daia started from his chair, "You dare to say so? The Emperor has commanded it."

"The gods, as you call them, are but stone and bronze, made by men's hands, whereas God is the creator of all things and alone must be worshipped."

Licinius was looking keenly at Giorgios. He had divined his purpose, though the others had not. Galerius was letting his temper get the better of him; "You dare to say that the immortal gods of Rome are false?"

"Yes. For I am a Christian and there is but one Lord and Saviour of Mankind, Christ Jesus, and Him only do I adore and worship."

Daia had risen to his feet, "You have condemned yourself. Not for three months has anyone in this city, anyone in this province, anyone in the Orient, dared to admit that he is a Christian, and now you defy the gods, defy the Emperor, defy the Caesar and defy the Consul, before all the people."

Licinius bent and whispered urgently in Galerius' ear.

"Do not arrest him. It is what he wants you to do."

Galerius half turned, "Why?"

"He wants audience with Diocletian, to be tried before him. Diocletian thinks highly of him and he is a Count of the Occident, under the protection of the Caesar Constantius who is still sympathetic to the Christians. He is the friend of Prince Constantine; all of this will weigh with Diocletian. Do not fall into his trap, have him followed and deal with him secretly."

Galerius continued to glare at Giorgios, but he was bringing his temper under control. He assumed an expression of judicial gravity.

"I have heard your appeal. You have not sacrificed to the gods and therefore are ineligible for public office. Your appeal is dismissed. You may now leave the court."

Giorgios saluted, turned on his heel and left.

Outside, he paused on the stoa to reflect. It was a stand-off. He had challenged Galerius to arrest him, but Galerius had side-stepped very neatly. There was nothing for it but to return tomorrow and goad him further. Out of the corner of his eye, and to his intense annoyance, he caught sight of Pasicrates among the crowd that thronged the steps. Deliberately refusing to catch the youth's eye, he strode away and began to cross the forum.

There was a large crowd around the podium where a notice board stood. A decurion and two of the municipal police were posting up a notice. Giorgios strode across and the crowd parted before him. The notice was a new Imperial Edict. Its provisions were simple and brutal. All Christian males were ordered to sacrifice to the immortal gods of Rome. Anyone refusing was to be put to the torture and ordered to sacrifice a second time. Anyone refusing a second time would be judged obdurate, condemned to death, and their property confiscated.

Giorgios re-read the Edict. His mind was numbed. Rome was slipping back into the barbarity of the Lex Talonica by which tyrants had destroyed enemies and rivals, and weakened for generations the Roman blood. On a sudden impulse he reached up and tore down the Edict. He stepped on to the podium and addressed the curious crowd which had gathered.

"Romans! I am Giorgios of Lydda and a Christian."

A murmur ran through the crowd. Someone shouted, "Deliverer of Alexandria", another called, "Friend of Constantine", at which a cheer went up. Giorgios raised his hand for silence.

"You are not slaves to be ruled by tyrants. This is a most profane and wicked Edict. without basis in law, inspired by tyranny, to plunder those who have committed no crime against Rome or the Emperor." He ripped the parchment in two, put the halves together and ripped again, and then again, scattering the pieces on the ground. There was a hubbub of cheers and protests.

The police decurion, collecting his wits, stepped forward. He appreciated that Giorgios far outranked him, and so spoke politely.

"Sir, you must come down. I must arrest you. It is my duty."

Giorgios smiled and stepped down.

"Certainly, Decurion, every one of us must do his duty."

CHAPTER SIXTY-EIGHT

The Prefect of Police, considering Giorgios' rank and the nature of the charge, thought it necessary to report the matter immediately to the Caesar. Galerius was with his nephew at the time.

"Execute him!" cried an exultant Daia. "No need for a trial, accusation is sufficient: condemn him to be burnt."

"You are a fool", Galerius snapped, "rushing in as usual. This man is more valuable to us alive than dead, more so because his execution would rally the Christians. This man is well known, he is looked up to by many. Let him sacrifice to the gods and the rest will follow. The sect will be scattered and then extirpated; I will succeed where Decius and Nero failed."

*   *   *

Giorgios found his prison cell quite as comfortable as the army accommodation he was used to. Left alone, he recited the psalms and meditated on each one. That night he slept soundly, and he was calm when, next morning, he was brought before Galerius. The Caesar was again flanked by Maximinus Daia and the Protonotarius of the court, but of Licinius there was nothing to be seen.

The Protonotarius read the charges and Giorgios immediately went on the attack, "I see in this court one who only yesterday declared a personal grudge against me. I appeal to the Augustus Diocletian."

Galerius looked down at him coldly, "I am invested with the full pro-Consular authority. Your appeal to the Divine Emperor is dismissed."

Giorgios opened his mouth to protest, but was cut short by the protonotarius: "You are Giorgios of Lydda?"

"I am, and the son of Anastasius, who was known to everyone here, a true servant of the Empire and a better Roman than many."

This sally was unfortunate: Giorgios had meant it purely in the moral sense; Galerius took it as a gibe at his Dacian origins. He cut short anything Giorgios might have to say to come straight to the point:

"Are you a Christian?"

"I am, and I will speak now for all Christians who are oppressed and persecuted by you. I proclaim their innocence of all the wicked slanders you have brought against them. I appeal to the August Emperor, to his clemency and justice, that my fellow Christians be freed of these slanders and be permitted to openly worship the One True God, so that the name of Our Lord Jesus Christ be praised before you all."

Galerius could contain himself no longer, "And what of the gods of Rome? Are they not to be worshipped?"

Giorgios gazed at him, long and hard. "Inimicus" or "hostis"? He must speak the truth, but try not to wound.

"Describe to me the objects of your worship. You call 'gods' either the vain imaginings of your own invention, or demons, polluted beings, who made neither the heavens nor the earth, who were cast down from heaven and ever since have practised to deceive men. We Christians worship the One God, who created all things out of nothing, by his Word, who became man, Our Lord Jesus Christ, through the Holy Spirit, to offer his life as a ransom for all. We worship One united Trinity, one Power."

Daia listened to this with a sneer on his lips, "We are not here to listen to lectures. Recant and sacrifice to the gods of Rome and you can walk free."

"None of my ancestors at any time has been a worshipper of idols, nor will I be", Giorgios answered defiantly.

Daia leaned forward, "Then you will be tortured until you do!"

"Then you must do as you will; but I count your tortures as nothing compared to even a single second in hell, into which I would undoubtedly fall were I to deny the Gospel, and of which all of you are in deadly danger for your crimes."

Daia was up on his feet, "Deliver him to torture", he yelled.

"Not so quick", Galerius said, "This young man is stubborn out of honour for his father. I, who have no son, envy that, and I honour him for it. I will speak with him privately and see if fatherly advice can persuade him to abandon this foolish refusal to sacrifice. Bring him to my cabinet."

"Sit down, sit down", Galerius said genially as soon as the cabinet door was closed. Giorgios sat and watched Galerius warily: "I knew your father well; there was a foolish quarrel between us and I wrongly suspected him of conspiring against me, but that was all the fault of that fox, Mansour – he was the culprit, I realize that now."

Giorgios interrupted him: "Mansour hatched no conspiracies, he looked after his people when they were threatened, he broke no laws, committed no crimes. But he was murdered, as my father was, and I know that that was your doing."

Galerius raised his hands in simulated horror, "These are lies spread about by subversive elements. Listen, if your father had stayed with Diocletian he would now stand where I stand, and after him you would stand in this place and wear the purple. Your father refused and left the way open for me. Why should I have murdered your father? I owe my rank to him."

"I know my father was murdered."

"Yes! Yes! That is past. As loyal Romans, and I know that at bottom you are one, we must think of the Empire. What is your opinion of my nephew Maximinus Daia?"

"I have no opinion of him."

"Neither have I, though in a different sense than you mean. He is a fool. He will bring ruin on the Empire if he succeeds me; you are worth ten of him. Now listen, and I swear this by Zeus and Apollo and by the unknowable God who rules over all, stand but once before the people and sacrifice to the gods, and I will adopt you as my son, I will be the father you lost, I will proclaim you Filius Augustus, with the rank of Caesar; I will give you the governance and revenues of a hundred cities and, when I am gone, you will be Emperor of the World."

Giorgios shook his head, "The army, the people, expect Constantine to be raised to the rank of Caesar in succession to you. The Augustus has declared that sons may not succeed fathers, but Constantine is not your son. It is he, not your nephew, whom you want me to supplant."

Galerius gave an expression of impatience, "Who is Constantine?"

It was the same question Diocletian had asked, and it received the same answer: "My friend."

Galerius stared at Giorgios. The violet eyes were deep, but utterly innocent; there was no glint of cunning or duplicity in them. He stood up, "I have crossed the floor to you to offer you not only friendship but adoption as a son, to offer you the greatest prize a man could desire or dream of, power of life and death, wealth to command any pleasure, and you have refused me, refused me for the sake of a pinch of incense and one you call a friend. Now I wash my hands of you. Politicians have no friends."

"Then I thank God that I am a soldier and not a politician, for I number my friends by the legion."

Galerius glared at him and struck a gong. Two guards entered and Galerius barked, "Take him to the torture chamber; let him be beaten with thin rods and his stripes rubbed with salt, then bring him back to the court to sacrifice."

*   *   *

Giorgios had passed the threshold of pain under the beating, but now pain returned as he half walked and half was dragged before the judgement seat. Galerius looked down at him in cold rage; Giorgios' submission and sacrifice to the gods had become an imperative, a battle of wills which he must not lose.

"Will you now sacrifice as commanded by the Edict?" he asked.

"I will not."

Maximinus Daia leapt up, "He is obdurate, he has refused a second time. Let him be judged obdurate and die!" Galerius gave his nephew such a look that he immediately sat down deflated.

Galerius spoke, "By the pro-Consular authority vested in me, I extend clemency to this misguided man, convinced that he is enchanted. Take him away and let him appear before us tomorrow morning."

Giorgios was not taken back to the police cell, but to a dungeon beneath the Palatium. It was dirty and stinking, with no furnishing other than a straw mattress. He was feverish with pain and shock, and only with an effort was he able to lie face down on the mattress. He became delirious. How long he had lain there he did not know, when he heard the key turn gently in the lock, the door opened slightly and a figure slipped in. So he was to be murdered after all, was the thought that came to him.

The man, whoever he was, uncovered a lamp which revealed his face. It was the battered, battle-scarred face of the trooper Scipio. The man drew a flask from his pouch.

"Here, Sir, drink this", and he dribbled some liquid into Giorgios' mouth. It tasted of wine and honey with a bitter undertone, and as his gullet began to work, Scipio increased the flow.

"What's in it?"

"A painkiller, Sir, old 'orse soldiers know it well."

"You mustn't get yourself into trouble."

"That's alright, Sir, the centurion winks an eye at me. There's no 'orse soldier in the Empire wouldn't help you Sir, you and Prince Constantine. Now Sir, just 'old still whilst I washes away the salt with this salve." Giorgios felt a soothing liquid on his back. "I'll be back tomorrow, Sir", Scipio said and slipped away into the dark. Giorgios felt himself falling into an uneasy sleep.

The arrival of his breakfast awoke him; a hunk of stale barley bread and a jar of water. He could not eat the bread but he was grateful for the water to wash the salt from his mouth and throat. The lock turned and Scipio slipped in, "A bowl of broth, Sir, not too 'ot so you can drink it quick."

He fed Giorgios with a spoon.

"You're good to me, Scipio; why, I don't know."

"I'm an old soldier, Sir, always ready to dodge the column, always lookin' for a cushy number. I never expected to be anythin' more than a trooper, but you made me a standard-bearer, that's as good to me as bein' made Marshal of 'orse would be to you, Sir. Now, 'avin' been a standard-bearer, I've got this cushy garrison postin' to see my days out, and that's thanks to you, Sir. Now, dip the bread in the soup, you'll need somethin' solid in you."

Scipio drew from his pouch a flask of wine, but before he could unstopper it the tramp of feet was heard. Scipio jumped up, picking up the bowl and spoon, "Why an honest soldier like me", he roared, " 'as to wait on criminals, bringin' their breakfast an' fetchin' an' carryin', I don't know." He turned toward the cell door as a decurion and two troopers appeared, " 'Ere am I", he cried, his voice rising in indignation, "A soldier 'avin' to bring breakfas' roun' like a common jailer."

The decurion looked at him with good humour, "Get out, Scipio, you rogue, what you're up to is none of my business; I'm not a jailer, either." He turned to Giorgios, "I've come to take you, Sir. Can you walk?"

CHAPTER SIXTY-NINE

To his surprise, Giorgios was taken not to the court, but to another cell, one which was clean, lit by a row of lancet windows, equipped with a couch and even a stool and a small table upon which stood two jugs, water certainly, possibly wine. Two physicians were awaiting him.

"He seems more recovered than I expected him to be", one of them remarked.

"These Christians have some magic or other to protect them", his colleague replied.

Giorgios smiled. Old Scipio had been called many things but never "magic". Yet perhaps in a way that was a true description of kindness. A soothing salve was poured over his stripes and they were sponged clean. One of the physicians held a cup to his lips, "Drink this and sleep."

Giorgios awoke as the evening light was falling through the lancet windows. He was covered by a soft blanket and knew that his wounds had been dressed. He sat up and, to his astonishment, saw Maximinus Daia sitting on the stool, drinking wine.

"Oh! So you're awake at last. I hope that sleep has done you good." Giorgios did not deign a reply, so Daia went on, "Look, this is an utterly stupid mess we've all got ourselves into: you, a noble Roman being beaten like a dog; it's not as if you were some sort of German or Arab." He paused but Giorgios still said nothing, "Well, look here, as far as I'm concerned we're quits now over that trough business, and now I come to think back on it, it wasn't your fault at all, it was that young beggar Constantine who started it all."

"Because you called him a bastard and his mother a whore", Giorgios replied, and swung his feet onto the floor.

"Well, that's just soldiers' banter, you know that, no real offence intended."

"It offended Prince Constantine, grievously; he's proud to be of the family of Claudius Gothicus, and who wouldn't be? He's also very close to his mother."

"Well, I'm sure it's all forgotten now, especially by me; but I'm not here to talk about Constantine, I'm here to talk about you and this mess you've got yourself into."

Giorgios had gingerly stood up, being careful not to stretch his back.

"Which mess?"

"Well, all this about not sacrificing. Oh I know how important it is to you and that you couldn't do it, whatever they do to you, but I've a plan of my own which should solve the whole thing and let you get back to that Lydda of yours."

Giorgios raised an eyebrow, "I can't think what that could be."

"Well, it's simple really. We both sacrifice together, like old comrades-in-arms, only I sprinkle an extra large pinch of incense on the lamp, and you don't sprinkle any, just rub your finger and thumb together over the flame: no one will be able to tell with all the smoke about."

There came a vivid memory of childhood. Giorgios was sitting on the stone bench with Grananna watching the fish in the pool, the scent of blossom in the air and the taste of honey in his mouth. Grananna was telling him the story of Eleazar and the unclean meat. He looked at Maximinus Daia.

"And you think so little of your gods that you would mock them, and so little of the Roman People that you would deceive them?"

Maximinus Daia stood up angrily, as if to speak. "No!" Giorgios exclaimed, "I have listened to you, so let me finish. Suppose I did as you suggest? What would my fellow Christians say? They would say, 'Here is Giorgios of Lydda, born into a noble family, a descendant, as they boast, of Joseph of Arimathea and so related to the Saviour, and certainly a descendant of Holy Giorgios, martyred under Decius; born into the comforts of wealth, educated, who has never known labour he did not choose to do, who has never known hunger or cold, favoured by God all through his life, yet for him the one sweetness we share with him, the sweetness of life, is so precious that he defiles himself by the worship of idols. If he degrades himself to buy a few more years of this life, can he really believe in the promise of the next? If he doubts, why should we be certain? If he sacrifices to save his life, why should not we?' I will try to believe, Maximinus Daia, that you have acted sincerely to save my life, but the price you ask is too high."

Maximinus Daia strode to the door, his face flushed with anger at the rejection of his "simple solution". At the door he turned, "You are obdurate! And you are a fool. Most of your fellow Christians, as you call them, have sacrificed and saved their lives and property."

"That is why I am here", Giorgios replied, evenly.

"And tomorrow you will be dispatched to your Elysium with all speed", Maximinus Daia snarled as he slammed the door behind him.

The proceedings the following morning were brief. Giorgios, stiffly but determinedly, walked the length of the audience hall and stood before his judges. The Protonotarius read from a scroll:

"Giorgios of Lydda, having been offered a second opportunity to sacrifice to the Genius of the Emperor and the immortal gods of Rome, and having refused to do so, the August Caesar Galerius has been moved to exercise his clemency to allow you a further opportunity to sacrifice. If you refuse this third time, nevertheless the Augustus will so extend his clemency as to deliver you again to torture that you may wisely consider your submission. Will you now offer sacrifice as should all true Romans?"

The little furrow of stubbornness creased Giorgios' forehead, and he drew himself up.

"I will not."

Galerius bit his lip. More than ever he needed Giorgios' submission. There was a mood growing in the city which he did not like. He spoke in measured tones, "Let him be delivered to the torturers. They are to rack him until he submits."

Scipio had contrived to be in the guard which marched Giorgios to the torture chamber. Walking beside him, Scipio spoke out of the corner of his mouth in the manner known to soldiers and convicts, "Pull against the rack, Sir, as long an' as 'ard as you can, otherwise your joints will be pulled out. Try not to scream, the torturers like to hear a man scream. It goads them on."

They carried Giorgios, half dead, into the court. Galerius was not there, his place taken by Maximinus Daia who asked harshly, "Do you submit, Giorgios of Lydda, will you sacrifice?"

Unable to rise Giorgios croaked, "No!"

Maximinus Daia glowered, "By the command of the August Caesar Galerius you are not to be judged obdurate, but given a further opportunity to submit. Take him away."

Giorgios was carried to the dungeon cell. He had pulled against the rack for as long as he could, and he had not yelled with pain until near the end. A surgeon had first stopped the torture, lest he expire, and then roughly, and agonizingly, re-set his shoulder sockets, and with cruel humour had remarked, "There, you're three inches taller". He was dumped on the filthy straw mattress and left.

How much more could he endure? His mind wandered and he felt the fear that he would, despite himself, submit. He prayed, "Out of the depths I have cried to Thee, O Lord", and had the strangest sensation of a presence with him in the cell. He had been wrong, he told himself, he had relied up till now on his own strength. He fell into a sleep from which he was awakened by the stealthy tread of Scipio.

"Here you are Sir, drink this, I've made it a lot stronger this time."

Giorgios drank. It was stronger, he wondered if he would become addicted to whatever was in it; he had heard of such things among the barbarians; then with a wry smile he recollected that it wouldn't much matter if he did, the addiction would be short enough.

CHAPTER SEVENTY

Galerius sat in his cabinet fuming.

"Perhaps you're using the wrong methods", Licinius suggested.

"Torture always works, sooner or later. Painful death is one thing, but torture which can be ended by submission is another."

"Well, you can't torture him much more without giving him a respite."

"And what do you suggest as an alternative?"

"He's an intellectual. Find a philosopher to dispute with him; if he can show this Giorgios that his beliefs are superstitions he will abandon them."

Galerius mulled the idea over, "You're a fool, Licinius. There are any number of men who can give you a hundred reasons why immorality is wrong, but put them in a brothel and they'll fornicate. But perhaps you're right in this case, unless the man's a prig. We can't have him die before he's publicly sacrificed."

The next morning Giorgios was carried to the baths and lowered into the tepidarium. Floating in the water soothed his inflamed muscles. He was taken to the ground-floor cell, served with broth, soft cheese, fresh wheaten bread, figs and wine, and finally left to sleep. He wondered what the next ruse would be.

When he awoke he found that he could sit, but not stand.

The door opened and a man entered and greeted him courteously, "I am Athanasius, a philosopher of Alexandria, but happy to be presently in this city and of service to the Emperor." Giorgios studied the man, he had a round, bland face with pink cheeks and curled hair. He was vaguely familiar. Athanasius smiled at his scrutiny, "We have met once, briefly, in Alexandria; you probably saved my life then, so now I hope to save yours."

Giorgios remembered: the deputation of philosophers who had come to his room to thank him.

"How can you do that?"

"By showing you the error of your beliefs", the man replied confidently, "I know that you are intellectually honest and will not cling to beliefs that I show you to be false."

"Where would you like to start?"

"Why, with your primitive concept of the Deity." Athanasius was, if anything, over-confident.

"Why do you call it 'primitive'?"

"Why? Because it is. The Deity is incomprehensible to finite minds; it is totally 'other', unutterable in finite words. Unknowable, yet you Christians conceive of Him – and you say 'Him' as though the Godhead were a man – as having the human attributes of intellect and will; you also speak as though it were possible for finite creatures to either offend or please the Deity. That surely is a narrow, shrunken, anthropomorphic concept of the Unutterable? One might just as well speak of a worm offending a man."

The little frown quivered on Giorgios' forehead.

"You are a follower of Plotinus, if I remember?"

"Ah yes! What lover of wisdom is not?"

"I prefer the incisive mind of Aristotle myself; but let us by all means use the terms of Neo-Platonism. You will agree that Plotinus teaches that, because all being is contingent – that is, things exist, but each thing need not exist – the source of being must be *incontingent*, that is, Being which cannot *not* be. He calls this 'The One'. Is that a fair statement of his teaching?"

"It is an excellent précis; I see I must tread carefully with you."

"We Christians agree with you that God is utterly Other and can be expressed only by analogy, as you yourself found when you used the word 'Him', in rebuking us for so using it. Such words as 'Person', 'Knowledge', 'Love', are but clumsy approximations, but they are all we have, and they carry as much of the truth as we can comprehend. Now tell me, Athanasius, if God is utterly 'Other' as we agree, how is it that contingent beings exist?"

Giorgios eased his feet onto the floor. Athanasius, not now so confident that Giorgios would be easy meat, gave some thought to his answer.

"The infinite Being of 'The One', overflows, as it were, into the *Nous* or *Logos*, undiminished in its Being, and so the Logos too overflows into the World Soul, in which indwell the Ideal Forms upon which all individual souls pattern themselves and from where they descend to impress their forms upon matter, which is but the shadow of reality."

Giorgios smiled, "That too, Athanasius, is an excellent précis of the teaching of Plotinus; but what are the attributes of Personhood in a Man?"

"Why! Intellect and Will, of course."

"And the functions of the Intellect and of the Will?"

"To know and to love."

"But we have agreed, Athanasius, have we not, that all beings pattern themselves upon the Ideal Forms? And we have agreed, have we not, that the Ideal Forms subsist in the World Soul, and that the World Soul proceeds from the Logos which in turn proceeds from 'The One'? Are we agreed on this, or do you wish to withdraw?"

"No, Giorgios of Lydda, for the present I will follow the argument where it leads."

"Then I think, Athanasius, that it leads to this: Knowledge and Love are attributes of 'The One', and therefore we are right in saying that God Knows and that God Loves. Will you dispute that?"

"I cannot, it follows from Plotinus' teaching."

Giorgios laughed, not unkindly, "Then take some comfort in this: I fully accept that the words 'Knowledge' and 'Love' are entirely inadequate to describe God, but you will remember that we agreed that they are attributes of personhood and therefore Personhood must be an attribute of The One. We believe in the Living God. We believe that God is our Father who knows and loves everything He has created. Will you accept that, however inadequate the words, our concept of the Godhead is in no wise primitive and narrow?"

Athanasius spread his hands as a token of defeat, "I will withdraw the charge; but you say your prophet is God become man. There are many barbarous religions in which a god is incarnated. For the philosopher, such notions degrade the purity of the Godhead."

Giorgios knew sufficient of the philosophers to know that their ideas did not arise from the moral sense, but were purely intellectual. For the Idealists, ideas were a brilliant abstraction of cosmologies, emanations and cycles. For the Materialists the universe was a storm of atoms, falling forever from no-whence to no-whither. He had met Athanasius on his own ground because there was no other between them. His task, as he saw it, was to demonstrate that the Christian was a match for the philosopher; he could hope for no more. He pondered, trying to choose his approach.

"I will endeavour to explain this in your Neo-Platonist terms, though they are not entirely in accord with ours, but tell me, Athanasius, would you agree that Man is a *genus*?"

"Of course."

"And that every genus has its Ideal Form?"

"That is what Plotinus teaches."

"Have you ever considered what the Ideal Form of Man might be like?"

Athanasius started. It was plain from his expression that no such thought had ever sullied the purity of the concept. For him, the Ideal Forms were beautiful abstractions.

"No! The Ideal Forms are beyond our comprehension."

"Then grant me this, that the Ideal Man, the *Autanthropos*, must be more perfect than all individual specimens of the genus."

"That is indisputable."

"Well then, let us suppose that we agree that the moral perfection of any man is Righteousness, will not the Ideal Man, the Very Man, be Righteous?"

Athanasius waved his hands, "I cannot dispute it."

"Let us go back to what we agreed about the Godhead, that our terms 'Knowledge', 'Love', 'Person', even 'Existence', are inadequate; yet there is one term which is adequate, 'Righteousness'. We do not need to say, 'Infinitely Righteous', or 'Perfectly Righteous'. It is sufficient to say, 'God is Righteous'. Now tell me, Athanasius, this Ideal Form of Man, whose nature you have never considered, if it exists, where does it exist?"

Athanasius smiled the smile of one who anticipates defeat, "Why, in the World Soul, of course."

"We would prefer to say in the 'Holy Spirit', but let that pass. Do you think that God could be less righteous than the perfect man?"

Athanasius laughed, "Of course not."

"Then, Athanasius, what does Plato tell us of the Righteous Man?"

"Why, if you are referring to *The Republic*, he tells us that the Righteous Man, not for self-esteem, nor for public esteem, nor to prove his righteousness, but for Righteousness' sake, will, though innocent, submit to judgement, though righteous will endure calumny, though just will suffer the scourge, though unresisting will. . . " – Athanasius stopped in mid-sentence. His eyes widened.

Giorgios, not noticing in his pursuit of the argument, continued, "And will God not do more than this? And does not Plato say that the sight of God is the greatest good? If God be Righteousness itself, will He not desire this greatest good for Man, more even than Man can desire it himself? Is it inconceivable to you, Athanasius, that the Logos will take to Himself the ideal human nature we agreed exists in the Holy Spirit, and, conceived by the power of Divine Love, be born, become incarnate, to reveal through sacrifice for others the Righteousness of God?"

Athanasius made no answer. Giorgios looked at him; in some subtle way his features had changed, his face had fined down, it was no longer bland, his eyes were shining with a new light.

Giorgios spoke quietly, "If He has not done so already, He will yet do so, for this Incarnation is the expectation of the Ages. What we teach is this: that He has done so, and that those who walked and talked with him saw His glory, the glory of God's only Begotten."

But Athanasius was not listening. He had no need to, for he had experienced one of those moments of the mind, variously but inadequately described as, "Understanding", "Illumination", "Insight", in which everything falls into place, in which depth is added to width and breadth in the mental landscape, but best described in the simple words, "Whereas before I was blind, now I see."

A long silence ensued, a silence in which Giorgios knew that the moral sense which had been lacking in the chain of dialectic by which he had sought to fight his corner and crush Athanasius had been filled from another source, the joyous presence in which he too shared. Yet he also felt ashamed that he had set out to crush the philosopher with the philosopher's own terms. That was vanity, and he had enjoyed it!

"I had forgotten", he said aloud, "that Righteousness is Love."

Athanasius looked at him, "I came here to mix a poison for your mind, but you have purged mine of darkness and error. I have a grandson named after me, his mother is a Christian – will he survive the persecution and carry on my name?"

"Will he? How can I answer?" Giorgios prayed silently for the right answer; and then it seemed that he was listening to his own voice from the outside, a voice speaking in prophecy, "Your grandson shall be as the Morning Star in a dark night of the Church, his name will live forever."

He came to himself with a start to see Athanasius crossing to the table and picking up one of the jugs. "Here is water. What hinders my baptism?"

"Nothing!" cried Giorgios and found himself able to stand.

CHAPTER SEVENTY-ONE

The next morning Giorgios was again taken before Galerius. Once again he was ordered to sacrifice and once again he refused. He was again delivered to the torturers. They brought him back to the court but still he refused. He was taken back to the dungeon cell. After a day's respite, if the conditions in the cell could be called that, the process was repeated, Giorgios standing before his judges supported by two troopers. This time Galerius exercised his "clemency", by ordering him to be to be tortured on the wheel.

*   *   *

Another crisis meeting was held.

"So much for your brilliant idea", Galerius barked at Licinius, "instead of Athanasius defeating him, he tied the old fool up in knots and sent him running back to Alexandria."

"You can extend your 'clemency' no further, uncle", Maximinus Daia protested, "it's becoming farcical. Judge him obdurate and behead him. Get it over with."

"You still know nothing", Galerius snarled as he snapped his fingers at Licinius. "How many certificates of sacrifice have been issued this week?"

Licinius searched among his scrolls, though he already knew the answer: "Thirty-three, Augustus."

"I'm not talking about the city, I'm talking about the province."

Licinius looked uncomfortable, "The figure *is* for the province." Galerius turned purple. "There is worse, Augustus."

"What? What worse?"

"A number of Christians have been appearing in sackcloth, with ashes on their heads."

Galerius trumpeted a laugh, "You can expect anything from these madmen; let's hope the ashes were red-hot when they sprinkled them."

"It means, Augustus, that they have recanted their sacrifice to the gods."

Galerius breathed hard. "Kill them! Kill them on summary accusation before a magistrate."

"Don't you see, uncle", Maximinus Daia protested, "the more this farce goes on, the worse it will be. Execute him; he'll be forgotten before the end of the year."

Galerius mused, "We will try once more, with the iron boots."

*   *   *

His feet bruised and bleeding, Giorgios was carried across the floor of the court. Before the question could be put to him, he raised his head and croaked, "I will not." He was hauled back to the dungeon cell and there, in the middle of the night,

Scipio brought him the drugged wine and bathed his feet, though Giorgios winced at each touch.

"Nothing broken, Sir, or at least nothing much broken; it's the soles they injure most, but the wounds will heal."

* * *

Yet another crisis meeting was taking place in Galerius' cabinet. A mob, not all Christians, had pelted the city Curia with stones and rotten fruit, though the curials had nothing to do with the case.

"You have to execute him, and it has to be tomorrow", Maximinus Daia stated it forcibly.

"It's no use putting him away secretly, as I advised", Licinius added. "People would believe he had died under torture."

Galerius got up and paced the room.

"He *will* sacrifice."

Maximinus Daia groaned.

"Wait! It will be proclaimed that Giorgios Theognosta of Lydda, Imperial Count, acknowledging his ingratitude to Rome and his disloyalty to the Emperor, and now spurning the superstitions which were the cause of his wickedness, will, before all the People, sacrifice to the Genius of the Emperor, two days from now. He will still not be able to walk, so two guards will assist him. He will wear a new white tunic, with long wide sleeves that cover his hands. The guards will carry him to the pedestal and stand him there. One will pull the sleeve so that it appears his hand has reached out to the lamp, and the other will sprinkle the incense. His pardon will be proclaimed and he will be hastened away for the treatment of his injuries." Galerius looked from one to the other triumphantly.

"It will never work", Licinius said without hesitation.

"Why not?"

"Because he will struggle all the way to the pedestal."

"Not if he's drugged."

"And when he is recovered, he will recant!" Maximinus Daia shouted in his frustration.

Galerius smiled blandly, "You both forget we have other charges against him, as yet untried. Defacing an Imperial Edict, abusing the Emperor's rule, and inciting rebellion. All carry the death penalty, but by the Emperor's clemency it will be commuted to solitary exile on some small island of the Aegean. Furthermore, I will have the Empress Prisca Alexandra there to witness the ceremony."

Maximinus Daia laughed aloud, "Uncle", he said, "only you could think of it!"

* * *

Even in his low state of pain and exhaustion, Giorgios felt grateful when he found himself conveyed first to the baths and then to the ground-floor cell. He had, like any Roman, found deprivation of bathing one of the most difficult things to bear in his imprisonment. Now he was bathed, and his soiled clothes had been taken away and replaced by a tunic with curious long, wide sleeves. The feel of clean linen was a luxury. He was served good food and wine, his wounds were dressed, and on the second and third mornings of the new regime he was again taken to the baths. It was after the midday meal on the third day that he felt strange. His head spun, his knees doubled under him, and he was unable to resist when two burly guards seized him under the armpits and carried him bodily from the cell to the audience hall. They entered at the side of the dais, so avoiding having to half-carry their prisoner the length of the great hall.

Galerius had choreographed the scene well. He sat enthroned, robed in purple silk and crowned with a sun-ray diadem. On his right hand sat Maximinus Daia, and on his left, Licinius. The legates of four legions were seated with them, two on either hand. Galerius' staff officers were ranged behind the chairs.

The Empress was seated, not on the dais but in the space immediately in front, so positioned that the Capitoline Wolf was between her and the bust of the Emperor. The auditorium was crowded with people. As Giorgios and his guards entered a hush fell and the Protonotarius stepped from behind Galerius' throne, scroll in hand.

"The Tribune Giorgios Theognosta, Count of the Empire, having repented the error of his ways has begged that, in the Emperor's clemency, he may now be permitted to offer before all the People of the Romans, incense to the Genius of the Emperor and in sacrifice to the immortal gods of Rome. Because of the weakness of his body, he has begged that he be assisted to the place of sacrifice, and to this the Emperor in his clemency has graciously assented."

As his two guards hoisted him up so that only his toes dragged along the floor and began to carry him to the pedestal, Giorgios' head cleared sufficiently for him to realize what was afoot. He tried to struggle, but his efforts were too feeble to break the iron grip upon him. He tried to cry out, but his mouth was dry. Desperately he prayed, "Judge me, O God, and distinguish my cause from the nation which is not holy, deliver me from the unjust and deceitful man."

They had reached the pedestal and stood before it. At a sign from Galerius, the guards lifted Giorgios slightly and, stepping forward, brought his weight and their own onto the paving stone upon which the pedestal stood. The long trail which Providence had laid when a bullying chamberlain had struck and kicked a lesser slave, reached its end. The rotten joist beneath the slab did not so much snap as crunch under the sudden weight.

The paving stone moved, and the pedestal, in front of the point of balance, slowly tilted forward. The two guards leapt aside, one dragging Giorgios with him. The silver oil lamp slid off the pedestal, splashing oil, and crashed to the floor. A film of blazing oil spread outward. Slowly, the pedestal continued to tilt. The bust of the Emperor slid forward, gathering impetus over the spilt oil, until it teetered on the edge of the pedestal and then crashed to the floor. The head broke from the shoulders and rolled away, scattering the onlookers. Beside the Capitoline Wolf, the Empress Prisca Alexandra let out a wild cry of terror.

Maxentius Daia was on his feet, his face suffused with rage.

"Magician! Necromancer! He has assaulted the gods! Their wrath will fall upon us. He is obdurate. Condemn him to death!"

Giorgios, deathly weak in knees and ankles, had fallen when the guard dragged him clear. Now the two pulled him to his feet and hauled him before the judges. Burning anger had cleared his head. He had endured all, but he would not endure this dishonourable double-dealing.

He glared up at Galerius and found his voice, "Thou foul and evil dragon from the pit, God has already judged thee."

His anger was such that he had, unthinkingly, addressed Galerius as an inferior. A hush fell upon the assemblage; never had an Emperor been publicly "thoued". Galerius, shaken by spasms of rage and shame at what he took to be an insult to his Dacian origins, and forgetting his determination that Giorgios should sacrifice before he was executed, rose to his feet. Anger and superstitious terror of the power that had brought the Emperor's image crashing to the ground struggled for dominance.

He raised his hand, "Giorgios of Lydda, all patience with you is exhausted. You are judged obdurate and condemned to death. Tomorrow you will be beheaded."

The two guards spun Giorgios around to haul him away, but he pulled himself back to face Galerius again. Standing to attention as best he could, he spoke clearly for all to hear.

"I beg the Augustus' pardon for addressing him in the familiar mode. There was no malice in my so doing, only forgetfulness of my duty."

Galerius still glared, his eyes bulging, "Take him away", he rasped.

As the auditorium swam before Giorgios' eyes, he saw Pasicrates in the crowd, but he was too weak, too weary, even to be annoyed.

That evening, once Pasicrates had reached the safety of the mansio and informed Lucius and Cyrennius, as he had done every day, of the events in the Palatium, he sat down to write his account of the trial.

"The Noble Tribune Giorgios, having been brought between two files of guards into the auditorium, marched fearlessly down the length of the hall. As he strode past, the idols on either side, in which the pagans foolishly place their trust, though they can neither see nor hear nor help them, fell from their places, crumbling into dust before the terrible gaze of Giorgios, and the Capitoline Wolf howled in terror."

CHAPTER SEVENTY-TWO

As no one had given any orders to the contrary, Giorgios was taken back to the ground-floor cell. Gratefully he stretched himself out on the couch and slept. When he awoke, dusk was falling. In a strange, detached way, he remembered that he was to die the next day. It would be twelve days since his arrest.

It was not what he had intended when he set out to gain an audition with the Emperor, but he had from the start regarded it as probable. He found that he could stand for short periods before his feet became too painful, so standing and sitting he recited the psalms and the Lord's Prayer. He was interrupted by the entry of Scipio.

"I managed to get your cloak, Sir, and your breastplate, but I couldn't get your 'elmet."

Giorgios gave a wry smile, "Well, it seems I won't be needing that, Scipio."

"You should go properly dressed, Sir. 'Don't let the bastards grind you down' as we troopers always say."

Giorgios smiled again. He took the cloak, his purse still inside an inner pocket. He drew it out, "Here's something else I won't need, Scipio. Take it and drink wine for me."

Tears were rolling down the honest trooper's face as he accepted the gift.

"I've bin thinkin' about your God, Sir. Ee's a rum un if I may say so, pullin' a trick like that on 'em, not that they didn't deserve it."

"I think it might have been a coincidence, Scipio."

"Well, if you say so, Sir, but I never found a god that was worth livin' for, let alone worth dyin' for. I've bin talkin' to some of the lads 'oo are Christians, an' they've told me a lot about it." The old trooper fell silent and began to shift from foot to foot, Giorgios looked at him quizzically.

"Don't be nervous, Scipio, what is it I can do for you?"

"Well, Sir, it's like this: they said any Christian can baptize, an' if I'm to be baptized, I'd take it as a great honour to be baptized by you."

"Are you sure you want this Scipio, do you understand who Jesus is?"

"Oh yes, Sir, I understood that right away, bein' an 'orse soldier like, when I 'eard about the ass's colt."

"The ass's colt?" Giorgios was startled, "Why, what's that got to do with it."

"The one no man 'ad ever ridden, Sir, an' 'im ridin' it unbroken with no saddle or bridle. 'Ee must 'av 'ad wonderful 'ands, Sir, more than any or'nary man could 'ave."

Giorgios crossed to the table and, picking up the water jug, said, "Bow your head, Scipio."

*   *   *

The guards had brought Giorgios a good supper, and now they brought him a good breakfast, but he could eat nothing. He was relieved when another visitor came, and overjoyed when he saw that it was one of his old tutors, Eusebius.

"I'm scribe to the Empress in public, fugitive bishop of Nicomedia in private", he explained, as he and Giorgios embraced.

"Is it true that the Empress apostatized?" Giorgios asked.

"Do not judge her too harshly; she was forced to take part in the ceremony by her position, but after yesterday she found the courage to recant, perhaps to her own great danger."

"Are there many bishops and presbyters in hiding?"

"A good many, Giorgios, and that's why this persecution will fail, why persecutions always fail."

"You think so? I can't see it."

"There are always men like Constantius who do all they can to moderate the edicts and mitigate the penalties. There are always ordinary decent people who hide the persecuted. There are always good neighbours who protect people where they can. There are always those who have a debt of gratitude to one being persecuted and come to his aid, and there are even the lazy and incompetent officials who turn a blind eye, so as not to make work for themselves. In the end, the persecution fails."

Giorgios shook his head, "You make me wonder why I'm to die in that case."

"Only God knows that, but perhaps it's to bring back the lost sheep, like the Empress, and perhaps it's to inspire the friends of the persecuted. Now, I must borrow your stool to sit in judgement and forgiveness. Kneel down beside me and confess the sins of your life."

*   *   *

As Eusebius raised his hand in absolution, tears were streaming down his face. He was to say later that it was the confession of a child.

Eusebius stood up, "Have you fasted?" he asked.

"From midnight", Giorgios replied, thankful that he had eaten no breakfast. Eusebius took from his cloak a small flask and piece of unleavened bread, consecrated at the morning liturgy. He recited the communion prayers, saying, as he placed the consecrated bread upon Giorgios' tongue, "Receive the Body of the Lord", and then, giving him the chalice, "Receive the Blood of the Lord." He left the cell as the tramp of the escort was heard. Giorgios drank water from the jug and, with the help of one of the guards, strapped on his breast-plate and donned his cloak.

The scaffold had been erected on the Field of Mars on the outskirts of the city, where for centuries the legions had been drilled. They took Giorgios in a cart to the gates of the field.

A pathway, lined by a cohort of the Imperial guard to hold back the crowd, led to the scaffold in the centre of the field. On the farther side there was a stand on which Galerius, Licinius, Maximinus Daia and half a dozen others were seated.

A decurion and two guards rode with Giorgios. As the cart started down the pathway, Giorgios had the strange feeling of another standing behind him. It was so persistent that he mentally counted: the decurion in front of him, the guard on either side, himself, and the driver – five, yet he sensed six.

He began to recite aloud the psalm,

"Give ear to my prayer, O God.
Hide not Thyself from my cry!
Listen to me and answer me,
I am overcome by my fears,
Desolate in the midst of the enemy,
Oppressed by the wicked,
For they bring terror upon me
And in anger they hate me."

They reached the scaffold and the guards helped him up, for his feet felt on fire. He took off his cloak and gave it to the decurion. The guards unbuckled his breast-plate of gilded bronze, and he joked, "There's only one; I'm sorry, you'll have to sell it and share the money." Again he had the strange feeling of someone close to him. He mentally counted again: five, with the executioner, but there seemed to be six. He turned to the decurion, "I will speak to the People."

The decurion stepped back, "I don't know that's allowed, Sir."

"Let me give my last order as a Tribune to you."

"Well, I don't know, Sir."

"Surely you will not deny a man his last request?"

The decurion pondered, "Very well, Sir, but don't speak too long."

Giorgios stepped to the rail facing the distant stand and gripped it with both hands, lifting his weight off his feet. A silence fell, and then he spoke.

"Romans! I am come here to die because I am a Christian." The faces were turned up to him and there was a murmur like the sea. "You have been told that we Christians are the enemies of Rome, that we plot the subversion of its laws and the destruction of its peace. This is not true, for we Christians are now the very defenders of the ancient laws and virtues of the Romans. It is we who uphold the Roman family. It is we who uphold the Roman marriage vow. It is we who denounce the perversions which have brought the Roman people to the pass where they must hire barbarians to defend their frontiers. It is we who defend Roman justice and the Roman way, even with our lives, against tyrants who rule without law. We honour and obey the Emperor as First Citizen in whom are vested all the ancient offices of the Republic. We honour and obey him as First Consul, as Tribune of the People, as Quaestor, as Censor and as Imperator of the armies; but we refuse to worship him as a god who may rule Rome according to his whims and in despite of its laws. We refuse because worship belongs to God alone, and God's laws are higher, and to His commandments the Laws of men are subject.

"The Senate has indeed deified Emperors after their death, and we have understood this as a declaration of the Senate that the Emperor was to be honoured and remembered as a righteous man in his government of the Republic, and as a lion in its defence. We have never refused honour to the memory of an Emperor honoured in this way by the Senate, but we have honoured him as a man."

Giorgios' voice had been rising, and now it sounded as a clarion, "But never yet have Romans been required to prostrate themselves before a living man, a man such as they themselves are, and this I will not do. I will not because I am, like you, a Roman, but more than that, I will not because there is but one Lord and Saviour of Mankind, Christ Jesus, whose Name God has raised above all names, and before him only will I prostrate myself, and Him only will I worship."

As Giorgios stepped back from the rail, a wave of approval swept through the crowd. Fists were shaken at the Imperial party, and there were shouts of "Justice! Justice!" The guards took him firmly by the elbows and, placing a hand on each shoulder, pressed him to his knees. The executioner began to swing his axe back and forth in a lengthening arc. The guards pushed him down so that his throat was on the block, and again he sensed the Other beside him.

Giorgios had instinctively closed his eyes, but now he made a conscious effort and opened them. Instead of the sea of faces he had expected, he was standing at the foot of a slope of goat-cropped pasture, dotted with bushes of the Rose of Sharon in full bloom. A hedge of the same shrub made a golden bank along the top of the slope. He was aware that the axe had reached the zenith of its arc and was about to descend upon him. Even as he sensed this, Justina appeared through a gap in the hedge and began to run down the hill toward him, her feet scattering diamonds of dew in the sunlight, her hair lifting in the breeze.

The hem of her silken dress, damp with the dew, rode above and clung about her ankles. She began to speak as she held out her hands to him, and he sensed as much as heard her words, as she uttered the ancient Roman marriage vow: "Whither thou goest, Giorgios, thither go I, Giorgia."

And then he was caught up into inexpressible light.

PART V
Saint George, A.D. 303 –

CHAPTER SEVENTY-THREE

As dusk fell on that 23rd April, AD 303, three figures moved silently toward the scaffold, two of them carrying a stretcher.

Dark shadows circled around. Forgetting caution, Pasicrates – for he, with Lucius and Cyrennius, made up the party – let out an angry shout, "Jackals!"

"Pray God they haven't mauled him", Lucius said.

"They're behaving oddly", Cyrennius remarked.

"They're whimpering. They're afraid", Lucius said.

"What's that perfume?" Cyrennius asked.

"Roses", ventured Pasicrates.

"Lilies", volunteered Lucius.

The body and head had been flung carelessly under the scaffold and left for the jackals and pariah dogs. Lucius ducked beneath, and came back, visibly affected. "It's Giorgios", he told them, awe struck, "the perfume's coming from Giorgios." Reverently, Lucius and Cyrennius edged the body from beneath the scaffold, wrapping it in linen. Pasicrates ducked beneath, and, tears streaming down his face, wrapped the head.

When they arrived at the necropolis, the slaves in charge, well paid to remain after dark, slid the coffin without ceremony into a cell in the honeycomb of wall tombs, bricked up the entrance, and plastered it over.

"You need an identification mark", one of the slaves said. Lucius scratched in the wet plaster the letters, Chi Rho.

*   *   *

Galerius was in his cabinet, with Licinius and Maximinus Daia in attendance.

"You're telling me that no certificates of sacrifice have been issued for the past year?"

"Not exactly, Domine, there have been a few."

"How many?" Licinius fidgeted with his scrolls. "How many?"

"Fifty-three, Domine."

"Fifty-three! You're referring to the province of course?"

"The Prefecture, Domine: Asia Minor and the Balkans."

Galerius' face darkened. "And you have worse to report?"

Licinius fidgeted again.

"Intelligence reports are that many who sacrificed have now recanted. We don't see them about in sackcloth and ashes any more; their Patriarch at Rome has granted what they call an 'indulgence'. They're permitted to wash and wear ordinary clothes in public."

Galerius seethed.

"Seek them out! Everyone who has recanted is be put to the torture and then sent to the arena."

Licinius nerved himself to speak, "Domine, we have killed fifteen thousand here alone. In the province it comes to thirty thousand. Thousands more have fled to Armenia, others have gone to Gaul and Britannia. You're bleeding the Empire to death."

Galerius rounded on him, "I will purge the Empire if it needs a million deaths." He stood up and walked to the window. "There is another way. We will seize the property of everyone who has recanted."

A thought struck him, "This is the doing of Giorgios Theognosta, opposing us still from beyond the grave. There is still one of the family left. I want Andrew of Lydda watched. If as much as a smear of ashes is seen on his face, seize his estates."

*   *   *

Another year had passed and the Eastern Empire was steeped in blood. Those without sufficient wealth to divert Galerius' wrath were executed in increasingly ingenious ways. The more wealthy had their property confiscated and were reduced to poverty. The slaves on many estates found themselves under new absentee masters who did not know them and who cared nothing for their welfare.

Andrew, filled with remorse when he learned of Giorgios' tortures and death, recanted. He was too cautious a man to proclaim his recantation openly, but eventually Galerius' spies trapped him. This time he stood firm. He was tortured, but escaped the death penalty by the confiscation of his estates. He now lived with the "Sisters of Perpetual Indignation". He had recovered his hoard of gold before his villa was seized, and had reburied it in the hypocaust of Kira's villa.

As a self-imposed penance, Andrew was writing the story of the life and death of Giorgios. Written in Greek, the scrolls were smuggled to Sylene, where Pasicrates, married now to Cleosolinda, made copies. Being Pasicrates, he could not but enliven the account with interpolations of his own.

*   *   *

Diocletian summoned Constantine into his presence.

"I intend to abdicate, as I pledged to do, and retire to my palace at Salonae."

Constantine was alarmed, "Is this wise, Augustus?"

"I am not such a fool as not to provide for my protection. A century of the

294

Imperial Guard will be sufficient, and you will command it, keeping your present rank."

Constantine successfully hid his frustration. He wanted command of a legion, and now he was being promoted for who-knew-how-many years, to chief night watchman. He drew himself up, "As you command, Augustus."

Diocletian was looking at him quizzically, "It is as I command, and believe me, it's for your own safety."

Galerius made himself senior Augustus by the simple step of asserting his right, as Diocletian's son-in-law, to name not only an heir to the Eastern Empire, but also to the Western Empire.

To everyone's surprise, he named the elderly soldier, Flavius Valerius Severus, as Caesar in the West, and, to everyone's indignation, his nephew, Maximinus Daia, as Caesar in the East.

*   *   *

That Constantine found his duties in Diocletian's palace dull would be to overestimate them; they were little more than dining with Diocletian and developing an aversion to cabbage. It came as a relief when, after six months, he received a posting to the Euphrates frontier.

"The Augustus Galerius has suddenly realized that you are only a short journey from your father's capital", Diocletian remarked wryly; "however, Galerius will not dare to murder you."

Constantine stopped at Drepanum to visit his mother and son. He found them in a great state of excitement. His father had sent for Helena and Crispus to join him in Trier, and they were to travel by sea to Arles.

Constantine's service at Callinicum on the Euphrates was even duller than at Salonae, and more awkward. The centurion in command resented what he regarded as the imposition of a superior officer. Constantine was well aware that he was being buried and that, if Daia had his way, he would spend his military career there. It was with relief and astonishment that a mere month later he received orders to return to Nicomedia.

With a light heart Constantine rode back to the capital. He reported to Galerius, who made no secret of his displeasure at seeing him.

"Your father wants you with him for a campaign. You can leave now, as far as I'm concerned, but tomorrow will do." He turned to a scribe, "Make out his orders and his warrant for horses and rations on the way."

Constantine saluted and, clutching the all-important documents, left. He was overjoyed to find Crocus waiting for him.

"Your father sent me to look after you; we're to join him at Gesoriacum – there's trouble in Britannia again – but we leave sooner than tomorrow. Sleep with your clothes on tonight. The less we are seen together now, the better. Listen for the words 'Chi Rho'."

Constantine was awake and reaching for his sword as soon as he heard his door creak. A soft voice said "Chi Rho", and he relaxed.

"Crocus", he breathed, "what is it?"

"Murder! Tomorrow noon, at the Byzantium ferry; only we shall be across it by dawn. I have horses ready."

So Constantine's epic ride from the Euphrates to the Tyne continued. In Britannia he was reconciled to his father and re-united with his mother and son. He was to rule over all the land he had ridden across.

Constantine's star shone in the Pictish war. Given command of the XXII Legion, in a daring move by land and sea, he invaded Pictland itself. For the first time the Picts were harried in their own territory and were soon persuaded to make peace. The army returned in triumph to Eboracum. Constantius, grey-faced, haggard and weak, was carried in a litter.

The physicians came to Constantine; he knew their tidings from their faces.

"How long?" he asked.

"A few days, at the most. Will you tell him? It is a son's duty." Constantine nodded and went to his father's sick chamber.

Constantius remained silent for a while and then summoned Eumenius, the protonotarius. His voice was weak but firm, "Order the court to attend on me – in the morning." After a pause he turned to Constantine, "Send for your mother and Crispus – and for Eborius."

"Who is Eborius?" Constantine asked Eumenius.

"The Christian bishop here. I'll attend to it."

Helena and Crispus came silently into the room and stood at the foot of the bed. Constantius motioned Helena to come to his right side and took her hand. Eborius arrived and Constantius spoke with an effort. "I desire baptism."

Eborius spoke gently but firmly, "Have you forsaken the woman for whom you deserted your lawful wife?"

Constantius sighed, "I maintain her and our children."

"That is only just, but do you keep yourself from her?"

"Since the death of Diocletian; but before that too, I have ailed long."

Eborius took a jug of water and said, "Help him sit."

After the baptism, Eborius took bread and wine, speaking the words of consecration, and Constantius received Holy Communion.

The following morning the legates of twenty legions filed into the chamber, forming a semi-circle opposite the foot of the bed, where Constantius insisted on sitting up. He seemed stronger, but still spoke with an effort. He took Constantine's hand, "This is my legitimate son, by my true and lawful wife, Helena."

He nodded to Eumenius who took out the scroll which Giorgios had carried from Diocletian, and read it aloud. After the customary opening declarations came the text, for so long kept secret:

"I now revoke my Edict that sons may not succeed their fathers as Imperators or Caesars. Upon his accession as Augustus, Caesar Gaius Flavius Valerius Constantius is, at such time as he deems propitious, to raise his son, Flavius Valerius Constantinus, to the Imperial dignity with the rank of Caesar, and is to name him in succession as Augustus and Imperator of Rome. This scroll is his witness."

"You are witnesses", Constantius said, and a murmur of assent arose.

Eumenius unrolled a second scroll. It named Constantine as Caesar with succession to the title of Augustus upon his father's death.

"You are witnesses", Constantius said again.

Crocus flung his arm up and said, but not too loudly, "Hail Constantine, Caesar." Every hand in the chamber was raised in the salute, and the words were like a whispering wind, "Hail Constantine, Caesar."

Constantius smiled; he took Helena's hand, and those present began to file out.

Constantius lapsed into unconsciousness, Helena and Constantine at his side. At one time he murmured something which sounded like, "Empire – was it worth it?" and then, "Helena", and then silence.

A physician glided across the floor, took his pulse and turned to Constantine, "He is gone – Augustus."

CHAPTER SEVENTY-FOUR

Galerius had calculated on the early death of Constantius and the elevation of Severus as Emperor. He would, Galerius intended, be a very junior Emperor indeed, and no heir would be appointed as Caesar. With Severus' early demise, Galerius would be sole Emperor. The acclamation of Constantine and its prior approval by Diocletian threw his schemes into disarray. Facing the choice between civil war and recognizing Constantine, he compromised by recognizing him as Caesar, subordinate to Severus as Augustus.

Aurelius Maxentius, still smarting at being passed over as Emperor in succession to his father, rebelled. In October A.D. 306, he triumphantly entered Rome, declaring that he would restore it as Capital of the Empire, and was acclaimed as Caesar.

In the April of 307 he took the final step and proclaimed himself Augustus. The following September, prodded by Galerius, the unfortunate Severus marched on Rome where his army deserted him, and he was put to death by the victorious Maxentius. To strengthen his position Maxentius forged an alliance with Constantine by consenting to the latter's long-delayed marriage to his sister, Fausta. Much to his chagrin, a condition of the alliance was that he acknowledge Constantine as Augustus of the West.

Galerius' dream of sole rule began to fade. He was Senior Emperor in name only, and by way of consolation he began transforming his capital of Thessalonica into a new Rome. On the outskirts of the city he built a magnificent twin-domed mausoleum, but chose on his deathbed not to be buried there. In the irony of history it became the church of Agios Giorgios.

In A.D. 311, Galerius was stricken by a disease, the accounts of which suggest that it was a particularly malignant form of cancer of the bowels. He became convinced that his suffering and imminent death were the vengeance of the God of the Christians.

He issued an Edict, to take effect from 30th April, A.D. 311. Its wording was curiously pious in tone:

"Great numbers of Christians still persist in their beliefs but at present they neither pay reverence and due adoration to the gods, nor yet worship their own God. We are greatly troubled by this lack of religious observance on the part of so many, for it cannot but be harmful to the good order of the state; therefore we have judged it proper that we should permit people again to be Christians, with this condition, that it will be their duty as Roman citizens to pray to the High God for our welfare, for that of the Republic and for their own."

The disease spread. The stench in the bedchamber, in spite of the sprinkling of perfume and of herbs, became intolerable. The physicians administered opium more frequently to counter his agony. Galerius died on 1st May, the anniversary of his elevation as Augustus.

Maximinus Daia was proclaimed Emperor. He decided it would strengthen his position if he repudiated his wife and married Galeria Valeria, daughter of Diocletian and his aunt by marriage.

Valeria, informed of this honour and of the necessity of her publicly sacrificing to the gods of Rome, declined. Her mother, Prisca, also refused to offer public sacrifice and both were exiled. In the October of A.D. 311, Maximinus revoked Galerius' Edict of Toleration and renewed the persecution. It was to last until his suicide in A.D. 313. He was remembered long after for his forgery of an anti-Christian document, *The Acts of Pilate*.

CHAPTER SEVENTY-FIVE

The news of Galerius' Edict was greeted with joy in Lydda.

It was a happy coincidence that the whole family was assembled. Kira, Martha, Claudia, Julia; Andrew and his sons, Andrew and Anastasius, and his wife Susannah were resident. Pasicrates and Cleosolinda had arrived on a visit with their children, as had Katherine and her family. Also present were Lucius and Cyrennius, both of the latter now married.

"We must bring Giorgios home", Kira exclaimed, "he must be buried at Lydda." There was a chorus of agreement, but Lucius looked troubled.

"We haven't the money", he said, "so much has gone in fines."

Cyrennius' face fell, "I can barely keep the hospice open."

"But why should it cost so much?" asked Katherine.

Lucius shook his head, "If we came overland, every night of the journey would cost money, not to mention new horses. If we came by sea we should have to hire a vessel and a crew willing to carry a dead body and they would charge a very high price: no sailors on an ordinary ship would sail with a body on board."

Kira was wringing her hands in dismay, "He must come home, my son must come home."

Andrew, grey-haired now and stooped, had said nothing. He got up silently and left the room, making his way to the hypocaust. He returned with a bag from which he spilled a shower of gold solidi. He was giving till it hurt.

*   *   *

The tomb was opened and the coffin slid out. Cyrennius levered off the lid and parted the linen. He started back, turning to the others, "He is incorrupt!"

"Thou wilt not suffer thy holy one to see corruption", intoned Eusebius who had accompanied them, almost in a whisper. They lifted the coffin onto a wagon drawn by two horses. Pasicrates took the reins with Eusebius beside him, while Lucius and Cyrennius rode on either side.

"There's a crowd at the gates", Lucius said.

"Are they hostile?" Cyrennius asked.

"Can't tell, but they don't seem agitated."

"Well, we can't go back", Pasicrates pointed out, "we'll just have to hope they'll make way for us."

As they approached the gates, the crowd parted silently. A woman threw a bloom of the Rose of Sharon onto the road before them. A sigh went through the crowd and a shower of blossoms strewed the roadway. A mother held her infant up in both hands and called, "Bless him – his name is Giorgios too." A man shouted, "I am Amon, once priest of Isis, he brought me to the light." Another called out, "He gave me freedom and a farm", and then another, "He saved our lives in a tempest", and another, "He saved Alexandria from sack, and I, Athanasius, am alive to tell it." Above a growing chorus of acclamation, a desert Arab called, "He gave us goats and hens, else we would have starved." An old soldier, gnarled and withered, cried out, "Ee was the best hofficer any soldier ever 'ad. If any one disagrees, let 'im come an' say so to Scipio."

Lucius looked in astonishment at Cyrennius, "Where have they come from? How did they know?"

Cyrennius looked at Pasicrates, who blushed, "I talked a little, but not to many."

Lucius patted him on the arm and turned to Cyrennius, "This goes far beyond anything Pasicrates could have done.

Eusebius turned from one to the other, "It is the Lord's doing, and it is marvellous in our eyes."

They took the road to the port of Nicomedia and the people came from villas and hovels to scatter flowers before them. Their journey became a triumphal progress. As they passed, those who lined the road followed, chanting psalms and prayers. As the coffin was hoisted aboard the galley, fifty pairs of oars were raised in salute. Here Eusebius left them, and the three brothers climbed aboard to be greeted by the captain.

"You honour us with your trust; every man aboard feels blest that he is to convey the holy martyr home."

Clear of the Aegean, the ship ran south of Cyprus. Arriving at Sidon, it followed the Syrian coast to Joppa. As the mass of Mount Lebanon rose above the horizon and the ship followed the sea-lane which had first brought the infant Giorgios to the land of his fathers, fishing boats put out from the shore. By the time they reached Joppa a flotilla was escorting them.

They were greeted by the magistrates and curia of the city, all wearing the toga. Andrew, with Kira by his side and the rest of the family behind them, received the body. The coffin was placed inside another of polished cedar with handles of gold and taken to Andrew's villa, now restored to him. He had cast his bread upon the waters and it had returned to him a hundredfold.

The Christian church had been burned to the ground and Andrew had replaced it with a temporary building. The grave had been opened and a place made beside Justina's coffin. Abba Theodore of Jerusalem celebrated the Aramaic liturgy – the "Liturgy of the Apostles" – offering up the holy sacrifice, the body and blood of the Lord. He then preached the Encomium:

"When persecution came, many denied their faith and their salvation, polluting themselves with the corruption of idols, abominable before the Living God. Many more indeed hid their faith, going in fear and trembling at the roaring of that dragon from the pit, Galerius, as he sought not the destruction of their bodies only, but the destruction of their souls also. In what dire peril stood the Church of Christ, its scriptures burned, its sanctuaries defiled, its priests and bishops imprisoned or scattered? Well might the enemy believe that its destruction was accomplished with no man daring to declare that he was a Christian. But God raised up this shining star, this Knight of Christ, Prince of virtue and compassion. Seeing the terror and misery of his fellow Christians, he went without fear before the very enemy himself; he alone adventured to confess the name of Christ, declaring 'I am a Christian. I believe upon Jesus the Christ, who only is both Lord and Saviour of Mankind.' Then, to the astonishment of those wicked men who sat in judgement upon him, he adjured them to cease their persecution, warning them of the wrath of God, boldly declaring, 'None of my ancestors has ever worshipped false gods nor bowed to idols.' God's heavenly grace infused him with such constancy that he not only warned the tyrants of their wickedness, but was contemptuous of their tortures.

"He was a comely man, beautiful of face, strong and athletic of body. He was a just man, a lord of courtesy, for never in his life did he seek to enhance himself by diminishing another. No cruel or heartless word passed his lips. He respected all men, the poor and lowly, the bonded and the free, equally with the rich and mighty. He was a true soldier, for though he would lay down his life for Rome, he would do no base thing to save her.

"He was wise and prudent, a learned man, filled with the Holy Spirit. He was also a modest man. He would have been amazed if told that he was remembered and venerated wherever he had sojourned. He would have been astonished if told that within a few years of the laying down of his life, his name would ring throughout all the churches, whether of Rome, of Byzantium, of Antioch, of Babylon or of Alexandria and Ethiopia. His sacrifice is known to all, not only to those here, but to men everywhere the Gospel has been preached. In so far as God needs human aid, Giorgios was the right hand of God. He saved the Church from its intended destruction. Not only thousands, nay, tens of thousands, renewed their faith and were restored to grace, but many were the pagans who, inspired by his constancy in suffering, sought rebirth in the waters of baptism. This was an abundant harvest, garnered by this Husbandman of God.

"But brethren, no man becomes a martyr who is not already holy, not already filled with the zeal for souls. We would have no Martyr Giorgios today if it were not for his parents, his mother who is here among us and the father so pitifully taken from him. They it was who lovingly formed him, by their example, in the virtues and prayer of the Christian life, so that indeed the zeal for God's Kingdom has eaten him up.

"I tell you now, that in the heavenly hosts he stands next to the blessed Apostles. Among the whole company of the martyrs there is none who is greater than Giorgios of Lydda, for by the shedding of his blood he overthrew the dragon, even as it was prepared to devour Christ's maiden Church, and led thousands to salvation."

They laid him beside Justina, and the mourners remained while the grave was filled. Kira replanted the shrub that Giorgios had set upon it so many years before, firming the soil around the roots with her own hands. Then she stood, grey-haired now, the beauty which had earned her the name "Rose of Sharon" faded by sorrow. She gazed around at those gathered there, and spoke.

"It was foretold to me before his birth that his name would be great, that he would do a deed which would overthrow the dragon, that he would be known in faraway lands and be held in honour second only to the blessed Apostles. His father at his birth was given the same foresight; but I did not think then, as I held him to my breast, that they spoke of his death, and that I should live to lay him to rest."

CHAPTER SEVENTY-SIX

Constantine was in conference with Crocus, now his chief-of-staff, and Hosius of Cordoba, a Christian bishop and his *magister memoriae*. They were studying the intelligence reports from Italy. A few months before, he had received a delegation from the Senate. They had informed him that, meeting secretly, the Senate had declared Aurelius Maxentius deposed and he himself elected Emperor. They had come to beg him to save Rome from the homicidal tyrant, who had murdered his own father. At Constantine's insistence they had sworn to his election as Emperor. They had also revealed that Aurelius Maxentius was preparing for an invasion of Gaul. After they had departed, Constantine had turned exultantly to Crocus. "Now", he had exclaimed, "I truly am the legitimate Emperor of Rome."

The three moved to the map table.

"All the reports point to a stockpiling of food, fodder and weapons at Mediolanum, for a strike through the northern passes", Crocus said.

"But not of men", Hosius remarked mildly.

Constantine gave him a quick look, "The very thing that struck me." He turned again to the maps.

There were three routes from Italy into Gaul. The first, along the coast using Genova as a springboard, could easily be blocked by a determined defence. The second, based on Taurinum, through the Mount Cenis pass, opened the way to Lugdunum and the heart of Gaul; while the third, northern route, based on Mediolanum, would bring the invader into the watershed of the Rhine and the Danube.

"Now, what would Aurelius Maxentius want to wander around there for?" Constantine had that ability of all great commanders: the ability to see maps as his opponent saw them. He pointed to the Mount Cenis pass. "The stock-piling is a ruse. We were meant to know about it. This is where Maxentius will strike. He hopes that we will have moved our forces north and be neatly trapped when he comes through here."

"It could be a double bluff". Crocus was cautious. "With his African cavalry he outnumbers us two to one. He could split his forces and come through both passes." He had put his finger on the one doubt that lingered in Constantine's mind. Looking at the maps he had been ninety-nine percent certain that he had outguessed the enemy. But whatever the quality of the intelligence reports, whatever his mental picture of the terrain and the battlefield, whatever his intuition of his opponent's thinking, in the last resort the commander has to gamble.

Constantine drew his breath in sharply: he had only one throw of the dice. If he concentrated his forces on the Mount Cenis pass, and Maxentius struck north, he could swing west to the Rhône and cut Constantine off. He turned to Crocus, "We can't divide our forces. Even stripping Britannia of the legions gives us only a hundred thousand men, and a quarter of those must remain to guard the Rhine frontier."

He remained silent as the minutes passed and then smothered his last doubt. "We strike through the Mount Cenis."

*   *   *

Drawn up, in the cold grey light of early dawn, outside the south gate of Trier, was the head of a column which stretched around the city walls and then, for mile upon mile, back along the road to the north. At the head was Constantine's household cavalry, the Imperial Guard. Three mounts at the front awaited their riders. Next came the Gallic light cavalry, followed by the auxiliary regiments and, after them, the legions, a sea of scarlet cloaks and a forest of eagle standards. After the legions, the supply wagons, the horse and mule trains, and finally the siege engines. Messengers on swift ponies flanked the column on either side. On the morrow the Gallic cavalry would leave the column to ride at high speed for Susa to seize the Mount Cenis Pass and hold it for the passage of the army into Italy.

At the side of the road, at the head of the column, a pavilion stood on some high ground. Constantine had spent the night there, and now he stood at the map table with Crocus and Hosius.

This, he knew, was the moment of decision, the moment of destiny, the moment which would shape history for a thousand years. All the evidence was that Maxentius would invade through the Mount Cenis pass and that any move through the northern passes would be a feint to lure and trap him between the Rhine and the mountains.

But, if he were wrong, if Maxentius did pour one hundred and forty thousand men through the northern passes while he himself was advancing into Italy, then all would be lost, there would be no second chance, and he knew the decision was his; he was utterly and entirely alone. The whisper of doubt remained, but he made his decision.

"Let us take our places."

Constantine, flanked by his companions, walked from the pavilion. At his emergence, resplendent in gilded armour and scarlet cloak, a shout went up from the Imperial Guard which rolled back along the column like distant thunder, "Constantine! Constantine!" It did nothing to allay that last, lingering unease. Putting it aside as firmly as possible, Constantine walked to his horse. It had been carefully placed, and held a head in front of those of Crocus and Hosius. Slaves assisted them to mount.

Constantine raised his arm, ready to give the command to advance; and the nagging doubt, grimacing and gesticulating, presented itself again, "What if you have guessed wrong? What if it is a double bluff?" Firmly, Constantine raised his head, looked down the road, and stiffened in the saddle, his arm held high aloft.

Some hundred yards ahead of him was a man, mounted on a white mare, a cavalry shield hanging by his side. His cloak was not scarlet, but gleaming white. On the left shoulder, in vivid red, were the Greek letters Chi Rho, superimposed. He wore no

305

helmet, and the morning sun was reflected from his golden hair in a halo of light. There was something familiar about the way his hair curled over his ears and along the nape of his neck.

Constantine's astonishment turned to irritation and then to anger. Who was this who dared to ride in advance of the Emperor? He sat unmoving, his arm still raised. His companions looked at him uneasily and followed his gaze down the road, but saw only the dappled shade of the roadside trees in the morning sunlight.

Crocus was aware of a tremor of anxiety starting in the ranks immediately behind and rippling down the column. Soldiers do not like uncertainty, and the Emperor's hesitancy was infecting them; but still Constantine held his arm aloft, staring fixedly ahead. And then the rider half-turned in the saddle and looked him in the face, a well-remembered smile about his lips and a slight furrow on his forehead, and Constantine's last doubt was resolved.

He dropped his arm and urged his horse forward, and as the column started, he said under his breath, "Lead on, comrade, friend, brother. Lead on, Giorgios, to the gates of Rome."

APPENDICES

BIBLIOGRAPHY

Books on St. George are numerous, though many are written from the standpoint of the author's special interest – St. George in art, poetry, literature, English tradition, etc. Most are unsatisfactory, to me at least, in that they neither place St. George in the context of the day-to-day life of the Later Empire nor in the Christian ethos of his life. This bibliography is far from exhaustive of either books about St. George or of the suggested reading for the historical context of his life.

Books on St. George:

Barnes, Philip, *St. George, Ruskin and the Dragon*, The Ruskin Gallery, Sheffield, 1992, with *The Golden Legend* as Appendix.

Budge, Sir E.A. Wallis, *George of Lydda: The Patron Saint of England*, Luzak & Co., London, 1930. Translation of indispensable texts attributed to **Pasicrates, Theodosius of Jerusalem** and **Theodotus of Ancyra**, with magisterial Introduction.

Bulley, Margaret H, *St George for Merry England*, George Allen, London, 1908.

Cooney, Anthony, *The Story of St. George*, This England Books, Cheltenham, 1999

Elvins, Fr. Mark, *St. George – Who Was He?* The Catholic Publishing Co., Ltd., Ascot, undated.

Hogarth, P.J., 'The Evolution of a Saint and his Dragon', in *History Today*, Vol. 30, April 1980, London.

Riches, Samantha, *St. George, Hero, Saint and Martyr*, Sutton Publishers, Stroud, 2000.

Royal Society of St. George, History of St. George, www.royalsocietyofstgeorge.com/history.htm.

Stace, Christopher, *St. George, Patron Saint of England*, S.P.C.K., London, 2002.

Thurston S.J., Fr. Herbert, 'St. George' in *The Month*, Vol. LXXIV, April 1892. A highly authoritative paper on the subject.

The Roman World:

O'Brien, P.K. (General Editor) *Atlas of World History*, Philip's, London, 1999

Barrow, R.H., *The Romans*, Penguin Books, London, 1949.

Boardman, Griffin & Murray, *The Roman World*, O.U.P., 1988.

Quennell, P., *The Colosseum*, Readers Digest Assn., London, 1971.

Stobart, J.C. *The Grandeur That Was Rome*, Book Club Associates, London, 1964.

Roman Britain:

Breeze & Dobson, *Hadrian's Wall*, Penguin Books, London, 1976. Useful for its clear and concise account of Roman military organization.

Dark, K. & P., *The Landscape of Roman Britain*, Sutton Publishers, Stroud, 1998.

Foord, E., *The Last Age of Roman Britain*, Harrap, London, 1925.

Richmond, I. A., *Roman Britain*, Penguin Books, London, 1955.

Scullard, H. H., *Roman Britain, Outpost of the Empire*, Thames & Hudson, London, 1979.

Wade-Evans, A. W., *The Emergence of England & Wales*, Heffer & Sons, Cambridge, 1959.

Treharne, R.F., *The Glastonbury Legends*, Sphere Books, 1967.

GLOSSARY

Ala   Auxiliary cavalry; the ala was comprised of sixteen turmae ('troops') of thirty-two men.

Centurion   Commander of a 'century' and backbone of the Roman Army. At the time of our story the 'century' had long ceased to have a strength of 100, and its official strength had dropped to 80, later to 60.

Cohort, Auxiliary Like the legionary cohort, an auxiliary cohort comprised six 'centuries' of about eighty men.

Cohort, Legionary A legion was divided into ten cohorts, each in turn divided into six 'centuries' of eighty men. The senior centurion of a cohort was the *primus pilus* and effectively commanded the cohort in battle.

Decurion   A petty officer in a century, but also a term used to designate deputy commanders of alae and cohorts. I have used it exclusively in the first sense.

Dominus/Domine A title meaning 'Lord' ('Domine' is the vocative form).

Notitia Dignitatum The record kept at Rome of appointments of governors of provinces, together with their insignia or badge of office.

Optio   Originally second in command to a centurion, though ranking below the standard-bearer. The term seems to have been applied to anyone in a position of minor command, for example a guard commander.

Excluding such obvious cases as Alexandria, Antioch, Byzantium, Rome, etc., the modern names of the Roman cities referred to are as follows:

Aquae Sulis	Bath
Deva (Legio XX Valeria Victrix)	Chester
Eboracum (Legio VI Victrix)	York
Genova	Genoa
Gesoriacum	Boulogne
Isca Silurum (Legio II Augusta)	Caerleon-on-Usk
Lugdunum	Lyon
Mediolanum	Milan
Noviomagus	Speyer
Porta Sisuntorium	Lancaster
Rutupiae	Richmond
Salonae	Salonica
Segontium	Caernarfon
Taurinum	Turin
Trier	Trèves

FAMILY TREE OF SAINT GEORGE OF LYDDA

(Derived from the Ethiopian texts, by Sir E.A. Wallis Budge)

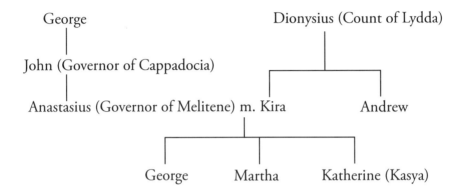

George
|
John (Governor of Cappadocia)
|
Anastasius (Governor of Melitene) m. Kira

Dionysius (Count of Lydda)

Andrew

George   Martha   Katherine (Kasya)